Advance

"*Life As We Show It* is a TiVo ~~~~~~~~~~~~~~~~~~~~~~~~~~~~~~~~~ that takes the form of Rebecca Brown musing on *Shane* and her father, or Dodie Bellamy fixating on *E. T.* and her mother; Lynne Tillman narrating the street life out her window like movie plots, or Wayne Koestenbaum recalling Elizabeth Taylor as a personal lesson in gender. The accumulated evidence is indisputable: we are what we watch. This collection of essays offers an early-warning system worth heeding."
—**B. Ruby Rich**, film critic and scholar, University of California, Santa Cruz

"Reading this book is like going down a rabbit hole of our collective cinematic imagination. These writers share with us in their own unique voices how watching movies can give us primal access to our fantasies, our histories, our fears, ourselves. Like a poem by Frank O'Hara, this collection erases the distinction between what we've seen on the screen and our own most personal memories. By the time you've finished this book, you have entered a fantasy world of the movies where Elizabeth Taylor and Joey Stefano and Ryan Phillipe and many more are all part of one fevered reverie of cinematic identification and desire."
—**Ira Sachs**, filmmaker *(The Delta, Forty Shades of Blue, Married Life)*

"Even in this age of universal cool, we're just as smitten by the movies as the kids who went to see them fifty, sixty, eighty years ago. Indeed, we may be even deeper into them than people used to be; for, as America disintegrates, and our real world(s) collapse and disappear, the movies, more and more, don't just stand out more vividly among our other memories, but permeate those memories, merge with them, become them; so that it's getting harder to be sure exactly where the movies stop and you begin.

So how, in so bewildering a borderland, does one write truthfully about the movies? In this rapturous anthology, many writers demonstrate the possibilities, making bold forays across generic borders of all kinds. *Life As We Show It* offers dazzling passages of memoir, drama, poetry, fiction and film history, philosophical suggestion and delirious analysis, and other writings that defy a handy name. Thus this remarkable collection helps us see where both we and the movies are today, and where we're going."
—**Mark Crispin Miller**, Professor Media, Culture and Communication at NYU and author of *Boxed In: The Culture of TV* and *Seeing Through Movies*

Life As We Show It
WRITING ON FILM

Co-edited by Brian Pera & Masha Tupitsyn
Introduction by Masha Tupitsyn

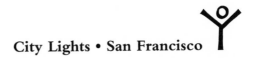

City Lights • San Francisco

First edition 2009

10 9 8 7 6 5 4 3 2 1

Cover illustration: frame enlargement, The Man with a Movie Camera (Dziga Vertov, 1929)
Reproduced by courtesy of The Austrian Film Museum, Vienna

Cover design: Stefan Gutermuth
Book design and composition: Linda Ronan

Page 293 constitutes an extension of this copyright page.

Library of Congress Cataloging-in-Publication Data

Life as we show it : writing on film / co-edited by Brian Pera & Masha Tupitsyn.
    p. cm.
  ISBN 978-0-87286-525-9
1. Motion pictures. I. Pera, Brian. II. Tupitsyn, Masha.
  PN1994.L4828 2009
  791.43—dc22
                2008035720

Visit our website: www.citylights.com

City Lights Books are published at the City Lights Bookstore,
261 Columbus Avenue, San Francisco CA 94133.

ACKNOWLEDGMENTS

Brian Pera wishes to thank: Fred Wilson; William Castle; Orly Ravid; Wash Westmoreland; Todd Haynes; Abby Levin; Phillip Roth; Kim Yutani; Gina Pera, Larry Rinder; Malcolm Futhey; Ira Sachs; b. Ruby Rich; Brian Sloan; Claire Patteson; Tom Cendejas; Konstantinos Kontovrakis; Denise Alvarado; Robert Sharrard, Sarah Silverman, Stacey Lewis, and Linda Ronan at City Lights. The authors, a number of whom contributed so consistently to lowblueflame.com during its life span and were just as game and giving when it came to the subject at hand here; and Masha Tupitsyn, for her energy and dedication.

Masha Tupitsyn would like to thank: Margarita Tupitsyn for her cover suggestions and, as always, her endless support; Victor Tupitsyn for his intellectual encouragement; Wesley Savage; Heidi El Kholti; Mark Harris; Mark Crispin Miller; Robert Sharrard, Sarah Silverman, Stacey Lewis, and Linda Ronan at City Lights; Rebecca Brown for her unique generosity of spirit; and the rest of the contributors. And to Fundación Valparaiso in Spain for giving me the time and space to work on the initial stages of this anthology as well as the essay I was inspired to write for it.

How can I know what is seen in this world?
Lidia Yuknavitch

CONTENTS

INTRODUCTION

The dismantling of the world's contents is radical. Even if it is undertaken only for the sake of illusion, the illusion is by no means insignificant.

Sigfried Kracauer

In the movie *The Blob*, a crowd of 1950s teenagers sits inside the Colonial Theater watching a midnight "spook-bit" in a small town in Phoenixville, Pennsylvania. On-screen, a sea of purple scrim frames a tiny black-and-white movie image. From it, a menacing, incantatory, voice booms, "Yes, I am here. The demon who possesses your soul. . . . I am coming for you. I have so much to show you." Since it has no face (sound and image are unsynchronized), it's as though the voice isn't tied directly to the horror on-screen, but to something beyond the theater; that the message transcends the frame it's in and is being communicated to the viewers inside the Colonial, not to the characters on-screen. It isn't until the very end that the blob targets the actual theater. Inside, rather than feel terror, the young viewers laugh at the on-screen horror. They're confident that whatever's on it is confined there and will never spill over into real life. Horror moves into the screen, and the screen moves out into the world.

Then a fuse is blown and the movie shuts off. The blob, a veiny mishmash of the bodies it's consumed, oozes out of the Colonial's projection room, the source of all movie theater images, and spreads itself across the room like a thick layer of icing. In this moment, the blob is primordial ooze in the shape of celluloid, and with its possession of the movie screen, horror shifts from cinematic to real. Within moments, a surge of movie viewers burst out of the Colonial in panic. The movie theater marquee above the frenzied crowd displays the name of the featured attraction, aptly titled *Daughter of Horror*, also known as *Dementia*. As the film patrons fall over like dominoes, a gooey, sepia-tinted mound known only as the "blob" (practically a palindrome) follows. It's reminiscent of Roy Neary's excremental replica of the Devil's Tower in *Close Encounters of the Third Kind*. In addition to blood and shit, the blob is also the same consistency as brownie mix, and not only does it literally fill the Colonial—the symbolic shape of celluloid—as it seeps out of the theater, the now enormous globule overtakes our frame and obstructs our screen. Like the double-bill spook-show, the idea of a shapeless life form feeding off the inhabitants of a small town is twofold. As it exits the theater, the blob is revealed as a monster that feeds not only off of flesh, but off the contained screen fantasies of 1950s B horror, or as Michael Wood puts it in his foreword to Peter Biskind's *Seeing Is Believing: How Hollywood Taught Us to Stop Worrying and Love the Fifties*, "The movies didn't make this happen, but they helped to make a particular set of values seem universal, and to make a partial account seem like the whole story."

Shot from outer space in the form of a pink meteor, or according to the two teenage lovebirds who spot it, a shooting star, the blob is a foreign entity that literally opens up the frame (America) and bursts a cultural bubble, so that everything after the 1950s becomes post-America. And, like the colored "special effect" silicone that was used to make it, the blob seals the gap between on- and offscreen. As a genre of possession, the structure of invasion in sci-fi, which typically masquerades sociopolitical anxieties over rivaling ideology, is usually expressed through the insurgent and indeterminate body. In the case of *The Blob*, however, a meta-picture, the dividing line is film itself. As one suspicious policeman puts it in the movie, "The bigger the blob gets, the bigger the story." And later, when Dave, Phoenixville's sympathetic cop goes into the Colonial to confront the monster, only to come right back out with the warning, "Don't go in. It's the most horrible thing I've ever seen in my life," is he referring to the blob or to *Daughter of Horror*? Finally, the best part: the blob rolls out of the Colonial's double doors and then, for a couple of seconds, fills our screen, looks right at us, and pulsates, throbs, a cake rising in an oven—as though breathing, until for a second it's up on the marquee, announcing itself as the true source of horror.

Released in 1958, *The Blob* marks the end of the official story of the fifties and its narratives of incursion. Signifying a break from centrist ideology, and a hairsbreadth away from the rebellions of the 1960s, the film ends, not coincidentally, with a question mark etched into the sky as the frozen blob is dropped like a bomb into the Arctic Ocean for safekeeping (that is, "If the Arctic stays cold," warns Steve McQueen's teenage Steve in a nod to global warming and atomic warfare). The form-defying blob thus becomes a strangely fitting analogy for the genre-defying approach *Life As We Show It* takes to writing about film. For, in the fifty-year interim since *The Blob* came out, the world has in many ways become what happens on-screen, and the screen has become the space where we wait for things to happen and plot the things we want to see.

When the great comedian Gene Wilder got his first big movie break, he ran around Lincoln Center ecstatically proclaiming, "I want everything I've ever seen in the movies!" With Reality TV currently reigning supreme, the symbiotic bonds that we have with screen fantasies and screen idols—that is, the way we contain, portray, and pursue images, rather than the way images portray us—have largely gone on to erode any kind of real civic alliance, making images the ties that bind. More than anything else, as a reflexive subcategory, Reality TV allows us to monitor and showcase the indelible impressions movies have made, in particular, our desire to be screened in the first place, making it a kind of twenty-first-century survey of 100+ years of cinematic mythmaking. As a recuperative ploy, Reality TV hijacks "reality" in an attempt to present it purely as a screen phenomenon even when the screen being used claims to democratize and elucidate ("expose") the star process, "underlin[ing] what be might be called the collusion or conspiracy that exists between Hollywood and American reality."[1]

If diegesis refers to the story world, or the world of the fiction, and the things that occur within it, then non-diegetic refers to that which happens outside a film's given parameters. Wikipedia defines a non-diegetic insert as "a scene that is outside the story world which is 'inserted' into the story world." Thus, the genre of assemblage and insertion, fictions about fictions, fiction from fictions, or more specifically, fictions affixed and inserted into already existing fictions—in the case of this anthology, the fictions of movies—might be an interesting and useful way to describe what the writers in this collection are doing. By emphasizing a movie's extra-cinematic narratives, that is, what one hears, says, reads, and believes about a visual medium, rather than what one simply sees, it becomes clear that images are not just shaped by the screens that transmit them, but by the viewers who inhabit and alter those screens, enabled by new digital technologies, which continually redefine and stretch the parameters of screen and viewer.

Given that movie theaters are no longer the primary viewing grounds for movies, movies are not confined to their "original" screen sources. They can be moved around, taken apart, and put into new frames; decontextualized and recontextualized at home in a variety of ways thanks to the internet and its user-friendly modes of revision. In *Death 24x a Second: Stillness and the Moving Image*, film scholar Laura Mulvey distinguishes the meditative, pensive spectator, who extracts and studies the film fragment in order to place it back into its original context with "extra understanding," from the more fetishistic and possessive spectator, who, with the availability of new technology, isolates the film fragment from continuity and context in order to gratuitously fetishize it à la YouTube. Through repetition and return, the critic's disruption of narrative flow allows them to find the "film behind the film"; to unearth hidden meaning.

But what exactly are the dimensions of the "story world" in today's new audiovisual culture, and what are the spaces and genres for its articulation? As much as readers and publishers alike would prefer that writers stick to a single mode of "extraction," to use Mulvey's term, in order to express a full range of responses and speak to the complexity of the current system of images—the role they play in our lives—is it really useful to limit ourselves to a singular genre or trajectory of writing? Moreover, what is being inserted into what, and can concrete—"1950s"—distinctions between reality and representation even be made in this hyper-age of media?

When Derek Malcolm, a former film critic for the *Guardian*, accused filmmaker Peter Bogdanovich of being "permanently hooked on making movies about movies"—for which Woody Allen, who did the same thing early on in his career was celebrated—he suggested that "the way back" for Bogdanovich would be to "make a film about real people instead." Malcolm's advice begs the question, what is a movie about real people? What does verisimilitude mean in the context of a fiction, in particular, an oversaturated twenty-first-century fiction? And what is reality and its representation in a world where "realism" and identity have proven to be nothing more than constructs? In his privileging of the real, is Malcolm referring to real people in movies or real people in real life—as in documentaries (if one can call documentary—of which the now rampant and psychoscopic Reality TV is a direct descendant—a mode of factuality)? This call for realness touches upon the futility and insincerity of categories in a market-driven society—as Eileen Myles puts it in *Chelsea Girls*, "You can't get money without a category"—which, in the case of Reality TV, merely unveils yet another layer of fiction. Reality TV is compelling precisely because it offers a template of reality that can be effected as strategy.

While categories have never been more enforced by the marketplace when it comes to what sells, the real incentives are brands, which rouse interest by establishing an audience correlatively, thus becoming the terms of consumption (audience before product). With the recent publication of her memoir, *Undiscovered*, leading actress of the 1980s—or "the indispensable 80s woman, a major focus for the return to the good old values of patriarchal capitalism and the restoration of women to their rightful place"[2]—Debra Winger becomes writer, sage, and self-help guru overnight. Simon & Schuster, the book's publisher, describes Winger's memoir as an "intriguing mix of reminiscence, poetry, storytelling, and insightful observation, a portrait of a life well-lived . . . strikingly rendered." As a star, not only is Winger permitted to don different labels in a way that results in lucrative film and publishing deals, but her writing and meditations on life take their inspiration from the genre of Hollywood fiction, so that the discourse of behind-the-scenes is appropriated as individual autobiography. Winger disobeys the "rules of art" by moving freely between genres and even non-forms in her writing. "Genres are necessities of the industry," writes film scholar Stephen Heath, "the optimal exploitation of the production apparatus requiring the containment of creative work within established frameworks." Winger's writing bypasses these necessities by fulfilling them in other ways.

Perhaps Bogdanovich's response to a similar critique of simulacrum in his 1975 movie *At Long Last Love*, a commercial and critical disaster, can offer some insight into this old-fashioned and ultimately unreliable distinction: "The New York of the thirties doesn't exist anyway. You know what [Ernst] Lubitsch said: 'I've been to Paris, France, and Paris, Paramount, and I prefer Paris, Paramount.' Most good movies are made on the backlot. I want to create an illusion of New York, an artificial New York." Similarly, much to the dismay of viewers and critics alike, in Stanley Kubrick's *Eyes Wide Shut*, the fantasy of place is linked with the "backlot" of desire by filming New York City as a blurry and generic artifice; a stage set hallucinated by Tom Cruise's character Bill. As New York becomes the specific scenery for Bill's libidinal fairy tale, the city sheds its identifiable morphology. But also, with New York in a constant state of flux due to gentrification, which makes the city more provisional theater than actual place, do any of us know what New York City really looks like anymore? In a similar vein, David Lynch's *Inland Empire* presents life as an unending movie role: the screen (the new ontological space) and, as a result, identity, is elliptical—an act with no beginning or end.

With the DVD special feature, the idea of a final cut is a thing of the movies past. Now, when thinking and writing about a film, one must take into account a much larger cinematic space that includes deleted scenes, outtakes, production photos, storyboards, interviews, and commentaries. In other words, what's "in" and "not in" the film, what is or could have been the story. The phenomenon of the movie commentary presents yet another break with diegetic reality, or a broadening of it, by having participants comment, as director and/or actor, on the experience of being inside a given story. DVD bonus features reveal that a movie, like any story, is also made up of cuts—the unused—demonstrating, yet again, that the story of a story is always part of the story.

With the home-centric devices of the new audiovisual age enabling new modes of address, viewers can reclusively reframe images and cinematic narratives in ways previously only available to industry insiders. DVD bonus features present narrative as not only wide-open, but variable. "Inevitably, today's stories are but prologues or sequels to other stories," writes social critic Todd Gitlin. "True and less true stories; stories that are themselves intermissions, stories without end."

The market of the addendum has led to an expansion of promotional discourse. Unfixed by institutional borders, the dispersal of information via the Internet has created non-structures, non-places, and non-genres of seeing and meaning. Gossip and offscreen discourse—or in the case of Heath Ledger, death—often generates more curiosity about an on-screen performance or performer, even going so far as to determine or rewrite its quality. In an appearance on *The View*, actor Aaron Eckhart, Ledger's costar in *The Dark Knight*, described Ledger's work in the film as a "performance of a lifetime," which, ironically, is exactly what it is. Ledger, along with the narrative of his death—an annotation—in relation to his last film, is an example of the auxiliary film text. Now, what was once left out of a film is put back in, thus dangling narrative, and its complex construction, in front of the viewer like a carrot.

When it comes to tabloid culture, fantasy and reality are one and the same. The last few years, especially (see James Frey's contested "memoir" *A Million Little Pieces*), have proven over and over that it rarely matters whether a narrative is actually "true"—a defunct distinction that stars today insist upon when it comes to the reported details of their lives off-screen. Stories of stories lead to more stories, regardless of the form they take, and in the case of James Frey, the plot of his "fake" memoir has become intertwined with the plot of his "real" life, which was falsified, or falsely classified, in order to land a publishing deal. A star's "good" reputation is no longer the sole ingredient of on-screen success, for the consumption of narratives isn't based upon rigid distinctions like true or false, real or fake, good or bad, but on consumption itself, in the same way that supermarket tabloids are stacked at checkout counters not only to be purchased monetarily, but to precipitate a social mode of consumption that has far greater currency. In their book *Channels of Desire: Mass Images and the Shaping of American Consciousness*, Stuart and Elizabeth Ewen write, "The politics of consumption must be understood as something more than what to buy, or even what to boycott. Consumption is a social relationship, the dominant social relationship in our society."

On a recent episode of *The Rachel Ray Show*, two female guests describe their experience with the company Celeb 4 A Day, a fake paparazzi service enabling people who are not famous to pretend to be by hiring fake paparazzi (up to six) to follow them around for two hours. The service also comes with a bodyguard and publicist as well as incriminating "evidence." One woman said she hired Celeb 4 A Day because she'd "always wanted to be an actress." Her confession is revealing. It records a major shift in the public's perception of acting as a vocation that transpires primarily outside the parameters of a film text (as something extra) and further, implies that the aspect of fame that is most dreaded by celebrities is the one nonfamous people want to experience the most. In the September 14, 2008, issue of *New York Magazine*, Emily Nussbaum's cover feature, "Man in the Bushes," looks at the rise of modern American celebrity through infamous paparazzo Ron Galella, without whom "there'd be no TMZ" and who "took acting classes at the Pasadena Playhouse, not to become a star himself," she writes, "but to learn to act like one." Fame, as Galella proves, is no longer a by-product or an extension of acting; acting is now a side effect of fame. A declared—or in the case of Reality TV *auditioned*—"talent" in one field can lead to success in an entirely different field, and an appearance on Donald Trump's *The Apprentice* as a wannabe business mogul, can lead to cohosting *The Tony Danza Show*, being on the cover of *Playboy*, or recording a hip-hop album. Celebrity stylist Rachel Zoe, who has changed the parameters of offscreen style by dressing stars for "every" occasion, claiming that "life should be a red-carpet moment," has also stated, "The nature of what, or who, is a celebrity has expanded. We aren't saving lives here, but we are creating images, and images create opportunities in a lot of areas."

When I met Brian Pera, my co-editor, in December of 2005, it was through email, the equivalent of coffee or drinks in the cyber world. Brian wrote me a missive in response to a formal inquiry I'd made about submitting to his online journal, Lowblueflame. The last issue he edited, which was still up on his Web site at the time, featured some of the writers in *Life As We Show It* and was dedicated to the movies. The untitled issue of Lowblueflame, which I refer to as the "déjà vu issue," was an exercise in cinematic hearsay. Tracing his own celluloid obsession, a curiosity informed in equal measure by movies seen and unseen, Brian asked each writer to describe a film based on what they'd read and heard about it. If I'd been able to participate, I would have recounted my own movie déjà vu (a word that literally means "already seen") of *Don't Look Now*, which I'd seen on TV but didn't remember seeing until years later, when I overheard someone describing what I thought was a private terror: a red-cloaked monster-dwarf haunting Donald Sutherland in the catacombs of Venice. At the time, my cinematic references were much more limited: I knew who Donald Sutherland was, but not Julie Christie. (I had not yet moved to London or discovered the British New Wave.) The name Nicolas Roeg didn't ring a bell. But based on the villain sketch, and the red hoody on the little girl next to me, I immediately recalled the iconic movie I'd seen a clip of as a six-year-old, rather than the private "memory" fragment I had catalogued it as all those years.

By confabulating movies they hadn't actually viewed, the writers in Lowblueflame concocted parallel pictures, plots, and narratives. In many of the stories, subtext is teased and stretched until it possesses the official narrative, filling and swallowing it like the amorphous blob. Lifelong *Jaws* fanatic and one of the makers of the yet-to-be released 2006 documentary *The Shark Is Still Working: The Impact and Legacy of Jaws*, narrated by Roy Scheider, Erik Hollander writes about the many different ways movies can be viewed:

> It was a full three years later when I finally got to see *Jaws* on the big screen during its rerelease in 1978. In the years between, I had obsessed about what I had come to imagine the film to be like. I based my "vision" of the scenes on three years of playground chatter from those lucky classmates that were allowed to see it—which was everyone else! Despite having conjured up a pretty impressive picture in my mind about the movie, finally watching the real deal with my dad on that fateful afternoon in July replaced my misinterpretations with imagery that exceeded my wildest expectations. That day has never left me. When *Jaws* finally aired for the first time on network television, my dad set up a cassette recorder and taped the audio for me, and for the next Lord knows how many years, I listened to that cassette every single day until the magnetic signal wore away. Every line, every sound effect, every music cue has been seared into my memory ever since. So, for me, *Jaws* has always been more of a personal life experience than merely a favorite film.

Looking at movies as representations of events and practices in his book *What Do Pictures Want?* W.J.T. Mitchell treats images as living things with personalities, demands, and desires of their own, stating, "To get the whole picture of pictures, we cannot remain content with the narrow conception of them." Whether or not the contributors to this collection are distinctly aware of their focus on the subject of cinema and media as a new genre or form of writing, I cannot explicitly say. But part of the incentive for *Life As We Show It* was to use film, and the culture that comes with it, as an ingredient for narrative impetus—for writing, for imagining, and for thinking. Movies are starting points, like any subject or theme, to enter into the culture that's inside of them. For me, film writing, as opposed to straight film criticism, is a way for an author to merge with not just the thing they write, but the film they're looking at, so that writing becomes both cultural analysis and personal revelation. Since on-screen and offscreen constantly overlap and get mixed up, writing about images becomes more interesting when it attempts to reflect this blurring through form and content. When writing is allowed to be transformed and shaped by what it writes about.

Masha Tupitsyn
New York City, 2008

NOTES

1. Thomas Elsaesser, Noel King, and Alexander Horwath. *The Last Great American Picture Show: New Hollywood Cinema in The 1970s.* Amsterdam Press, 2005.
2. Robin Wood. *Hollywood from Vietnam to Reagan*, Columbia Univ. Press, 1986.

1

Genre Pictures

OTHER MOVIES

Lynne Tillman

Along Tenth Street, it's pretty quiet. The beginning of the night and the taxi people opposite my building have four limos out front waiting, probably, to drive to the airport, but no one's gunning his engine. The motorcycle club is out of town, the ten bikes that are usually parked next to each other and which take up one and a half car lengths, they're probably rolling along a highway somewhere, or they've pulled over to the side of the road and the bikers are drinking beer and listening to the radio, something I know about from road movies like *Two-Lane Blacktop* or *Easy Rider*.

Roberta's walking her dogs. She's got three of them, two very small poodles and one big mutt. At first, I couldn't stand Roberta. Along with her dogs, she owns three cars, all of them in bad shape, and she moves them daily. In this way she participates in a major block activity, car parking. There are people who sit in each other's cars, or move them, or just look after them. Roberta spends about three hours every single day waiting for the time one of her cars will be legal in the spot it's in. Alternate side of the street parking means nothing to you unless you have a car in the city. Then, if you don't have the money to park your car in a garage, it controls part of your day.

As I say, I took an instant dislike to Roberta, because she raced her engine, turning it over and over late at night under my window, and because of the way she looked. She has a huge mass of dyed black hair, eyebrows tweezed into startled half moons, and she wears sausage-tight pants

13

stretched over a big stomach and ass. But by now we've taken to saying good morning to each other and she doesn't look so bad to me anymore and I guess she's all right. She probably never suspected that I had put a desperate and angry typed note on her car window saying I'd report her for noise pollution if she continued racing her engine at two a.m.

That was a while ago, around the time Richie got put away. Now he's down the block, drinking coffee from a styrofoam container, not worried that those containers cause cancer, just calmly looking at the setting sun. Richie's out of the hospital again and on lithium. The new people on the block didn't know about him then, didn't know that his screams weren't serious, and he probably woke them the way he wakes everybody at first. You learn not to pay attention. You learn to distinguish his shouting from anonymous and dangerous screams or from calls for help and you fall back to sleep. But these new tenants called emergency and Richie disappeared again. It took weeks to find out where he'd gone. Jeff, who's been on the block longer than almost anyone, hung a sign in his storefront window and many along the street, on telephone poles. WHERE'S RICHIE? The signs lined the block. We all missed him. Maybe Jeff's lover Juan didn't, but I never talk to him, he's very unfriendly.

Richie usually stands in front of the door where he sleeps. The rock group gives him a bed and food. He stays outside during the day, rain or shine. When Richie's in one of his moods, having a psychotic episode, he walks back and forth and shouts: "Where's the sixties?" "Where's Central Park?" "Who killed Kennedy?" Sometimes he just howls like a wolf. When he comes out of it, he washes and combs his hair, cleans himself up, smiles at you and says, "Hi, how are you?" Makes small talk. If you can make small talk, that means you're well. One time I dreamt he was my boyfriend. Maybe because he's so steady in his own particular way.

It takes time to discern behavior different from your own. When I first moved in, I called the police because there were strange and loud noises on the street. I thought someone needed help. A cop said: "You'll learn to tell when they're funnin' and when they're serious." I think the neighbors below me used to beat each other up. A tall, thin, black woman, a tough blonde white woman, and the black woman's adolescent daughter. Sometimes I'd run out my door and stand in front of theirs, ready to knock loud. But I never did. Two years later I saw the blonde go into an Alcoholics Anonymous meeting on Saint Mark's Place. There's always a big mob of people outside just before and after meetings. "A good place to meet men," I heard one woman say to another as I strolled past. The fights downstairs have stopped. We've exchanged names—Mary, Jan, and Aisha—and now we complain together about the landlord and the super. I like the women, there are always wonderful cooking smells coming from their apartment. Their daughter seems OK, but it's hard to tell how kids will turn out. Maybe in the midst of those fights, the little girl cowered in her room, on her bed, or was protected by an imaginary friend. Rescued by someone like Sigourney Weaver in *Aliens*, who kind of looks like her mother.

Not so long ago, Telly Savalas was filming here. The dealers down the end of the street yelled to him, "Hey, Kojak, how's it going, man?" Savalas gives the high five sign, and the guys are content, even proud to be, if only for a second, part of the big picture. We're accustomed to our block being used as background, local color, for TV movies or features, even commercials. Cops and robbers. Drug busts. Hip and trendy scenes, the location for galleries, weird boutiques, that kind of thing.

If I were to make a movie of the block, one version could be based on *Blue Velvet*, titled something like *Under Tenth Street* and starring Roberta as the Isabella Rossellini character, one of the rock and roll guys as the boyish voyeur, and Richie as Dennis Hopper. It might open with a shot of a large rat on a roof blinking its eyes at the camera and some country and western music playing on the soundtrack. The big city romance of the small town set in a big city.

Sandra might be from a small town in Utah. I see her about once a week. She could be the daughter of a farmer and his hardworking wife, long dead, Gothic American types carrying pitchforks. I figure Sandra escaped to the big city years and years ago. She's down on her luck, without a home and with a drinking problem.

Sandra's emaciated. Walking along the block, she's carrying two tote bags and clutching a cardboard box to her thin chest. She heads for Susy, a punked-out seventeen-year-old, and says, "I'm sixty-seven, can you give me a dollar?" Susy gives her a dollar, then counts her money to make sure she's got enough. As she counts her money, someone moves up on her. Susy shoves the money in her pocket and jumps in the other direction. The guy behind her, one of the rock and roll guys, is rushing and he shakes his head but doesn't look at Susy. He looks at Sandra. When Sandra notices him, she asks for another dollar.

What I think happens to Sandra as she walks off the block, or set, is that she goes to the B&H for a bowl of soup. It costs $1.35 and comes with two slices of bread. Afterwards she'll reluctantly spend the night in a shelter where she'll have to hide her money because somebody might steal it. It's safer on the streets than in a shelter, but at her age it's too cold and she might freeze to death in her sleep. I don't know why, but Sandra has an inordinate fear of being buried alive. She keeps a notebook—she used to be an editor for a Condé Nast publication before she started hitting the bottle—which details her life on the street and her fears. After she dies of hypothermia or malnutrition, the notebook might be found and published in the Sunday New York Times Magazine.

Susy's about fifty years younger than Sandra. To me she looks a little like Rosanna Arquette in Desperately Seeking Susan, when the Arquette character dressed up to look like Madonna. After Susy pushes the wallet into her pocket, she looks again in the rock and roll guy's direction, needing a bed, or a fuck, a little love. Maybe she's a teenage runaway.

Susy enters a door near where the dealers hang out and where they, in gestures and movements as choreographed as any ballet, walk past each other or a client and exchange small plastic envelops for money. Susy disappears behind a dark grey steel door. Behind this grey door the girl might be shooting up, doing her nails, abusing her child, or talking to her mother on the phone. On the other hand she could be a lab technician. From across the street I follow her disappearance, the door an obstacle to my camera, not, of course, to my fantasy.

I think: Susy's in her room, or someone else's room, or in a hallway on the third floor. I try to picture her. I ask myself, what's she doing? If I could I'd follow Susy inside, and stand invisibly next to her, then maybe I'd rob her story, steal it away to look at and consider.

Recently I watched a TV program about a woman robber who did her breaking and entering in Hollywood in broad daylight. She said steel doors were practically impossible to get past but she could open anything else. She still loved the thrill of being inside somebody else's house, knowing that at any moment the owner might walk in and that she might get caught. A variation on the primal scene, I suppose. Part of her punishment, in addition to going to jail, was to be videotaped teaching cops how to catch a smart thief like herself. She enjoyed telling what she knew to people she outsmarted more than four hundred times. She enjoyed being on camera, caught by it, performing for the cops, her captors. But like Susy's story the robber's story, even though documented, is hidden from view, blighted by incoherence and the impoverishment of explanation. Still, I can see her on the job. Maybe I'm another kind of thief with desires just as strong as those that compelled the Hollywood woman to break and enter in broad daylight and to want to get caught. I don't want to get caught.

Suppose Susy's caught up with a crowd, as in *River's Edge*, a crowd so alienated and detached they don't report the murder of a friend by a friend. Every day they go and look at her body decaying. They watch her skin turn yellow and green, her lips dark purplish black. Perhaps Susy's the one who wants the movie's good guy to tell the police. Perhaps she's as fascinated with the rotting body as I am with her story. Or maybe she's more like the dance instructor in *Dirty Dancing* who needs to get an abortion because one of the young, rich patrons at the hotel where she works got her pregnant but he won't help her out. Now Susy's on Tenth Street, a runaway, carrying a baby she doesn't want.

Watching her with me, I'm sure of this, is a man in a wheelchair who lives on the ground floor behind a plateglass window. He has as unrestricted a view of the street as you can get. We never speak, nor do we say hello. I don't know his name, but I think of him as Jimmy Stewart in *Rear Window*. Except for some reason he's the predator, not the victim. It may be that he's collecting their stories too and we're natural competitors. He lives next door to the man with seven dogs and ten cats. I know Jimmy Stewart watches Susy because his wheelchair moves ever so slightly when she walks down the block and he bends from the waist to see her better. He seems sinister to me, his fascination a little like mine. When I look in his plateglass window I see him and a reflection of myself, in fact I'm just to the left of myself.

Suppose Jimmy Stewart leads a secret life, is not actually handicapped, is in fact a murderer, and has his eye on Susy. Or on one of the rock and roll guys, or on Roberta. Funny Roberta. She passes a lot of time in front of Jimmy's window. Many of her parking spots land up right in front of it. Or maybe Jimmy's a Vietnam veteran who got shot in the legs. Most likely he was at My Lai, that's where I see him. His actions during that massacre live with him daily, and he will never, never forget or get over them. Like the machine he was supposed to become in training, like the boys who become men in *Full Metal Jacket* by learning to kill and then doing it to rock and roll songs on the soundtrack of the movie, Jimmy Stewart was transformed at My Lai into a human monster more terrible than he could ever have dreamed or than could ever be shown in horror movies. What was inside him was as destructive and grotesque as what was around him. His thoughts then. His thoughts now. Maybe he sees nothing when he looks out his window. Maybe it's all just a big blank. On the other hand, he reads the *New York Times* every day.

I pass by his window. He's gripping his head in his hands. Roberta's on the sidewalk struggling with her mutt and trying to clean up the shit from her two poodles. Richie's in a doorway three buildings from this scene, and he's humming a tune, which sounds like Sinatra's version of "My Way." Usually he sings Motown classics. This could turn into a musical comedy, with Richie, all cleaned up, a Marlon Brando-type hood in *Guys and Dolls*, or maybe Richie'd get the Sinatra role, Nathan Detroit, since he's singing one of his songs already. Roberta could be the heroine and work for the Salvation Army. Jimmy Stewart could be one of the guys, a third-rate mobster looking for a crap game. Better yet, it's *The Buddy Holly Story* and instead of Gary Busey as Buddy Holly, he's played by one of the rock and roll guys, with Richie the acoustic bass player for the Crickets, and Jimmy Stewart as a record executive who wouldn't, of course, do any singing.

Actually, I don't think the man in the wheelchair would ever get cast for a part in a musical, rock or otherwise, not even *Pennies From Heaven*. He's a Bruce Dern type, a bitter man with a dark past. Or, as he's already in a wheelchair, he could be Raymond Burr in *Ironside*. Nothing like a courtroom and a trial for that intense excitement, drama, and awe once found in the church or theater.

When the sun goes down, people either stay in and watch TV or go out. As I said, Sandra disappears. Richie stands in the doorway till pretty late in the evening, then wanders. The neighbors below me cook and listen to music. Larry and Martin, a couple who run the Thrift Shop on First Avenue, usually pick up Harvey, who has a bad heart, and take him to one of two hangouts, B and Seventh or Bar Beirut. Every neighborhood needs a couple of bars, every neighborhood movie or TV series needs a meeting place, where the richness and complexity of human life unfolds in a series of interlocking vignettes. The bar on Avenue B and Seventh is my choice since it's already been used for numerous Miller Beer ads as well as for Paul Newman in *The Verdict*.

Imagine the place. A corner building. Red and green glass windows on two walls of the bar, so that the light filters through in color and it's always dark, even in the afternoon. Pinball machines. A locked toilet that costs 25 cents to use, to keep junkies out. A TV above the door. A horseshoe-shaped bar. The jukebox is good and loud, draft beers still cost a dollar. It's *Cheers* or *Archie's Place* except the ethnic groups are different. For the regulars, it's a home away from home.

Tonight at one end of the old horseshoe-shaped bar sits Harvey, unemployed salesman, a *Death of a Salesman* type, except I don't imagine he's had children. Just out of the hospital—another heart attack—Harvey hasn't stopped smoking or drinking. He's with Larry and Martin, and they're not fighting with him about it. Since AIDS hit the block—two young men died recently—and the city, so many people are sick, I don't see them arguing as much. Larry's got his arm around Martin's back. To me Larry looks like James Woods, especially in *Salvador*. Martin doesn't look like anybody. He waves to Susy when she walks in. No one waves to Roberta but me. Her cars must all be parked and the dogs walked. Now she can relax, drink a whiskey sour and shoot the breeze, if anyone will talk to her. Richie never comes in. He sometimes stands outside, like a watchdog, acting protective.

I take my place at the other end of the bar from Harvey and watch him flirt with Kay, a relative newcomer to the neighborhood. Larry and Martin are talking animatedly to Susy. She certainly doesn't look pregnant. I've heard that Kay's boyfriend took a walk, a permanent one. Tonight she'll even put up with sad, chubby Harvey.

Kay's wearing a cut-up T-shirt with a Bruce Springsteen logo on the back. She reminds me of Sally Fields. Her small breasts are encased in a pushup bra. She likes wearing a pushup bra, to get a little cleavage. I watch Kay look at her breasts resting in their cups of cotton, silk, and lace, then she looks at Harvey. Tomorrow she's going to have a mammogram because she's over thirty-five. One out of ten American women, she tells him, gets breast cancer. Then she drinks a shot of vodka and rolls her blue eyes at him, as if she were Demi Moore in *St. Elmo's Fire*. They talk about disease. His heart. Her breasts. AIDS. Kay's good friend Richard died two months ago, and she still can't believe it. Life, she tells Harvey, wasn't supposed to be like this. Kay slides off the barstool, goes to the jukebox, and plays "Born in the USA" and "Girls Just Want to Have Fun."

Joe the bartender is nothing like Archie or Ted Danson, the guy from *Cheers*. He's a tall black guy, sort of like the lead in *The Brother from Another Planet*. Joe lived in Harlem before moving down here. He's friendly but cool, suggesting that when he works, he works. He keeps his eyes on the couples and singles around him. Sometimes I watch the scene through his seasoned, professional eyes as they pan the bar, scanning the crowd for trouble and requests for more drinks. He doesn't betray much. He tells Larry and Martin the rumor is that Edouardo, who lives two houses from Susy, got caught dealing heroin, and he and his older cousin are in jail, probably at Rikers.

Edouardo's about eighteen, Hispanic, the oldest of seven children. Seven children from the same mother—she moved to New Jersey about when I moved in—and three different fathers. Their grandmother, who always looks tired and usually carried an open can of beer in a paper bag, lives with them and takes care of them. In their crowded apartment Edoduardo—or Eddy—screams at his brothers and sisters, controls the TV set and leaves the lights on all night so that the youngest ones find it hard to sleep. On the block he plays the big man and struts his stuff, even holds doors for the "ladies." Then he laughs behind their backs. I wondered why I hadn't seen him around lately.

Standing outside the bar is his sixteen-year-old sister Maria. Months ago Maria and I were in the corner bodega, the one run by three Syrian brothers. A man walked in and in front of everybody started shouting at her: "I'm your father. I don't want you on the streets. ¿Comprendes? I'm your father." As if we were watching television, a soap like *Dynasty* or a docudrama about a family in trouble, the Syrian grocer and I pretended not to hear, pretended to go about our business. When Maria left with the man who claimed to be her father, she didn't look at us, stood up tall, stretching her small frame, and projected a sullen dignity which I respect. Ahmed says to me, *Family Court.*

I'm pretty sure Maria is working the street. Tonight she could be dealing herself or dope. This is a crack and cocaine area, unlike Tenth Street, which is primarily grass. Anyway she never comes into the bar, maybe because it's mostly white, then black, hardy ever Hispanic, or maybe it's because she respects certain traditions, like a girl doesn't go into bars alone. Maybe it's just that they won't let her in, she looks her age, or they know she's a hooker. I'm not sure. Edouardo used to come in sometimes. Both of them frequent Bar Beirut on First Avenue where the motorcycle crowd hangs out when they're in town.

Joe hands me a draft beer and says, conspiratorially, "I couldn't see you living in the country. You're a real urban woman." He's never said anything like that to me before, and since I'm there invisibly, a kind of Hitchcock walk-on, I'm reluctant to become part of the action. Kay, who's never really talked to me before, overhears Joe's remark, and for reasons I'm not sure of, doesn't go back to her seat next to Harvey but sits down close to me. She does most of the talking, and I realize she's flirting with Joe. They talk about real estate—what landlord has bought which building, which ones are being warehoused—and about the squatters on Ninth and C, the closest Manhattan comes to having a tent city for the homeless. It looks something like England's Greenham Common.

Kay orders a martini and Joe, to lighten the mood, says he's just heard on the news that martinis are the favorite drink of 11 percent of Americans. Kay says martinis make her think of thirties movies, a different time. What about *Moonlighting*? Joe asks. Roberta takes a stool next to Kay and talks about a story she heard on the news. A pet psychologist refused to divulge the name of the golden retriever she was working with "because of the confidentiality of the doctor/patient relationship." Then Harvey, still chasing Kay, wanders over and pretends to be talking only to Joe about the porn he's been renting from the video store, the one that's also a dry cleaner, owned by Kim, the Korean who's got a lot of good selling ideas. That's the way Harvey puts it.

Highlights from the Iran/contra hearings play on the TV above the door and everyone but Joe turns to watch, listen and laugh. One old guy screams support for Ollie North. He's drunk, says Martin. But he's not alone, says Larry. Roberta switches from pets to vets and tells the story of her window washer, a Vietnam vet who said he wouldn't ever fight again unless they were landing on Coney Island. If I were really part of this movie, I'd ask who are "they"? But I don't and instead think about the man in the wheelchair who never comes in here, but has been known to go to the pasta restaurant on Avenue A and sit in the window glowering.

Kay remarks that Freud once said Coney Island was the only place in the US that interested him. This gives Harvey a chance to talk to Kay again, and he says, "You one of those Freudians?" She throws him a disgusted look. Now he realizes she'll never sleep with him. Martin and Larry probably are aware that Harvey, who gets very aggressive when he drinks, is about to lose it, having lost an opportunity with Kay, and they take Harv by the arm and lead him out of the bar.

It's not such a hot night at Seventh and B. Kay says Bar Beirut is better on weekdays. She says she's just gotten a part in an independent film being shot in the neighborhood. The mood changes when Susy strolls by, her arm around another young woman. Joe, in an uncharacteristic gesture, takes out a teddy bear from behind the bar and hands it to her. Susy's friend looks angry, as does Kay. It's all in close-up: their anguished faces, Joe's mischievous grin, Susy's sense of her own power, her hands on her slim hips. Sets of eyes dart back and forth. It turns into a rock video, something like Michael Jackson's *Beat It*, and I see them all moving around the bar, snapping their fingers, taking positions and pulling knives out of their pockets. What's going to happen? I ask myself, wandering home. How's it going to end? Will Susy sleep with Joe and desert her girlfriend? Or will Kay outstay Susy and land him, if she really wants him?

I've often wondered what it would be like to shoot a bar scene using as extras all those actors who work as famous look-alikes. These characters could wander back to the block, each to her or his own particular place on it, with their own thoughts about the night they've just had. If Susy were the dance instructor in *Dirty Dancing*, and Joe turned into Patrick Swayze, and Kay into Jennifer Grey, they'd dance out of the bar and into the street, exploding in an ecstasy of pelvic thrusts and utopian feeling. The extras, of course, would all join in. Or, as in *Hill Street Blues*, it could end in a freeze frame with Susy opening the steel door, while Kay and Joe kiss in the foreground.

I don't like endings. Besides, though the night has drawn to a close and is a natural ending, the next day Tenth Street bustles again. Roberta's revving her engine. Richie's upset and is shouting about Bush and the CIA. The thrift shop has opened a little late, because Martin's hung over. Jimmy Stewart's in the window, staring. And Kay and Susy pass each other on the street, but don't say hello. I decide that Susy did sleep with Joe. When an ambulance pulls up next door, its siren blasting, I run to the window, wondering whose life might be in danger. Last week an apartment house went up in flames, the fire engulfing and destroying three floors within minutes. Everyone watched. Disasters bring people together. I hope they're not taking Richie away again.

OUTTAKES

Lidia Yuknavitch

FADE IN:

INT. 7-ELEVEN SOMEWHERE IN SOUTHERN CALIFORNIA. **1:00** A.M.

ANGLE ON:

The name tag of the clerk reads, "Zeus." He's scratching his elbow; some kind of skin disease. His hair punked and bleached. Tongue stud. Tattoos sneaking out from the sleeves of his green uniform.

> **ZEUS**
> Yeah, I can see her as clear as day, man. She was a hottie.
> A real pocket rocker (laughing). Her lips, man. I never seen anything like 'em.

STOCK FOOTAGE of famous women from the nose down

> She had this little tattoo sneaking up her neck too, dude, it
> was some kind of snake or serpent shit or something . . . What?
> Are you sure man? Fuck . . . well was she the one then who
> was kinda old, like thirty or some shit like that, the one with
> the spiky hair bleached at the tips that kinda looked like
> Shania Twain on acid? No? Fuck . . . well what'd she look
> like, anyway?

INT. GOLD'S GYM SOMEWHERE IN SOUTHERN CALIFORNIA

We see a punch to the face as if it has hit us dead on. Two supermodels in Nike clothing and kick-boxing gear, one stunned on the floor, one looking down at her. Black and red Nike clothing. Red nails. Red lips. Both about a size zero. One of the supermodels, the one on the floor, wears a gold necklace in the shape of her name, "Kate." The other has her name stitched on the ass of her Nike Lycra pants, "Mew."

> MEW
>
> You OK?

> KATE
>
> Yeah. Swell.

KATE gets up off of the floor, shakes her head some.

> MEW
>
> Cool.

> KATE
>
> Actually she trained with us for about six months. Wasn't it?

> MEW
>
> Yeah. I think so.

> KATE
>
> We all had the same trainer. Sensei Marc.

> MEW
>
> He had the idea that we train together. Threesome.

STOCK FOOTAGE of *Charlie's Angels*

> KATE
>
> Perv.

> MEW
>
> Fucker.

KATE

Anyway. We got good enough to spar. All of us.
And instead of sparring with people in the other
classes, we sparred with each other. To practice.

MEW

She was definitely the best of the three of us. She
nailed me in the head once so precisely my ears
rang for about a month. I think my equilibrium was
off for a while too; I kept misjudging doorways and
table corners, almost falling when I got up out of
chairs.

KATE

Yeah, I remember that . . . it was a spinning knife kick, wasn't it?
You'd be surprised how high we can kick with these legs.

MEW

What do you want to know?

KATE

Definitely. She could have taken a guy . . . particularly if he
wasn't expecting it. Like some fat-ass bank guard,
no problem. Or a security guy off his doughnut break.
Yeah, I think she could have stunned or even taken a
guy out.

MEW

Or she could have dosed him with a series of blows,
then kicked the shit out of him. I mean, some of these
moves can be lethal, you understand? This isn't
aerobics. You'd be surprised.

KATE

So did she? Did she take a guy out? I mean, I'm just
curious. I just want to know. Did she do any damage?
Because if she did, I mean, I'd just really want to know
about it. I always thought she could take someone out.
The first thing anyone ever noticed about her was those
lips. Drop-dead gorgeous. But she could drop you dead

for real. I guess I'd just once like to see that. You know?
So what. Did she?

INT. 7–ELEVEN SOMEWHERE IN SOUTHERN CALIFORNIA. 1:00 A.M.

ANGLE ON:

ZEUS still trying to remember. Helping a customer or two, having trouble giving them correct change since he is stoned.

> ZEUS
>
> Wait. Dude, was she the one with the nasty blonde
> dreads and that pierced shit on her face? Oh man. Cuz
> if it was her then shit yeah, I got a story to tell. She
> was one crazy bitch. There was this one time, I'm pretty
> sure she was methed out . . . she had that hyper twitch
> speed thing going on, and she came in with this other
> chick, some Asian hottie, and it was REAL near closing
> time. They brought all this beer and shit up to the counter
> and she says, get this man, she says, uh, we don't have any
> ACTUAL money (stoner laugh). And I say, well, I don't
> have any ACTUAL beer to sell you. But hey, I could maybe
> DONATE this VIRTUAL beer to you two, because, I mean,
> dude, they were both HOTTIES, man, their tits alone could
> have lit that fucking 7-eleven neon sign up . . . what?

We see slow MOTION ACTION of the tits of two women.

> ZEUS
>
> Oh. Sorry man. Then which one was she?

INT. PSYCHIATRIST'S OFFICE. NIGHT.

The gold and fake wood thing on the desk reads "Dr. Freed." There are
more books in the office than probably anyone has read, arranged stylishly on bookshelves from Pottery Barn. All the furniture in the office
is from Pottery Barn—black leather mostly. Clever area rugs. Silver and
black framed photographs peppering the room. His diplomas and credentials are also arranged in an almost excruciatingly aesthetically

pleasing way on the walls. He is of course smoking a cigar; the smoke curls around his mouth and face just like in a movie. SLOW MOTION.

> **DR. FREED**
> You understand of course that I cannot divulge any actual information about our relationship, either implicit or explicit . . . you understand that I am bound to a set of ethical codes with regard to her as a patient.

ANGLE ON:

DR. FREED watching the interviewer take her seat, unable to take his eyes away, standing for a moment directly in front of the couch, his crotch staged at eye level, his hand resting briefly at his hip.

> **DR. FREED**
> What I can do, however, in an effort to help you, is narrate the surrounding information, or add to the information you have already presented me with, in a kind of "roman à clef." Do you see? Particularly if she is in some kind of danger, or, perish the thought, worse . . . I often thought that her tremendously sexual presence would draw . . . well, you know the world we live in. You are a beautiful woman, you must understand your environment, the world of men, of sexual predation, with a certain complexity.

STOCK FOOTAGE of rape threat scenerios

> **DR. FREED**
> What? Yes. I am well aware that she was a black belt.

STOCK FOOTAGE of men being emasculated

> **DR. FREED**
> Let's get on with things. What was it you were saying earlier? If I am not mistaken, you said something about her bisexual tendencies. You wanted a professional rather than secular account. I admire your efforts. Most people are only interested in tabloid renditions of reality these days. Bad B movies.

There is a way in which bisexuality, theoretically at least,
saves the Oedipus complex from simple gender
determinism, yes? We've come a long way in the
last century. In our better understanding we see that
bisexuality shifts its meaning and comes to stand for
the very uncertainty of sexual division itself. It is,
if you will, an in-between zone, a place between
choices. Once the patient resolves this uncertainty,
either as a heterosexual or as a homosexual, for
we of course no longer treat homosexuality as a
disease, as a condition to heal oneself from,
they can almost always achieve a full and happy
relationship, complete with commitment.

DR. FREED strokes his beard and licks his lips.

> **DR. FREED**
> As with you, it was the case with her that a young
> woman so beautiful . . . that is, it would be a shame
> to lose her.

DR. FREED smiles while stroking his beard. He almost winks.

> **DR. FREED**
> What? Good lord. I'm merely attempting to answer
> your questions. You asked me about her inclinations,
> her sexual predispositions. That IS why she came. To see
> me. Her unconscious desires were making a mess
> of her life, and she wanted to resolve things, one
> way or another, as I stated. You see, today we
> understand bisexuality in quite sophisticated ways.
> It can be said to be either a theoretical wish, or a
> socialization practice, more crassly put I suppose as
> a trendy stopgap for the young, akin to grunge music
> or the modern primitive impulses of tattooing and
> piercing. You see it everywhere; it is a fashion. But
> more seriously for some, it is the obstacle in the way
> of normal and long-lasting human relationships.
> This "either/or" condition. This wavering between things.

DR. FREED waves his hand back and forth in the air, then makes a little fist with it.

> **DR. FREED**
> She came because she was lodged so tightly in an
> in-between world as to almost be paralytic. Do you
> see? A beautiful young woman in the prime of her
> life. But the literal reason was that she was having
> stalker fantasies.

Clips from STOCK FOOTAGE of famous stalkers

> **DR. FREED**
> Hmm? No. She was not being stalked.
> She was having fantasies of stalking someone.
> But it really begins before that. Inside of a deeper
> story. You see, she had an obsession. No. That is
> incorrect. She had a complex fixation based on the
> obsessions of her dead brother; she was thus obsessed
> with the obsessions of a dead man obsessed with another
> dead man. I see already that you are perplexed. Let me
> narrate. It seems that her brother, with whom she may
> have been in love, but certainly with whom she
> developed an obsession after his untimely death in a car
> accident, her brother was obsessed with James
> Dean—this you know.

DR. FREED licks his lips.

> **DR. FREED**
> As you may or may not know, Dean was a bisexual. Though
> he preferred to be referred to as an "explorer," in this as in
> all his adventures, and of course biographers and busybodies
> debate this business as a marketing ploy. But what is important
> here is that Jimmy, her brother, identified with Dean both
> as a young man in the midst of authority battles and as a
> startlingly beautiful man attracted to both men and to women.
> On the face of it one might not think this makes much of
> a difference; however, if you go back and study the film

Rebel Without a Cause, if you, in effect, "re-read" the scenes
that might be relevant to a man obsessed with Dean as a
love object and second self, well, I think you would agree with
me that the movie takes on a myriad of possible meanings.
For instance, the scenes between Jim and Plato.

James Dean FILM FOOTAGE

Yes? And once you have understood that relationship,
you would then need to probe deeper, for L.'s love for her
brother was predicated on his love for Dean; therefore, what
L. loved was not Dean's representation, but the representation
of a representation. And what she wanted more than to have
her brother, who of course wished to be Dean, was to be her
brother wishing to be Dean. Are you getting the picture?

Oh, he enacted a whole list of small-time crimes, probably
inspired by the movie of course. Petty theft, stolen cars,
a feeble attempt at a bank robbery. They were a bit like
parodies of a delinquency that no longer has currency.
He raced cars, too, I mean after hours with friends, for money
and testosterone highs, no doubt. And in the end, he died
in a kind of aestheticized repeat of Dean's famous car
wreck. Same car, only the whole accident was constructed,
almost staged. You know, money can buy you anything
these days, even your own death, even a story of your
death.

What? Yes. She was not your average client from the get-go.
There was a point in time where I began to be concerned
about her in a professional sense. Her tales about her
brother, combined with her narrations about her inability
to center herself in her own present life, and perhaps most
importantly her fantasies about stalking a man—an actor
it is reported to be true has been signed to perform in the
film biography of Dean—as well as stalking a woman—
the girlfriend of her dead brother—left me wondering if perhaps
this beautiful and clearly brilliant girl had perhaps a
more disturbing disorder than I originally thought. It

wasn't so much the fantasies themselves, but rather the
stories of action she narrated . . . they were positively dreamy,
as seductive as any roman à clef. Why, I remember watching
her leave the office on occasion after one of these stories
with the distinct feeling that a deep seduction had occurred,
one from which I might not be able to break the spell.

DR. FREED is looking off into space, almost dreamily. The smoke from his
cigar is perfectly suspended in the air. He has the look of pleasure on his
face.

DR. FREED

What? Good lord no. What has caused you to ask such
an insulting question? Ridiculous. I did see her after
the abrupt termination of her visits. At the market, where
she appeared to be in some kind of trance or daze over
the meat; another time I saw her very late at night in the
park near her apartment. She was sitting on a bench
talking to herself. And there was the time I saw her
downtown; she took a cab to a popular alternative bar, then
another to an Indian restaurant where she dined alone.
The third cab she took that night went into an area of
the city where I have heard after-hours clubs host all kinds
of troubled people. What? What are you suggesting? Look
I don't have to talk to you. Look you have misinterpreted
what I have said. You come in here, you tell me on what
now appear to be false pretenses that the girl is missing,
possibly dead, you come in here dressed like that . . . What?
How dare you. Get out of here. This "interview" is officially
over. You are very rude. Have you no integrity? This is
an ethical issue. You have no idea. Get out.

INT. 7–ELEVEN, 1:00 A.M.

ZEUS shooting spit wads at the ceiling. Pausing for an instant as if he has
had an epiphany.

ZEUS

Oh shit man, what are those things called when you remember
something? You know when you get that kind of bolt of

lightning in between the eyes shit? Yeah dude, epiphany.
I'm having one of them. Dude. She had big lips, right?
And her eyes kinda had that glazed-over look like she was
on Dilaudin, correct? Eh? Am I right? I got her, baby. I got
her fixed in my mind's eye now. All right now. You're gonna
love this shit.

                                                    CUT TO:

JEM walking into a 7-Eleven where ZEUS is working.

                        ZEUS
Aren't you kinda late man?

                        JEM
Zeus, baby, you might want to ease up on the visual aids.
I'm an hour early.

                        ZEUS
Oh, right, shit yeah. O.K. Dang woman, you look all hot
and shit.

                        JEM
Calm down before you rupture something.

                        ZEUS
So you ready?

                        JEM
Yes Zeus. Maybe we should talk about it like this for a while
first so the cameras get the whole thing on film. Huh?

                        ZEUS
What?

                        JEM
Nevermind.

                        ZEUS
Oh, shit . . . that's a joke, right? DUDE. I get it.

JEM

You know, Zeus, sometimes you look just like Jiminy Cricket.

ZEUS

You mean that little insect dude with the top hat and cane?

JEM

That's right, brainiac.

ZEUS

Kinda Hannah-Barbera you mean.

JEM

No, kinda little cartoon cricket with oversized head singing a surrealistic song.

ZEUS pauses, not knowing whether or not to laugh. JEM and ZEUS stare at each other.

JEM

Are you looking at my tits, Zeus?

ZEUS

No, man, Jesus . . .

We see a close up of Jem's tits.

STOCK FOOTAGE of women's tits.

JEM

Let's do it.

ZEUS

Fuck yeah.

JEM quickly pulls a 9mm 92FS Beretta from her inside coat pocket and points it at ZEUS's face.

JEM

Give me everything you got or I'll blow that fucking dumbass grin right off of your god damn face.

>   ZEUS
>   I don't want any trouble, lady.

ZEUS begins to give her the money he has access to in a kind of exaggerated cartoon way. JEM stuffs it into a paper bag.

>   JEM
>   Stop grinning, Zeus. You look like an idiot.

>   ZEUS
>   Yes Ma'am!!

JEM takes the bag and walks out of the store. ZEUS watches her, mutters "thank you for shopping" underneath his breath, then calls the police.

>   ZEUS
>   Then we'd meet back up at my place around three a.m. and
>   fuck like bunnies.

>   CUT TO:

ZEUS's ratty-ass little studio apartment where he and a woman whose face you can't see bust in kissing and groping each other. Then the SHOT FREEZES.

>   ZEUS
>   No, wait man. That wasn't her. I mean about the bunny
>   fucking. But we did get it on, in my car. Always in my car.

>   CUT TO:

ZEUS's beater-mobile of a car in an abandoned parking lot. All kinds of shit litters the inside of the car . . . old 7-Eleven bags and plastic cups, Jack-in-the-Box stuff, etc. . . . . ZEUS is in the front seat and a woman whose face we can't see is riding him for all she is worth. Zeus moves to grab her tits. Then the SHOT FREEZES.

>   ZEUS
>   Oh fuck. Maybe we got it on in the bathroom of Denny's. . . .
>   Or was that that other chick with one leg shorter than the
>   other?

ZEUS appears lost in thought in 7-Eleven.

> **ZEUS**
>
> Anyway, things went like that. What? Once a month. For about
> four months. Practice runs. Dude, I almost got fired even.
> Well she made herself look different every time. One time
> she even did it as a man. No, dude, I'm serious. And
> every month like clockwork I got my cut underneath my
> car—strapped to the axle. Killer, huh?

INT. CALIFORNIA PRISON

A television in a day room with the movie *Rebel Without a Cause* on.
The names of men who have visitors can be heard over a loudspeaker.
Men raise their hands one at a time. When the name "Buzz Stark" is
called, a man separates himself from the crowd of orange-suited men,
steps forward. He has a scar across his right eye. He is handsome in an
old movie star way. He is smoking a Camel cigarette and his walk looks
almost rehearsed. He walks over to a table and sits down.

> **BUZZ**
>
> I don't know why I should talk to you. I don't even know
> you. I don't care about you. Like at all. Why should I talk
> to you?

BUZZ looks up at the television for a while. Then back to the interviewer.

> **BUZZ**
>
> What do I get out of this deal? I'll tell you what. Jack shit.
> Look at you. With your little tape recorder. You look
> jack-astic is how. Fucking cunt. Who do you think you
> are? I don't have to tell you diddly. What?

BUZZ looks right and then left.

> **BUZZ**
>
> Are you telling me you're holding?

BUZZ reaches a hand underneath the table. He stares straight ahead. The
interviewer jerks away and he pulls his hand back up.

BUZZ

You come prepared. Maybe there is something I can tell you.
She had a sweet pussy. She had the sweetest pussy I ever
saw. And her tits. Man. Like perfect champagne glasses.
Her nipples round and hard in your mouth. Look, if you
wanted the "G"-rated version you shouldn't have come
here. I mean, look around you. Cuz every guy here is
looking at you the same way. You are the SHOW, baby.
We're the audience.

No, man, I met her by accident. Her brother used to
be my outside connection. Then he suicided or something,
and BANG, she just shows up to visit one day. It was
kinda eerie, I have to admit, because I knew who she was
the second I laid eyes on her.

CUT TO:

Inside a California prison visiting area. JEM is picking a scab on her arm.
BUZZ walks up and sits down.

BUZZ

Well what the fuck do we have here.

JEM

Nothing to get excited about. Sit down.

BUZZ

You Jem? You Jimmy's little piece of tail sister? Well I'll
be a god damned son of a bitch. What are you doing here,
girl? You got no place here.

JEM

I got a place here. I got the same place my brother had. You
still need someone on the outside, right?

BUZZ stares at JEM, smiling.

JEM

I'm your man.

> **BUZZ**
>
> You're no man, tits.

BUZZ leans over very close to JEM, close enough so that the stubble on his face is magnified to cinematic proportions.

> **BUZZ**
>
> Listen here, tits. You don't know how things go down in this line of work. You can't just waltz in here and act like you own the place. So you can just turn around and take that little pink ass out of here.

BUZZ gets up to leave, laughing under his breath.

> **JEM**
>
> I got a twat full of something that says I do know how things work. You gonna pass up the chance to feel me up?

BUZZ stops. Turns around. Comes back. Reaches underneath the table between them until his hands are making their way up JEM's skirt. JEM spreads her legs.

> **BUZZ**
>
> Talk to me, tits. You gotta talk or they'll hassle me. Come on now, little sister, that's right. Just open up.

> **JEM**
>
> Your mamma says to write her more. She's sick. She's got the flu. She's got a fever.

BUZZ manages to get a plastic bag filled with dope extracted from between JEM's legs. He smiles.

> **BUZZ**
>
> That's good, sister, real good. Now what do you want. Cuz I know it ain't my birthday. What's the dope.

> **JEM**
>
> Information. I want you to tell me step by step how to make an explosive device serious enough to take out a building the size of a movie theater.

> **BUZZ**
>
> You want to blow up a movie theater.

> **JEM**
>
> No, braniac. That's just the size of the building.

> **BUZZ**
>
> What, a bank? And just what does little miss twinkle
> twat think she's gonna do then?

> **JEM**
>
> It's not a bank, and it's none of your fucking business. And
> that's not all.

> **BUZZ (V.O.)**
>
> Then she takes out this list, and on the list are five crimes.
> Crimes she says are the most popular in the eyes of society.
> The most popular. She's got car theft, robbery, drug smuggling,
> murder, and bombing on the list. She tells me she wants
> a shot-to-shot script of how to accomplish each one.

> **JEM**
>
> Look. I got what you need. I got what my brother had and
> more. I'll be here once a week, with dope every time. I believe
> that keeps you where you want to be. You educate me and I
> give you what you want.

BUZZ stares at her for a long minute and then starts to get up and leave.

> **JEM**
>
> Baby, don't go yet. I got something else for you.

> **BUZZ**
>
> What's that?

BUZZ sits back down, laughing. JEM grabs his crotch underneath the table.
She unzips his pants. She takes his dick out, gives him a hand job. Eventually he closes his eyes.

JEM

I'm gonna talk to you so nobody harasses you. Think about these lips wrapped around your cock. Oh yeah. Think about sliding your dick down my throat some, giving me a pearl of come. I can taste you. Can you feel me tasting you baby?

BUZZ

Oh yeah baby sister . . . give it to me. . . .

JEM stops.

BUZZ

No baby, you don't stop now, give ol' Buzz the works. . . . Think of it as a first installment. . . .

BUZZ grabs her hand and tries to return it to his crotch. JEM jerks it away.

BUZZ

What the fuck? You some kinda prick tease?

JEM

I'll be back next week . . . what, don't you get it, Buzz? We were just playing chicken. I just had to prove my manhood.

CUT TO:

Present interview in prison.

BUZZ

So that's how we met. And that's how things went down for about three months. Every time she came in she looked different too; once I almost didn't recognize her. But it turned me on, I mean it kept things interesting. It was like a new *Playboy* calendar pinup coming every week. Why? Because it felt good. No. Not just getting each other off. It was more than that. It's like she understood something about a man. Once she took a photo of me. She brought it to me . . . black and white. In the picture I was laughing. I've never seen myself laugh. You don't understand what it is to never have anything but shit reflected back to you. Every damn day of your life. Every man likes to feel like they are worth something. Like they are good at something. Like somebody gives a fuck. She was a good woman. Inside and out . . . and she kicked ass on her brother, no doubt. Yeah? Well if what you are telling me is true, then I was a good god damn teacher, wasn't I. They oughta fucking give me a diploma or something. Yeah? Then they oughta give her an Academy Award. Fuck yeah.

INT. BAR IN L.A. NIGHT

From floor level we see the feet of regular patrons in the bar. Cowboy boots, old worn-out shoes, work boots, shoes of all sorts. Underneath one particular table we visually climb a pair of white go-go boots. At the knee we shift to a view of hands on the table. Large fake gems decorate the fingers of a WOMAN who is very clearly about 80 years old. Up her arms are bangles. Her hair is dyed red. Her chin juts out since she is holding her head high. She has the look of a kind of sassy, classy rodent; small features and quick eyes. Behind her head is a sign on the wall of the bar that reads: "If you need to know my name you came to the wrong woman." She is drinking scotch on the rocks and sizing up the interviewer.

> **WOMAN**
> There's something about you. No, I'm saying, I can't quite put my finger on it, but it will come to me. Don't say anything. Let me just look at you for a minute. I said don't say anything for chrissakes. I'm using some of what you call women's intuition. Don't interrupt me.

The WOMAN closes her eyes.

> **WOMAN**
> You ever been to Del Mar? To the tracks? You ever do the ponies?

The WOMAN opens one of her eyes.

> **WOMAN**
> No? Well it'll come to me. Just talk to me for a while. Eventually it'll pop up just like a strudel.

The WOMAN claps her hands together and laughs.

> **WOMAN**
> A person could say I was the only eyewitness to the accident.
> No, really. While the rest of the beach-world was doing that
> kind of late summer swelling into fall thing, you know, the
> smell of coconut oil and beer fading to bonfires and wool blan-
> kets, I had my metal detector out, my earphones on, my mind
> as clear and wide as the ocean.

Southern California beach scene, ANGLE ON an old woman in a kind of
muumuu wearing metal detector gear, a broad straw hat, and stylish sunglasses, panning the sand.

> **WOMAN (V.O.)**
> I like to close my eyes when I'm hunting for metal. Let my
> intuition lead me, let my conscious mind slip back, my
> subconscious lean forward. You know what I'm saying. That
> day I'd already scored what appeared to be a working Rolex,
> quite a find, really, and some change, and then I hit on a
> larger object, which is always a little exciting, you understand.

The WOMAN looks as if she is zapped with electricity; she stops in her
tracks and toes the sand with one foot.

> **WOMAN (V.O.)**
> I'm not saying I saw the thing itself, mind you. I'm not saying
> I saw it shot-to-shot or anything like that. Why, it was up the
> bluff from where I was hunting metal for one thing, and the
> sun was high enough in the sky to blind anyone looking up.

Image of the ocean. The sand. The blue of the sky. Little glittery things
in the sand.

> **WOMAN (V.O.)**
> What I'm saying is that I found scraps of metal like breadcrumbs
> leading from me, down on the shore, to her, up the bluff. One
> at a time. After about the third object, part of a side mirror, I
> realized what was what. Objects just don't fall from the sky in
> patterns like that is what I'm saying.

Image of a side mirror falling from the sky in SLOW MOTION, landing in the sand.

> WOMAN (V.O.)
>
> I'm going to be honest with you. The first thing I thought was that I was going to find a body. A young, male, beautiful body. Because the beach is filled with young beautiful males all summer, like some never-ending movie. No really, it's like a constant supply of gumdrops or pennies from heaven. They're just luscious.

Images of beautiful boys on the beach—playing Frisbee, carrying surfboards, scoping chicks.

> WOMAN (V.O.)
>
> And you know they're all on dope and dreamy and moving through their youth like shooting marbles. So what I thought I was going to find was one of those beauties wrapped directly around a telephone pole or something. Going 80, 90, 100 miles an hour around that bluff in Daddy's car, Ray-Bans and shirtless and hair blowing like magazine advertisement. Dashful of pills, some girl's panties in the back seat. When you do what I do for as many years as I have the whole world sets up like little pieces you can track and collect.

Image of the woman finding metal objects from a car one at a time.

> CUT TO:

Back in the dimly lit bar, the WOMAN swirling ice around in her glass, drinking, holding the liquor in her mouth a few seconds before closing her eyes and swallowing.

> WOMAN
>
> A lot of the people that live in So. Cal. are role playing. The whole area is like a veneer or Hollywood set, and people sort of move around artificial-like, like they are trying to fit a story of themselves. I'm not sure when it happened exactly, but once it did it was as if the whole population had been strangely anesthetized or knocked out. Out there.

The WOMAN gestures toward the door with her glass.

> **WOMAN**
>
> Alls you have to do is listen, watch. What you'll see is people
> acting like people . . . no, I mean acting. Everything out of
> their mouths sounds scripted and flat, like you could push
> a rewind button at any moment, or change the hair on the
> blonde to red with a few clicks of a button.

STOCK FOOTAGE of Southern California babes in rapid succession.

The WOMAN leans in closer to the interviewer.

> **WOMAN**
>
> Wrecks on that particular turn were frequent; well, not
> frequent in terms of the way you young people experience
> things. But frequent when the definition meant something.
> I mean, since I've been here there have been maybe ten
> crashes, each more glorious than the next, almost always
> young, beautiful men, drunk, high, or depressed. But the
> way things happen now . . . I mean, speed's the main thing
> now. There are ten stories of violence a night on the nightly
> news, so one car wreck can hardly carry weight, now can it.

We see a talking news head on the television above the bartender's head.
The images are of some random car wreck.

> CUT TO:

Smoke just visible over the crest of a hill in the road. People in nearby
apartments poking their heads out of their doors, looking at each other
and in the direction of the smoke.

> **WOMAN (V.O.)**
>
> One thing that pissed me off, I mean it really got my panties
> in a wad, was that people around here started claiming to
> know her after I found her. And so when the television
> trucks stationed themselves outside our apartments everybody
> who was usually inside hiding like moles came out to
> shoot their mouth off, to blab out some fiction that made them

feel important, hoping for a "spot." Christ. This is the world
we live in.

                                                      CUT TO:

Bar scene.

> **WOMAN**
>
> I mean, don't you find it repugnant how people claim
> ownership of violence after the fact? Forget slowing down
> to do the peeping Tom number on a car crash, now people
> want in on the action. They want to say they knew her
> therapist. Her lover. They want to say she was working
> on a movie, that they had her car done at their garage, that
> they saw her with someone mysterious looking at some
> shi–shi–ass restaurant. I mean what I'm saying is they wanted
> her to be someone famous so that they could talk about knowing
> someone famous.

We see the image of a famous person selling something in a commercial
on the bar's television.

> **WOMAN**
>
> Pieces of human excrement. That's what I'm saying. Because
> not one of them knew her. Not one of them saw the wreck.
> Not one of them was there when I found her crumpled like
> a wadded-up piece of paper in her car, her boot toes setting off
> my detector like a siren.

Image of feet and the sound of a metal detector going nuts.

> **WOMAN (V.O.)**
>
> But what I was thinking as I was making my way up the bluff
> was that one of these little Greek gods had gone and fucked up.
> And I was thinking how all those little Greek god deaths sort
> of repeated and accumulated. How they stood for something
> that maybe was the other side of the teen idol. . . . Look, you
> can't live in Southern California without understanding that the
> central symbol for life down here is the movie star . . . maybe
> for everyone everywhere. Only in little pockets or on the sides

of actual roads they're lining up like road kill. Always have.
I don't mean in a big huge cinematic tragic way. I mean in an
ordinary way.

I remember my live-in beau at the time was a retired smack
addict—horny old bastard I'll tell you what—I don't know if
that Viagra is a blessing or a curse—anyway. We were watching
videos one night and I turned to him and said Wayne, you
know what I think? I said I think it all boils down to those
god damn Greeks. And Wayne said, what the hell are you
talking about. So I turned the sound down for a minute and
said the Greeks—the way they made out like the young naked
boy was the height of art. The purest form of beauty. I think
we've been stuck on that feed for a long time. But nobody
wants to admit it. And Wayne said, get out of here. Nothing
is more prevalent in popular culture than tits and ass and
blondes. And that ain't Greek. That's American.

I had to admit he had a point. But then I pointed out how all
the popular movies had these male leads that were either very
young, or very virile even if they weren't young. (You got your
Mel Gibsons and your Kevin Costners, for chrissakes. God help
us.) And I added that the tits and ass are only there so that
more young men will go see movies about themselves. And think
of all the popular movies with no women in them at all, Wayne,
like sometimes what the men are doing is so fucking fantastic
you don't even need women at all. I was thinking of old movies,
new movies, and everything in between. I mean, I can name em,
can't you? I know that you can. Wayne went silent at this and so I
turned the sound back up. I think we were watching *Apocalypse
Now*. Or maybe it was *The Usual Suspects*, *Butch Cassidy and the
Sundance Kid*, *Cool Hand Luke*, or *Goodfellas*.

So when I walked up that bluff and located the car and came
around to the driver's side and my detector went berserk and
I saw blonde hair undulating with the wind, I was a little
stunned. I mean I stopped in my tracks a bit. And the first
clear thought I had upon seeing her was my god, what an
oddly beautiful image, since she was smiling, I kid you not.

And I can't be sure of this, but I think her eyes were open. And the second thing I thought was Jesus Christ, that's a Porsche Spyder, isn't that the car James Dean died in? And the third thing I thought before I could stop myself was, aren't they making a movie about his life, and wasn't Brad Pitt up for the part?

Of course then I snap to and run like a banshee back down the bluff to a phone and I call the police and get my ass back up that god damn bluff but you know what? There's no woman in the car anymore. She's out of the picture entirely. But on the car seat is a pile of silver jewelry, quarters, dimes, a compact mirror, a little tin box filled with pot, and enough metal to let me take a few days off and sit by the pool drinking mai tais with my feet propped up.

You think she's out there? You think she just got up and walked away? Because I don't mind telling you, that's one woman I'd like to meet. See these boots? I bought em the very next day. Let's drink to that. Let's you and me drink to that. You know, I kind of like you. There's something about you. There just is.

IN A JUNGLE

Veronica Gonzalez

In a jungle . . . —OK, not a jungle like you'd expect, not with monkeys
and so much vegetation you can't see, not like in the stories we've all
read where it is dim and shadowy in the midst of all that lush and crawling life, even in the harshest of the day, or like in the movies we have
seen—Aguirre marching mad while his men slash at inundating plant life
just to move two steps ahead, or Terence Malik's *Thin Red Line* where
the slightest turn of a camera catches a toucan here, slight turn, a panther
there—but in a jungle, nonetheless. Though it is true I thought of it as a
jungle only because I'd read it in the brochures.

It might actually be better to call it the tropics, more accurate. Because that I was sure of, and not just because I'd read it somewhere; it was
tropical. There were several things to assure me of this. For instance, it was
extremely hot, yet every day between the hours of four and six it rained
for about forty minutes, the humidity having built to a point where it finally congealed into big clean drops that fell on us from out of the sky. We
all waited for that rain with anxious eagerness, for before it came to cool
things off we moved slow through the thick and humid air, made worse
by our own sweat. And then there was the vegetation, all those plants that
I didn't know the names of, some of them familiar, to be sure, for it's not
like I was really in a jungle, we've decided. Those plants did mostly look
like things I'd seen before: a strange and giant hibiscus with flowers bigger
than any I'd ever seen on a hibiscus. And big banana trees. A whole series
of bushes with long red penile-shaped flowers. Lots of flowering, creeping

47

vines, purples and pinks and bright yellows. Some bougainvillea—these I knew by name. And there were countless birds, also in wild and screaming colors. They screamed in a literal sense too, squawks and screeches and yells. And there were more butterflies than I was used to seeing, in pale greens and yellows and oranges, gathering together in big packs and then fluttering up all at once when I snuck up on them that first happy morning, like Easter confetti that rose instead of fell.

I saw buzzards too, twenty or thirty the next day, heaped atop something on the road down the way, and then as we approached in our tiny car we smelled first what that something was, and as we got closer the huge black clump of buzzards scattered and, yes, we saw it was in fact a skunk, dead there in the road, and my eyes, my husband's eyes too, burned from the intensity of the gas—the only thing still emanating from the pecked-at creature—as we drove by.

It was in this jungle (?), these tropics (!), that I began to decompose.

We had rented this car we were presently riding in. The rental company had dropped it off at the hotel for us that morning and now we were venturing out on our first day trip, some recently unearthed pyramids—hands cupped over noses, eyes squinted almost shut. Yes, at this point there was still a childish dark pleasure in our animal adventures, our oooohs and yells, the buzzards flapping up around our small red car as we drove screaming through that gas.

To be sure there are other things that confirmed these were the tropics; there were countless other creatures, not merely screaming birds, confetti butterflies and dead skunks. In fact, the following night, as he was tauntingly terrorizing me with scenes of approaching snakes, the snakes that were most certainly creeping in and out of bushes, he said, slithering underfoot, we saw a tarantula, as big as the palm of my hand. Not smaller than my hand as I had always imagined those things to be; intense and hairy and black, yes, I had pictured all that, but I had never imagined them so large. It crossed our path, slow and stealthy as we were on our way to the hotel restaurant for dinner, and we stood and stared for a full minute, the light from the flashlight we'd been provided unwavering, the two of us mesmerized and silent until it was well gone before he pushed me hurriedly on. And then he whispered my name as if it were the tarantula doing so, "Elena ... Elena ..." and every 1950s mutant giant creature horror film I've ever seen came into focus in my mind's eye.

Well, that had been something. I was pretty tipsy, now. It was a beautiful night. I imagined that it was always a beautiful night here. Actually, it was slightly oppressive, all that unknown closing in on one, all that insistent and overbearing tropical beauty. Still, the margaritas were big and I liked drinking them and into my second one, brave now, I called out to our waiter: "Guess what we saw," I began. He nodded. So I got louder: "It was huge, hideous!" And I went on to explain where we'd seen it.

"There is nothing hideous about tarantulas," he answered in his formal tone, and continued very matter-of-fact: "They're not horrible. You shouldn't be scared. They eat the Tabanoh, the biting fly." He looked into my eyes as he poured our water.

Two tables away a wealthy Mexican woman was sending her food back. At breakfast she'd done the same thing. Too spicy, she'd said. She was the same woman who laughed along when the Spanish owner talked to the workers as if they were children. Behave now, he'd say; be good or you'll be fired. He called them niñas and niños, these grown Mayan men and women, and she prodded him on with her sinister laugh.

I looked away from her and back at my waiter, "Oh yes, I know that fly! Giant horsefly. It's nasty," I took another sip of my drink, "I couldn't sit by the pool today for more than five minutes before getting a bite . . . I've read they actually take a little bitty piece of you each time. Well, I've completely given up the pool!"

"And besides a tarantula is not interested in you," he went on, ignoring my outburst. "They look scary because they're so dark, so different from you, all those slow limbs, but they want nothing to do with you."

I looked at his Indian face, the curve of the nose and that black hair, the politeness in the mouth contrasted with the suddenly harsh intonation of his words; or maybe it was not meant to be harsh; I looked away, confused by the realization that I had lost my ability to discern intention; nonetheless, I was suddenly ashamed. And in my shame I recalled a film I had seen a while back, *Chocolat*. In it a little colonial girl, France, loves the African caretaker, Protée, and he loves her too, gives her good things to eat, tells her stories when they're alone. She is only a child and she can move in and out of the Cameroonian's world, though she is reminded by an old African woman that she is not one of them. She will turn black, spending so much time with them, she says. "Your father will scream," she says. There is a sexual tension between Protée and her mother, but they are different, will always be different, and there is no broaching that. These are lines that cannot be crossed, the film tells us, because both sides risk losing something, as if only madness lies on the other side. But here, in Mexico, in a very different time, I hated the idea that because I was afraid of tarantulas, somehow, in my waiter's eyes, I was like the rich women at this hacienda. And here's the thing: Oscar didn't mind. He liked the service, he said. He was going to tip them when we left, he said. I cringed when he elbowed up to the Spanish owner of the hotel, and another woman who spent a lot of time complaining greeted Oscar with a big and open smile. Yet I looked like them, was with them. Was them. In that moment my waiter was the Incan Indian clearing the path for Aguirre, and I was, in his eyes, the mad Spaniard in search of mythic gold. With tiny arrows the Incas had killed Aguirre. And I had felt that they were right. But my allegiances did not matter here, me on this side of the table, my waiter on that.

I was drunk and embarrassed now, and I again began thinking about the snakes he'd been terrorizing me with. Last night another waiter had told us all about them. And Oscar knew I was frightened: coral snakes, not so large, but deadly for sure. And then there were the jaracas, arboreal snakes. Not deadly, but large, five and six feet long and as thick as your arm, and though they really only eat rats, they could very easily dip their heads down at you from a tree. That would be something. And there were others this man had talked of. The tzabacan, and the eyelash viper—a cute name for a deadly poisonous snake. And you better be sure you know what bit you if one does, the waiter said, because if you don't know which one it was, how are they going to give you the right antidote? Oscar smiled at him and all I could do was laugh along. Though I read what the waiter had put there, in that question of his, and knew too that Oscar was having fun with him at my expense, and that they both heard right through my own lame and sorry laugh, my attempt to join in the fun. And I knew too that Oscar didn't have any of these issues I had with the waiters, my place in relation to them, and that somehow that made it easier for him to interact. The boundaries were clear. And together they laughed at me.

That night, the frogs that the hotel used to keep the mosquitoes under control (they used bats too, and there is a lot I have to say about those bats), were especially loud. There was one, well, it could have been one, or it could have been many with a similar voice and coming from the same direction, this one or many was really going at it and since there was no way I was going to be able to sleep, I turned on the light, picked up my copy of *Wide Sargasso Sea*, and began reading. It was hard to focus with my head so full of margaritas and that image of Oscar and the waiter laughing at me, but after rereading the same paragraph several times (or was it only twice?) my eyes actually began shutting. It was then, there in the rafters, that I saw a shadow, and when I focused on that shadow it became a rat. It was walking upside down! How it could possibly walk upside down in the middle of the ceiling like that I don't know, but I swear I saw it do it. And I wanted to wake Oscar, from his deep snore there next to me, but was embarrassed at my own fear, how easily it could take hold and overwhelm me, so I struggled to be reasonable, looked away and tried to begin reading once again. But no, it was too difficult; I was much too preoccupied with looking up for that rat, even long after it had disappeared into a corner. I continued staring at the ceiling even in the dark, once I'd forced myself to turn the light off, after giving up the book. It would surely end up on my chest at some point in the night, I thought, unless one of those big jaraca snakes happened to crawl by.

I lay awake for hours, still and again wanting to wake Oscar, but too ashamed of my own stupidly racing heart—what would I say to him was the matter? And besides, how would I look in his eyes, panting and full of fear at a silly little mouse? Barely able to mouth the word, help? So I lay awake for hours, knowing but not believing that no snake would be crawling up to where I was . . . crawling, slithering, tongue darting in and out, fangs exposed, ready for the attack.

Who knew how I finally fell asleep, but I must have at some point (probably only an hour or two ago) because now he was waking me, calling to me from outside, calling me to come and look. He was happy and eager, completely unaware of the torturous night I'd passed. The lack of sleep in that hazardous night.

"Take a look at this," Oscar yelled, his big tan arm drawing me forth, to the side of the dipping pool outside our room, on the edge of which he stood, tall and contented, looking in.

I was tired and annoyed by his enthusiasm, his inability to read my growing despair without making me have to speak it; nevertheless, I dragged myself over. And then I saw them, hundreds of little tadpoles darting about in that pool. All that new life. It was a full minute before I spoke, near a whisper: "They were awfully loud last night, kept me

awake till dawn, the parents." I looked over at him, "Do frogs get especially loud when they plop out those eggs?"

"Maybe it was some kind of frog orgy you heard," he answered,
unwittingly continuing to make light of my sleepless night, as he walked
over to the coffee that had been left for us outside the room.

And then I did feel rather stupid, or hollow, maybe. The beautiful
day all around me, and me unable to make sense of what I felt. I crouched
down to get a closer look at all of that new life and started thinking
about the frogs' partners, the bats. They were great, really. I knew this, was
convinced by this. They ate mosquitoes; the frogs ate the larvae—thank
god for this new batch—and the bats finished off what the frogs hadn't
gotten, five or six hundred a night each. So they were our friends, really.
I am a magnet for mosquitoes, a huge welt every time they bite, so bats
are my friends. But the thing is, they flew right at you, or, rather, right at
me. The night we got to this place—the hacienda cum hotel, and really
it was beautiful here—two of them flew right at my head as I climbed
the stairs where the owner was waiting to greet us. Flew right past the
owner's grey-haired head and at mine. They never hit; at least I've been
told they never hit. Still, having these little rats with wings and bared teeth
flying right at my head was nothing pleasant. It happened again a few
days later when I went into an abandoned colonial house in downtown
M. with a realtor and Oscar. The two of them walked right through this
house—making tentative deals, exchanging information, the bats ignoring them, while I trailed behind dodging the beasts left and right, my
excitable heart racing from all the action, all that agitation. This realtor
would lean right into walls covered in guano when she wanted to point
out some feature, covered herself in guano just to point out some Italian
tile, or a baroque cornice for christ's sake. I wanted to pull her away from
those walls and scold her, tell her that Bob Dylan, yes, the Bob Dylan, had
almost died when the bacteria from bat guano entered his bloodstream
not three years ago. It was true; I'd read it in *The Post*; but a bat flew at my
head and I forgot my train of thought.

We'd just gotten married. We were on our honeymoon. And I was
starting to doubt everything.

The other thing about bats is that their guano looks like bloodstains.
All over the walls of the old colonial buildings there were what looked
like the stains of millions of squashed insects. Bloody walls. Streaked red
bloody walls. The owner of the house we were shown just before this

one had explained them to me when I asked what those stains were. But they do eat the mosquitoes, the owner reminded, and this woman told me I really shouldn't be afraid of them.

When we weren't looking at houses in M., the main town, we would drive around in our rented red car, going from tiny village to tiny village, in all of them a cathedral built from the very rocks of the ancient pyramids. The Catholic Spaniards had the Mayans tear down their own temples, I learned, then rebuild churches with those already sacred, in a different language, rocks. And often, en route from town to town, we'd see dozens of those buzzards, circling and circling there in the distance, so that we'd have to imagine something dead there under them, or nearly dead, the buzzards waiting for it to hurry up and go.

And it was here that I began to see myself.

And when we got back after five or six hours on the road, that second day, the skunk we'd seen splayed there was nothing but a sack of fur, the buzzards having done their job. And as I stared at this fur I tried to tell myself how important the buzzard is, how it is an indispensable component of that cycle we are all a part of. But I was not convinced.

For it was then that I began to formulate the image. Began to feel myself a blip. Could see us from way up there, engulfed. Could follow the empty and meaningless tiny red car I sat in far below, crawling through that vast and endless landscape, as seen through the buzzard's cold eye.

The first night, the night we'd arrived, there were some spiders in the room. Big but not too scary. I told myself to remember to check my shoes before putting them on in the morning, though I knew even then that I would forget. So I said it aloud, to him, "Remind me to check my shoes for spiders before I put them on in the morning." Aloud.

I had read some information about the hotel, where they kind of gave their philosophy, all organic, eco-friendly. Every creature serves a purpose. Sure. That was okay, admirable even, just remember to check the shoes. Then, in the bathroom, I saw this ant. Huge. It was red, and my husband, Oscar, my brand-new honeymoon husband, told me he'd heard of cows that'd been killed by swarming fire ants. Goats too. Really big things. I myself had seen a show on the jungle once in which there is a big rain, and a catfish joyfully ventures out for food in the new water. But the water eventually dries up, of course, and this dumb fish is stuck in a puddle, which is now separated from the other puddles that eventually lead back into the lake or creek or river or whatever by patches of dry land. This catfish and all the other catfish who have stupidly wandered out have to work their way back to bigger water by twisting and pushing and tossing themselves from puddle to puddle. They showed one that made it. Smart strong fish. Then they showed the typical one, the one who got tired in his twisting and shaking. Was tired. Couldn't take it anymore. Was sick and tired and terrified and could not take it any longer so that in his weakened state he got found by one ant. Then more ants, of course, and more ants and many more ants. Till he was all aswarm. And then I had to look away and even so I pictured it in my mind's eye, that poor dry dead fish. And as I was trying not to recall this fish any longer, feeling sick and sorry for her, a surge of nervous electricity ran through me and I remembered something else which had been lost; I shuddered as I saw myself, a girl, and there in the distance, in the middle of a field sits my dog, like she is paralyzed. My sisters are there too now, and we are standing, our hands by our sides covered in mud. We are serious but happy, a pause in our play, looking toward our new dog who is a German shepherd and is only four months old, and then we walk together slowly to see what Diana is doing, what game our goofy dumb puppy is playing, sitting so so still; and as we approach we see she is covered in ants. We scream in horrible unison and then the oldest, Marina, runs and begins to swat them off, and then the other two of us join in, reluctantly at first but then with more conviction. Six small arms flailing, bits of mud flying up around us.

What was it that had made Diana sit like that? Why had she not found the strength to move when it all began? Didn't she know what it would turn into? She had not even yelped out—cried for help. But we had seen. In that moment of need we had seen.

"Naaaah," he said when I excitedly called out this story. "That's too strange. Why wouldn't you have told me that before?"

"I don't know," I answered, "I just remembered it . . . or maybe it was a dream," I added, suddenly doubting myself.

When I walked back into our room from the bathroom I managed a smile, "It's possible that I only just dreamt it," I repeated, confused now as to whether it had happened, his doubt turning into my doubt, and I made a mental note to ask Marina. Then, an hour later, after Oscar had turned over, was already snoring, I got up to pee and saw another of those ants. And then another, and then two more crawling out from under the sink. I had to remind myself of the philosophy of the hotel, everything a purpose, all a part of this small world, this big cycle . . . blah blah blah. Tried not to worry about those ants, shut the bathroom door good and tight, and turned off the light. Though I woke up more than once that night, wondering at the number swarming there around me, were there thousands now?, afraid to get up to pee again, afraid to leave my safe-island bed, there in the middle of that menacing night.

And then in the still tired morning I crept into the bathroom and it was the same ten ants as the night before. Probably just looking for water, he said. Last night you said they could eat a cow, I answered, upset. Then I went out and put on my shoe without looking in it first and had to fling it away from myself with a scream when I felt the slight moving legs there on my toes. "Christ! I only told myself about a hundred times last night to remember to look in the shoe."

Oscar laughed at me, peeked in at the now empty shoe, and handed it back to me.

"Don't laugh," I said. "You know," I went on, "I know someone who lost a leg from a spider bite. He owned the gas station by my old apartment. I saw him one month, two legs. The next month he was on crutches with one leg missing. When I asked one of the guys who worked for him he said it was a spider bite. So don't laugh!"

"Naaaaah," he said. "That doesn't happen." He took a bite of his apple.

"Okay, then, nah," I answered as I finished putting on my shoes. And then, standing straight and with fisted hands down at my sides, "Why do you always doubt what I say?" I cried.

For Herzog, the jungle was a fetid, stinking place, all things spoiling, rotting. "It's the harmony of perfected and overwhelming murder," he said.

And here. The ants. And that dead skunk. The attacking bats, and too loud frogs. Rats in my room and snakes surely not too far behind. And don't forget the tarantula—who cared if it ate the fly who took a tiny chunk of you with each bite. It was A TARANTULA!

And now I was in bed, not sleeping again and my heart was rushing. No, this was not just a normal rushing heart. These were palpitations. This could be the indication of some large and possibly unfixable problem. Arrhythmia. I knew what that was. Holes in my heart. I could have a heart attack. Here in the middle of all of this unknown, all alone, Oscar snoring through it all. Today we had gone to look at more houses, there in downtown M. It was a ploy. We sometimes did this at home. We would call a real estate agent, let them know we were looking for a house, give our specifications, and then, voyeurs, see how other people lived. But today Oscar had said: It would be great to really move here. It's so beautiful and rich and full of so much life. He had spoken it like that, all formal and flowery. A pitch. Then he'd gone on: It wouldn't be too hard to do. All either one of us needs for our work is a computer and the mail. Something like that. He'd said something like that—but I couldn't be sure because my head had begun spinning after he'd spoken the first sentence. No, I'd returned, hyperventilating. It's all too much. We just got married. I'd like to figure that out. You know, live inside it a bit before I start jumping to another world, to another puddle. No way. I repeated it, my head shaking involuntarily. I need to be around people I know. People that can see things. I need Marina.

But I saw that there was something in his eyes, as if things had already been decided.

And then I was scared. How had I not seen it before? Me and him. People think these things before they settle into a union, no? They see things that need to be seen. Change their minds even. Walk away. Why hadn't I? I had never seen, worried, never felt myself disappearing, never felt myself so doubted, discounted, engulfed. And maybe, maybe there had not been anything to see before. But now, that look in his eyes.

And as we were driving back to our hotel, there in the distance I saw another pack of those infernal perpetual buzzards, and I was afraid that it was me who was going to die, and it was then that I clearly saw myself there under that swarm, my body all laid out. And now after another big dinner and a few margaritas I was in bed and my heart was rushing—no, palpitating, and I was, again, ashamed to wake him with: Oscar, I think I'm having a heart attack. I think I am going to die. And it was me in that jungle—it was a jungle—the swirling swirling sounds and the bigness of the world outside my room, no, not outside, my room a part of all of that and me, my self enveloped by the darkness of that moonless night and all the breathing life around me, the fetid, rotting life. And my heart was rushing and racing with all of this and I wanted to wake him so I reached out to him and began to rub his big shoulder but he did not awake so I lifted myself up and crawled over to him and began to kiss at his neck—I needed him awake—and when he turned from his side onto his back I crawled very slowly on him. Hello, he whispered. Hello, I trembled back, unable to open myself up, unable to ask for help. And as I moved on top of him I saw myself—tied there to our bed, snakes and rats slithering and running all over me. Shut my eyes and saw myself stepping on a mound of those fire ants, was unable to will myself to move and then felt as my body went numb and then stopped feeling, finally, when I was fully paralyzed. And then I am up up up, floating high above it all, and when I begin my descent, fast and sudden into the jungle from out of the sky, I see that there are vine-covered pyramids there and lots of claustrophobic green green lush, down, down below me, and again I see a pack of those big black birds circling and swirling all about.

And as I fall I hear his voice from very far away:

"Hey, are you crying," it asks.

"I'm just so . . ." is all I can bring myself to say back.

YOUNG GOODMAN BROWN EFFECT

Kevin Killian

In Hawthorne's 1835 fable of Puritan guilt, Young Goodman Brown leaves Salem Village and his whitewashed cottage at sunset, the pleasant voice of his young wife, Faith, lilting through the air while she scrubs dishes or churns butter. . . . Alone he sets out on a path narrowing into the forest, red leaves crunching underneath and the last rays of the sun disappearing overhead as he trudges on, one doesn't know why yet. . . . He meets a distinguished stranger who agrees to walk with him a ways, and little by little we discover that this kindly old man is really the devil, guiding Brown to a witches' Sabbath. Brown had the intellectual curiosity, perhaps, to wonder what evil feels like; but he didn't know the experience was going to be so universal, large enough to envelop just about everyone he's ever known. As he proceeds into the heart of night, the exalted status of his companion impresses all those they encounter: the "good" people of the town, teachers, ministers, jolly grandpas, mothers, and virgins: all are on this pilgrimage together, and all of them are hooked on evil. It's that thing where what you thought you knew is different once the lights go out. Brown's feeling ill and horrified, but then they get to the clearing and who's there, in a bridal gown, but Faith, his wife, eager to marry her Satanic lord at midnight, while the graves creak open to reveal the souls of the damned. "The husband cast one look at his pale wife, and Faith at him. What polluted wretches would the next glance show them to each other, shuddering alike at what they disclosed and what they saw! 'Faith! Faith!' cried the husband, 'look up to heaven, and resist the wicked one.'" Our young hero blacks out, and when he comes to, in the morning, all seems well in the village and Faith seems innocent, but how can he believe his senses? I guess we've all had those days where our wits give us opposite accounts of the "real," but in the supermediated age we live in, the Young Goodman Brown effect, if I may isolate it with a name, has increased geometrically. Let me tell you a little story about a boy I know, and how I became aware of his double life and how I felt when it found me out.

My downfall, like Goodman Brown's, stemmed from pride. I always thought that being a novelist necessarily entails sharp wits and better yet, a good working knowledge of men and women's ways. As a novelist I should be able to see more accurately other people's relationships, know their innermost thoughts. I'm usually wrong, so wrong in fact that I have been questioning whether the novel in fact does know any more about human relationships than, say, that abandoned pair of sneakers, knotted and dangling over the telephone wires at the foot of my alley. For too long the novel has privileged itself, and the joke may very well be that it is clueless. At least insofar as I am a practitioner, I confess I don't have all the answers, in fact I have never had one. But my modesty, false modesty or whatever, jumped up and bit me in the ass a few months back. This anecdote will show you how I don't know life, but video does. Fall 2007, another semester teaching at the art school, and having the strangest feeling that one of my students, a young man of exceptional talent, looked somehow familiar, as though I had known him, known him intimately.

This was Jason Marais, who had come to San Francisco from Delaware, back East, landed like a refugee with a broken wing. Delaware's the one U.S. state that I'd never met anyone from before—that I know of, unless it's a guilty secret in the shadowy background of some of my friends, but why cover it up? Why not just look me straight in the eye and say, "I'm from Delaware"? I'd look at him over my clipboard with what must have been, had a third party been watching us, a strange expression of suspicion crossed with guilt, lining my face. I'd continue talking about how to write an essay, and I give myself credit that not once did I actually stop talking, but I came damn close. I looked down and the clipboard was shaking in my hands, betraying a—I couldn't figure it out, but some sort of deconstruction was taking place right before my eyes, like it was Michael J. Fox who was holding up that clipboard in that wobbly way he has that's actually quite charming. Or a scene from *The Exorcist*, the 1973 movie adapted from the controversial best seller of the same name, where Linda Blair plays disturbed adolescent Regan, who hasn't been herself lately. "She's acting like she's fucking out of her mind, psychotic, like a . . . split personality," says Ellen Burstyn, her equally distraught mother. At night, the words HELP ME appear across Regan's stomach. During the day, she levitates, taunts the young priest sent to help her, and beats mother Burstyn senseless, stabbing herself with a crucifix. Yes, that's rather how I felt when I talked with Jason, wobbly and self-conscious, only I didn't know it with my "mind"; only my hands knew.

What my mind knew was that my young student, as it happens, is a superb stylist masquerading as a writer. Some of us who burn bright at age twenty-three may burn out by the time we're thirty, but it might be that this Jason, my Jason, has it in him to write something great and to keep up with it. In other areas his life, as I tried to piece it together, seemed makeshift, his background blurry and partial, a smudged fingerprint. He'd throw out enough backstory that you could just about piece together into one master narrative, but there'd be leftover pieces that seemed to fit nowhere. (But that would be true were I to tell you about my life, wouldn't it? It's not as though we each have one story, one life to live.) Jason's family had some money, or had lost their money through the generations. I got the picture that the father was a withholding, disapproving type, but sometimes I thought he was dead, other times alive. The mother was more visible, hovering around Jason's broad shoulders like a fog of charm, cellophane crinkling in the sun. She was more permissive, didn't mind him being gay, wasn't trying to get him to go straight. But she was no angel either. She had a series of flower shops all throughout Delaware. I wanted to meet her; then I thought, well, it's always weird when writers' parents turn out to be my age or even a bit younger, and they look at me thinking in horror, this bohemian man might be what my boy or girl becomes most like! I could ask her what the state flower of Delaware is and if she found it more popular than ordinary flowers, like roses.

At my office I was asking people about Delaware, for it's funny how many people will confess things at an office that they won't in the outside world. There's a French expression for the phenomenon I'm about to describe; it's a version of our "open secret," a fact about someone so obvious that it's never mentioned and thus becomes invisible to those not in the loop. In France they call it a *secret de Polichinelle*, a secret that's known to all the world, except for the person who doesn't know it. Polichinelle was "Punch" in the Punch and Judy puppet shows of France, and his secrets were "stage whispered" by the narrator to the entire audience, though he remained his benighted, wooden-headed self. I started asking people if they had a twin, and what d'you know, many acknowledged this straight out. In fact one girl at my office is one of three triplets! This was the dominant fact of her young life up till now and yet I would never have known it because it was exactly too obvious. Strange Chestertonian paradox, you have made my life more interesting than it deserves! "Are you adopted?" produces a few reactions, though there's something more charged about this question, and people get skittish when they're asked. This woman in our accounting department, Elena, was adopted, and with a girlish moue she said that as a child she'd fantasized about having royal blood like Princess Diana. In her sharp three-piece suits and Cuban heels, Elena does look a little like Diana, though a dark-haired version of her. And I could picture her kissing AIDS patients or walking through land mines like Diana. The scenarios are endless. I suppose the truth of it is, almost any of us could be adopted and not know it. But Delaware you would think one would remember, and one wouldn't be ashamed to have hailed from any particular state, and yet no one copped to Delaware—not a soul.

At school functions Jason would return my gaze with an utter lack of curiosity, rather the way a cat will look at you, those impenetrable eyes flat and inexpressive. Thus I couldn't read him, couldn't read him reading me. Did he know I found him sort of sexy? That isn't to say I wanted to fuck him—which, I will say, I sort of did, but I sort of didn't for all sorts of reasons. It wouldn't really be cool because of liability issues, as well as the outright prohibition of sexual congress between teacher and student. I'm always reading on TheSmokingGun.com of the tidal wave of pretty, twentysomething high school teachers who give themselves to their junior high students, texting them, "U were a stud last nt, A plus," and wondering, how did these women let themselves go like that? Often as not they have husbands and toddlers themselves, yet they're going down on their 15-year-olds in the broad daylight of Smithtown Middle School. Why, how, what happened to the proprieties? Could it be that every time you make a new rule, whatever you're condemning just grows dearer to those who now can't do it freely? How did boys become men in the long huts of Margaret Mead's Samoa? Anyhow that's the reason I didn't want to go there, I just shudder at being perceived as "one of the crowd."

He surveyed me with what I came to think of as his Delaware look.

He was used to the gaze, that was obvious, and yet he'd go red at the oddest times, blushing a hot red all up and down his face, even the patch of forehead that peeked through his thatched blond fringe. For on top he sort of resembled one of those old-time thatched cottages you sometimes see in old prints of medieval France. He's not a big guy; he's slightly built but with long legs that allow him to run faster (I would think) than the ordinary man.

Afterwards, dissecting particularly purple patches of writing by Joan Didion, around the seminar table we would sit, thinking, and Jason would be squirming in such a way that if he were your dog, you'd be thinking he must have worms. Really rubbing his ass into the hard purple plastic of the chair. This was a wonderful sign to me, that his cool surface could agitate where writing was in question. He could be positively expansive when it came to his own ambitions in that direction.

I remember at Walzwerk, an East German restaurant near my apartment, with wonderful pot roast and Wiener schnitzel and pear soup, the waiter was even more attentive when I brought my class in as a special treat. We had a table for six and Jason sat on the very far end from me, he got drunk really fast and started talking about how much he loved Samuel Fuller movies. How he wanted to be the gay Sam Fuller, except in writing, that he would join the spirit of Denton Welch with that of Sam Fuller. My waiter, Mauritz, was all like, that boy you are with is famous online. Big porn star him.

"Oh really?" I murmured, automatically, not really thinking.

Then he dropped his voice, dropped the clue. "Why don't look you at Extreme Remedies, the Web site? Look up under 'Scottt.' Scott with three T's," said Mauritz, handing me back my credit card.

"Okay, I will."

"Why isn't there a gay Vollmann," shouted Jason, imitating the famous author firing two guns over his own head like Yosemite Sam capturing your attention. "A gay fucking Vollmann, with balls and not just, you know, a quaint French cottage in the Lorraine."

"Be prepared for another side to your friend," whispered Mauritz. I didn't know what he meant but, of course, it was the *secret de Polichinelle*. At home I clicked open the laptop, meaning to write something else, but my guilty fingers found themselves spelling out "Extreme Remedies." A site of vast capacity, "Extreme Remedies" isn't free, but with dozens of free tours, you could easily spend hours on it without having to enter your credit card number once.

My cat, Sylvia, prowled around my ankles, hoping to rouse me from my detective activity, give her some food. But in fact I couldn't say if she ever ate again. Such considerations seemed utterly distant when I typed in the single name "Scottt" with three T's, and then presto, in an instant, I was transported as though by a genie to the very site of Jason's other life. The picture moved and bulged, occasionally some pixels blurred and burned together, but all in all it was a remarkably sharp image of the boy, Jason my student, in profile, on his knees. He was naked but for a wristwatch, like one of Colter Jacobsen's drawings, bent along a bench, his head touching the bench, his face turned to the camera, thus to me. His cheek mashed against the wooden width of the bench, as though an invisible boot was pinning him by the throat.

I could see his face appealing to me for help, his mouth mumbling some words or stentorian breaths. Hard to make out what he was "saying," but it was the sort of thing you yourself might mumble if it was your ass up in the air being spread and pounded by what looked like an enormous grease gun. At my kitchen table I looked this way, that, hastily, for what I was seeing seemed so raw it seemed wrong of me to see, and of course we feel implicated when the moving image, relentless as the piston-fueled dildo machine manipulating his butt, moves into our line of vision. A ring of dampness rose inside my collar.

I can't believe he did this, I thought, and then: or let himself be filmed like this, for anyone—I suppose!—might want to try a fucking machine if you thought you could actually accommodate the dildo at its working end. In private, in the spirit of scientific inquiry, one might put it in an inch—an inch and a half—then slide it out gingerly, saying no thanks, too ornate. But in porn you can't say no thanks; there might be "safe words" but no thanks isn't among them. On-screen Jason's tongue flickered all around his lips and he drew up one hand from the floor—was it supposed to be a garage or auto body shop?—and his mouth sucked in his thumb, as though for comfort. Spittle glued his blond hair to the bench beneath his cheek; his eyes had gone blank, flat buttons of blue and white, through which you might delude yourself into thinking you were reading messages of hurt or lust. Meanwhile the thing, nearly alive, like a

Giger maquette from *Alien*, or a Sten gun reengineered into a pile driver, made further assaults on his smooth, oscillating ass. His chest heaved, rattling like a torn muffler. I could see his cock, dangling down from his elevated hips, nothing special there, a glistened red-brown tube good for shaking, responding, quivering, but he didn't seem hard. Not hard-hard. Oh, whatever. You can go and judge for yourself if one of the most talented young writers around is hard or soft in his video clip. It's moving so fast it's hard to tell, but to me what I saw was beyond phenomenology. His appearance in this video threatened to explain some aspects of Jason, but otherwise it only complicated him, made my knowledge of him more fleecy, the way you might dissolve the picture you had painstakingly etched on "Etch-a-Sketch" by shaking the red square toy with your hands. The connecting lines disappear and only grains remain.

I guess Jason's secret life explained that peculiar dog thing he does in class, rubbing his ass along the chair, as though it were sore, as though it were raw or wet. Poor guy, and yet, if this intrusion was so awful, why then did he return and make a sequel a little while later? And a second sequel, not a solo this time but a duet with a second, more vocal boy on the far end of the bench, a boy called Willie. Where "Scottt" suffers in silence, Willie's panicked screams ring through the dungeon, glissando, like Joan Sutherland in one of those Rossini roles, imprisoned for a crime she did not commit and yet free as the air at the same time, for her voice could part bars. And this boy's voice is like a pair of hands that pulled himself out of danger with the solace of musical theater. The tape is called "Scottt and Willie Meet Mr. Machine." Meanwhile Jason just kneels in perfect silence while, this time, an electrical charge is mounted to the oscillating dildo inside him, and you can register the sudden shifts in voltage only by his abruptly shocked and numbed eyeballs, glistening, unblinking. He is the lizard to the other boy's lark. Jason can't talk, for the sheer mass inside him preempts his thought, indeed his identity. But Willie finds surcease in sound, in moving into a realm of spiritual and physical bird noise.

Well, you couldn't stay all day watching the same brief clips over and over, you had to pony up if you wanted more of this spectacle—this series of mini-spectacles—so I became a member of course. You could have DVDs mailed to your home or just have these full-length videos "streaming" (and was there ever a better word!) down one's screen from morning to night all month. Something like thirty dollars a month? At the time it seemed very reasonable. The devil had brought me to this place, but I was curious. And then when I wanted to look away, something in the very transactional fact of my gaze made that a no can do. I had given myself up for good. It did remind me of the days when the Internet was brand-new for us, and me and Dodie would go on and look up sites, and the first thing I looked up was the "Anagram Generator." We tried making anagrams out of our names, and then when that palled, we thought of our cats, Blanche and Stanley, who were playing on the rug nearby. And when I typed in "BLANCHE AND STANLEY" the program spat back hundreds, thousands of combinations, but oddly—horribly—the first one that came back, lo, leading all the rest—was "CHANNELLED BY SATAN." I looked down at the cats and they seemed to pause in their play and stare at me with those flat cat eyes as if to say, you have reached the subhuman, how may we help you?

I couldn't tell whether or not "Scottt" was a star within the confines of the "Extreme Remedies" world, or whether he was but a featured player. He had made a sizable number of punishment videos, but five or six boys on the site had made more. And in fact in some clips he appears in the background, almost as an extra, like Harry Carey Jr. in the later John Ford films. In some he doesn't even take off his clothes but sits there in his "Jason" clothes, outfits I recognized, looking sullen or bored—that "Delaware look"—while some other twink like Willie takes it for the team. And just as he was sometimes not where you thought he would be, he could sometimes be found where one didn't expect him—as a sort of guest star in other people's videos. It wasn't just a gay site, it was open to anyone with $29.99 a month and the taste for discipline. In fact, counting it up, there were probably more girls than boys being punished, some of them with credits long as my arm.

You could flick from here to there on thumbnails, and in one of them I thought I saw Jason in the background of an otherwise all-girls orgy, set in a hospital ward with cheerful white hospital screens, yards of rubber tubing, cold steel stethoscopes, and what looked like real knives. In the center of the action was the star, "Diana," on her back, resplendent in what apparently was actual electroshock treatment mode, electrodes glued to the sides of her head, and you, the viewer, could control how many volts she was going to get, for the video was apparently at some previous time a live experience, now presented as sort of a souvenir of good times gone by. "I can't believe people pay for this shit," said I—the hypocrite, the distasteful spectator. Jason was dressed as a doctor in operating room gear with big pale green gloves of rubber, and seated on what looked like a metal bar stool in the corner of the operating theater. While the camera focused on Diana's jaw and eyes, and the sizzling burns of wire just above her temples, Jason extended his gloved hands slightly and looked at them with that goofy grin of the stoned, as if to say, what are these plastic things on my hands? Diana's screams filled my kitchen, and then I realized she was Elena, the girl from my office. I had just never seen her lying down. Elena, the one who looked like Princess Diana except a brunette, the one who was adopted, she said. I saw her every day, her nimble fingers massaging a calculator or flicking the coffee machine to decaf.

And you know, ever since that weekend I spent as a member of "Extreme Remedies," I haven't really been able to trust my own senses. I call it the Young Goodman Brown Effect. It's where from the time your alarm clock wakes you in the morning, to the dark hours of the night where sleep mercifully releases you from concern, you don't know who your fellow beings are. They all seem normal on the outside—most of them, that is: I mean you always have characters!—but the moment you turn your back, they're getting plugged from behind for all the world to see; it was only you their demure smile was meant to fool. And maybe I'm the same way, a polluted wretch who shudders to disclose his own sin. Shakes you up it does, when you see something out of the way. Of course God invented porn, and probably the entire concept of cinema, to drill this lesson in us. Those on-screen aren't exactly real people, of course, they're simulacra and thus shouldn't be asked to meet ordinary standards of humanity. Meanwhile I see Jason from time to time at poetry readings, and he was there tonight at Scott Heim's San Francisco launch for his new novel. Elena from my office is getting married in September, from what I understand—I put five dollars in the office pool to buy her a shower present. I can't really look either of them in the eye—I've seen too much of them, and I resent them giving away to a mass audience what should have been kept for me. Behind every good secret, resentment lurks: no wonder Punch and Judy were always hitting each other over the head with those rubbery phallic bats. At the end of my days, when I'm borne to my grave a hoary corpse, they will carve no hopeful verse upon my tombstone, for my dying hours were gloom.

FROM *WHAT EVER: A LIVING NOVEL*

Heather Woodbury

Skeeter and a New Acquaintance Uncover a Spate of Coincidence

Skeeter finds himself by the side of a highway in the gray light of a waning day. Potato fields stretch flat on either side. He stands, thumb stuck out, mutters "shit" as each passing car swooshes by. A '70s-something rust-red Mustang comes into view, tears down the narrow highway, going at least ninety. It screeches to a halt a few yards past him and he runs to catch it. A red-haired guy with bushy eyebrows and a beard is inside puffing on a huge hand-rolled cigarette. He leans over and opens the low-slung car door.

MOCCASIN: How far ya goin'?

He has a voice like someone holding in a big toke on a joint and you can almost hear a swagger in it.

SKEETER: Wull, all th' way tuh New York City, but on th' penultimate swipe, tuh Indiana.

MOCCASIN: I'm headed north up through Montana and then tuh Rapid City, South Dakota, take ya dat far.

SKEETER: Most appreciated, dude.

MOCCASIN: Hop aboard,

The man rolls his eyes sideways at him as they speed off.

MOCCASIN: *Private Idaho.*

SKEETER: Heh, heh heh. Yeh-up.

MOCCASIN: You look like you're about sixteen, what the cosmic fuck you doin' in the middle of Pocatello, Idaho, scout?

SKEETER: Hitchin' rides, you know.

MOCCASIN: Runaway?

SKEETER: Nuh.

MOCCASIN: No?

SKEETER: Nope. Just walked.

MOCCASIN: Yup. 'At's your generation. Walkaway. Huh. 'At's funny. You look like dat kid who died. Good actor, though. My old lady rented the movie after dat kid OD'd. Yeh-up. I don't care for dat homo shit and I fell asleep during 'at Shakespeare poetry bull but I have tuh say, all in all, I enjoyed it. I liked the kid. You look just like 'im and here you are hitchin' in Idaho. Strange. D'you see dat movie? *My Own Private Idaho*?

SKEETER: Naw.

MOCCASIN: Oh. Well it's called *My Own Private Idaho*. You look like 'im, you should see it. You look just like 'im.

SKEETER: Yeah, lotta people say I look like River.

MOCCASIN: Who?

SKEETER: River Phoenix? The dude that died?

MOCCASIN: Dat's his name. You *saw* the movie?

SKEETER: Nuh nuh I just know who he is, was, 'sall.

MOCCASIN: Yeah. P-p-p-people tell you you look like 'im?

SKEETER: Yeh-up. *Girls* do. All the time.

MOCCASIN: Hey, SCOUT! I ain't no homo!

SKEETER: Null that implication at the base, dude. No one said det you were—are. What. *Ever*.

MOCCASIN: Right!

SKEETER: Right.

MOCCASIN: Name's Joe Moccasin, kid, yours?

SKEETER: Ezekial. But my friends call me Skeeter 'cause I annoy 'em in a mosquito-type manner.

MOCCASIN: Yeah, why?

SKEETER: Ah, I wager I talk overmuch.

MOCCASIN: Don't do dat to me, Skeet, not if you wanna ride all the way tuh Rapid City. I HATE people who talk too much.

SKEETER: Most assuredly. I won't, then.

MOCCASIN: Yeah, some people can never stop talking'. Picked up a kid near L.A., sposeta take him to Salt Lake, dropped him in Vegas. Ugly little bastard. Punk rock pimple head, you know?

He puts out his cigarette in a cloud of exhalation disgust

MOCCASIN: An' he wouldn't stop talkin'. 'Bout anarchy. Said he got thrown out of some crash pad in San Francisco 'cause he stole a little chick named Brigit's antique bread box. But he wouldn't admit he stole it, refused to recognize ownership.

Moccasin looks back and forth between the road and Skeeter as he rolls a new cigarette with both hands, propping his hands against the wheel as a precaution.

MOCCASIN: He said they were all *uptight*—part of the po*lice* state 'cause they believed the antique bread box belonged to Brigit.

He sticks it in his mouth.

MOCCASIN: I left 'im to the loose slot machines in Vegas. And I stole 'is lighter.

He takes a Zippo off the dashboard, clanks it open, lights up, clanks it closed, and tosses it back down.

MOCCASIN: Little *fuck*.

SKEETER: Was 'is name Cyrus?

Skeeter rolls his eyes slowly toward Moccasin, inclining his head slightly more in the man's direction.

MOCCASIN: Yeah! How'd you know?

SKEETER: I know that asshole. Useta float the punk scene in Frisco. He's terminally theivin' girls' shit.

MOCCASIN: You don't look like a punk rock.

SKEETER: No more, friend, 'at was when I was twelve'n shit. Now I rave, brother.

MOCCASIN: Yeah? I heard about dat. Dat's col. We did all dat back in the sixties. All dat stuff you kids do? We did all dat thirty years ago.

SKEETER: What.

He looks out the window.

SKEETER: Ever.

Moccasin glances at him.

MOCCASIN: We did. It's all a repeat. We got high. We got higher 'an you. We *balled* everyone.

He clears his throat.

MOCCASIN: I mean, we balled all the chicks. See, I'm hep, I just don't like to hear this political bull. I'm inta gettin' high, ballin'—dat's cool—but when people start takin' about takin' other people's property, livin' without money, not workin', 'at's when I start to get pissed. We got to return to our tradi*ti*onal values we GOT to, I mean, we got to keep *jobs* for Ame*ri*cans you know? And we got to keep our borders *clean*, you know? You *know*?

SKEETER: Sure, dude.

MOCCASIN: Two problems. Immigrants and politicians. Those're the two main problems we have. Dat's why I voted for Ross Perot. An' I haven't voted since. Why bother? Close the borders. And vote out the politicians. Make America a real place again. You *know*?

SKEETER: Dunno. Ain't votin' age yet. Tuhhh.

Skeeter gazes at the scenery. There isn't much, as night falls on the flat fields.

MOCCASIN: Yep. You ain't even seventeen, right? You a runaway?

SKEETER: Nuh, goin' tuh visit m'aunt in New York City. My ma knows.

MOCCASIN: What business you got in Indiana?

SKEETER: Figure I'll stop in, see a dude I know.

Skeeter leans down, elbows on his knees, and looks as far out the window as he can.

MOCCASIN: Where?

SKEETER: Marion?

MOCCASIN: They got a federal prison there.

SKEETER: Yeh-up.

MOCCASIN: Your old man locked up there, Private Idaho?

SKEETER: Yup

MOCCASIN: Drug oh-fence?

SKEETER: Marijuana smuggle.

MOCCASIN: What's 'is? Maybe I know 'im.

Skeeter's neck stiffens with skepticism as he turns toward his driving companion.

SKEETER: Bruce. Bruce Frye?

MOCCASIN: Heheehehheh. See dat? I know Bruce. Heh. Yep!

SKEETER: How do you know Bruce?

MOCCASIN: Drug business, scout, get wise, boy.

He sticks his middle finger under his eye and pulls down the skin in some coded signal of criminal complicity that Skeeter is not yet familiar with.

MOCCASIN: Got a shipment abroad right now. Ha-haah! Bruce Frye's little runt. How 'bout dat? Small fuckin' cosmos, man.

He touches his chest and holds out his hand to Skeeter

MOCCASIN: Arnie McManus, pleased tuh meet ya, Skeet.

SKEETER: Er!

Skeeter regains his composure but chooses not to shake hands.

SKEETER: What.

He looks ahead at the road.

SKEETER: *Ev*er.

A Nephew Expresses His Affection

Back at the wall.

JEANETTE: Ezekial, there you are, come on, get in the cab, I've been looking for you for a week. What happened?

SKEETER: I dunno, I been subject tuh vagrancies. Aunt Jeanette, meet my . . . frien—er, associates. Jasper, Spaz meet—

JASPER: Spare any change, lady? I can see you got it.

JEANETTE: Oh, really?

Jeanette takes an angry pull on her cigarette.

JEANETTE: Well, I earned *my* change sucking the cocks of the rich white male corporate elite for ten years. If you want some goddamn money, I suggest you go suck some cocks of your own.

SKEETER: Whoah, Aunt Jeanette, yur waxin' perilously scandalous!

JEANETTE: Ezek-Skeeter, whatever your fucking nephew name is, get in the damn cab and get away from these drunks.

She yanks him off the wall.

SPAZ: We're anarchists.

JEANETTE: Alright, then, *anarchist* drunks! Come on.

JASPER: Fuck it, Squeezo, yuh not gonna get in dat bourgeois cock-sucka's cab, are ya?

SKEETER: Er, with pleasure.

He quickly gets in the cab and turns to wave.

SKEETER: Bye, associates! Bye, Jasper, bye, Spaz, bye Pork Rind, say good-bye to Giraffe and Mr. Spam and Chito.

SPAZ: ANARCHY!

JASPER: ANARCHY!

SKEETER: What. Ever.

They pull into traffic. The cab driver looks back at Jeanette.

ANATOLE KOMALSKY: Where to?

He has a thick Russian accent and a deep, no-nonsense voice.

JEANETTE: Now back to where you picked me up—Seventy-eighth and Park.

SKEETER: Is 'at true, Aunt Jeanette, did you? Is that how you get yer apartment an' everything?

JEANETTE: What? You think I bought that place teaching my sacred crystal seminars?

SKEETER: I pondered.

JEANETTE: No, you know. You asshole. I've been worried sick about you on top of Paul having a heart attack and deciding to go back to his idiot wife Polly.

SKEETER: Wull, 'at's why I stayed away, Aunt Jeanette, I figured I was in yer path an' all like that, what with yer emotional decrepitude an'—

JEANETTE: So you just went down to Avenue A and stayed there without calling for a week?! How did Linda raise you?!

SKEETER: On th' road? In a bum like fashion.

JEANETTE: Was it the letter from your dad, Bruce, in prison that Linda forwarded to you? Is that what sent you off?

SKEETER: Nuuhhhhhh.

JEANETTE: Ezekial.

SKEETER: SKEEEETERRRRR! I burned it.

JEANETTE: What?

SKEETER: I burnt 'is croakin' letter. See? Hur.

He removes the remains of the letter from his mood-hat and shows them to Jeanette.

JEANETTE: Why did you save the ashes then?

SKEETER: Never. Mind.

JEANETTE: Ez-Skeeter, I realize I haven't been a very available host.

SKEETER: 'At's fine. No problem, Jeanette dude.

He wipes back tears.

SKEETER: I hate my dad anyway. I only defend him tuh piss off Linda. I can't believe all those years you sent us money orders an' all like that you were bein' a, a, p-p-p-prostitute.

JEANETTE: But now I'm a healer, Skeeter, and I do fine.

SKEETER: Tuhhh. 'Cept you won't help me put a spell out on Clove 'n Sable fer whom I am waxin' MOST pinish and melancholic an' you can't keep help yourself with your own twisted heart troubles. Yur just like my ma Linda, all Wicca-er than thou with her crafty ways, but she's still th' same fuck-up with men an' jobs 'et she's always been. An' I'm her son, an' now I get a letter from Bruce. "Dear Ezekial, I'm sorry." Yeah, so am I. Tuhhhh.

JEANETTE: Skeeter, Linda might be a flake but she loves you and she is a good witch, she is a magic healing lady. And I-I may have had a hard life—

SKEETER: 'At's fine, no judgmentality 'bout yer *checkered past* on *my* slope.

She cuts him off.

JEANETTE: But I'm not a flake, okay? I might have emotional problems but I'm working on them and even Bruce, your dad Bruce, might be on the wrong side of the law and was a big partyer, but he's—he's, what can I say, Bruce is Bruce and I wish he'd been around more because he's a unique guy and you remind me of him only you're not an asshole. I didn't mean that. Yes, I did! Come here, come here, Ezekial.

She holds out her arms to him.

SKEETER: SKEETERRR!

He pounds his chest, but in a second he breaks down and is crying on her stomach.

SKEETER: Aunt Jeanette, Aunt Jeanette. I been drunk for a week and I don't even have alcoholic tendencies.

She strokes his head.

JEANETTE: I can tell—you're a stoner from way back.

SKEETER: Right on, oh Aunt Jeanette, you feel so good, yur just like my ma Linda but even prettier an' you understand me better. Yer married boyfriend is such an asshole tuh desertify yer fineness.

JEANETTE: Oh, Skeeter.

SKEETER: Ohhh, Aunt Jeanette.

He is drawn to her full breasts.

JEANETTE: Stop it, Skeeter, honey, don't get sexual.

SKEETER: Puuuhlease, Aunt Jeanette.

JEANETTE: No, stop. Gaia!

She pushes him off.

JEANETTE: I told Linda to stop letting you sleep with her after age seven.

ANATOLE KOMALSKY: Excuse me, you are going to make incyst in my cyab, I drop you at the kirb. Nobody make incyst in my cyab.

JEANETTE: No, I am not going to "make incest"! I'm a grown woman, I can resist the sexual attractions of teenagers. Unlike *men*. My name is not Roma*nette* Polanski!

ANATOLE KOMALSKY: Oh, Roman Polanski, good director. I am fy-ilmmaker. You *know* Roman Polanski?

JEANETTE: Sure, *Knife in the Water*?

ANATOLE KOMALSKY: Oh yeah—*The Tenant*?

JEANETTE: Oh yeh. Sure. *Macbeth*?

ANATOLE KOMALSKY: Huh, oh you know that one? You really know!

SKEETER: Er, who?

JEANETTE: Ah, never mind, Ezekial. Let us off here, here on Lexington. Let's go to the Blue Ship Diner to eat bloody steaks and fries, do you want to?

SKEETER: But, uh, Aunt Jeanette, the food there sucks, and wur both kinda sposeta be vegetarians, aren't we?

JEANETTE: Yeah, so let's go, let's go, and eat it all!

She hands the driver a twenty.

JEANETTE: Here you go, keep the change, thank you.

ANATOLE KOMALSKY: You arre welcome. Uh. What's your number? You want a date?

JEANETTE: Sure.

She looks at his name and picture on the hack license.

JEANETTE: Uh, Anatole Komalsky. I'll call you when I'm in the mood to cuddle up and rent *Rosemary's Baby*. Bye!

SKEETER: Er, have a nice day!

Skeeter shuts the cab door and follows Jeanette to the Blue Ship.

Paul Pursues His Heart

It is midday in midtown Manhattan. Paul catches Jeanette just as she exits a building through a revolving glass door.

PAUL: Jeanette.

JEANETTE: Paul! What are you doing here? Did you come for a seminar at the Epiphany Institute?

She tears down the street through the streams of lunchtime pedestrians.

PAUL: Jeanette, don't be sarcastic, I was waiting here because I knew you were probably teaching one of your seminars.

He chases after her, bumps into someone.

PAUL: Excuse me.

He calls to Jeanette.

PAUL: Can we talk?

JEANETTE: No, I'm in a hurry, I've got half an hour to meet Skeeter at Chase Manhattan and give him the money to buy our plane tickets to Portland.

PAUL: Your nephew. Fine young man. He was there at the apartment when I came to explain to you.

JEANETTE: I'm sick of explanations, Paul.

She bumps into someone.

JEANETTE: Excuse me! I told Skeeter to tell you that I never wanted to see you. Why are you still in New York? Go back to Virginia.

PAUL: But Polly's, my wife's left me, she's having an affair.

JEANETTE: Good. First time she's done anything impressive that I know of.

They stand at a corner, waiting for the light to change. Jeanette begins to cross.

JEANETTE: Send her my compliments and go back to Virginia and rot!

PAUL: But, Jeanie, it's you I love—

JEANETTE: Stop calling me that! It's Jeanette! I'm not your Jeanie, I don't live in a bottle, and I'm not here to grant your every wish. In fact, tell me your heart's desire and I'll use all my crystal powers to make sure you get the fucking opposite.

PAUL: Don't hate all men on my account.

JEANETTE: Don't flatter yourself. There was a long line of bastards before you, starting with my father. You don't know about that, do you?

They are crossing another intersection. Two young men in extremely baggy trousers walk ultraslowly ahead of them, trading rhymes.

KID 1: Over to da *si'*,

I sad you gonna *be* fly.

see how I *move* you *like* they is no *otha* guy.

over on the *take* out

got to *gimme* stooped *make* out
No *blem*ishes, no *false* kisses,
pro*mise* this is no *fake*-out.

KID 2: Whoopsie—whoopsie-*o*
girlie-*girl* I am your *rome*-eo,
I'm *fat* like *dat,*
like *tit* for *tat*
an dat you alrea*dee* know—
over on da *scat,*
you *look* like a *kitty*-cat,
dat I want to *pat,* an' pat
aw, *don't* gimme dat—

JEANETTE: Excuse me, we're trying to pass here.

PAUL: Why do these kids these days walk so slowly?

Jeanette thinks about it a minute, distracted.

JEANETTE: I don't know.

Without missing a beat, she plunges right back into her rage.

JEANETTE: Anyway, as I was saying. If you want to know the real truth, Paul, the first man to betray me was my father.

As she rushes down the sidewalk and Paul struggles to keep up, a horn sounds alongside them repeatedly.

JEANETTE: He came back from the Korean War a sick man, okay? When I was ten, he pushed my mother down an ice hole. Then he put a gun in his mouth. My mama was an Eskimo. How do you like your little Eskimo Pie, Paul? All my life I wondered if my mother was still there under that ice, and then I realized she was, she was frozen inside me.

The horn blasts and Paul looks over.

JEANETTE: I kept her intact. Until you came back and you said, "Jeanette, I don't care about the past, let's be real this time, I want to know you" and then I gave in, I opened up, I thawed out, I let the ice break and dissolved my mama in the warmth of *trusting,* of being available to YOU, of *loving you,* goddamnit. You SHIT, you SHIT, A CURSE ON YOU!

She hammers his chest with her fists as the horn blasts again. Annoyed pedestrians, utterly disinterested in the scene, have to alter their hurried courses down the sidewalk to get around them.

PAUL: Jeanette, that man is—that cabdriver is honking at you, look.

JEANETTE: What?

Anatole Komalsky is leaning out his cab window.

ANATOLE: Hey remember me? I picked you up with your horny nephew who tried to make incyest with you?

PAUL: What? Skeeter tried? And I'm fond of the boy!

ANATOLE: Remember, we were going to go on a date. Roman Polanski, hmm? How about the new one, *Death and the Maiden*?

JEANETTE: No, thanks, I don't think I could handle Ben Kingsley as a South American fascist these days. I'll get in touch when there's a revival of *Repulsion*.

ANATOLE: Okay, well, I'm in the book. Anatole Komalsky.

JEANETTE: Right.

Jeanette tears off again and Paul chases her; by now he is out of breath.

PAUL: Who the hell was that?

JEANETTE: Anatole Komalsky!

PAUL: What was all that about Roman Polanski? Have you dated him?

JEANETTE: What? No, I'm too old for Polanski: I'VE GOT PUBIC HAIR!!! Remember?

PAUL: No, I mean the cabdriver.

JEANETTE: Of course not, Paul. Oh, why am I reassuring you, you infidelitous scumbag!

A little twentysomething woman in a smart business suit and sporting pert pageboy haircut bumps right into Paul.

KIT: Paul Folsom?

PAUL: Huh?

KIT: Kit? Kit Fisher? Barston, Levey and Axtheiler?

She speaks rapidly, rushing allherwordstogether and has a high, squeaky voice like a kid. She plays with the pearl necklace at her throat.

KIT: I met you at the New Cycles for the Next Millennium Conference? You were awesome?!

She glances back at the fast-receding figure of Jeanette.

KIT: Is she all right? Ted Ryan says you resigned from Axnell Board?

PAUL: Oh yeah, I'm great, fantastic, nice to see you, Kit, give my regards to Ted Ryan, tell him I've become an anarchist.

KIT: Excuse me?

PAUL: HA! Just kidding. Got to go. I'm having the most important, HORRIBLE conversation of my life.

KIT: Wooo-kay! Nice to *see* you.

PAUL: Jeanette, wait up, I've never seen that kid in my life.

JEANETTE: She said she knew you, Paul.

PAUL: From a conference. It's like your seminars. I mean, what are you teaching today?

JEANETTE: Cornucopia of Chakral Light Workshop.

PAUL: What? That sounds like a lot of malarkey!

JEANETTE: You asked me! Don't ask!

PAUL: Okay, well do you remember the name and face of every student?

JEANETTE: Yes, because only three people signed up! I'm broke! Now, go away, I'm almost at the bank and I don't want to have a scene with Skeeter.

PAUL: But we've been having a SCENE in front of HALF of NEW YORK!

JEANETTE: That doesn't make any difference. THEY'RE JUST EXTRAS! SKEETER IS A MAIN CHARACTER! NOW GO *AWAY*!!!

He runs after her, gulping down breath, pushing people out of his way.

PAUL: I love you, Jeanette. What do you want from me? I'LL STOP MAKING DONATIONS TO THE GOP! I'LL BURN INCENSE TO A GODDESS OF YOUR CHOICE! I'LL EVEN WEAR ONE OF SKEETER'S MOOD-HATS.

As he catches up to her, she stops and turns to face him.

JEANETTE: No, Paul, it's over, you let me down too many times.

She walks away.

PAUL: I hope you don't hate men because of me, Jeanette, you deserve the best.

She turns again.

JEANETTE: I don't hate *men*, Paul. Hatred requires energy. I *relinquish men*.

PAUL: That's worse.

They both think about this.

JEANETTE: I know.

PAUL: Good-bye, then. I'm glad I at least saw you one last time.

She gives him a final, loving, rueful once-over.

JEANETTE: Good-bye, Paul Folsom.

PAUL: Wait.

JEANETTE: *No!*

PAUL: No, I mean, look, isn't that Skeeter those cops are dragging through the bank lobby?

JEANETTE: Where?

They rush to the bank entrance.

PAUL: Hey, hey stop that!

COP ONE: Who are you?

PAUL: I'm Paul Folsom, retired CEO, Axnell Corp. Until recently, I served on the board of Chase Manhattan and I'd like to know what you're doing with my ex-girlfriend's sister's—with my—uh-grandson! Grandson!

COP ONE: Uhhhhhhhh.

SKEETER: 'At's right, along comes a corpret dude and post-haste I'm reprieved o'yer hoaxish accusations!

2

Living Images

PHONE HOME

Dodie Bellamy

E.T.'s chest glows red with fear as faceless agents chase him through the forest. My mother and I sit in her living room and watch. A week ago she called me in San Francisco and said she couldn't breathe right, that she felt like she was suffocating. The doctor was going to stick a long needle in her chest and drain out the fluid from around her lungs. "I'm afraid," she said. And then she started crying. "Please come home." The procedure didn't help. My mother's breaths are loud, a jerky bellows over the movie's soundtrack. Compared to the swimming pool–studded terrain Elliott crazily pedals his bike around, our Indiana neighborhood is modest. Still, I'm reminded of my recurring dreams of racing my blue Schwinn down Oakdale Avenue. I'm hungry, so while Elliott scatters a trail of M&Ms in the woods, I dart into the kitchen to make a salad. Washing my lettuce I stare out the window at the apple tree in the front yard. The tree looks like a man bending forward with his arms outstretched. Like in a fairy tale, I think. "Dodie!" my mom calls out. She's having an anxiety attack. She had one yesterday and the day before. I give her a Xanax and sit beside her on the couch. She's gasping for air. All through my visit she's been talking about a neglected neighborhood cat—Fred—my mother lets him in when it's cold and feeds him. Last night when Fred came to the door scratching and meowing, she said, "All he wants is a human touch, he's craving a human touch," and I knew she meant herself. She's hunched over in her sleeveless nightgown, shaking. So frail. I awkwardly put my arm around her. She lays her head on my shoulder and holds my hand.

My mother's lung cancer has returned. We don't have an official diagnosis yet, but we both know it. She calms down a bit so I nod to the TV and say let's watch *E. T.* Elliott's just lured E.T. into his bedroom. Elliott places his fingers to his lips, then E.T. places his fingers to his own lips. Elliott sticks one finger to his ear, ditto E.T. Elliott smiles, then holds his left hand up with all five fingers spread apart. E.T. raises his left hand with his three fingers spread apart. Elliott makes a fist and points his forefinger up. E.T. does the same. They both wiggle their fingers. My mom says, "I love this movie."

Nothing about my reaction to my mom's situation is unpredictable. My mind is frazzled trying to figure out what to do, I rehearse one scenario after another, I couldn't possibly drop everything and move here—but who else would take care of her—and if I did who would teach my classes and how could I abandon Kevin. I feel overwhelmed, swallowed. I'm compulsively task oriented. I'm numb—then tears well up. I take a walk during a tornado warning, the sky is a chiaroscuro of white clouds fluffy as cotton candy jammed against ominous dark patches, I'm elated by the drama of the light flickering between sunny and shadowed, the intense cool wind tousling my hair about. I go to a supermarket, the place is huge and unintuitive—too many things too many choices—tears get caught in my throat. For the lung fluid removal my mother is hooked up to a heart rate monitor, I watch as the LED number continuously changes from the upper 80s to low 100s—it's like her heart is convulsing—and I try not to let her see how freaky her arrhythmia is. I drive over to Walgreen's to pick up her prescription and feel tenderness and compassion for each sad, fluorescently lit person standing behind a cash register or idly wandering the aisles. The horror of old age and illness and being alone surges, I call Kevin and wail, "I want to go home, I can't do this, I'm too weak." My mother panting, my mother gasping, unable to walk more than a few feet at a time. First thing in the morning, I've been up for like two minutes and she wants me to feed her cats, I'm so groggy and she's directing me like I'm a puppet—not that dish, the other dish, and don't forget to rinse the can and wipe up the floor around their bowls, don't stack so many dishes in the drainer and the litter needs to be changed, and when you do that take the garbage out to the alley—and I want to scream "Be quiet!" so I can make some tea and wake the fuck up—I say "okay" with a bit of snippiness in my tone, and she starts crying, saying I'm getting irritated with her, saying "please don't be mad at me," and apologizing. I sit next to her on the couch and put my arm around her—it's not you, I say, it's me, I'm always grouchy in the morning, ask Kevin—and she puts her head in her hands and says she knows why people want to die. It's almost impossible to focus on anything outside my buzzing thoughts.

E.T.'s turned whitish gray and he's lying on the bathroom floor. The soundtrack fills with the labored in and out of his breath. A windy rattle. My mom and I grow silent and stare at the screen. Then E.T.'s in the hospital tent, hooked up to oxygen and machines that monitor his vitals. Elliott's lying on an adjacent table, desperate, reaching out for E.T. "You're scaring him," he cries as the E.R. team frantically prods and pummels E.T.'s body. "Leave him alone, leave him alone. I can take care of him." But E.T. keeps slipping away. Some version of this is going to happen to me and my mom. Soon. The only question is, how soon. Of course Elliott's devotion eventually brings him back to life and E.T. ascends into the night in a spaceship that looks like a many-toothed Mirakami beastie. The night sky in *E.T.* is never black, but a vibrant dark blue, an ink-stained cerulean. As the closing credits roll, my mother tells me about my grandmother's death. Even though it happened eighteen years ago, this is the first time I've heard the story. On a Wednesday my grandmother started to whistle when she breathed. My mom took her to the hospital and they kept her there. On Saturday they told mom she was breathing her own carbon dioxide, meaning she was poisoning herself. My grandmother complained—where's my breakfast—and the nurse said they were afraid she'd choke on it. Grandma kept staring at the right corner of the ceiling when she spoke. Aunt Squee came into the room and my grandmother stared at the corner and said, "You are so beautiful." Squee said, "Thank you." "But," my mom said, pointedly, "I don't think she was talking to Squee!" Then Grandma went to sleep and died five hours later—her breathing slower and slower. On the phone that evening Kevin reminds me that the one time he met my grandmother we watched *E.T.* with her. I think back, squeeze my eyes to focus my memory, and exclaim, "You're right!" There were so many of us back then, moving in and out of the living room, Mom, Dad, Kevin, so many people talking over the movie, throbbing with life. It was summer and Grandma was sitting in Mom's chair wearing a purple muumuu. Her soft liver-spotted arms, her I love you unconditionally smile. She hugged me good-bye and said, "This is the last time I'll see you." She said it so matter-of-factly, never stopped smiling, and she was right, she was gone in a month or two.

My mother is nauseous and fluish but has to sit upright because any kind of incline tightens suffocation's vise. Her foot is huge and puffy with edema. Numb. I fetch her a chocolate milkshake and drive home though a glorious sunset, the sky rippled with grays and yellows and then at the bottom a sharp edge of azure blue. My own needs feel petty, selfish. When I bring her home Chinese take-out she makes a face and says, "Why'd you get me so much food." Tears swell, but I don't cry—it's like there's this dam inside my head that the tears bounce up against and then fall back. I try to produce more compassion, but remain detached and listless. Hard to sleep. Mom has a panic attack, she tells me she doesn't feel right in the head. I give her a Xanax and fix her tomato soup and egg salad. I have one of those primal "what the fuck is existence all about" moments—which haven't changed much in quality since I was a child. The fact that we are here at all makes less sense than we will no longer exist—and that thought is still terrifying to me. The results of the labs on my mother's lung fluid are dire. The pulmonologist says she'd never handle chemo and suggests hospice. My mother calls her friends. "The cancer's back," she says, panting. She can't breathe and talk at the same time. When I arrived she could fix food but now she can barely pour out a bowl of cereal. I feel guilty and guilty and guilty and guilty. She shows me where her will is. I can't quit thinking about *E.T.,* the coincidence of it being on TV right before my grandmother died—and then when my mother takes a turn for the worse it reappears. I'm afraid that because we watched the film, this will be the last time I'll see my mother alive. In my journal I write, "E.T. is the angel of death."

Thursday I return to San Francisco to prepare for an extended stay in Indiana. Sunday my mom's taken to the hospital in an ambulance, and the following Wednesday morning the pulmonologist calls and says to come home—immediately. It's Halloween. Six hours later I'm sitting on the plane, wearing velvety orange-and-black cat ears. No other passengers are in costume except two little girls in matching satin dresses and purple capes. The headband of the cat ears presses into my skull, a dull soreness, but I leave them on. The cabin's oddly empty—I have a whole row to myself, with no one in the row in front of or behind me. I feel ridiculously lucky, turn sideways with my back to the window and my legs luxuriously spanning all three seats. Nibbling on a spiced sugar cookie in the shape of a pumpkin, I open my journal. "In the mad dash to get washed up and packed this morning," I write," I couldn't quit thinking about *E. T.* Watching it with my grandmother then watching it with my mother, it feels like I'm living a variation of *The Ring,* that film where you watch the videotape and then in nine or ten days you're dead. In my version you watch *E. T.* on TV with someone you love, then E.T. harvests their soul and you never see them again. The Halloween scene in *E. T.*—in clown shoes and white sheet with eye holes cut out, E.T. the ghost hobbles in plain sight among the living. And now I find myself—unexpectedly—flying home on Halloween—the parallelism is laughable." I look out the window. Darkness ahead, glowing vermillion strip of sunset behind us. No turbulence, no sense of movement, it's as if the plane were being absorbed by the night. "The cabin is dark," I write, "and I'm sitting in a halo of light—like the beam from the spaceship's open chute. E.T. phone home. When my mother dies, home will no longer exist." Then I try to take cute pictures of my cat-eared self on a Boeing 737, but the digital images look old and haggard, like the flesh of my cheeks and jaw is melting.

It's well past midnight by time I get to the hospital. The room is blurry—a couple of nondescript chairs, something turquoise—on the far right by the window my mother pops out in a focus so sharp it pinches the eyes. I stand beside her bed and watch her sleep. The nurse taps her shoulder and says, "Winnie, look, Dodie's here." My mom opens her eyes, confused and remote, as if the inside of her skull were enormous and she was peering out from very far away. The left eye's glazed over and her head wobbles. She doesn't recognize me. She doesn't recognize anything. When I called her that morning she was still *there.* I told her I was coming, and she said, "Good." You're such a fuckup I think, why didn't you come home yesterday, and when you got here why didn't you rush right over instead of dawdling at the house, unpacking. Her lips have disappeared—a thin band around a mouth drooping into an O-shape, never closing. She noisily gulps in air and then her head twitches back and to the right—gulp/back/right—pause—gulp/back/right—pause—her movements mechanical and rhythmic as an antique wind-up toy, the circus monkey banging cymbals as his tin head swivel-jerks left and right. Clear oxygen tubes drape softly from each nostril. The nurse says, "Touch her, talk to her. That's still Mom in there." I take her nonresponsive hand and say, "I love you Mom."

An aide brings in a cot for me. I take off my shoes and lie on my back. Millions of holes in the ceiling tiles. The dimmed bulbs cast a yellowish aura, there are the expected mechanical beepings, voices from the nurses' station across the hall. On the other side of a thin cottony curtain, my mother's arduous breathing. My eyes produce their own light, flash spangles of pixilated gold pink and green—no lines, no sharp edges between figure and ground, image and memory, thought and vision, it all tumbles together in a gravity-free frenzy until my mind grows woozy. As I anxiously toss in and out of consciousness, my mother radiates aliveness, her aliveness tingles the air like the scent of roses, the bouquet of yellow roses I bought her on my last visit, a gesture she took to heart, the roses said you're not a pain in the ass, the roses said I'm happy to be here, the roses sat on the coffee table in the living room as she hunched over in panic, a superfluous flush of beauty, she had me put them in the closet at night to protect them from the cats. I'm seized by this primal love a mother has for her child—it's not directed at me, it doesn't even feel personal, it's roaring through me, this vicious, unreasonable, gut-love—a love that would rip apart predators with its bare teeth—and it becomes clear to me that nothing could stop the violence of this love, that it was always there, every second of my life it was there, even when she acted like she didn't like me. Then the atmosphere switches to calm—no transition—the turbulence of the racing mind clicks off. Click. Calm. Behind my mother's struggle to breathe lies a seductive stillness, she's ushering me into that stillness, and I feel ecstatic lying there beside her. Time lurches rather than proceeding with its typical metronome—bleep somebody comes in to check her vitals—bleep I'm sitting cross-legged on the cot in the middle of the night, the nurse has pulled up a chair and is telling me about her own mother's cancer death, we have the intimacy of adolescent girls at a sleep-over, sharing secrets—bleep she's putting a hot towel on my mother's waxy blue feet—bleep I'm lying down again—bleep another nurse says we can roll her on her side if you'd like, rolling them on their side fills their lungs with fluid, it makes them die faster, I stare at her without answering—bleep I'm home taking a quick shower—bleep I'm patting her head saying "I love you" over and over, her hair's thin and scraggly, a few wisps that feel soft to the touch, her smooth head beneath it, so small—bleep the breathing therapist puts a clear plastic cup over my mother's nose and mouth, flips a switch, the machine makes a loud whooshing noise and pressurized steam bubbles and billows within the cup with such force my mother's head shivers with it, her eyes remain closed, her mouth slack and open—bleep my mother's love blankets me—bleep the pulmonologist arrives and offers morphine to speed up her dying—bleep I'm calling my brother and saying come right now—bleep I sit in a chair at the foot of her bed, blankly watching her convulse for air. I've seen this before, I think—the cramped O-mouth, the gasps and head jerks—but where. The relentless spasming is exhausting. On the phone Halloween morning the pulmonologist said, "I don't know how long anybody could go on like this." Anybody. Any body. And so I flew home. My own breaths become deep and irregular, as if my autonomic system were in upheaval, trying to realign itself with my mother's. Where did I see this before. It must have been in a movie, but what movie. I observe her for maybe an hour when I realize it was *E.T.,* the part where E.T. turns white and is dying—and all the kids are sobbing—E.T.'s round lipless mouth gasping for air—this is what my mother looks like, E.T. dying. Spielberg must have based E.T.'s death scene on someone he observed dying, I think, someone he loved, dying. I'm stunned how accurate the film is, how graphic. As my mother continues to die the flesh around her mouth stiffens and her lower face wrinkles a bit, so she looks even more like E.T. Her gasping eventually gets slower and more shallow and the jerking less pronounced. Her hands turn cold, and then her head, purple mouth. She stops breathing and I think it's all over, but then there's these waves of tremors on the left side of her neck and underside of her chin. It looks like little animals are scurrying about there. Her body absolutely still, her eyes closed, round mouth open, and these scurrying tremors. It's the Day of the Dead, I think. November 1, 11:05 a.m. Bleep.

I was worried about staying in her house, that it would be macabre. But it's calming to be among her things, I can feel her energy—in the walls, in the air, in her stained Pyrex coffee pot, her Italian blown-glass clowns. I try to log on to the Internet but a dialogue box says "No dial tone detected." I check my mother's cordless phones. The screens on both handsets read LINE IN USE. I turn them on and off, remove and return them to their charging docks, but the screens still read LINE IN USE. I give up, brush my teeth, take some Ambien, lots of it, so I pass out. I wake up in the middle of the night to a pulsing green circle—it's coming from the desk, from beneath my bathrobe, a lime green ball of light expanding and contracting—I realize it's just my iBook under there in sleep mode—but I see this luminous respiration, the same size, the same shrinking and swelling rhythm as E.T.'s glowing red chest when he comes back to life. His love, his magical thump thump always homing in on home. The space heater's power light glows orange. E.T.'s belly button. Breast on desk, belly button on floor—everything's fractured and jammed back together. When I was growing up I couldn't wait to get away from here—but now I cling to the hush of its wall-to-wall carpeting, its dust-free surfaces, its doors with locks I was always given keys to. In the morning I reach into a cupboard for a bowl and find that someone has stacked the dishes differently than how my mother did it. This is all wrong. I take them all down and put her plates, her saucers, her bowls back in her order. I pick up after myself, I wipe the counters. On my last visit when I suggested throwing away her battered Tupperware measuring cup, my mother said, "No, I've always had that cup." She paused to breathe. "That cup is a part of me." I stick the measuring cup in my suitcase. As I walk through her living room, as I boil water for tea in her kitchen, my mother's love is freed up, can circulate through me unhampered by the aging, gasping shell I was afraid to touch—but I did touch it, I held her in my arms. My mother's radiant green heart still throbs, I glimpse her in the periphery, these green trails of light. Phones begin ringing. Constantly. In the hospital, at the funeral home, the credit union, the Mexican restaurant I go to with my brother, in the car. Sometimes the ring is faint, like it's in my head. Other times it's clamorous but muted like it's a cell phone buried in my purse, but when I dig mine out, the phone is silent with no messages or missed calls. As I stand in front of the cat food section of the supermarket, I'm plagued by a ringing so shrill and insistent I look around to see what idiot it belongs to, but find I'm alone in the aisle. Sitting at my mom's kitchen table I hear a voice coming out of my closed cell phone, very distinct—it sounds like my mom—"Dodie pick up the phone." Even though I know it makes no sense, I open my Samsung and say, "Hello." No one answers.

A spray of yellow roses crowns the coffin, dozens of them. My mother's stringy deathbed hair has been set and styled just like in the picture I provided. I smile at the playful crystal cat pin on the neck of her sweater. I'm wearing its mate. She loved animals, volunteered at the thrift store for the local humane society. The crowd is small, but devoted—neighbors, a handful of relatives, former cafeteria ladies my mother worked with, other thrift store volunteers, a couple of carpenters from my dad's union. Everyone says she looks really nice. My mother was losing a pound or two a week. Her clothes hung on her, but she was too weak to buy new ones. She told Linda that in the coffin they'd have to bunch the clothes up under her. So I went to Carson's, where I'd shopped with her many times, and bought her a pair of comfortable Laura Ashley black stretch pants and a cornflower blue mock turtleneck sweater—blue was her favorite color. I also brought to the funeral home a bra and underpants, socks, slippers for her feet—and her new diamond earrings, her splurge from hitting a $1,000 royal flush on the poker slot machine. My mother cherished those earrings, but earlier that day, in a burst of greediness, I had decided to wear them myself—and I set aside a pair of gaudy emerald teardrops for her. The emeralds instantly disappeared. After searching room to room in vain, I was stricken with the conviction my mother had spirited them away. She was always so stubborn. A favorite story from her childhood: she was walking somewhere with Grandma, and Grandma wouldn't give her what she wanted, so my mother threw herself down on the sidewalk and held her breath, she held it until her face turned red, until she was about to pass out, until Grandma finally "hauled off" and slapped her. "I'd cut off my nose to spite my face," my mother said, laughing. In the chill of the funeral parlor, the blue of her sweater adds a cheerful note—I feel proud of how nice my mother looks. But I also tell Kevin that isn't my mother. "That's not her in the coffin that everyone's interacting with," I say. "It's a big doll." I don't touch it.

The Lutheran funeral service is stern. We're all sinners in need of salvation. The satin-robed pastor remembers visiting my mother in the hospital on Tuesday. "I told her that I knew her cancer had returned. We both acknowledged the reality that the Lord was calling her. She said being baptized and becoming a part of the church was the best decision she had ever made. And I told her that I knew that when the Lord was ready for her, that Winnie was ready for the Lord. And she said without a moment's hesitation, 'I'm ready now.'" My mother was telling everybody she was ready to die. Her friends say, "Winnie willed herself to die." The pastor continues, "That was the last I saw Winnie Bellamy on earth. But I know that because of the faith that was hers, I will see her again in heaven." He gets to see my mother again, but I won't because I'm such a miserable heathen. In *E. T.*, Dee Wallace, the mother, reads *Peter Pan* to Drew Barrymore. Tinkerbell is dying: "She says she thinks she could get well again if children believed in fairies." Drew and her mother clap and clap, just as I clapped in 1960 for Mary Martin on our round-cornered black-and-white TV. Whenever you clap Tinkerbell glows brightly. After the doctors have given up on reviving E.T. and they've packed him in cold storage, Elliott cries out, "I'll believe in you all my life. Every day. E.T.—I love you." E.T.'s heart glows crimson and he reawakens from the dead. I'd do anything to see my mother again—anything short of becoming a Lutheran. The pastor points out she died on All Saints' Day. "Very early the Christian Church recognized the need to remember and give thanks to God for all the humble saints who lived and died in the faith whose life and witness are not remembered by many but are known by God. How fitting it was that Saint Winifred Bellamy should be called by God to His presence on All Saints' Day." I turn to Kevin with this look of "what????" on my face. I thought saints were these special ultra-holy people with miraculous powers, not widows with cancer in Hammond, Indiana. "And now she is in the presence of our Lord worshipping Him and singing His praise with all the saints in glory."

After the service I walk up for my last look at her. The mortician, bizarrely, has painted her fingernails the same Crayola "flesh" color as her skin, and he's stuffed her oversize bra so these huge showgirl boobs poke up beneath her blue sweater. My mother swam in her bras. Last summer I was with her when she bought some. She didn't try them on, she just grabbed D-cup underwires because that's what she always wore. She pointed at her chest and said, "There ain't nothing but skin there anyway." When she sat topless on the pulmonologist's examination table, not just her breasts but her entire torso sagged, waves of it bunching up at her waist. The nurse said, "You two look alike," and I winced. The pastor is planted beside the coffin, his hands clasped together in front of him, like a bodyguard. I feel self-conscious and frozen, the three of us cast together into a tableau. I blurt out, "Bye, mom." He gives me a look that says, "That's it?" The weather was unseasonably warm when my mother died, the trees still green—then suddenly the temperature dropped and overnight the leaves burst aflame with oranges and reds. We drive to the cemetery through a palette of glorious excess, as if all of nature were celebrating the new saint, Saint Winifred.

That evening Kevin and I go to see *Lars and the Real Girl*—to lighten up. Lars has a life-size sex doll that he thinks is real—and the entire community goes along with it. Somehow this is supposed to be good for Lars. His sister-in-law dresses the doll in sporty Midwestern slacks and shirt, and the hairdresser gives her a more contemporary bob. The doll gets a job modeling at the local department store, visits children in a cancer ward, gets elected to the school board. The doll develops such a busy social life, she has a schedule on the refrigerator door. Lars gets jealous and declares she's dying. The doll is rushed to the hospital in an ambulance. It takes days for her to expire. The funeral service is Lutheran. Neighborhood women visit the grieving Lars. "We brought casseroles," they say. The food Lars scoops on his plate—fried chicken, lurid red pasta, coleslaw, squishy rolls—reminds me of my mom's funeral lunch, catered by the local supermarket. Kevin leans over in the theater and says, "He's eating the same food. This is awesome!" My tacky comment about my mother's corpse being a doll is literalized on screen—her rush to the hospital, the deathwatch, the Lutheran funeral I'd been to eight hours before. I sit in the theater weeping.

As soon as I return to San Francisco, I order a DVD of *E.T.*—the two-disk collector's edition. Four months later I still haven't watched it. It's February, and I have to return to Indiana yet again—to open an estate bank account and to finalize plans for putting the house on the market. I take the DVD with me—its cover is playful, the iconic shot of Elliott in hooded cape, flying his bicycle across a giant full moon, E.T. resting precariously on the handlebars. I'm planning to watch the film on my laptop in my mother's house, on the last night I'll ever sleep there—an eerie ouija-type invocation—I'm planning to fan my grieving to a frenzy and write about it. The house is gradually shutting down. The newspaper and cable TV have been cancelled, the phone disconnected. My brother has emptied the cupboards and scavenged anything he thinks is valuable. After this visit, he's planning to put up a notice on the bulletin board at Inland Steel, to sell what's left over to fellow steelworkers, who are always on the lookout for cheap furniture and appliances. Linda, the next-door neighbor, has been coming in periodically and running water so the pipes don't freeze. Her husband's been snow-blowing the sidewalk. It snows my entire visit and everybody says it's the coldest week of the winter. Just darting to the car is brutal, yet exhilarating—crisp, muffled, slippery, eye-clenching white.

It's below zero outside as I sit in the phoneless, TV-less, newspaperless living room and sift through my mother's photographs. She sits in an armchair, our pet squirrel beside her, hanging from the curtains. She found him in the front yard, a starving baby, and nursed him back to health. She's a grinning ten-year-old in a drop-waisted dress, freckle-faced with blonde bangs cut ruler-straight. A little girl with Ds on her report cards and an alcoholic father, a little girl with scrapes and pleasures she took to her grave. She's toasting the camera with a glass of champagne, her huge pregnant belly full of me, who she's planning to name Nancy. She's sitting on the couch, her chemo-bald head covered with a triangular scarf. I went with her to chemo—once. Patients sat in easy chairs in a circle, IVs dripping into their arms. People chatted casually, the Game Show Channel blasting from the adjoining waiting room. Mostly she would drive herself there and back. And be sick all alone in this house. "What if I fell in the bathtub," she'd say. "Days could go by before anyone would find me." So much of her life had nothing to do with me—I always knew that, and I resented it. Her hair's teased into a sixties bouffant as she stands in a white uniform at the far left of a long line of cafeteria ladies arranged from tall to short—she was five-foot-eight back then—the photo is a glossy black and white, printed in my high school yearbook. She was popular among the cafeteria ladies—because she was a hard worker, because of her sense of humor, her willingness to take part in zany cafeteria pranks. She's the prettiest cafeteria lady. Did the male teachers flirt with her? Did she have secret crushes? Since birth I've judged her by how well she did or did not fulfill my needs, my tremendous need. I pick up a snapshot of her wedding day—she's stepping down the church steps, eighteen years old in a suit and corsage, holding my father's hand, ecstatically smiling. My father was a biker. Was she worried he wouldn't settle down? Did she fear his violence, his moodiness? So much of my mother's life is obscure to me, there were so many questions I could have, should have asked her. In the seventies when it was in fashion to "rap" with the old folks, I asked her if she had orgasms—she said she did, but she was married for six months before she had her first one. I think of the octagonal mirror Kevin pointed out at the foot of my parents' bed. "That could only be for one thing," he said, with a look that implied his ever-imaginative head was filling with sex kinks. She asked me questions too, but I lied. "Yes I tried marijuana, but only once." These photos, which I've glanced at many times before, have become charged with mystery. In them my mother pops out with the radiant otherness of a celebrity. When I was a teen I read that existentialists compared a person's life to a sausage—each instant, each choice is a slice of your sausage—but you don't know what the whole sausage looks like until you die. Looking at the boxes and half a dozen albums of random, jumbled moments, I think *there is no sausage.* Just flash upon flash, slice upon slice, of loss. I give up my sorting and haul all the photos to the car, along with a set of letters she and my father hand-wrote to apply for gun permits, her loose-leaf notebook of recipes, her blown-glass clowns, the engraved tray she kept on her dresser, and the Christmas and birthday and Mother's Day and Thanksgiving and Easter cards I made for her in grade school. I drive over icy roads to FedEx and pay $300 to ship the stuff to San Francisco. I never take *E. T.* out of my suitcase. When I think of watching it my emotions say *no fucking way.*

In March I choose a night Kevin's out, rush home from yoga with a take-out salad, and load *E. T.* into the DVD player. I need to view it alone, in secret, because of my mother and my grandmother. It would be too dangerous to let Kevin see it. He doesn't even know there's a copy in the house. Elliott meets E.T. and falls in love. E.T. gently touches Elliott's tears, brushes the hair from his forehead. Elliott wraps a scarf around E.T.'s neck in a tender embrace and their eyes meet. I'm nervous Kevin's going to appear unexpectedly. He's having dinner with Raimundas—what if Raimundas doesn't show up, what if Kevin comes back early—what if he barges through the door before I can click off the movie. He can't glimpse even a second of it, for *E. T.* could cast one of its death spells and I'll never see him again. Finally what I've been waiting for yet dreading—E.T. falls ill and wastes away. But he does it like Ali MacGraw in *Love Story,* gently, beautifully. It's 10:00—I should have heard from Kevin by now, he always calls on his way home. When I dial his cell phone, voice mail picks up immediately. I leave a message. E.T. lies on the bathroom floor, grayish white. Elliott: "I think we're dying." E.T. slowly rolls his head from side to side, he groans, he screams, he whispers, "Home." No gasping, no jerking. It's nothing like the merciless spasming of my mother. The sounds of labored breathing come from the government agents lumbering about in their bulky bubble-headed space suits. Maybe this is the wrong scene, maybe it's the next scene, in the medical tent. Cut to E.T. on a hospital bed, oxygen tubes drooping from his nostrils. The doctors run about manically, but E.T.'s movements are subtle, elegant, his mouth closed as his chest silently lifts and collapses, lifts and collapses. Again, he doesn't gasp or jerk. Where are the images I remembered in my mother's hospital room? Where's my mother's death? I press down number 5 and speed-dial Kevin. No answer. My stomach is tense and queasy, and my heart's beating faster. What if something's happened to Kevin, what if my

watching *E. T.* in his home, in his absence, is enough to destroy him. E.T.'s
spaceship has arrived. E.T. and Elliott face one another, eyes locked. E.T.:
"Come." Elliott: "Stay." Pain on both their faces. E.T. lifts his fingers to his
lips: "Ouch." Elliott: "Ouch." Elliott touches his pointer finger to his chest
then his lips, then he flips his finger outwards as if throwing E.T. a kiss of
ouch. Tears in eyes. I leave Kevin another message. E.T. and Elliott hug,
cheek to cheek, E.T. massages Elliott's back, puts a glowing finger to Elliott's temple. "I'll be right here." E.T. comes back to life, but death wafts
off of him like steam, like the scent of yellow roses. In the aura of death
all the bullshit dissolves—the one dying is vulnerable, aching for touch,
the dying body pulls both of you into the present moment. Fear drops
out pretty quickly. Your emotional life is reduced to grief and love, to
waves of clinging and letting go, your heart spirals open, a sloppy vortex
in the center of your chest. Glowing red. Kevin calls—he's fine, they went
to a bar afterwards—but the tension doesn't leave. I'm lightheaded, my
breathing's shallow, my jaws clenched as E.T.'s spaceship ascends above the
spiky fairy-tale forest. By the time Kevin gets home, I'm on the computer
looking up E.T.'s death scene. I discover there are two *E.T.*s—the original
from 1982, which I've just watched, and a slightly longer 2002 edition.
In the later version, E.T.'s facial expressions were computer generated to
give a broader range, the government agents' guns were replaced with
walkie-talkies, and the word "terrorist" became "hippie." Fifty shots were
digitally tweaked. So maybe I watched the wrong one, maybe the death
scene does match my memory. "Did you write tonight?" Quickly I quit
Firefox as Kevin walks into the room. "Did you work on your piece?" He
thinks I'm writing about Vietnam, as seen through the lens of *The Deer
Hunter* and *Coming Home*. "I did research," I answer, vaguely.

The next evening, as I pull out of the San Francisco State parking
garage, I think about my class, how when I mentioned I was writing
about *E. T.*, a collective shudder rippled around the room. Ali: "*E. T.* was
the scariest movie ever." Matt had an E.T. doll. "It was too creepy," he
said. He looked down at the floor as if his childhood doll were going to
materialize out of the ethers of memory, and squinted his face in disgust.
"I never played with it." Though celebrated for his cuteness, E.T. gave my
students nightmares. At a red light I take out my journal and start jotting
down notes. I scribble at the next stop and the next, and when the light
turns green too quickly, I continue writing while steering with one hand
and I wonder if I'm breaking the law—is it against the law to write while

driving?—probably not because the idiots who make the laws wouldn't imagine anyone doing it—night comes on—the moon is huge, round, opalescent, the sky a vivid fake computer-generated blue. I imagine my Subaru lifting off of 17th Street, hovering for a moment, shooting up and flying across the neon bright moon. I am the Wicked Witch of the West on a broomstick, I am a hooded boy on a bicycle racing to get E.T. home. I sleepwalked once as a child—in the living room I opened the front door and walked into a spaceship—I stood in the cockpit with all its dials and knobs and circular gauges and looked out on the serenity of space—then my mother grabbed me on the curb outside our house and dragged me back inside.

As E.T. runs through the forest, a ghostly woman is superimposed over him, huddled on the couch, drinking tea. I pull down the shades—my reflection in the TV screen is too distracting, too fertile for bad symbolism. Other than the added bathtub scene, the film looks pretty much the same. Including the death scene. It's still hard to accept E.T. didn't die the way I remember it—some irrational, desperate part of me is still hoping to find a third version of the film where E.T. does gasp and his head does jerk back and to the right, his lipless mouth and my mother's lipless mouth, one. I'm more relaxed this time through—Kevin's at work, he's reachable, he's not going to barge in. I get a little erotic frisson from sneaking, like I'm having an affair with E.T.—like Elliott, I'm hiding him in my closet. The darkened room is making me drowsy. My eyelids droop as these pictures I shared with my mother flutter in the subdued afternoon, her sitting across the living room, snared in cancer's slow terrifying suffocation, her saying, "I love this movie." I click to the bonus features. The scenes were shot in chronological order. This created more tension, provoked reactions from the child actors that were spontaneous, unrehearsed. Real doctors frantically try to revive E.T.—Spielberg's internist and his doctor buddies. E.T. convulses from the shock of their electric paddles. Startled, Drew Barrymore jumps back, tears streaming down her face. Clip of Barrymore after the scene is over, still bawling, Spielberg trying to comfort her. E.T. is a collage of fragments. He's rarely seen as a whole—bits and pieces of him pop up unexpectedly, his head peeks out from among the dolls, his long knobby fingers crawl up from under a table. His hands were performed by a woman mime, hired for her unusually long thin fingers. His puppet-self was operated by a dozen men, who sat in a separate room, watching E.T. on a video monitor as they expertly synchronized his movements.

The sets were built on a platform so E.T.'s cords and wires could run under the floor. Spielberg: "There was no full movement except when we had our little people and our young boy without legs inside the E.T. costume." Clip of E.T.'s body topped with a woman's head. The woman makes a goofy face for the camera. She/E.T. are wearing a plaid bathrobe. Clip of legless boy in a blue T-shirt and larval-looking padded vest. A handsome, dark-haired boy. He's sitting on a flesh-colored pillow, so it looks like his body has melted and he's sitting in a puddle of flesh. His hands are on the floor in front of him. The boy winces as helpers begin to lower E.T.'s floppy purplish body over his head. Drew Barrymore: "E.T. was absolutely real to me. I understood that it took mechanics and some people being in his suit and a woman doing his hands to make him manifest and come alive, but I just thought that he was a guardian angel. And a good friend. He was a very real, tangible being." That evening when I go to hear Linh Dinh at U.C. Berkeley, I'm still sleepy. I've been looking forward to the reading, but I keep dozing off, right there on a wooden chair in the drafty auditorium, my head drops forward then jerks upright, I have to pinch myself to stay awake. It's as if the movie has thrust me into unconsciousness, a narcoleptic spasm of too much meaning, the way Elliott passes out the first time E.T. enters his bedroom. Afterwards in the California cuisine-y restaurant, Linh Dinh sits across from me. Kevin's asking him if he's written any poems about boxes. The walls are decorated with original art, bold black ink washes in frames. I point at the one above my head, a blobby face wider than it is tall, with big hollow white eyes, and say, "Look, it's E.T. It looks like E.T." Lytle Shaw says, "Yes it does—but an academic E.T., with spectacles." I twist around, craning my neck upwards, and indeed he does have glasses, the thinnest of wirerims. Bits and pieces.

I walk down Ninth Avenue sipping an "I Am Worthy," a juice blend the bluish red of vein blood. I have the urge to write down everything, to embalm the trivial against the onrush of death. It's a beautiful day, sunny with a hint of distant ocean, a moisture verging on scent, I approach a bottlebrush tree, pruned compact and round with dense red brushes, it's perfect, I think, and I don't even like bottlebrush trees. I want to capture atmosphere, the quality of light like in a bad Iowa poem, the crisp glare of cool and breezy at three o'clock in the Inner Sunset. I remember walking through the park in Indiana, what an odd fall it was, the weather shifting and shifting. My mother said we might as well spend her gambling money on groceries because she'd "never go to the boat again." She was telling me she was dying, but I didn't listen. I should have stayed with her, should have said fuck to my responsibilities in San Francisco and stayed. I'm on the couch, my arm around her—so frail and angular—she awkwardly puts her head on my shoulder. After a few minutes I move to an armchair across the room. She flinches when I get up, and that flinch keeps playing in my head over and over, my pulling away from her in that moment of need—and in the hospital, I sat against the wall at the foot of her bed, every once in a while walking over, squeezing her unresponsive hand, patting her head, but not lingering too long—I could have pulled my chair up, could have leaned right in, could have held her while she passed. It was enough, I rationalized, for her spirit to know I was in the room. I wasn't perfect. I wasn't perfect. It's like my mother's death is a tape I long to rewind, do over, get it right. But every time I rewind it's always the same—me fucking up, getting it wrong. I swallow a mouthful of "I Am Worthy." It's thick and bitter but cloyingly sweet. I'm wearing her diamond earrings—after the viewing, the funeral home removed them from her ears. I soaked them in saltwater by moonlight and cleaned them with alcohol, still I hesitated to put on a corpse's jewels. Spears of light bounce off the diamonds, cool, breezy light. I wear them every day.

My iBook's battery has become sluggish, so I unplug it. I've heard that if you totally drain the battery, its charge will last longer. As I type, the bar of the battery icon grows shorter and shorter, then turns red. I'm wearing headphones, listening to iTunes. During *Midnight Oil*—how can we dance when our earth is turning—a staccato, affectless male voice talks over the music, I can't understand his words, but he speaks one sentence, intent as a command. It's eerie. Is iTunes/my headphone acting as some kind of receiver? I'm reminded of an art installation I once saw, headphones mounted on the wall, you put them on and listen to record-ings of ghost voices emerging from static. This is called Electronic Voice Phenomena. "The voice or voices of the dead are embedded onto mag-netic recording tape by a process that we do not understand." The voices spoke German, crackles emerging from another world. I listened to them for like 30 seconds and ripped off the bulky headphones. The voices sounded demented, like Artaud in hell. They scared the shit out of me. "If the speech is difficult to understand, remember that the spirit talking may be talking in a language or dialect that is not in common usage today. The voice can also be in reverse, you would need a computer to reverse this to hear it." I replay "Beds are Burning." No ghost voice. The battery icon bar is a mere slice of red. My computer's deathwatch makes me nervous. Really. I can feel my heart. A dialogue box appears: YOU ARE NOW RUNNING ON RESERVE BATTERY POWER. I have to pee, my colon's rumbling, but I sit here, not wanting to miss the event. It's going to die during Phil Ochs's "Crucifixion." I await its final words. The screen collapses to black. My iBook's final words are "So dance." I plug in the power cord, push the On button and the machine bounds back to life. In *E.T.* love equals resurrection. E.T.'s love heals Elliott's cut finger, E.T.'s love perks up the dying potted plant. When E.T.'s dead and packed in cold storage, Elliott delivers a show-stopping soliloquy of mourning: "Look at what they've done to you. / I'm so sorry. / You must be dead / because / I don't know how to feel. / I can't feel anything anymore. / You've gone someplace else now. / I'll believe in you all my life. / Every day. / E.T. / I love you." Then E.T.'s heart beams red and his eyes spring open.

To avoid doing class prep, I fart around with my cell phone, deleting obsolete entries from the address book. So many contacts are from Hammond. I leave in my mom's next-door neighbor, her housecleaner/companion, the estate attorney, my brother. I remove Commander's, our favorite Greek diner—their chicken soup was all she'd eat at the end—and Community Hospital, where she died. Each number I expunge feels like a mini-death—and then there's the brutal finality of erasing her home number from speed dial. At any time I could grab the phone, hold down 4 to contact HOME—the most ancient voice I know would answer, and love would flow towards me through thousands of miles of wires, or it would beam to me from satellites orbiting the earth, huge towers broadcasting love to me. The original voice, hands on either side of her big round belly, speaking to me when I was still floating inside her. Kevin doesn't excise people from his address book when they die—he just types in DEAD, all caps, bold. DEAD is a tombstone beside their name, a remembrance. Writing this piece is keeping my mother alive for me, when I finish it I'm afraid she'll really be dead. I don't remember her last words to me. We were on the phone, 24 hours before her death, almost to the minute—I was coming, the conversation didn't seem important enough to remember. Did she tell me she loved me? Normally she would have, but she was breathless and terribly weak. She told me she loved me so often those last few weeks, she said my love meant the world to her. I wonder if she suspected how much I'd miss her. E.T. points to the sky with his long knobby finger and croaks, "Phone home." If human emotions developed to promote the survival of the species—attraction and its ensuing horniness ensures we propagate—what possible use is mourning. Mourning slows us down, draws us inward, takes away our will to go out and club a woolly mammoth for dinner. Time is no longer linear—it's more like a chord that flashes in and out of being.

In the film's original opening sequence, E.T.'s flight from the government agents is created by a light bulb that zooms in a straight line on a rail. In the 2002 reanimated sequence, E.T.'s glowing red chest bobs up and down through the forest, to show "these things *can* run." But do we really need the bobbing? Some viewers dislike E.T.'s computer-generated face lift, claiming that his lack of expression added to his character, his adorable alien stiffness. We need so little to believe. Before the enormity of death, meaning implodes and fractures—rationality buzzes out of the room like a swatted fruit fly. One walks around in a daze, stumbling upon clues. Phones ring, computer lights throb. *E.T.,* with its surplus symbolism, is loaded with clues. Online I read that the title credits are purple because purple is the color of spirituality. I read that black and red are associated with the antagonists, while the colors of innocence are blue and white. Over and over E.T. is wearing a white hooded cloak like a holy person. Drew Barrymore: "E.T. was like a guardian angel watching over us—there to teach us the deep meaning about people and a way of life." Throughout the film Elliott and E.T. wear blue and white, Elliott's blanket is blue. Right before Elliott's brother Michael becomes an ally he takes off his red football jersey to reveal a blue shirt beneath. In the hospital scene, when government agent Peter Coyote switches from antagonist to friend he dons—surprise—blue and white. With Coyote sympathetic, a new antagonist must now be created in order to maintain conflict in the story. In this scene DEATH itself will serve that function, DEATH, which threatens the life of E.T. Elliott: "Look at what they've done to you. I'm so sorry. You must be dead. I . . . I didn't know how to feel. I can't feel anything anymore. You've gone someplace else now. E.T., I love you." E.T. dies with his head resting on a piece of blue cloth. When E.T. and Elliott hug goodbye they're surrounded by blue and white lights. Of course I'm thinking of my mother's blue sweater. The clues don't add up to an answer or solution—*there is no sausage*—they just echo and reverberate. *E.T.,* the text of my mother's and my grandmother's deaths, infiltrates everything. It melds with and mirrors my life the way E.T. and Elliott become mirror images, one being. E.T.'s frightened, Elliott gasps; E.T. drinks beer, Elliott belches; E.T. falls asleep, Elliott passes out; E.T. turns whitish gray, Elliott says, "We're sick. I think we're dying." E.T. is always a "we," never an "I." Inside E.T. is twelve-year-old Matthew De Meritt. De Meritt, a lively boy who skateboarded around the set, was born without legs. Since he had to walk around on his hands, he couldn't control the arms of the costume—still Spielberg liked the legless boy's "alien, unnatural gait that always looked as if E.T. were on the verge of being off-balance." One of the funniest scenes is when De Meritt as a drunk E.T. waddles around the kitchen and topples backwards with the slapstick ease of a round-bottom doll, the kind that when you knock it over, pops right back up. His performance so impressed George Lucas, he offered De Meritt the role of Admiral Ackbar in *Return of the Jedi*, but he turned it down. At first Spielberg was resistant to dwarfs—he wanted to stick with legless people. To convince him, optical effects put the young daughter of one of *E.T.*'s lawyers inside the rubber suit. "She hated it. She was screaming and crying the whole time. But the videotape looked great." Inside E.T. is Pat Bilon, who was 2'10" and weighed 45 pounds. Bilon wore the fifteen-pound latex suit three to four hours at a time inside. His head barely came up to E.T.'s chest, he couldn't see, and it was sauna hot in there. Between scenes assistants removed E.T.'s radio-controlled head and cooled Bilon off with a hair dryer. Bilon died suddenly on January 27, 1983, of complication from pneumonia—eight months after *E.T.*'s premier at the Cannes Film Festival. He's buried in Calvary Cemetery in Youngstown, Ohio. My mother never visited my father's grave. "Why should I," she said. "He ain't there." Inside E.T. is 2'7" San Franciscan singer Tamara De Treaux, who also played Greedigut in *Ghoulies*. De Treaux's close friend Armistead Maupin based his novel *Maybe the Moon* on her *E.T.* experiences. She died of respiratory and heart problems on November 28, 1990, and is buried in Forest Lawn Memorial Park in Los Angeles in the Courts of Remembrance, wall crypt 5542A, above Andy Gibb. My mother's buried beside my father. Not there. Inside E.T. are Tina Palmer, a legless girl; Nancy MacLean, who played Ewok in *Return of the Jedi;* and Pam Ybarra. E.T.'s voice was performed by Pat Walsh, a 65-year-old speech teacher who smoked two packs of cigarettes a day. She was paid $380 to record for nine and a half hours—with her dentures removed to make her raspy vocalizations sound more alien. Fifteen minutes after the fact, the doctor pronounces my mother dead. Her lips have shriveled, exposing the perfectly even white teeth of her dentures. Her mouth is too small—everything about her—except her swollen feet and legs—is too small. E.T.'s scream is the electronically altered cry of an otter. Designer Carlo Rambaldi modeled E.T.'s eyes after the eyes of Ernest Hemingway, Carl Sandburg, Albert Einstein, and Rambaldi's Himalayan cat. E.T.'s hands shake because mime Caprice Rothe drank too much coffee the first day of shooting. "I made a joke about E.T.'s D.T.s, but Steven liked the tremor and asked me to keep it in." My mother's hand too shaky to sign a check. "You do it for me," she said. "Sign my name." Caprice Rothe puts on her E.T. gloves, lies on her stomach and cants her arms upwards and out, like the arms of a praying mantis. The position is grueling to hold. E.T.'s going home. Rothe/E.T. hugs a tearful Elliot goodbye. My final visit—as soon as I opened the front door my mother was there, wrapping her bony arms around me, reaching up to me—how did she get this short—clinging to me like a child or my cats, like she never wanted to let go. "I'm so happy to see you," she said. I wish I had spent the entire ten days hugging her, absorbing the last drops of her. E.T. puts a glowing finger (a tiny quart lamp in its fiberglass tip) to Elliott's temple. "I'll be right here." Death entrances like a lover, like an ex-lover you can never quite get over—wherever you go you see fragments of the lost one in others—that person has their eyes, another their laugh, another that quirky cock of the head, another says "whatever" with the same intonation. You cling to those slivers, heart speeding with excitement, even though they're never going to add up to anything. Dee Wallace, with her short blonde hair, looks like a younger version of my mother, especially in her gray sweatshirt—time shatters and fragments—when she sits on Drew Barrymore's bed reading *Peter Pan*, she's not Barrymore's mom, she's mine sitting on my twin bed reading a Golden Book, *The Little Engine that Could,* to chubby little blonde me. Before the enormity of death I can no longer synthesize a whole, I can only marvel at reflective flecks, I wait for them, expect them. Kevin and I settle down to watch a DVD of *Mr. Brooks.* Kevin Costner and Dane Cook drive around in a car looking for someone to murder. Costner looks over at Dane in his hooded sweatshirt, and says, "You look a little bit like that E.T. guy—you remember that movie—he flies on the bike." Dane Cook: "Yeah yeah. Yeah, I like that movie." E.T.'s death *is* my mother's death, whether he gasps or not—the film and life exist simultaneously, each dipping in and out of one another. The cat ears I wore on the plane, the cat ears Dee Wallace wears for E.T.'s first Halloween. My mother directing me in the kitchen—do this do that, not like that, do it exactly this way—as if I were a puppet. Inside E.T. it stinks of sweat and silicone. It's airless, sweltering. And so heavy. Soft whirring from the mechanical head up above. I can't see a thing it's so dark in here, so tight, like being buried alive. My mother lying in her bright blue sweater, putty makeup, too angular face—from the waist down, dark wood-grained coffin, giant spray of yellow roses my brother and I picked out at Solan's Florist. E. T. / Stay with me. / Please. / Stay. / Together. / I'll be right here. / I'll be right here. / Stay. / Stay. / Stay. / Stay. / Stay. Flash of myself in my bedroom putting on the turquoise dress I got for my eighth-grade graduation. The heels were white satin, which I dyed turquoise to match the dress. Even though my mother was there, orchestrating the scene, paying for it, I have no memory of her. She's white noise in the background of the grand opera of Dodie. Nauseating scent of cigarettes and Estée Lauder emanating from the bathroom as she stood in front of the mirror in her white cafeteria lady uniform, smearing on blue eye shadow. I'm in the kitchen, yelling, "I don't want to wash the dishes, why do I have to wash the dishes." I'm yelling at her, but I can't see her, she's an incidental prop eradicated by my rage. Glimpse of her on the porch, making a face and mouthing to me as I walk by, "You're fat." Glimpse of her running barefoot across the front yard, soaking wet, throwing another water balloon at my friend Ralph. She rarely drank—but here she is, drunk as a skunk with me and my girlfriend on New Year's Eve. She pulls over to the side of the road, jumps out and squat-pees in the snow. Janis and I buckle over with laughter. As I lie on my stomach on my bed, writing in my diary, I can hear her in the living room telling my father she thinks I'm mentally ill—because she found a cache of my poems and all of them were about death. My last visit, sitting at the kitchen table, she complains about the Chinese takeout. I get all silent and stiff, like she's a pain in the ass, and she starts crying, saying don't be mad at me—or maybe that was when I acted irritated with her first thing in the morning. Like a scolded child she sat there eating fried rice she clearly found revolting. I should have said that's okay, Mom, what do you want—I'll give you anything you want. Anything. The antagonist is death itself. Elliott frees the chloroformed frogs in the school science lab. "Back to the river, back to the forest," he cries. "I gotta save you." Elliott doesn't analyze, he lets the moment wash over him, possess him. E. T. watches a man and woman kissing on TV, Elliott grabs a girl in his science lab, spins her around and kisses her passionately, their movements choreographed to match the movements of the couple on TV. Dee Wallace: "I truly never thought of E.T. as a puppet. He was very real to all of us." No matter how much I research, remember, shred, E.T. is still real, death is still real, still everywhere. Cutting up a dead frog into little bits and pieces will never contain it. The bits blow apart and scatter like a dandelion puff. E.T. calls us back to the pre-symbolic, the burden of otherness we've carried ever since we left the primal ooze of our mother's body. *I-think-I-can! I-think-I-can! Choo, choo! Choo, choo! Choo, choo!* As we watch *E.T.* fragments coalesce and point in one direction: Home. Home is a place of perfect belonging, wholeness. Home is an instinct, a yearning that has never, ever been satisfied, that can never be eradicated, an itch we will scratch until the day E.T. comes to harvest our souls, until we walk with him into the blinding light of his spaceship and ascend into the heavens to join Saint Winifred and all the rest of God's minions. Into your hands, O Merciful Saviour, we comment Your servant Winnie Bellamy. Acknowledge, we humbly beseech you, a sheep of your own fold, a lamb of your own flock, a sinner of your own redeeming. Receive her into the blessed rest of everlasting peace, and into the glorious company of the saints in light. I'll believe in you all my life. / Every day. / Mom / I love you.

DESIREE, DANEAL, AND THE DEVIL
Some Thoughts on Disembodiment, Image, and Possession

Donal Mosher

These notes have been shaped from the diary I kept while shooting October Country—*a film documenting the lives of my family from one Halloween to the next, made in partnership with Michael Palmieri. These passages concern my nieces Desiree and Daneal.*

Oct 27/07 – Herkimer, NY

Arrived, unpacked, then settled down in the traditional family way—sitting around the TV. At this time of year of course *The Exorcist* was on. We watched the scene where Ellen Burstyn walks home through Georgetown. Leaves, nuns' habits, and bedsheet ghost costumes flutter in the chill air. For years I thought this segment of the film really captured the ephemeral spirit of Halloween as I remembered it growing up. It seems heavy-handed and clumsy now, and the music, once so evocative, has become blunt and dated. I feel robbed of a dear childhood memory.

Scene 32 – Oct 28/07 (Desi views footage of herself)

We are filming Desi watching a DVD of herself shot at Halloween last year. She leans in as her own image fills the TV. She's dressed as the devil. Her costume is vivid red—a color pulsing with High Definition, weird, plastic life. Cut. She applies carmine glitter lipstick. Voice-over (in exaggerated little-girl manner): "This might be my last year trick-or-treating 'cause I'm growing up." Then she's out the door racing and laughing through the monster-filled streets.

Viewing intently, Desi seems pleased by what she sees but giggles shyly at a slow-motion shot in which she pulls a dollar from her treat bag, kisses it, then lets it fall. The image continues in real time as she chases after the bill across the frosty grass.

★ ★ ★

Later we review our scene within a scene. The effect is hallucinatory. A girl and her diabolic double face each other, one year and a screen between them. On the couch, Desi's watchful eyes jump and flutter. Her smooth face pulses with light from the screen. On TV, her doppelganger flickers with video-on-video grain. In repetition Desi's corporeality scatters and shimmers into ghostly textures, as if the layering of time within the frame (rather than the flaws of the recording media) caused a disintegration of her form. The strangeness of the scene eclipses its original subject. The clip now appears to be a fragment of a film, or perhaps even the memory of a film, that has nothing to do with Desi or our documentary. Family and memory disperse into cinema and phantasm.

In *The Remembered Film*, Victor Burgin describes a similar effect as two film segments merge in his memory. "Detached from their original setting each scene is now a satellite of the other. Each echoes the other, increasingly merges with the other, and I experience a kind of fascinated incomprehension before the hybrid object they have become."

Poor Desi, a hybrid object.

Scene 68 – Oct 30/07 (Desi in her bedroom)

Desi on her bed, high on candy corn, blood boiling with fructose. Her legs kick. Her hair flies. She bounces as if hurled from the mattress, making guttural noises, gibberish, and high, wild laughter. She's Linda Blair in *The Exorcist*—a film she's never seen because she is too frightened to watch horror films, especially those involving young girls.

The trick to getting Desi to talk seriously is to film her at play first, sometimes for an hour or more. When she calms we broach the troubling subject of her mother's relationships. We ask if she's liked or trusted any of her mother's boyfriends.

"I trusted my dad once but not anymore," she says growing somber.

"Why?"

"'Cause he's in jail?"

"What for?" We expect drugs, maybe domestic abuse—usual problems in the family. But she turns her head away and hides her face in her hair before asking, "Do you really want me to tell you?"

"Yes."

She turns. There's an unhappy power in her expression. She knows she's giving us something serious. "Child molestation."

"Did he touch you?"

"No, older girls, and sissy, just once."

Then she's up, full of energy and angry life. "Where's my kitten?" No more questions. We're left to reconcile what we've just heard and permanently recorded.

Scene 71 – Nov 2/07 (Daneal talks of Desi's father)

Daneal is surprisingly open about the subject and speaks with hard but lazy scorn. "He's a fucking shit, perv. He used to take me places and act like he was my real dad. Then when I was twelve he started climbing in the bed. I put Desi next to the wall so I could always be between him and her. He would have gotten round to her too if I hadn't been there."

Feb 18/08 – Portland, Ore.

Reviewing the scene of Desi on her bed with a slide bar we choreograph her convulsive antics. Whenever we pause a clip, her body appears twisted in some incredible way. Using still frames, we could illustrate the lineage of images of mad and possessed women. Pause, she's one of the bewitched girls from Salem. Pause, she's one of Charcot's hysterics from La Saltpêtière. Pause, caught falling backwards on the bed, frozen in midair, levitating—again, a scene from *The Exorcist*.

The Exorcist has been haunting me since I heard the story of Desi's father. The infamous crucifix scene flares up in my mind whenever I ponder him climbing into the bed with the girls—quick cuts of a hard-edged crucifix, gnarled fingers, and the bloody hem of a nightgown. Beneath these movie images, another image, the imagined image of the incident plays out unseen, like a filmstrip moving through a darkened projector.

I've always thought the crucifix scene was a particularly repulsive way of representing the onset of menses and sexuality and very cruel to the character of Regan. It's strange then that this gratuitous segment has become a kind of protective talisman against my own imagination—a version, perhaps, of the Freudian "screen memory" with "screen" to be taken in a cinematic sense. The graphic power of those few gruesome shots overwhelm and deflect any picture I might form of what happened to the girls. It makes me queasy that Friedkin's notorious scene and a very real, very traumatic portion of my niece's lives, have saturated each other.

★ ★ ★

Apparently it is common knowledge to the rest of the family that Desi's father was imprisoned for molestation and that it was Daneal who helped convict him. Daneal speaks openly, though bitterly of this, grunting off this incident as if it was par for the course in dealing with men, like the beatings, pregnancy, and abortions she's lived through at age nineteen.

Desiree however is not made of the same tough fiber. She bounds her world with cartoons, video games, and all the dense, sparkling décor of young girlhood. At age twelve (the age of Regan in *The Exorcist* and the age of Daneal at the time of the molestation) Desi plays the preadolescent, though her body is growing and dragging womanhood along with it. She will never achieve the innocent state she seeks, let alone maintain it. An unclean spirit entered her innocence long ago. It inhabits her and tells her terrifying secrets. She will not speak of sex or her own body and says the worst thing she knows is how babies are made. Since this is life, not film, the spirit that haunts her body is not an outside, disembodied force, but the memory and knowledge of what bodies do and have done unto them. There is no ritual expulsion to rectify this form of possession. At the end of *The Exorcist*, Regan has no memory of what has happened—neither Daneal nor Desi will receive this forgetful blessing.

FROM *DON'T LET ME BE LONELY*
Claudia Rankine

EVERY MOVIE I saw while in the third grade compelled me to ask, Is he dead? Is she dead? Because the characters often live against all odds it is the actors whose mortality concerned me. If it were an old, black-and-white film, whoever was around would answer yes. Months later the actor would show up on some late-night talk show to promote his latest efforts. I would turn and say—one always turns to say—You said he was dead. And the misinformed would claim, I never said he was dead. Yes you did. No, I didn't. Inevitably, as we get older, whoever is still with us says, Stop asking me that.

ONE NIGHT we discuss at great length the movies *Boogie Nights* and *Magnolia*. The consensus is that both movies are motivated by the theme of the disappointing father figure. In both movies men old enough to be anybody's father do bad things to people who are younger than they are, people who could be their children, people who are their children, people who if these father figures had behaved better could have looked up to them for the slimmest of reasons. Tom Cruise is convincing as the disappointed son in *Magnolia*. There is another character with my same name who is also bitterly disappointed. Though the subject of cancer did not come up in our late-night conversation about the two movies it did for him, for Tom Cruise's character in *Magnolia*.

I LEAVE the television on all the time. It faces the empty bed. I don't go into the bedroom during the day once I've dressed. Sometimes when I am wearing a skirt and feel like putting on pants or vice versa I go in there and people are conversing. Occasionally I sit on the edge of the bed and listen. I listen for a few minutes only. One day there is a man interviewing a boy caught in the penal system, a juvenile offender—

> Man: He is deceased?
> Boy: He is dead to me.
> Man: So he is not deceased?
> Boy: I don't know. He could be dead.
> Man: Is he or is he not dead?
> Boy: He's been dead to my life.
> Man: Someone wrote in your file that he is dead. Did you tell someone that he is dead?
> Boy: All right, he is dead.

CORNEL WEST makes the point that hope is different from American optimism. After the initial presidential election results come in, I stop watching the news. I want to continue watching, charting, and discussing the counts, the recounts, the hand counts, but I cannot. I lose hope. However Bush came to have won, he would still be winning ten days later and we would still be in the throes of American optimism. All the non-reporting is a distraction from Bush himself, the same Bush who can't remember if two or three people were convicted for dragging a black man to his death in his home state of Texas.

You don't remember because you don't care.

Sometimes my mother's voice swells and fills my forehead. Mostly I resist the flooding, but in Bush's case I find myself talking to the television screen: *You don't remember because you don't care.*

THERE IS a button on the remote control called FAV. You can program your favorite channels. Don't like the world you live in, choose one closer to the world you went to live in. I choose the independent film channel and HBO. Neither have news programs as far as I can tell. This is what is great about America—anyone can make these kinds of choices. Instead of the news, HBO has *The Sopranos*. This week the indie channel is playing and replaying spaghetti Westerns. Always someone gets shot or pierced through the heart with an arrow, and just before he dies he says, I am not going to make it. Where? Not going to make it where? On some level, maybe, the phrase simply means not going to make it into the next day, hour, minute, or perhaps the next second. Occasionally, you can imagine it means he is not going to make it to Carson City or Texas or some-where else out West or to Mexico if he is on the run. On another level always implicit is the sense that it means he is not going to make it to his own death. Perhaps in the back of all our minds is the life expectancy for our generation. Perhaps this expectation lingers there alongside the hours of sleep one should get or the number of times one is meant to chew food—eight hours, twenty chews, and seventy-six years. We are all head-ing there and not to have that birthday is not to have made it.

PECKINPAH'S *THE WILD BUNCH* is worth watching because the cowboys in it have nowhere to get to. They're older and they don't have to make it anywhere because where they are is all there is or rather the end of a genre. Theirs is not the Old Testament—no journey to take; nothing promised; no land to land in. For them, life and death are simultaneously equal and present. The simultaneity of the living who are already dead is filed as sexy.

Peckinpah gives the final shoot-out in which they all die a kind of orgasmic rush that releases all of us from the cinematic or, more accurate-ly, the American fantasy that we will survive no matter what. Though they are handsome, white, leading men not dressed all in black, he liter-ally shoots the life out of all anticipatory leanings. Once the orgasm is over we can just lie back, close our eyes, and relax, though we are neither liberated nor fulfilled. They are dead, finished, no American fantasy can help them now.

LAST YEAR this close friend was in the depression of his life. He had to take a medical leave from his job as a speechwriter. He could barely get out of bed. That's what he said so he might have meant he wasn't getting out of bed. He said he felt like an old man dying, the old man dying. The leaves on the trees outside his window rattled within him.

Before his breakdown we had DVD evenings. I'd go over with a bag of Doritos and a bottle of wine. After the breakdown, he didn't wish to see anyone. He wasn't answering the phone. I called; I left mes-sages—sometimes to break into the general silence and sometimes to check on him. Finally, he agreed I should come by. I walked the thirty-six blocks to his apartment. By the time I reached his place I was anxious but optimistic. I thought the apartment would be a mess; the apartment was dust free. He seemed fine.

We sat on the sofa in front of his television. He crossed his legs and seemed excessively silent, though I had no real grounds for comparison having never noticed the quality of his small talk before. He had rented *Fitzcarraldo* from The Movie Place. They pick up and deliver. Herzog is his favorite director. He refused the glass of wine I poured for him.

His body couldn't take alcohol and drugs at the same time. He was on lithium, one capsule four times daily. There was a red sticker on his medicine bottle warning against alcohol use. He handed me the bottle.

While watching the movie, tears rolled down his cheeks. Apart from their use in expressing emotion, tears have two other functions: They lubricate the eyes so that the lid can move over it smoothly as you blink; they wash away foreign bodies. It is difficult to feel much tear-worthy emotion about anything in *Fitzcarraldo,* as it is about having outlandish projects and achieving them in the name of art, but since the tears kept coming long after smooth blinking would have been restored and foreign bodies washed away, I decided that apparently my friend was expressing emotion and was not fine, not OK, no.

WE HEAR on the television that a thirteen-year-old boy is convicted of first-degree murder for killing a six-year-old girl when he was twelve years old.

I, or we, it hardly matters, seek out the story in the *Times*. The girl had a torn liver, fractured skull, and broken ribs—perhaps there was more. In any case, her time is done. The boy was tried as an adult or he was tried as a dead child. There are no children anymore, at least not this boy—this boy who is only a child. But then, what child behaves like this? What child behaves like this, knows the consequences, and still insists he was playing at being a wrestler? To know and not to understand is perhaps one definition of being a child. Or responsibility is not connected to sense-making, the courts have decided.

In this moment we are alone with the facts as he will be when he understands. In the time it takes for the appeal to happen he will be a dead child in an adult prison. He will be alive as someone else. He will be there with adults and because his life is happening in this way, he will forever happen in our minds as a dead child. I see the tears have run relatively parallel down his mother's cheeks. What I have is a headache. On the Tylenol bottle someone has made the distinction between adults and children. I, as an adult, am allowed two tablets. As I stare at the label from somewhere a voice whispers in my ear: Take comfort in our strength.

ON THE BUS two women argue about whether Rudy Giuliani had to kneel before the Queen of England when he was knighted. One says she is sure he had to. They all had to, Sean Connery, John Gielgud, Mick Jagger. They all had to. The other says that if he had, they would have seen it on television. We would have seen him do it. I am telling you we would have seen it happen.

When my stop arrives I am still considering Giuliani as nobility. It is difficult to separate him from the extremes connected to the city over the years of his mayorship. Still, a day after the attack on the World Trade Center a reporter asked him to estimate the number of dead. His reply—More than we can bear—caused me to turn and look at him as if for the first time. It is true that we carry the idea of us along with us. And then there are three thousand dead and it is incomprehensible and ungraspable. Physically and emotionally we cannot bear it, should in fact never have this capacity. So when the number is released it is a sieve that cannot hold the loss Giuliani recognized and answered for.

Wallace Stevens wrote, "The peculiarity of the imagination is nobility . . . nobility which is our spiritual height and depth; and while I know how difficult it is to express it, nevertheless I am bound to give a sense of it. Nothing could be more evasive and inaccessible. Nothing distorts itself and seeks disguise more quickly. There is a shame of disclosing it and in its definite presentation a horror of it. But there it is."

Sir Giuliani kneeling. It was apparently not something to be seen on television, but rather a moment to be heard and experienced; a moment that allowed his imagination's encounter with death to kneel under the weight of the real.

MY GRANDMOTHER tells me that since the doctor told her to stay away from cigarettes she now smokes the longest ones she can find. Actually she continues to smoke a pack of Marlboros a day. I tell her Philip Morris is thinking of changing their name to Altria. From behind a screen of smoke my grandmother says, We should all change our names when we don't like what we see in the mirror. It's an easy way to distance the self from the self, I say for the conversation's sake. She and I sit outside in the sun during the dead of winter smoking cigarettes, chewing gum, and watching the cars go by. Sitting here, chewing Juicy Fruit until the taste evaporates, makes me think of the last line of that movie *Secrets and Lies*: "This is the life."

MY WESTERN

Rebecca Brown

If only I'd known what to look for.
　　If only I'd known how to read the writing on the screen.
　　A private meaning just for me
　　but I was looking wrong

Then he was gone.

　　This is how the movie ends, the scene we won't forget: The child is facing away from us and watching someone leaving. ". . . And mother wants you! I know she does," the child shouts, "Come back!" But the man does not. "Come back!" the child shouts again, "Shane, come back!"
　　Come back come back come back.
　　My father can't come back because he's dead, and no one's really sure about the lone man on the horse. He came from far away and then he left.
　　He looked, far away, like a silhouette, first black and white, then color. Although the book said he was dark, in the movie[1], he is blonde, as is the kid, who could have been his child and wished he was, though he already had a father. The kid was looking out, before the stranger came, at a deer he wanted to shoot except his rifle had no bullets. (His mother hated guns.) The kid was also looking up at the Wyoming sky—it's 1889 —as wide and high and blue and vast as anything we've ever, ever seen

or ever will. There's mountains too, both far away and crisp and cold, but also close, like everything. The kid is looking out at them and at the giant, lonely world.

Does everybody always want to be somebody else?

At first they wanted Montgomery Clift for Shane, but he was "not available," like what they say about the kind of men who can't make commitments (why don't they just say what they fucking mean?), so they got Alan Ladd and now no one can imagine Shane as anybody else.[2]

As if the way it ended was the only way it could.

At first they wanted William Holden for the father, but he was also "not available," so they got Van Heflin. Van Heflin was part Irish, born in Oklahoma, went to O.U. and was a Navy man. All of this is exactly like my father.

They tried to get it right but you can't do everything. Some things they did but others not, you have to read between the lines, I mean the frames, or put in things you might not see but know are there because it was all there, if you knew how to look, if you looked right. Then you could see the way it was or would be. It tried to tell you, and it was not what you thought.

At first they wanted Katherine Hepburn for the mother, but she was also "not available," so they got Jean Arthur. Jean Arthur, like my mother, once lived in Jacksonville, Florida. We all did when my father was stationed at Pensacola. This was a good posting, at least for me, because it meant he got to be mostly at home as opposed to away on a naval carrier when we might not see him for months. He was a pilot for the Navy, though we did not know where he flew, and a photographer. My mother taught grade school in Florida, having given up her college dream of acting.

They brought Jean Arthur (who named herself after two of my favorite childhood heroes too, Jean [Joan] of Arc and King Arthur) out of retirement for it. She was fity-three by then, eight years older than Van Heflin, and long past her heyday as a screwball comic. In her prime she'd also had a few romantic roles, including once as Cary Grant's love interest in *Only Angels Have Wings* (Howard Hawks, 1939), where she falls in love with the dashing pilot Cary Grant the way my mother fell in love with my dashing pilot father. My mother always referred to Cary Grant as "the world's most perfect man," and though Cary leaves Jean, it's only for a while because later he comes back.

My father didn't.

("Come back! Come back! Come back!")

Brandon De Wilde played the kid. He was blonde and fair and small, like Shane and me and my dad. Actually my father wasn't short, he was 5'10" or so, but built compact and wiry like Shane. Brandon De Wilde also had severely deep-set eyes that looked a little weird. I had, if not exactly the same thing, at least a "lazy eye" that had to be corrected with a patch. At first I hated it. I hated looking weird with the weird eye, then the weird patch, but then I liked the patch because it showed I was a cowgirl and I'd lost my eye in a fight. Or at the Alamo (*The Alamo*, John Wayne, 1960, starring himself), where I almost died while defending it with Davy Crockett. Or to an Indian[3]—not a nice, wise one, I was friends with them—an Apache or Comanche who had shot me in the eyeball with an arrow that I had to pull out myself.

I could have done Brandon De Wilde's part. Why didn't they pick me? True, I wasn't born till five years after they made it, and I was a girl, but they had already changed the name of the kid from Bob in the book to Joe in the movie, so why couldn't they also change Bob into a girl? I could have played that part. I could have done it better. I could have said "Come back! Come back!" so wonderfully he'd have to.

Van Heflin invites Shane to dinner. Mom dresses up, sets the table for four, and makes a special apple pie for the occasion. After dinner, Shane helps Dad remove a stump from the yard. The men decide he'll stick around to help the family on the farm. Shane becomes part of this nice domestic farmer's life as, around the valley, ranchers grumble about "sodbusters" fencing the range. After he's been at their home a while, little Joey asks the gunman to teach him how to shoot. He hesitates, then takes the kid to the corral and is showing him how to hold a gun when Mom comes out and stops them. She doesn't want her child to play with guns.

My father taught me how to shoot. He took me to the range where he practiced shooting "skeet" or "trap," clay pigeons, not something I could—with a bungled shot—maim, hurt, or cause to suffer. I remember him telling me to squeeze the trigger evenly—don't jerk it—and always aim a bit in front of a moving target. I remember the weight of the gun in my arms, the cool of the metal, the buck of the blast, my shoulder sore for days.

Later he took me duck hunting. I wore my brother's hand-me-downs—a corduroy cap, the flaps folded down over my ears, too-big boots, and camouflage pants and jacket. We were in a brown field and the air was cold and the sun was coming up. There was the sound of men's and boys' and my boots on the crunchy, almost frozen ground, and also the sounds of calls and cries, the whup of wings because the ducks knew what was up. This was in Spain, where we were posted after Florida.

I think I remember this, but maybe I don't. Maybe I only think I do because I saw a photograph of me in such a field on such a day, holding my father's gun. I must have been eight or nine because the gun was about my height. I do not remember firing a gun on this or any other trip at any living thing, although I'm sure I begged my father to.

Did my mother see to that?

After he retired from the Navy, Van Heflin had a successful career in the movies. After my father was piped over[4] from the Navy, he kind of went to hell.

Van Heflin did, however, play a failure in his last major role, which was in *Airport* (George Seaton, 1970). He played a husband who tries to blow himself up so his wife can get the insurance money. So, a heroic failure then. Whereas my father just plain old died of "natural causes."

They scattered his ashes at sea.

(Van Heflin's and my father's.)

Shane gets wounded in a gunfight. Shot in the gut in the saloon in town by the bad ranchers who are mean to good farmers like Van Heflin. Van Heflin had planned to go to fight them, but Shane, in a valiant and self-sacrificial move, socked him good so he couldn't go because if Shane got hurt by the bad guys, no big deal, but if the father got hurt, then who would take care of his wife and child?

Shane is not so wounded, however, that he can't come back to the farm after the fight to play the poignant scene we want to see. He looks down at the kid and the kid looks up at him and there's all of that "Come back! Come back!" etc.

I don't remember when my father left. He was away "on tour" with the Navy most of the time I was a kid. Then after he was piped over and got civilian jobs, he traveled a lot. Then after he lost those jobs he stayed away for other reasons. So when it became official, through their divorce, that he was really leaving, it was like he already had. There wasn't any specific time or scene in which he walked or drove away or rode out on a horse and then did not come back. There was no time that I or anyone yelled after him, "Come back, Come back! Come back."

He was already gone.

What if, when Joey cried "Come back," he did? What if we saw his face close up, his sudden recognition, then his tenderness, and then he turned his horse and looked back at the child? The child brightens! Full of joy! But only for an instant because the guy's been wounded after all, and on his face is not a shining, all-forgiving, all-forgetting smile. No—No—He turns back with a gasp, a gag, a gurgle in this throat and starts to fall. He's slipping in the saddle, back and stomach twisted. The child sees him fall, but only partly because his feet are in the stirrups so he's stuck half-on, half-off the horse which might be funny somewhere else but isn't here. He's trying to right himself but can't. He's writhing like an insect, like a centipede, a worm—Wait. We can't do this to them.

Okay. Then how about this: Let's say he turns, but in this version his feet slip out of the stirrups so he can actually fall all the way off the horse and into the child's arms. The child catches him, holds him. The wounded man's bent over now, exactly the height of the child, which might seem nice at first but isn't because now the child can see, close up, at eye level, in garish, gruesome Technicolor, the man's blown-apart skin and his guts gouging out and brown stuff and red stuff and oozy stuff. This wasn't in the script. This isn't stuff a child should see. The dying man is trying to hold or push his guts back in but they keep oozing through his fingers and over the tops of his hands. Now his face is moving, he's sputtering, gagging, trying to tell the child something. His mouth falls open and he makes these bubbly hacking awful noises and blood starts burbling up then, shooting out of him, red at first, little splatters like drops of rain, big thick lines of it then clots, black, viscous, thick, and then a great big glob of it that splatters against the child's face.

The kid is so fucking terrified that it can hardly breathe.

The guy makes another gurgly noise and his face goes white and his eyes roll back in his head and he shivers like he's got the D.T.'s. He clenches, falls. The child holds him up.

How long does the child hold the man?
How long will this go on?

Is this why Shane did not come back?
Is this what his departure spared the child?

For a while my mother wanted to be an actress. She got away from Oklahoma, where she, like everyone else in my family except me was born, to study speech and drama at Sophie Newcomb Women's College in New Orleans. She performed in plays (the screwball gal? romantic lead?) and studied radio during an era when such a study could have led her to the movies. But she suddenly returned to Oklahoma. I don't know why. Is the answer in a scene that was deleted? An outtake on the cutting room floor?

After my mother returned to Oklahoma, she transferred to O.U. where, through his younger brother, Stanley, whom she was dating, she met my father.

Kind of like how Hallie does in *The Man Who Shot Liberty Valance* (John Ford, 1962). Hallie (Vera Miles) is a nice girl, the illiterate daughter (unlike my mom who loved to read) of the immigrant couple (isn't everyone white in America some kind of immigrant?) that runs the local canteen. At the start of the movie, she's sweet on handsome, swaggering, gun-toting Tom Doniphon (John Wayne). They're not exactly engaged, but everyone assumes she's promised to him. Then slender, earnest, Ransom Stoddard (James Stewart), a vest-wearing guy whose head is always in a law book, comes to town. Ransom is beaten up by the Liberty Valance gang and John Wayne rescues him. The two become friends and John treats the gentle, bookish guy the way an older boy might treat his little brother. He calls him "Pilgrim," meaning "greenhorn," because he thinks he'll always be his sidekick.

My father called my Uncle Stanley "Little Brother" all their lives.

Uncle Stanley told me once that he remembered their father coming home from World War I and teaching him and his big brother how to take apart and clean and put a gun back together, then how to shoot it. My father was better at this than Stan. Stan's pursuits were quieter; next to his confident older brother he was shy.

What my father remembered about his father was how he was henpecked by his wife. She ran away to New York once (to be an actress?). My father remembered his father washing dishes at the kitchen sink, a hero and a veteran diminished by his wife.[5]

John Wayne was not John Wayne until the movies.

His name at birth was, after his Irish mother, Marion. Marion Robert Morrison. Needless to say, he wanted a nickname. When he was a child, he went everywhere with his dog, a huge thing named Duke. People started calling the boy "Little Duke." When he got older it became just "Duke."

He kept that name and got another when he started playing heroes in the movies.

My father's name was Vergil (spelled with an "e," not an "i" like Dante's guide) Neal Brown, Jr. after his Irish father. He hated the name and he swore he'd never name a child that. When he was a kid they called him "Hershey." I don't know why because I never asked. What else did I not ask about? What else did I not think about until it was too late?

Perhaps the first kind thing my father did for his son was to name him plain old Bill.

Everyone else, besides John Wayne, calls Jimmy Stewart "Rance." Because he helps out in the kitchen, wears an apron, likes to read, and is terrible with guns, they treat him like he isn't quite a man. Though Rance is grateful for John Wayne's help, he wants to fight his own battles and turn the gun-happy Wild West into a law-abiding state. Rance doesn't want to carry a gun, but John insists, for his own safety, that he learn to shoot. He tries to teach him but he's a miserable shot, so when the evil Liberty Valance (a leather-clad, whip-toting, Lee Marvin!) challenges Ransom to a gunfight, John has to rescue Rance a second time. As Jimmy is about to fire, John, hidden in the shadows, shoots Lee Marvin dead. Unaware of who really killed him, gun-shy Stoddard Ransom becomes famous as the man who shot Liberty Valance and, riding this law and order reputation, is elected Representative at the territorial convention. After Stewart is voted in, John Wayne tells him that it was he, not him, who shot him.

Jimmy Stewart feels awful that he's been given credit for something he didn't do, but he's already made a commitment to the convention. Drunken, angry John tells Jimmy not to tell—the people need to believe in something. Rance goes to Washington and is eventually elected Senator. He also marries Hallie.

Which brings us back to my parents. Hallie starts out with the bigger, charismatic guy who's going to turn out bad and switches to, then marries, his less showy greenhorn sidekick who is going to turn out good. This is the opposite of my mom, who started out with the less showy guy who is going to turn out good (Uncle Stanley), then switched to, then married, the older, charismatic one, who kind of went to hell—my dad.

When Tom sees Hallie taking care of the traumatized Pilgrim after the shoot-out with Lee Marvin, Tom thinks she's sweet on Rance. Tom freaks out, drinks too much, burns down the house and basically, for the rest of his life, kind of goes to hell. In the movie he falls apart because he loses the girl. But my father didn't lose the girl, so why'd he fall apart? Uncle Stanley married, had kids, kept a job, did not become a boozer.

After John goes to hell, the only person who can stand to be around him is loyal Pompey (Woody Strode), a former slave. It was the early sixties when we lived in Florida. Years later, my mother told me about how, when she was teaching there, some white parents wouldn't ever let their kids be absent from school because then enrollment would go down and the school would have to integrate. These white parents would send their kids to school even when they were really sick with things like impetigo. I don't remember this, although I do remember—and it's one of my most shameful memories—preschool me, after one of my father's friends had come over to our house to visit, referring to his friend with the "N" word. My father firmly, carefully, quietly told me to never, ever use that word again and why. My father may have been a troubled man, but he was right about a few important things.[6]

The Man Who Shot Liberty Valance is a frame narrative. It starts with the Senator and his wife returning to a little town to mourn the passing of some old drunk. When local newsmen ask the Senator why he has come back to mourn the dead guy, he tells, at last, the story of who really shot Liberty Valance. He wants the paper to print this story and finally honor the man who'd done such a heroic deed back when. The editor refuses. "This is the West, sir," he tells the Senator, "When the legend becomes fact, print the legend."

Tom Doniphon had never told anyone else about who really shot Liberty Valance, and he suffered for that. Is that what happens to the guy who knows the truth but has to keep it secret? Was this the real reason Tom Doniphon went to hell?

Some things about John Wayne

John Wayne hated his birth name.

John Wayne never actually fought in a World War, but he loved the military. John Wayne was very pro-gun.

John Wayne was asked to be George Wallace's running mate when Wallace ran for Governor of Alabama. He turned them down so they got Lester Maddox.

John Wayne was married three times.

John Wayne smoked packs and packs of cigarettes a day.

John Wayne got cancer.

John Wayne died.

Some things about my father

My father hated his birth name.

My father never actually fought in World War II, but he loved the military. My father was very pro-gun.

My father went duck hunting once with Lester Maddox.

My father was married three times.

My father smoked packs and packs of cigarettes a day.

My father got cancer.

My father died.

Does everybody always want to be somebody else?

To be from some place they are not?

To always be arriving or departing?

Shane did not come back to Little Joey. But when Brandon De Wilde grew up, he got to be John Wayne's son. It was, oddly enough, not in a

Western but in a movie about World War II, *In Harm's Way* (Otto Preminger, 1965). John Wayne is Rockwell Torrey, a Navy officer who left his family years before because he couldn't be both a family man and a Navy man. Brandon De Wilde is an only child and, in the way that can only happen in Hollywood, is stationed near his father, John Wayne. Exactly like in *Rio Grande* (John Ford, 1950), a son whom he hasn't seen in fifteen years is stationed near his father, John Wayne. This time, however, it's 1965 and although the war in Vietnam isn't quite as hated as it's going to get, the son hates being in the Navy. He's only in it to eventually become a journalist or something, and we already know from *Liberty Valance* how untrustworthy journalists are. But then Pearl Harbor happens and the son sees his father in his element and comes to understand, in a way I and my anti-Vietnam peacenik siblings never did, why a father has to leave his family. The son and father also double-date.

John Wayne's love interest is the no-nonsense nurse Patricia Neal (my father's middle name!), who is roommates with a younger nurse who goes out once with Brandon De Wilde. Patricia Neal is also kind of the crush interest for modern cowboy Brandon De Wilde when he plays bad Paul Newman's shy, younger cousin in *Hud* (1963, Martin Ritt).[7] (Is there some kind of Freudian thing going on here? The boy gets a crush on his father's girlfriend after she becomes his cousin's almost girlfriend?) Paul Newman is the bad cowboy—violent, yelling, crashing around drunk—who almost gets her but she gets away in time.

I never saw my father violent and I don't believe, at home, he ever was. My mother always said if he had ever laid a hand on any of us she would have left him in an instant, and I believe she would have.

But my sister, seven years older than me, remembers times when we were small and our mother, hearing our father outside, bustled the three of us to our room at the back of the house and told us to stay there no matter what happened. My sister had to keep us quiet as she listened to our father yell and the sounds of breaking things.

I don't remember any of this.

Come back come back come back!
No, don't. No—Please. Do not come back.

The movie *Shane* was adapted from a book by Jack Schaefer that begins "...in the summer of '89," which was sort of the beginning of my family too. Eighteen eighty-nine was the year of one of the great Oklahoma Land Rushes. (See *Cimarron*, Charles Walters and Anthony Mann, 1960, for a version of April 22, 1889, when, at high noon, with a gunshot and a bugle call, some 50,000 [mostly] white people ran or rode on horseback or in wagons or on trains to try to claim a piece of the two million acres the U.S. government was giving away, having wrested it with bullets, blood, etc., from the people who had lived there previously but were not white. This was the beginning of the state of Oklahoma).[8] I don't know if anyone in my bloodline took part in this 1889 Land Rush, or snuck in earlier as Sooners. I do know that my maternal grandfather was born in Canadian County, Oklahoma Territory, one year after the Land Rush and my grandmother two years later in Blaine County, Oklahoma. Then a generation or so later, my father and my mother and Van Heflin were born in Oklahoma City.

Does everybody always want another set of parents?
Does everybody always want to hear "Come back"?

I wasn't born in Oklahoma like everyone else. I was born in California when my dad was stationed there, but I was the kid who really loved the West. I wanted, longer than most kids do, to be a cowboy or cowgirl. The important thing was the riding and shooting and being free. We lived in Spain in the mid-sixties, the era of the great TV Westerns, so we didn't get to see them first-run, but "Bonanza" was so famous that they dubbed it into Spanish. I remember a story from that time about my father going drinking with Dan Blocker (Hoss). My father came home and told us that Dan Blocker was a very, very huge man and he could really hold his drink. I couldn't believe my father had met Dan Blocker and hung out with him. I was thrilled. I couldn't keep my mouth shut. I told everyone.

John Wayne's last movie was *The Shootist* (Don Siegel, 1976). It begins with a bunch of old black-and-white clips of early John Wayne movies. We see the young man—handsome, clear-eyed, confident—ride and shoot his way through the ranges and mesas, canyons and plateaus of the classic West, a stranger or a loner or a soldier who will save us. Then we see him age—his suntanned face gets wrinkled and his girth expands. His walk becomes more measured, slow. By the time the black-and-white runs out, he's old.

He rides into a town—buggies in the background, a primitive street-car—and buys a newspaper that announces the death of Queen Victoria. It's 1901, the end of an era of history and the beginning of the end of this man's life. John Books has traveled for days to see the one doctor he can trust, a man he knew when they were young, James Stewart. Doc Stewart, no longer a greenhorn like Rance Stoddard was, tells John that the pain in his lower back is cancer and that he's going to die of it.

"How bad is it going to be?" the old man asks, and Doc tells him he doesn't want to know.

But John insists, so James tells him it's going to be bad, very bad, and gives him a bottle to take a nip of whenever he needs it, the way my father carried a flask. Assuming a false identity, John rents a room in Widow Rogers' house, where he expects to die. Widow Rogers is actually Lauren Bacall, who had lost her husband, Humphrey Bogart, to cancer in '57. She's a single mom with a now fatherless only child played not by Brandon De Wilde, who is dead, but by Oklahoma-born Ron Howard. Ron Howard's name is "Gillom," a name I'd never heard before, which is perhaps why I first heard it as "William," like my brother, who was often called "Guillermo" when we lived in Spain or Texas near the border.

Gillom learns that his mother's boarder is the notorious gunman John Books. He is so thrilled he can't keep his mouth shut and he tells everyone. In a familiar rite of passage scene, the kid asks the man to teach him how to shoot. Gillom is a better shot than Jimmy Stewart was back when the place was still a territory, and the teacher has grown up too. He's older and wiser, recites his cowboy code of honor and tells young Gillom that shooting is less about your technique than your mental state. Then they go and blast the hell out of some targets.

The Shootist ends when John Wayne, after bidding a poignant fare-well to the Widow Bogart, goes to the saloon to confront the trio of outlaws he's arranged to meet there. Then, rather than from the filthy, slow and long decay of cancer, he goes down in a blaze of bullets, taking all the bad guys with him. Gillom sees this scene and we know he will tell of it (his future as a movie director is just around the corner), so John Books will not suffer, as Tom Doniphon did, by having his heroic deed kept a secret.

John Wayne died three years later. (Cancer.)

Brandon De Wilde was already dead (a motorbike, a rainy road) and so was Alan Ladd. The man whose nickname had been "Tiny" as a kid (he hated that) finally went down, at age 50, with an overdose of booze and pills, an "accident" like Hemingway's. He'd also tried to shoot himself before, just ten years after *Shane*, which was ironic considering that during the filming of *Shane* he was so gun-shy they had to do more than 100 takes of the scene of him trying to teach the kid to shoot.

The Mom and Dad, Van Heflin and Jean Arthur, died, peacefully, of heart attacks.

My father outlived all of them.

My brother told me recently our father had a secret.[9]

Our father said, years afterward, that when we lived in Florida, he'd flown a mission over Cuba and was chased by Russian planes. I don't know if my father fired back. I know, because my brother told me, that our father had been sworn to never tell.

My brother had not thought much of this—our father had told us many things when he was in his cups—until he saw a movie.

Thirteen Days (Roger Dolandson, 2000), based on a true story, begins with a series of aerial photos. A nameless military pilot flying over Cuba has found something that looks to him like a missile buildup. It's October 1962, and J.F.K. is in the White House. (My father always hated J.F.K.) The military brass tells J.F.K. they think the Soviets are planning to place missiles in Cuba that can hit the USA. Having recently come off the Bay of Pigs mess, Kennedy is skeptical about his generals' interest in invading Cuba again. The president orders more flights, more photographs. Kevin Costner, J.F.K.'s second right-hand man after Bobby, makes personal phone calls to the pilots down in Florida to tell them that even if they are fired upon, they must not return fire because if they do, they'll start another war, which will be nuclear, and all of us will die.

The two pilots, also nameless, are shot at but they don't fire back. Or maybe there's only one pilot. And maybe he goes down? I can't remember and besides, it's just a movie only based on a true story, it didn't say it was a true story. In any event, they get more photos, then J.F.K. and Bobby and Kevin Costner stand up to the Russians and avert world war. Also, Bobby makes a deal under the table for us to get rid of some of our bases near Russia so they can save face, but all of this has got to be kept secret. Was my father the one who took those pictures? Was he chased by a Russian plane and did he see his buddy die? Was he the shootist who did not shoot back?[10]

My father didn't like the West. He always called Oklahoma City the most godforsaken city on the planet. He only retired in Texas because he wanted to be near the Gulf (great fishing) and a Navy base. He shopped at the PX until he died.

To my father, the term "cowboy" was an insult reserved for mannerless brutes, uneducated clods, or rednecks singing twangy, unsophisticated ditties. He was more the nightclub or juke joint type.

A few years before my father died, his wife (his third, already a widow when she married him) gave my father a Humphrey Bear-gart teddy bear, complete with raincoat and fedora. He pretended it was ridiculous but he loved it. It sat on the mantel over their fireplace in the den along with some of my father's German drinking mugs and photos of her grandkids and kids.

My father did not go down in an airplane or in a blaze of bullets, but died of "natural causes," which, in his case, could have included lots of things. In the years before he died, he had been sick with slurry speech and memory loss, a stroke or two, blood pressure problems, too much booze, and, the thing that would have got John Books, the old man's illness, prostate cancer. If my father had lived long enough for his cancer to progress, I suspect he would have been, like John Books or Tom Doniphon, an awful patient. By dying before his cancer made him bedridden, he made it easier for everyone around him. Did my father somehow will himself to die so that his wife wouldn't have to go through that? Was his death then, in his small way, heroic?

My father forbade his wife to have a funeral, but we wanted to remember him so we all flew down to see her and have a big meal, with a lot of booze, in our father's honor. We went around the table and said things we remembered. My brother couldn't say much without crying but finally he got out something about how our father, when he took him hunting, taught him to love the out-of-doors. I didn't have much to say from childhood, but I said how glad I was when Dad accepted my partner so lovingly when I took her to meet him.

At the start of *Shane*, the book, there is this dinner scene:

We sit down to supper and a good one. Mother's eyes
sparkled as our visitor kept pace with father and me. Then we
all leaned back and while I listened the talk ran on almost like
old friends around a familiar table, but I could sense that it
was following a pattern. Father was trying, with mother helping
and both of them avoiding direct questions, to get ahold of facts
about this Shane and he was dodging them at every turn. He was
aware of their purpose and not in the least annoyed by it. He
was mild and courteous and spoke readily enough. But always put
them off with words that gave no real information ... no news
about himself. His past was fenced as tightly as our pasture.
All they could learn was that he was riding through. . . ."

A classic western sunset and a stranger on a horse is passing through. We
fall in love. With him and with the stories we imagine he could tell but
won't. We fill his secret past with our desires and the things we are afraid
we cannot do. We do not want to know what he is not. The stories we
will tell of him will save us from our lies.

I tried to see him everywhere
in places he was not
but didn't look in places he would be
a stranger here from far away
forever coming back

NOTES

1. *Shane* by Jack Schaefer (Houghton-Mifflin/Bantam, 1949).
2. Most of the stuff about the making of *Shane* comes from *Code of Honor: The Making of Three Great American Westerns (High Noon, Shane,* and *The Searchers* by Michael F. Blake (Taylor Trade Publishing, 2003). I have to confess I never saw this movie when I was a kid. I saw it for the first time a year or so ago. By then everybody was dead.
3. To shoot John Wayne's *The Alamo* they had to build a fake Alamo in a little town in Texas (Brackettville) that didn't really have much going on before the movie, though what town would with a name like that? Like your whole existence was in brackets, like you were just an afterthought, a second-class or minor thing, a footnote? But then, after they made the fake Alamo in Brackettville, it became "Alamo Village," as if it was something from the olden days. It wasn't, but that didn't stop it from being used a million times after *The Alamo* as a movie set thereby making the former nothing town a star of stage, screen, and television.

The John Wayne material comes from *John Wayne: The Man Behind the Myth* by Michael Munn (New American Library, 2004) and from *John Wayne: American Legend* (produced by Van Ness Films/A&E network, 1998), and from some of the 169 movies he made.

4. Piped over is when they get rid of you from the military because you can't stay at the rank you are forever but they aren't going to give you a raise because you're a mess. Or at least this is how I was given to understand it later. What I remember is going to the base somewhere, into an airplane hangar, and my father was there in his dress whites and a couple of other Navy men and my mother and me and then the sound of the whistle like they have on ships and it was over.

My brother remembers this differently, although it may be he remembers another time entirely. What my brother remembers is a ceremony and my father being given a medal for something but he does not remember for what. Are my brother and I remembering two different events or just different versions of the same event? Both of us know we remember poorly.

5. I'd never actually thought about the word henpecked until recently when Chris and I were taking a walk near her son's house outside Phoenix and came across a peacock farm. It was a poor farm—scrappy, dusty. You could tell it used to be out in the country but the suburbs had grown up around it. The peacocks were beautiful and strutting their amazing fantails. Then a peahen came up to one of cocks and started pecking at its head. It pecked and pecked and pecked. The male's beautiful feathers went down and he made these pathetic squeaky noises and tried to skitter away from the female. The peahen was brown, dowdy, dusty-looking, as scrappy as the farm and stronger than the male. She chased him around and pecked at him, punishing him for something, for being beautiful maybe, and he couldn't fight back. He was, with all his pretty finery, useless. The hen was the power and the brains and she'd have had him by the balls if he had them.

My mother said about my father's mother: "She never washed a dish in her whole life." Her husband, my father's father, did the dishes. I have this image of him standing in an apron by the sink. I don't know if I ever actually saw that, or if that's just an impression I inherited.

My father had a terrible work ethic, never wanted to do anything around the house. I never saw him wash a dish, or even do men things like mow the lawn. Whenever my mother said anything about the lawn, my father said his back was acting up—some mysterious wound from "the war"—so, although he was able to go out hunting or fishing or ride around on his boat, one of us kids would have to go out and mow the lawn. I wonder if his father's being henpecked was a reason.

6. I remember, also shamefully, in junior high, going on a Girl Scout outing and being in the car with our leader and her saying, very primly, "Lock your doors, girls, we're going through Nigger Town!" and no one saying anything, just locking the doors and looking down into our laps mortified that anyone would hear her, or maybe worse, see that we were with her on an outing, i.e., that though we were in junior high, we were still in Girl Scouts. I also remember taking "care packages"—hand-me-down clothes and old toys—to people there before Christmas and being mortified that we'd recognize some of the black kids from school. There weren't many black kids in school so even if you didn't know them, you knew who they were if you saw them and they

saw you, you both would have to admit that you knew where they lived and that they were poor and that you were a do-goodie church kid going around with do-goodie white church ladies and that even if you didn't call it that yourself, everyone called it "Niggertown" and that you didn't do a thing at all about that.

7. Why couldn't I have had just some of what Brandon De Wilde got? Why didn't I get to meet Patricia Neal? I could have had a decent crush on her. Why didn't I get to meet the Beatles, like Brandon De Wilde did when he flew to the Bahamas when they were shooting *Help!* to bring them some pot? He can keep Gram Parsons and Emmylou Harris writing that song about him after he died, "In My Hour of Darkness" (from *Grievous Angel*, 1973). I recognize Parson's genius, of course, but I can actually kind of take or leave Emmylou Harris.

8. My grandmother had a kids book she read to us from, about the western migrations. It had a picture on the cover of a Davy Crockett type (bearskin hat) leading his women and children and wagons west assisted by his faithful Indian (feather headdress) guide. My grandmother had made written notes in this book about things her ancestors had done. I thought my mother got this book from her when she died then I got it from her when she died but I couldn't find it. So, for Oklahoma history I went, I admit, to Wikipedia, but I checked all external links. The best link was: www.library.cornell.edu/Reps/DOCS/landrush.htm.

I don't know who to ask anymore about where that book of my grandmother's might be because everyone is dead.

9. Our father had a secret that he told my brother, as opposed to a secret he didn't know although someone else knew it about him which is the kind of secret Van Heflin had. I found out about Van Heflin's secret when my research came up with this book called *Eleanor's Rebellion* by David Siff (Knopf, 2000), who, it turns out, was Van Heflins' secret son he didn't know he had. Siff grew up to be an actor and when he learned that the man he had always thought was his father was not his father, but Van Heflin, he became obsessed with Van Heflin. Heflin was dead by then so the son wrote a book about it.

I wonder what it's like for a man who fathers a child but doesn't know it. Maybe the woman doesn't know who the father is or maybe she does but doesn't tell the guy. Does the guy know it somehow somewhere?

10. The pilots were unnamed in the movie, but it was easy enough for me to find their names—even in a kids' book (*The Cuban Missile Crisis,* Catherine Hester Gow [Lucent Books, 1997], pg. 8). Neither name was Vergil Neal Brown, Jr.

Then I thought, so what if the book said guys named Major Richard Heyser and Major Rudolph Anderson, Jr. photographed surface-to-air missiles in Cuba on Oct. 14, 1962? Maybe my dad shot photographs on other days. Maybe my dad flew on another day or several other days! Maybe my father was sent out as bait, to see if the Russkies would chase him and they did! Then maybe my father had to do amazing plane maneuvers that only he could do! Then, after he had tempted the Russkies out and been chased by them but escaped, then maybe my dad came back and reported in secret to J.F.K. and J.F.K. was chicken at first, which was why my dad hated him, but then when the other guys around J.F.K. realized, after my dad's report, exactly what we, the U.S.A. and the entire free world were dealing with, they decided what to do and then they did and they told my father to not tell ANYone, EVER, which he didn't, until years later when he told my brother.

Or maybe they entirely made up the names Major Richard Heyser and Major Rudolph Anderson, Jr., who never existed at all, were only made-up names, invented to protect the real hero, a man as heroic as—no, even more heroic than—John Wayne or Shane or anyone—my father, Lieutenant Commander Vergil Neal Brown, Jr., the man who had, secretly, and thereafter tormentedly, (would he have been better off if he had told?) saved the entire world.

FROM *THE RED PARTS: A MEMOIR*

Maggie Nelson

MY MOTHER had always told us that Jane had been the rebellious, out-spoken daughter, while she had remained the dutiful one. Jane was going to change the world by becoming a fierce civil rights lawyer; my mother was going to get married, put our father through law school by teaching high school English, then stop working and raise two kids. Jane had said all the things to their parents that my mother couldn't or didn't say—the big Fuck You (or, in 1969, You racist pigs). As a result, Jane was no longer welcome in their home. If Jane hadn't been estranged from her parents, if she hadn't been worried that they wouldn't accept her decision to marry a leftist Jew and move to New York City, she wouldn't have been coming home alone on March 20, 1969. She wouldn't have advertised for a ride on the ride board, and she wouldn't have ended up with two bullets in her head, stretched out "puffy and lifeless" on a stranger's grave in Denton Cemetery the following morning, her bare ass against the frozen earth, a stranger's stocking buried in her neck.

> Dear Jane,
>
> It makes little difference whether it is two nations or two people with conflicting opinions, not much can be done to settle the dispute unless some form of communication is established. It is in this hope that I am writing this letter. I'm sure there is no question in your mind (and in mine) that the contacts we have had in the past year or so have been very disturbing and

anything but pleasant. I also recognize the fact that differences in opinion between daughter and parent is a normal situation and fortunately time reduces most of those mountains into mole hills. I'm sure that will be true in our case. But the last few times we have been together have been traumatic emotional experiences that have accomplished absolutely nothing. I have no intention of maintaining that kind of relationship.

So wrote my grandfather on March 4, 1968. But things between them did not improve—indeed, as Jane's relationship with Phil deepened, and as she elaborated her plan to elope and move to New York, things worsened. A year later she was dead. Time did not get its chance to reduce "mountains into mole hills." Instead her death froze these mountains into mountains, and froze her father into a state of perpetual incomprehension about her, and about their relationship.

DURING THESE years my mother and I went to the movies together quite often. It was an easy way to spend time together, sitting in dark places, staring in the same direction. On weekend days we would drive across the Golden Gate Bridge into San Francisco, find a good art-house theater, pay one round of admission and then sneak from film to film: her trick. But a problem recurred—she couldn't tolerate scenes that involved the abduction of women, especially into cars, and she couldn't watch women be threatened with guns, especially guns pointed at their heads.

Try going to the movies with this rule, and you will be surprised at how often such scenes crop up.

I left home at seventeen, for college, and for New York, where I soon discovered the deep pleasure of going to the movies by myself. Yet whenever such a scene arose I immediately felt my mother close beside me in the dark theater. Her hands spread across her face, her pinkies pushing down on her eyelids so she can't see, her index fingers pushing down on her ears so she can't hear.

I felt her this way acutely when I went to see *Taxi Driver* at the Film Forum in Greenwich Village several years ago. I was excited—it was the first screening of a new print, a classic I'd never seen. Waiting in line my excitement dampened a little upon noticing that I was one of the only women, and certainly one of the only solo women, at the theater. The crowd was solid boy film geeks, probably NYU film students, who had apparently come prepared to treat the screening like a performance of *The Rocky Horror Picture Show,* screaming out in chorus the movie's many famous lines seconds before the characters spoke them. This was tolerable, sometimes even amusing, until a passenger in Travis Bickle's taxicab embarked upon the following monologue, which the passenger—played by Scorsese himself—delivers while watching his wife through the window of another man's house:

> I'm gonna kill her. I'm gonna kill her with a .44 Magnum pistol. I have a .44 Magnum pistol. I'm gonna kill her with that gun. Did you ever see what a .44 Magnum pistol can do to a woman's face? I mean it'll fuckin' destroy it. Just blow her right apart. That's what it can do to her face. Now, did you ever see what it can do to a woman's pussy? That you should see. You should see what a .44 Magnum's gonna do to a woman's pussy, you should see.

Sitting alone in a sea of young men hollering, *Did you ever see what a .44 can do to a woman's pussy?* was not amusing. Perhaps it was not tolerable, or perhaps I should not have tolerated it. I sat through the rest of the movie, but as I walked slowly home down the dark cobblestone streets of SoHo toward my apartment on Orchard Street I found myself thinking about my mother, and about Jane, and about my sister, with tears streaming down my cheeks. *That you should see.*

ON ONE VISIT back to San Francisco in 1996, my mother and I returned to one of our old haunts, the Opera Plaza Theaters on Van Ness, to see a movie we knew virtually nothing about, save that it was a "dark comedy" titled *Freeway.* In its opening scenes a wayward teen played by Reese Witherspoon steals a car and runs away from her truly screwed-up family. Her car then breaks down on a California freeway, and a seemingly well-meaning yuppie, played by Kiefer Sutherland, pulls over to help. In his car they have a wide-ranging conversation, which takes a turn for the worse when he starts talking about wanting to rape her dead body. She then realizes that he is the so-called "I-5 Killer," and he intends to make her his next victim.

By this point in the movie—just about ten minutes in—I could see that we were going to have to pack up. But as we started to gather our things, the movie took another turn. Witherspoon gains control of the situation by pulling out her boyfriend's gun. She asks Sutherland if he believes that Jesus Christ is his personal Savior, then shoots him in the neck several times. Then she throws up, steals his car, and leaves him for dead on the side of the road.

I don't think he actually dies, but to be honest I remember little to nothing about the rest. What I remember is the moment in the small dark theater, right before Witherspoon pulls out her gun, right before we stood up to leave, when my mother leaned over and whispered to me, *Let's give it one more minute—maybe something different is about to happen.*

AMERICAN TABOO

THE FIRST E-MAIL I receive from *48 Hours Mystery* comes a few months before the trial from a producer who addresses me as "Mrs. Nelson," unwittingly conjuring up an identity held but fleetingly by my mother many years ago. In his e-mail the producer says that he hopes I will consider working with them, as he feels strongly that "my family's story of struggle and hope" has great relevance to their audience.

I ponder this phrase for some time. I wonder if he is imagining my family as the kind to print up T-shirts with Jane's picture and a "we will never forget" slogan on them, as I have seen some families on these TV shows do. I wonder if he read the article in the *Detroit Free Press* in December 2004 in which my grandfather likened the reopening of Jane's case to "picking a scab." I wonder what he would think if he knew that after the January hearing, when [my grandfather was asked] what he thought of the court proceedings thus far, my grandfather said he found them "boring."

I agree to meet the producer for dinner at a restaurant on the Upper West Side of Manhattan.

• • •

THE NIGHT before we meet I stay up late perusing the Web site for *48 Hours Mystery*. I learn that *48 Hours* used to focus on "human interest" stories of varying degrees of social importance—the international sex trade, the pros and cons of the "Subway Diet," the risks of gastric bypass surgery. But as ratings for investigative journalism plummeted and ratings for true-crime shows began to soar, *48 Hours* became *48 Hours Mystery*. At times they attempt to take on deeper topics within the "murder mystery" rubric—a recent show, for example, investigates the topic *Who Killed Jesus?* and stars Elaine Pagels.

As I scroll down the long list of show titles I feel my spirits start to sink. There are a host of stories about missing or murdered girls and women, with panic-inducing titles like *Where's Baby Sabrina? Where's Molly? Where Is Mrs. March?* Others feature high-profile cases—*JonBenét: DNA Rules Out Parents; Is Amber Still In Love with Scott?*: *Her Father Says She Has Never Gotten Over Him*—while others strive for a more poetic effect: *Dark Side of the Mesa: Did Michael Blagg Murder His Wife and Daughter?* I try to imagine the title they'll choose for Jane's show but come up dry.

I FIND the producer on a street corner on Broadway, talking outside the restaurant with some of his college friends, all of whom graduated just a couple of years ago. I'm surprised—I had imagined dinner with a slick patrician, a hard-boiled veteran of the TV business. The surprise is apparently mutual: when we sit down, he tells me that I look way too young to be a professor, and he's taken aback that I'm not married. I have no idea why he thought I was.

We are meeting early in the evening because he has to fly to Los Angeles first thing in the morning to cover the Michael Jackson child molestation trial. I am not very interested in the Jackson trial, but I try to make small talk about other famous trials. I bring up Gary Gilmore and Norman Mailer's *The Executioner's Song*; he says he hasn't heard of Norman Mailer, but will definitely look him up. He orders us a bottle of Sauvignon Blanc and appears perplexed when it arrives. *I thought I ordered us a red*, he says, decanting with a shrug.

Over the wine he asks me if, while writing *Jane*, I felt as though I were channeling my aunt. I say no. He looks disappointed. I try to explain that *Jane* is about identification, not fusion. That I never even knew her. That in the book I don't try to speak for her, but rather to let her speak for herself, through her journal entries. And that although I have tried to imagine her death, there's really no way of knowing what she went through—not only because I don't know what happened to her on the night of her murder, but because no one ever really knows what it's like to be in anyone else's skin. That no living person can tell another what it's like to die. That we do that part alone.

Our entrees arrive—stylish piles of monkfish—and he shifts gears, says it's time for the "hard sell." He says that although *48 Hours Mystery* strives to entertain, it always keeps a serious social issue at stake. When I ask him what the issue might be in this case, he says this episode will be about grief. About helping other people to mourn. He says that my family's involvement could really help other people in similar situations.

All those viewers who thought they lost a family member to a famous serial killer, then are told thirty-six years later that DNA from the crime scene matches both that of a retired nurse and a man who was four years old at the time and grew up to murder his mother, I think.

With less graciousness than I'd hoped to display, I ask if there's a reason why stories about the bizarre, violent deaths of young, good-looking, middle to upper-class white girls help people to mourn better than other stories.

I thought it might come to this, he says good-naturedly but warily, re-folding the napkin in his lap.

After dinner we walk a few blocks up Broadway together and pass one of the gigantic, brightly lit Barnes & Nobles that now sprawl around so many New York City street corners. He lights up with an idea—he says he's going in to find the Mailer book I told him about, which he will read on the plane to California tomorrow morning. *Good idea*, I say, not mentioning that it's 1,056 pages. He beckons me into the store, says he'll buy me anything I want, on his CBS account.

I know I should decline. But a wicked you're-using-me-so-why-shouldn't-I-use-you feeling has already taken root.

We browse for a bit on our own, then reconvene at the cash register. I have James Ellroy's 1996 "crime memoir," *My Dark Places*, in my hand.

My Dark Places is a sinister, engrossing book about the 1958 murder of Ellroy's mother and his subsequent sexual and literary obsession with vivisected women. I had furtively skimmed this book in various bookstores while working on *Jane* over the past few years, but had always felt too ashamed to buy it for myself. It seems the perfect memento for this evening.

In parting the producer hands me a sample videotape of his show, which I deposit into my plastic Barnes & Noble shopping bag.

I take the train back to Connecticut the next morning and stuff the shopping bag under my dresser as if trying to forget a one-night stand I'd prefer never happened. The bag sits there for over a month. When I finally pull it out, I stack the book and videotape on top of each other on my desk in the Ponderosa Room, where they sit untouched for several more weeks.

The label on the videotape reads: *American Taboo: Who Murdered a Beautiful Peace Corps Volunteer in Tonga?*

At long last, one night I pull my TV out of the closet, curl up on the couch, and insert *American Taboo* into the VCR.

The show opens with a photo of a truly gorgeous brunette chewing playfully, erotically, on a long piece of grass. Then a true-crime writer who has written a book about this woman, whose name was Deborah Gardner, appears against a mountainous backdrop and explains why he became obsessed with her. He says it had something to do with the combination of her beauty and the horror of her 1976 murder. He then quotes Edgar Allan Poe, who once declared the death of a beautiful woman to be the most poetic topic in the world.

I'm taken aback: I used this same Poe quotation in *Jane*.

The show then vacillates between more lovely photos of Gardner and photos of her blood-splattered hut in Tonga, where a fellow Peace Corps volunteer stabbed her twenty-two times. (He is later found not guilty by reason of insanity in a Tonga court.) The camera whirls around her hut in a restaging of her murder, first from the perspective of her deranged killer, then from that of a panicked, dying Gardner, fighting hopelessly for her life. There are several stills of the long, serrated hunting knife apparently used to do the deed.

I can't make it to the end of *American Taboo*. I try on a few other occasions, but every time I end up symptomatically falling asleep, or shutting it off in despair.

THE SHOW about Jane, which will air on Thanksgiving weekend, 2005, will be titled *Deadly Ride*. I won't watch it either, even though my mother and I will ostensibly be its stars. People will assure me that we brought some dignity, some depth, to the genre and to Jane's life, and I will be glad. That was the point of participating, as they were going to do the show with or without us. But I don't want to see the crime scene photos flashed over and over again on TV, nor do I want to think about millions of Americans flipping by Jane's corpse under its bloodstained raincoat while channel surfing at their in-laws, up late, still stuffed from Thanksgiving dinner.

IT TAKES ME even longer to crack the Ellroy memoir, but I manage to finish it in one sitting. As with *American Taboo*, there are some discomfiting parallels.

Ellroy's mother died when he was ten. Exactly thirty-six years later he decides to research and write about her long-repressed murder. Eventually he is able to reopen her case, which he works on with a homicide cop from the LAPD.

Ellroy also suffers from murder mind, but his turns him on. The titular "dark place"—the fantasy that nearly drives him to insanity—is that of fucking his mutilated mother. *Her amputated nipple thrills me.*

Despite all his hard work on the case, Ellroy's mother's murder remains unsolved; at the end of the book he provides a contact number for tips. *I'll learn more*, he promises his dead mother on the last page. *You're gone and I want more of you.*

It's a disappointing ending. Not because the case doesn't get solved, but because Ellroy never seems to grasp the futility of his enterprise. Instead his compulsion to "learn more" just smashes up against this futility with increasing velocity. He knows that no amount of information about his mother's life or death will bring her back, but somehow he doesn't really seem to get it.

I don't get it either.

I've never had the desire or need to bring Jane back—I never even knew her. And while the unsolved status of her murder may have once haunted me, now a man has been arrested for it, is being held without bail, and will soon be brought to trial. And yet, daily, while in faculty meetings or paused at traffic lights, I find myself scrawling lists of potential avenues of further inquiry. Should I visit Leiterman in prison? Interview members of his family? Find Johnny Ruelas? Spend more time with Schroeder? What on earth for?

Conventional wisdom has it that we dredge up family stories to find out more about ourselves, to pursue that all-important goal of "self-knowledge," to catapult ourselves, like Oedipus, down the track that leads to the revelation of some original crime, some original truth. Then we gouge our eyes out in shame and run screaming into the wilderness, and plagues cease to rain down upon our people.

Fewer people talk about what happens when this track begins to dissolve, when the path starts to become indistinguishable from the forest.

THE GOSPEL OF LARRY

Myriam Gurba

One, Two, Three, Four, Five: Virgins, Smell, Addictive, Nitrous, and Hole

The very fist scene in *Kids* upsets people. It's a pornographically up close look at two maybe middle schoolers, maybe high schoolers, French kissing in their chones. They're obviously in the little girl's bedroom, you can tell from all her teddy bears and stuffed animals, and the boy stops the make-out session to tell the girl that she's beautiful and feed her all the other bullshit that will enable him to fuck her. He gets on top of her and starts to do her and you can tell from the look on her face that it doesn't feel good and you learn the boy's name is Telly because she grimaces and says, Telly, it hurts, and Telly does a voiceover that exposes what you've been suspecting about him for, like, the past minute and a half of grossness, he's just some horny little asshole who wants to de-virginize girls, all he cares about is pussy.

Folk Implosion's *Daddy Never Understood* begins to screech and pound as the title credits roll in a Satanic red-on-black color scheme and the scene you've got a few seconds to recover from proves that director, some say pedophile, Larry Clark is not above pandering to clichés: Do you know where your daughter is?

Okay, so the punk rock credits are done, there's action on-screen again and it's Telly hurrying outside to meet his homie Casper. He's an ugly fuck and he's sitting on the steps of the de-virginized girl's brownstone reading a comic and sipping a forty. Casper gets up and they walk and as they go, Telly (who's an ugly fuck, too) brags to Casper how good the fucking was and how he's getting addicted to sex and he lets Casper take a whiff of the "butterscotch" pussy residue on his fingers. Casper stops to drain his bladder all over a brick wall, you can practically smell the piss as it runs down the sidewalk and into the gutter, and he zips up his fly and as they head south, they shuck and jive about their horndog Christopher Columbus mentalities, deflowering girls is about being the first guy there, very NASA, very colonial, very Plant That Flag, Bro!, and then the guys duck in to a store to shoplift lunch.

Afterwards, they crash at some beaner-in-a-beanie's pad, the guy reminds me of Suicidal Tendencies, and Telly and Casper are in a den full of boys that are Tommy and Prescott, doing things I know Tommy and Prescott did.

Tommy and Prescott.

Telly and Casper.

Casper catches a buzz off a nitrous-filled balloon, he's kicking back on the couch, and all the skate rats there are skate rats from Santa Maria, who's Larry Clark kidding? These ain't no mothafuckin' New York boys, I know these boys too well! The walls are tagged with tags I've seen before and the boys are watching Mark Gonzalez videos and getting stoned and their clothes are hella baggy, especially their pants with their boxer shorts poking out the top, and these boys look like they smell sweaty, alcoholy, and cigarettey and there's fast food trash and empty bottles all over the place and Tommy and Prescott are there because they are Telly and Casper and all those other Zoo York boys, New York boys, are really straight up Santa Maria boys.

Santa Maria boys. That's what this is really all about.

First Epistle to Thrasher, Fall 1990

Dear Editor,

This is the Zodiac speaking. I am writing to let you know that I am coming out of high bear nation. Nothing but faggots on the cover of your publication is the reason why.

Shogo Kubo:
On the cover.

You have one year.
Three hundred sixty five days.
To fulfill my request.

I know where you faggots live.

Thank You,
The Zodiac

Santa Maria, CA

Six: Diseases

Jennie, who is played by Chloë Sevigny and whose Chloë-ness is so over-whelming I'm just not even going to her call her Jennie, I'll call her Chloë, is the star of *Kids*, sixteen and totally not a slut. Her friend Ruby, who's played by Rosario Dawson, and who I'm gonna call Rosario for the same reason I'm calling Chloë Chloë, is seventeen and a straight-up ho. Rosario is worried she might've gotten AIDS from fucking some skeevy guy in the heat of the moment and so for moral support, innocent Chloë goes with her to get an AIDS test at some Manhattan free clinic.

Chloë thinks she's got nothing to worry about, she's only ever fucked one guy (Telly!), and little, white, skinny her, she is so pure, so virginal compared with hobag Rosario who's all curvy and Latina and thick-eyebrowed and shit that the duality is absolutely brilliant; it's Betty Grable and Rita Hayworth joining forces, like what David Lynch did with Naomi Watts and Laura Elena Harring in *Mulholland Dr.* Pairing up girls who're opposites like that looks great on film but I'm not sure about the consequences in real life.

Take the summer I turned fourteen for example. My cousin, Coquette, who was fifteen, rode the bus to our California hick town, Santa Maria, to stay with us for a couple of weeks. She was from L.A. and into gangbanging and had a street name, a placa, La Green Eyes. She looked like the consummate scary-ass chola, like that stupid picture you can file share that's got Elvira-looking homegirls posing for a cheapo mall glamour shot. Across the bottom, this racist caption warns, Keep Sharpies Away From Mexicans.

If you get a chance, check out this picture. It's actually kinda funny.

I'd like to think I was the Chloë to Coquette's Rosario, the flat-chested one who was all innocent and shit. I swear I was virginal and unlike Coquette, I didn't wear any makeup and I'd just barely come into my own subculturally. I did goth and mind you, it was goth-casual, not ultra-goth, not makeup thicker than porridge goth. I wore The Cure T-shirts and leggings and sandals that all just happened to be black and the white kids at school and in my neighborhood, which we'd only recently moved to, called me creepy and a slut. To them, all Mexican girls were stinky, creepy sluts. Plus, this freckle-faced white boy at school claimed he'd fingerbanged me but he was such a liar. He got mad at me because I wouldn't kiss him so he went around telling the eighth graders the fingerbang lie and calling me nigger lips. All the kids thought this was funny, even the little freak crew I hung out with. Never mind that white women like Barbara Hershey were getting collagen injected into their skinny ass lips to make them puff up like exotic fruits. People like Mexican girl lips so long as they're not on a Mexican.

Epistle to the Santa Marians, Summer 1990

Dear Miriam,

Hey what's up? Its just me, your cousin, Cokie. I'm tripping out cuz my mom is sending me to stay with your family this summer. I can't believe I'm going to spend the whole summer in the country. Well, its not totally country but you know what I mean. We're gonna get real close!

Guess why my moms sending me to your house? Because she hates my new friends. She thinks they're all druggys and gangbangers. And she also found the box under my bed. It had letters that I wrote to guys who were in jail and stuff. It was just for fun. They were my penpals. Everybody likes having a penpal.

See you soon cuz!
Love,
Coquette

Deleted Scene: How Chloë met Telly

The summer that shit went down was the summer before I started Catholic high school. My mom and dad sent me there to keep me under lock and key and get me away from the weird white kids I'd started hanging out with in junior high. I was crushed out on one of them. A tall white girl with a big butt, an unusually big butt for a white girl. I think she knew I liked her. I think she used it to her advantage. To make me her little minion. Her little gopher. Her little yes girl.

At the Catholic school, I took four years' worth of religion classes and one of the priest-teachers taught us about something called the apocrypha. The Greek word means "those having been hidden away," and for Catholics, it refers to stories that never made it into the Bible's final cut. An example? *The Acts of Paul and Thecla*. Thecla was a female apostle the Church has always kept very hush-hush about. Of noble lineage, she dressed up like a guy to follow Paul after hearing him preach about chastity. Her mom and fiancé got so pissed about this decision that Thecla was ordered burnt at the stake. The joke was on them, though—her virgin flesh repelled the flames. After being released, Thecla was reunited with Paul and went to Antioch. There, a nobleman named Alexander tried to rape her on a city street. She fought him off and guess what? She was condemned to death again. Stripped naked, Thecla was thrown to wild beasts who should have ripped her to shreds. They couldn't, though. A blessed virgin, the girl was unsinkable.

The story of Chloë and Telly's meeting is Harmony Korine's apocryphal gospel. He's the mad genius skater boy who wrote the screenplay for the movie. I heard Harmony said Jennie's character was inspired by Chloë and she was his real-life girlfriend. Maybe that's why he didn't tell the details. He wanted to keep something private. Everyone wants to keep some things private. The only kernel that Harmony gives is that Telly is the only guy Chloë's ever fucked. Chloë is sitting on Rosario's bed, chilling with a bunch of Puerto Rican–looking chicks, swapping teenybopper sexcapades, and Chloë tells how Telly devirginized her last summer, talked all this mad shit to get her to do it with him, and then disappeared.

Also, she adds that she didn't even bleed when it happened.

How weird.

Since this story is all about apocrypha, I won't keep how me and Tommy met private. I didn't meet him at summer camp or at school or at the pool. I met him at the mall. And I wasn't supposed to be there. I lied my way there. Me and Coquette told my mom that we wanted to go hang out at the library and on her way to work, she dropped us off at the entrance with the palm trees. We waited for her to drive away and then we walked across the street, to the Town Center, and hung out under the clock by the cookie shop with the white girl with the big butt. Her name was Sara.

Sara walked us to this spot by the Salvation Army where there were concrete steps and rails and the curb was high. Lots of Filipino skater boys were hanging out there, practicing tricks, my ears still perk up when I hear that sound, the sound of a wooden deck hitting the pavement. There were two boys there who looked twinsy but opposites, that lovely duality like Chloë and Rosario, me and Coquette. One boy was tall, the other short. One boy was white, the other brown. One boy was hairy, the other smooth; loud, quiet and so on and so forth. They were opposite twins. Now you see what I mean.

We made a habit of deceiving my mom and going to this spot to hang out, and Sara and Coquette urged me, encouraged me to talk to the brown guy. They said he liked me because he looked at me a lot. I offered him a piece of gum and we spoke and it turned out his name was Tomás but he went by Tommy. When he'd show up in the middle of skate sessions, he'd bust up everyone's rhythm by hollering, Heeeeeere's Tommy!, and when hard tricks frustrated him he'd beat his skateboard against the sidewalk. Like lots of Santa Maria kids, Tommy was embarrassed to be Mexican so he told people his last name was McGuire but it was really Aguirre. He sported blotchy tattoos on his arms and legs and his arms and legs were hard with muscles although he still had a baby fat belly. It wasn't big, you only noticed it when he skated a certain way that he still had a bit of a paunch.

Tommy liked reading and heavy metal and he was really into the Zodiac Killer. Because he liked him so much, he sharpied astrological signs across the bottom of his deck and when he popped his board just right, I could see my sign, Cancer.

Me and Tommy held hands in the urinal-stinky mall stairwell once. That was as far as he got with me. Hand holding. His hands were enormous. He hugged me once, too. I felt so small that day, like I was a rabbit or something that a polar bear was playing with.

Tommy's best friend stared hard at Sara and Coquette and hardly ever talked. He was bitter because of how he looked. He had a giant port wine stain like someone had spilled Merlot all over his face. He sulked a lot. With that constant sour ball face, it wouldn't surprise me to learn that he grew up to become a mass murderer or something.

Acts of Myriam, Coquette, and Tommy

Dear Diary,
Tommy met me and Cokie at the library. He told me he had a present for me. He
gave me a tab of acid. I have never done acid before. I waited until I got home to
open it. In my bedroom, I unfolded the tin foil that wrapped it. Cokie said it was
one dose and you are supposed to put it on your tongue. It was just a small piece
of paper with the Rolling Stones lips printed on it. It surprised me for acid to look
that way. It looked funny. I put the tab inside of my jewelry box. Cokie scoffed at
it. It is the kind with the ballerina inside that spins. Tommy embraced me.

Book of Revelation or AIDS as a Plot

When Chloë goes back to the clinic to get her results, she finds out she's
HIV positive, and of course, she's shocked. She's not the ho, Rosario's the
ho but Rosario's clean. *Kids* builds steam through this viral revelation and
the movie becomes the story of a quest: Chloë, the messenger, must find
Telly to declare, You've got HIV, asshole. It's really fucking pressing that
she tell Telly immediately because he's on his own quest, to fuck a new
virgin, thirteen-year-old Darcy. Following Chloë and Telly's journeys,
you bite your nails, chomp, chomp, chomp, praying that they'll dovetail
soon.

Me and Sara's quest was scrawled all over a flier Sara xeroxed at the
library. She was sad summer was ending so she planned this big-ass party
at her house. Me and her passed out the flier to all the kids from the mall
and the kids from school we still saw and she passed them out to the kids
in her neighborhood which was a weird place, out in the country, full of
fancy houses. Hers was designed by her dad, an architect, and she had a
pet pony who lived out back.

Ha, ha, something was wrong with those houses and they all had to
be abandoned, including hers. Those fancy houses were built on soil that
literally bubbled with oil, and now that neighborhood is a condemned
ghost town.

Coquette made me call Johnny and personally invite him and I
almost peed my pants as I spoke to him on the phone. I wasn't allowed
to call boys on the phone. That was something my parents were all
Mexican and strict about. Boys. They didn't want me getting pregnant

and talking on the phone with boys could somehow lead to my hymen ripping and a baby growing inside me.

Chloë and Telly's stories finally dovetail at this one party, but before then there are a couple of party scenes that are important. One is where Telly and some other boys break into a pool with some girls they picked up and they go swimming and you can see the girls' nipples through their wet bras and some of the boys are actually skinny-dipping. Two girls make out with each other, putting on a show, and it's so fucking lame, it's every guy's fantasy to see two chicks make out. Telly is putting the mack on Darcy, trying to be the sensitive guy as she talks about how her mom is strict and won't let her have a boyfriend and it's for the same reason that my parents wouldn't let me talk on the phone with guys, pregnancy. There's also a scene where Chloë goes into this club, there's a rave type thing going on inside and Harmony Korine makes a cameo appearance. He gives Chloë some kind of unidentified drug, which sets her up for the grand finale, the fiery pit.

So, back to my party. My mom dropped me and Coquette off at Sara's before her parents left. We told the parents bye and they drove off and then people started showing up. Coquette wanted beer so I took her to the kitchen to show her where the refrigerator was and we got beers. I sipped mine but then I saw kids going in and out of the pantry so I went in there, too. I saw a big bottle of vodka and I thought about how I'd seen my parents drink vodka and tequila and wine so I poured myself a tumbler full of it without anything to chase it and I gulped it like I was a fucking man.

To get the gasoline taste out of my mouth, I tore open a pack of cookies and stuffed a fistful of them into my mouth and got crumbs all over my face. The alcohol hit me fast and I ran all over the house like a retard, a happy drunk, with my arms out like an airplane. In the living room, someone had put on Depeche Mode videos and someone was trying to turn off the video, people were fighting, and Coquette told me, Where's Tommy?

I don't know, I said.

I kept running around the house like I was the nun from *The Sound of Music*, twirling, and went back to the pantry for more liquor and I guzzled more clear liquid and then Sara called me, Myriam! Phone!

Panting, Yes?

It's Tommy. Meet us at the ditch at the Frontage Road.

All right, out of breath and hanging up. Coquette. I need to go get Tommy. Will you come with me?

Yeah.

She slipped the bottle of vodka into her sweatshirt and we headed out together and walked the mile to the ditch. We sat inside of it, getting filthy, and waited. We waited so long, it turned dark and bugs started to eat us. Coquette handed me the bottle she'd snagged. I took a swig and felt dizzy.

We need to get back to Sara right now, I said.

Okay.

I bolted out of the ditch and did a drunk girl run through a thistle covered field, brambles ripped at my legs, I was wearing cut-off jeans, it was so fucking hot out, and I could hear Coquette scream, Wait! but I kept running because my heart was beating so fast and I was confused and I felt like I had to be back at the house.

I saw the party happening in Sara's house from the main road, it looked like something out of a movie, and I climbed a fence to get there and stood on the driveway to catch my breath. Then I felt it hit me. Whap! Something hard slammed the back of my head and I reeled forward, into a dusty patch of dirt beside the driveway. I fell on my knees and looked up. Coquette was standing there.

Don't you ever fucking leave me alone like that again! she raged.

She was crying. I'd never seen her cry. She was a tough as nails girl. She fucking plucked all of her eyebrows out and used eyeliner for lipstick. Her fucking pen pals were in prison. She wasn't supposed to have tears.

Don't you ever fucking leave me alone like that again, she said and kicked me in the ribs. The wind sailed out of me and she kicked me again and again and then sobbing, she headed alone in the direction of the backyard.

I spit onto the ground and then dragged myself up. I staggered back into the house and into the kitchen. I found a glass and started to drink from it. I don't know what was in that glass. I could no longer taste anything.

The Gospel of Judas

It had to have been past midnight. I wiped my face with my T-shirt's hem. There wasn't much else I could do to fix myself. I walked down the hallway.

Tommy waited for me, grinning. He was a Joker dealt from a stack of poorly shuffled cards, and as my Joker, he'd use me as the butt of his prank. Feeling dizzy, I leaned against the stucco for balance. The vodka, the mystery liquid, and the fight did me funny. Shrinks call how I'm about to tell it disassociation:

"Hi," says The Joker. He hands the girl a long can. It's a forty, King Cobra. The girl accepts his gift with unsteady hands.

Someone, somewhere: "Dude, she dropped the fuckin' can, man!"

Malt liquor pools on the expensive carpet. The girl crumples into the wet spot, the alcohol soaking her shorts, but The Joker won't let her stay down for the count. He peels her off the floor and hoists her over his brawny shoulder. Her head looks like it throbs.

The Joker chuckles, "This bitch totally wants me."

He takes her to the toilet with him.

He drops her onto the bathroom floor, and she opens her eyes. She presses her hands against the tile. She looks down and sees her naked chest. The lights go out.

Meaty hands wrap around her neck and guide her to a dank spot between legs.

"You're pretty like this," The Joker tells her. "I love lesbians."

It's hard to breathe with a dick in her throat, and she has no idea what to do so she just lets her face get fucked. Finally, he pulls out, she breathes, and then she's hoisted back into the air and feels trapped. Her body is pinned upright, her rib cage smashing against a towel rack.

The tom-tom drums beat and the tomcat screams, "This bitch is just like a puppy!" The crowd outside the door roars. "She just keeps coming back for more!"

The Joker turns her over and chews her nipples for supper. Kids bang on the bathroom door, and one of them, a very excited one, says, "He's fucking that green-eyed chick in there! Dude, he just passed her underwear under the door."

They have hearts on them, and they become a party souvenir, displayed like in that scene from Sixteen Candles.

Twenty-three: Rape

Once Chloë arrives at the final party, Telly has already fucked Darcy. It's too fucking late, he's already spread his AIDS around. Chloë looks like shit, drugged and awful and beautiful, and she passes out on a couch. It's pure post-party apocalypse, there're kids passed out on the floor, kids passed out on chairs and there's empty plastic cups and bottles everywhere, like how Sara's house got. The only one awake and staggering through the mess is Casper. He finds pretty Chloë like a little gumdrop someone dropped on his doorstep and there's no one looking so he touches her, tentatively at first, to see if she'll react. Then, very carefully, he undoes her pants. He takes them off her and takes of her chones and lifts both of her legs over his shoulders and arranges her rag doll legs and you see his back and his hips pumping and her white socks, anklets, and she's falling all over the place and he whispers, It's Casper, and her feet are straight up in the air and he pumps and it's necrophilia, total necrophilia.

Now they're both gonna die.

I'm not totally sure of how mine went down because I only remember bits and pieces of it. I do remember being hoisted over a shoulder and shouts coming from outside the bathroom door. The morning after, I had bruises and hickeys and bite marks but I couldn't remember how I'd gotten each of them. So I made up in my head, with time, a story of how I got them. I told one girl that something bad happened to me at a party, and she must've had a big mouth because when I ran into Tommy when I was sixteen, he went off on me. He was like eighteen or nineteen by then.

You think I fuckin' raped you? he yelled. He was standing outside the men's room at Lyon's, this restaurant that truckers dined at a lot and where freak kids would order coffee and smoke at and annoy the waitresses on Friday nights. I never raped anybody! he yelled. You—

I ran outside and into the parking and into my friend's car, shaking.

That was the one and only time I saw him after he took my virginity, which is weird for a small town. Maybe a santita, like Saint Thecla, was looking out for me or something. The summer that I turned 18, I left Santa Maria to go to college and went with a bunch of my dormmates to go see *Kids*. I almost barfed when the movie was over. I think it caused a little PTSD but a weird kind because how can you have flashbacks of an event you blacked out during?

Kids did great things for Chloë. She became the it-girl and she's still kind of an it-girl and Rosario Dawson is a big star now but the movie fucked the guys. Like Casper, he hung himself. And Telly got shit everywhere he went because people couldn't separate him as a person, he was just the butthole "virgin surgeon" and got his ass kicked everywhere he went. The black kid from the skinny-dipping scene, Harold Hunter, OD'd. I wrote a book about the summer of 1990 and it got rejected by a couple of publishers and then I wrote another one that had nothing to do with the summer of 1990 and it got published. Out of the blue, maybe because he heard about my book, Tommy emailed me.

First Electronic Epistle to Myriam

Date: Tue, 7 Aug 2007 22:35:20–0700
To: xxxxxxxxxx
Subject: Hi
From: xxxxxxxxxx

I just wanted to say hello.

tommy

THE WOUNDED MAN

Abdellah Taïa

We had broken our fast about two hours ago. It was getting dark. Et Hay Salam was unusually calm. It was as if all the inhabitants of this working-class neighborhood in Salé had suddenly moved to the other side of the Bou Regreg River, not far from the beach in Rabat, everybody who lives here, except for my family. The place was deserted. It made you think that something extraordinary was about to happen, something that would drastically change the entire country, disrupt the land and the people still on it. A huge thunderstorm that would bring hope, rain, and a successful harvest. Or else the Apocalypse: the end of the world, starting right now.

My mother, M'Barka, was sound asleep.

Ramadan was an exhausting month for her. Even though fasting made her very tired, on a daily basis and all by herself, she had to prepare rounds of sweets, crêpes, and of course, *harira,* a soup she always loved, very tart with lots of tomatoes and lemon juice. In the past, my sisters were happy to help her make every day of this holy month a spiritual and gastronomic celebration, a never-ending ceremony. Now the house was empty. Three floors with nobody living there.

Everyone had gone off somewhere, somewhere far away, some other city, some other country, left for another world, to live there among strangers, people I'd never know and never really accept. The only people left in the house were my mother, my younger brother, Mustapha, whom we almost never saw, and me. M'Barka was afraid to be alone now, quite often afraid, and time and again she'd repeat herself by telling me how solitude is a slow and dolorous poison.

That always made me sad, very sad. I never managed to completely share her suffering. On the other hand, I felt like crying every time I heard her talk like that. Every day, she would beg me not to tarry in the city once my classes ended at Rabat University, plead with me to come home early, before it got dark, beg me to catch the early bus and get home fast so the house seemed full again, so I could keep her company, help her get through her everyday tasks, cheer her up just by being there, put some life back in her, share a warm moment, make us feel like a family again before night fell.

At night, just when it came time for us to separate again, she'd never want me to retire to my bedroom. She'd want me to stay there beside her until she had fallen asleep. Sleep was death. And since my father's brutal disappearance one year ago, she suffered from bouts of fear and panic attacks. That's when she'd cling to me. She used to sleep in the living room, where the television was king. She didn't like that "apparatus," as she called it, but it wound up being the companion who got her through the day, this machine that emitted sounds, voices that somewhat reassured her, though not all the time.

Thanks to the price of satellite dishes coming down, we had just started to pick up the French channels, the ones that really interested me. When I could get it, I really liked watching Arte.

That channel made me think of myself as someone important: this intellectual and with-it student who was interested in things that people around him found boring or hard to understand. I was proud. I acted proud, like I was one of a kind.

That's the part I was playing that night, after I devoured a good amount of the delicious Ramadan food my mother made. I turned on the television. There was this movie on Arte.

I missed the beginning. Locked in the bathroom of some train station, Jean-Hugues Anglade was crying his eyes out. Obviously, he felt abandoned too. He was battling something as well, maybe solitude. I was instantly moved by him, by the actor and by the character he portrayed. Thanks to my knowledge of movies, it only took me about a minute to recognize that film, one I'd never seen before. It was *The Wounded Man* by Patrice Chéreau. A French film from 1984. A cult film. Something off-limits.

My mother was sound asleep. And right there on the screen, they were showing this movie that no one in Morocco could do anything about, whether that meant stopping it entirely or interrupting it to give a lesson in religious morality to this young hero who lived beyond the rules, wore his hair a little too long, and loved other men. This hero who was in love with one particular man.

I was faced with a dilemma. Faced with desire. Ready to watch that movie right to the end.

Watch it with my stomach knotted with fear. Constantly on the lookout. My mother, asleep in back of me, could wake up at any moment and catch me in the act. Then she'd know my secret, my one big secret, know about my other life, the object of my desire. She'd make a big deal out of it. The whole thing would be a scandal. I'd be so ashamed, I wouldn't know what to do, what to say to her.

My stomach hurt. I ate too much when we broke our fast and couldn't digest it all. I was aroused by the level of desire that permeated the film, that had taken over Jean-Hugues Anglade and the other characters. It was the only thing they lived for, the only thing that kept them alive: sex, love, and the danger that went with them. They'd feel attracted to someone, approach him, try to pick him up, flatter him to no end, pay for him, play with his head, rape him, toss him aside, kill him little by little. I was fascinated, hypnotized by what I was seeing. And I wanted to live like one of those characters, to be just like them. Outside the law. I wanted to love just like they did. Love another man. Just one. Alone. Illicitly. I wanted to touch myself. Stroke myself.

Lick myself. Bite myself. I wanted to go right up to the toughest one and give him everything I had.

My stomach was heaving. I was getting hard. And I didn't know what to do because I was still afraid in spite of the level of desire the television beamed right at me, this urge that overwhelmed me and soon drove me almost crazy.

Now my mother was snoring. Regular exhalations, loud snoring one minute, quiet snoring the next. But once or twice she stopped. I changed the channel immediately. I couldn't help taking this cessation as a sign that she was returning to consciousness, about to wake up and catch me watching this banned movie. Somewhat reassured after waiting an endless minute and turning toward her to make sure her eyes were completely shut and she was still miles away from me and all those images, I went back to watching *The Wounded Man* and his story. And suddenly my desire became uncontrollable and my fear came to the forefront.

Jean-Hugues Anglade was in love with this tall, handsome guy I seem to remember was dark.

A little like Gérard Depardieu in the early eighties. This virile, sensitive, hard-edged, merciless man.

A king. A dictator. A pimp.

Anglade fell for him the minute he saw him. And from that moment on, life revolved around this man who made him forget everybody else. No one else would ever matter as much as he did.

Almost from day one, he gave up everything, his former life, his family, just to chase after this guy. He'd turn up on the street, in train stations, in parking lots, trail after him, pursue him, clumsily try to seduce him, anything to have a minute of his time, a minute of his body. To have him, love him. And it never happened. Anglade lived on passion alone. The kind of passion that could only be heartbreaking and tragic.

Patrice Chéreau's film, in the same tumultuous and brutal way it took hold of me that night and has remained forever in my mind, is extreme in the way it depicts the exacerbation of romantic feelings, extreme in the way it reveals how sex dominates the body. This film comes complete with slaps to the face, quarrels, pursuits, every kind of trafficking, tears, orgies, blood, sperm, down-and-dirty moments, obsessions, and death. It shows the never-ending slide of a young man with blood on his hands, a man doomed from the start, toward this crime he commits for love.

I forgot his first name. He was the one I identified with. In love and frustrated, just like him. Ready to give up everything for some wild dream, some rock of a man, some emotion rarer than hen's teeth, some exceptional human being. And constantly afraid. Constantly in hopeless pursuit of the only person I desire. The man I love. The man the Americans call "The One." One man and one man only. Someone older than me, so I could learn something from him, relive parts of the past with him, together becoming this couple people wouldn't recognize. A spiritual leader, a master, a baker, a man of God who prays five times a day, an enlightened man, a parent, an uncle, a cousin. . . .

The film played out in front of me, and lodged its force, its hopelessness and its religion in the back of my eyes, in the back of my mind. Without even knowing it, I had become a believer, someone prone to indulge in this lifestyle on a regular basis, someone adept at perceiving, at wandering about, at banging into bodies, at exploding with joy before I went crazy, even beyond crazy. What was forbidden stood right there in front of me, touching my scrawny and suddenly emboldened body. And what was forbidden stood right in back of me too.

I kept getting harder and harder, my heart even more confounded. My eyes were turning red. I was both happy and sad. Fired up and chilled to the bone, as if some gust of northern air, some blast from Tangier, had passed over me. At one point, I wanted to wake my mother up and get her to look at these images, get her even more involved in this movie that moved and, for that matter, totally overwhelmed her well-mannered son. Wanted to move in toward her, snuggle up to her, find room on her lap, lift her hand to my stomach, feel her breath on my back, on my neck, recognize her smell in my nose and against my skin. Wanted to go back to where I began, the first door, the first opening that brought me into this world, that let me find life and light.

And there, back in the place where it all started, back at my original threshold, I'd hollow out a space, a depression, and sit there crying while I watched this wounded man, this young man, this brother disoriented by love's searing intensity, sit there crying, crying over him and right along with him. Wanted to gently move my mouth across his eyes, slowly run my tongue across each one until I finally drank the slightly salty water that flowed from them and ran down his cheeks and across his skin.

I knew just what he was going through. I dreamed about it. Fantasized about it. I stopped thinking. Couldn't think anymore. My eyes hurt, my thighs hurt, my knees hurt, my cock hurt. I snapped out of it. The wounded man was still walking the Way of the Cross that all lovers walk. That's where this hero would fulfill his destiny, right here in front of us, here in this house that had no father, here in our almost empty living room, here in the privacy of our lives, so filled with silence and obscurity.

I used to think I was sophisticated, but as I watched Patrice Chéreau's movie I realized for the first time what an inexperienced movie fan I really was, since I watched all movies the same way I always did. And by that I mean, the way I watched them back when my childhood years were ending and, still programmed by others, the religion of Indian films and Chinese karate movies became part of my life forever. I started to rediscover myself. I guzzled images in dark and public theaters, sitting there with prostitutes and thugs. And those images delivered me from the shackles of my homeland, linked me to an art form that little by little gave me a reason to live, a way to see above and beyond things. I could leave the world, go beyond its gravity, see my own nakedness, then return to fight my battles.

I was in the heat of battle. In full revolt. Just days away from Ramadan's holiest night.

Suddenly my mother's music stopped. Not a sound came from her mouth, no wheezing, no humming, not a single breath. Was it apnea? Was she dead, beyond all fear, no longer afraid, gone off to join my father? Was she awake now? Was she sitting there with me watching *The Wounded Man*? Would she figure out what these strange scenes meant, these pictures from another world, these images from hell? Was she suddenly going to jump up and start yelling at me, yelling in that voice she always used when things turned ugly, start pulling my hair, punishing me, pinching me, cursing me out? Would she try to castrate me right then and there?

With my heart in my throat, I turned to face her. Her eyes were open but she was staring at the ceiling. She was dreaming. She was still entangled in the sequence of images that sprang up in this dream that only she cultivated. Somewhat at ease, I changed the channel and asked her, in a quiet voice brimming with respect, if there was anything she needed. Her response was immediate, as if she had been preparing it for a long time, had fallen asleep thinking of it.

"I'd love a glass of water, honey!" I ran to the kitchen to get her one. She was very thirsty, had just returned from some long voyage. She wanted another one. "I will die, child, if I don't have have another one . . . Oh, my sweet son, may God . . ." She didn't have to ask me twice. I almost ran back to the kitchen, already happy that she would pray for me, remember me in prayers that were always the same, prayers that pictured heaven as someplace real and not some fictitious abode.

Her thirst quenched, M'Barka went back to her sleep, back to tending her dreams. But right before closing her eyes again, she gave me this blessing that absolutely bowled me over and still does: "My son, you need to watch, watch what you want on television . . . I will not get upset . . . Watch what you want. . . . "

I turned the sound down and waited for my mother to start snoring again before I went back to watching *The Wounded Man*, finally catching up with the film's wounded hero. By now, he had completely run out of patience, was tired of love that cruised a one-way street, tired of humiliation, tired of aimless wandering, and all that time, crazed with love, crazed. He was almost at the point where his path to crime would end, the moment, that single and final moment, when he'd have his way with the other man, finally possess the object of his desire.

Only death could give meaning, purpose, and structure to this young man's tragic story, to his sublime love.

Naked, pressed against the man he loved, he was strangling him with his bare hands, snuffing him out while he made love to him. That's how he gave him everything he had: his body, his heart, his mind, his skin, his blood, his breath. He gave up his life by taking the life of the man who, right up to the end, refused to unite with him in that great religion of feelings and shared embraces.

It was tragic.

Love, like life, which at certain miraculous moments burns with light and intensity, is a tragedy. I knew that, knew it intuitively. I was twenty years old. *The Wounded Man* taught me that, taught it to me once and for all. I had been warned. The choice was mine. Would I give up? Never.

At the end of the movie, the credits flashed in front of my eyes. The name Hervé Guibert came up. He was the guy who wrote the script along with Patrice Chéreau. I had forgotten about him. This movie, this story, they were his too. Part of his life. The way he lived. A lifestyle I discovered and came to love when I read his books. He'd been dead for four or five years now.

Tears started running down my cheeks. Finally. But why was I crying? Who was I crying over?

I didn't exactly know what to say, couldn't really answer my own question. Was it for Hervé Guibert, this man I knew inside and out after reading all of his books? Was it for the hero who in the course of that movie turned into a criminal, a brother, a friend, turned into me? Was it for my father who left too soon, who never got to see my life become a book, a story put into writing?

Was it for life itself, life, which when you come right down to it, is sad and terribly lonely despite what happiness Ramadan brings?

Even today, I still don't know. Even today, I still cry when I think of what actually happened back then, think about how the movie ended, think about Guibert, think about myself . . . and think about my mother who cried out in silence. And I cry for all of us.

The next day, I woke up very late. I only had one thing in mind. I was in a big rush to find my favorite cousin, Chouaïb, the cousin I was sort of in love with. I ran off to find him, seduce him, corrupt him. I hurried off to hang all over him, talk him into breaking the fast before sunset, breaking it by letting both of us talk about sex. Then we'd climb that hill in Bettana, his neighborhood, and from up there, right next to the old cemetery, we'd be able to see the opposite shore of the Bou Regreg River, see Rabat, the Hassan Tower, the Kasbah built by the Oudayas, the public beach where poor people swam. Both of us would smoke a little hash. Then I'd put my head on his thighs. And in that state of silence and contemplation, I'd tell him all about the movie last night and gently, but directly, invite him to sin, to transgress.

To deliberately sin.

God would be watching us.

We'd do it anyway. Right through to the end. Right down to the sea. Right up into the sky.

Unlucky, one day I'd be unlucky in love, just like *The Wounded Man*. In the meantime, Chouaïb, this cousin with a moustache, this bad boy with a body big enough to wrap around mine, has a place in my heart and that's how I drag him off to the movies almost every day, then sit there under the bright lights, my eyes completely shut.

Translated from the French by Frank Stock

SOMEWHERE, OVER

Daphne Gottlieb

My mother is in her bed, in two worlds. She is watching movies on the ceiling. There are ants and chipmunks. "I want to go home," she says.

"You are home," we tell her.

The tumor has bloomed like poppies, has spread to her liver, streams through her blood, is rooted to her lungs. The tumors are in there with my mother. "Who's that?" She asks. "Who was just here?" There's a man in the corner that only she can see.

"I need my coat," she says. "I have to go home."

"I have the earrings," she says. She's holding two Ativan in her hand, small pearls of peace. "There's so much to do," she sighs.

Sepia tones and Auntie Em—this is a real, truly live place. Some of it wasn't very nice. But most of it was beautiful. She sleeps in a field of poppies; a red halo on her white pillow, all her hair fallen like a red rain from her head and she's in the movie now; she's no one's mother.

"Things don't make sense." "I get confused." "Sometimes I'm in the movies," she says.

The yellow brick, the bedroom. She's smoking a technicolor cigarette that only she can see, drinking from a glass only she can hold. What are you drinking? "Château Le Monde," she says, rolls the glass under her nose for its bouquet, sips deeply. She's drinking from the house of the world today. "Is it good?" we ask. She nods and smiles. Yes. Very.

I had this dream that wasn't a dream. If I ever go looking for my

162

heart's desire again, I won't look any further. I'm drinking Château Le Monde.

The power to go back to Kansas, with pills for pain, pills for sleep, pills for function, pills to alleviate secretions, pills for pulses and blood pressures. Pills in two places at once, earrings. "I have to go home," she says.

Somatic death, the death of the body, involves a series of irreversible events that leads finally to cell destruction and death. Here come the flying monkeys. I'll get you, my pretty.

"Can you help me sleep?" she asks. We have pills for sleep. "No," she says. "I don't want to wake up. I want to go home." She wants the Asian coat, she says. And her shoes. "Where are my shoes?" she asks.

Click your heels together three times.

Physiological death is preceded by an irreversible cessation of all vital systems. "I'm crazy. I might as well be crazy," she wails. She pulls the pillow over her head, sobbing. All I kept saying to everybody was, "I want to go home." I'll get you, my pretty.

One at a time, systems shut down. Poppies close in the dark. The dying person turns to the light. Blood backs up into the lungs and the liver, causing congestion. As for you, my galvanized friend, you want a heart. You don't know how lucky you are to not have one.

A dying person turns toward light as sight diminishes. Glinda floats down in a bubble, chases chipmunks on the ceiling. And they sent me home. Doesn't anybody believe me? All I kept saying to everybody was, "I want to go home."

The heart becomes unable to pump strongly enough to keep blood moving. Hearts will never be practical. Blood backs up first throughout the heart and your little dog, Toto, too.

My father, she says, will be home soon, even though he's been dead 13 years. Those magic slippers will take you home in two seconds.

Now?

Whenever you wish.

Stay with us, Dorothy. We all love ya. We don't want ya to go. The body surface cools. "I'll never get home," she cries.

She's planning menus. There's so much she needs to do. She's in the movie, at work, she's throwing parties. She points out where the bar will be, where the hors d'oeuvres go. She's working so hard. Oh, scarecrow. This could never be like Kansas. What am I gonna do?

She forgets how to eat, stabs bread with a spoon, doesn't want food. She wants scotch on the rocks. She drinks one, then another, then nods out in the poppy field.

She opens her eyes and says, "Thank you for the party. I had a wonderful time."

Hearts will never be practical until they can be made unbreakable.

Those magic slippers will take you home in two seconds.

"Thank you for the party. I had a wonderful time. But now I am very tired and have to go home."

Now?

Whenever you wish.

This is my room—and you're all here! Oh, Auntie Em, there's no place like—

Overnight, the wind picks up, rattles through her chest.

It's the tornado, going, going.

THE FORGOTTEN MOVIE SCREENS
OF BROWARD COUNTY

Richard Grayson

University Cinema 4

This four-screen theater, in a small strip shopping center at the corner of Pines Boulevard and University Drive, was where Mom and Dad took us to see *Kramer vs. Kramer* one night during Christmas vacation in 1979. Our family had just moved to Broward County the month before.

We drove down University from our town house in Davie, passing orange groves and cow pastures. In the dark we couldn't see any cows or the creatures Mom called their mascots, the ducks who would sit on their backs.

Soon after the scene where Dustin Hoffman throws the little boy's French toast into the garbage, Edward got up and went out of the theater. We assumed he was going to the bathroom, but when he didn't come back, we started getting worried.

Finally Dad went out to look for Edward, but he wasn't in the men's room or at the candy counter or in the tacky little lobby. Eventually Dad found Edward watching Steven Spielberg's *1941* on another screen.

Later I'd think that as young as he was, Edward knew that something was up between Mom and Dad. He didn't want to see a movie about divorce. It was easier for him to watch something from the past.

The University Cinema 4 was torn down in 1994 and replaced by a warehouse and storage complex.

Lakes Mall Cinema

A year later we all went to see *Coal Miner's Daughter* at this six-screen theater at the Lakes Mall at the corner of U.S. 441 and Oakland Park Boulevard.

Before that we'd had dinner at Pumpernick's in Hallandale and then went to the Greyhound track. Rachel thought the way they treated the dogs was cruel, so we left after a few races even though Dad had picked two winners.

Maybe that's why he seemed annoyed as we aimlessly drove up 441, through Hollywood, Plantation, and Lauderhill. In the back seat, we all noted that Mom and Dad had spoken to us, but not to each other, all night.

When Edward saw the theater marquee, he nagged so much that Dad made a sudden illegal U-turn and lurched the station wagon into the mall parking lot.

We had to wait almost an hour for the next show. After we got our tickets, Edward and Rachel and I walked around the mall, Rachel holding Edward's hand, till we joined Mom and Dad on line at the theater.

They had been talking about something while we were gone.

Even though none of us were country music fans, we agreed afterwards that *Coal Miner's Daughter* was a great film.

It was the last movie we saw as a family.

The Lakes Mall got decrepit and finally closed, replaced by some low-rent big box stores.

Last year the Magic Johnson Development Company opened one of the Starbucks stores they put in African American neighborhoods across from where the theater was.

Dale and I go there on Sunday mornings to sit on their patio, drink overpriced coffee, and read the *Sun-Sentinel*.

Broward Mall 4

This four-screen theater, which was 14,000 square feet on 3.6 acres, opened in 1978, the same year as the Broward Mall across the street from it.

It was the movie theater I went to the most. It was where I saw *Pretty in Pink* and *Making Love* and *The Last Emperor*.

Sean and I saw *Victor/Victoria* here at a Saturday matinee on a rainy weekend around the time we were graduating Nova High.

While Julie Andrews was singing a sentimental song, Sean's hand reached for mine. It was the first time I ever held hands with a guy and I felt a little paranoid about someone seeing us, like the black twins from school who worked as ushers there.

But I wasn't paranoid enough to let go. In a couple of months Sean would be heading for Tallahassee and I'd be going to Gainesville.

We made plans to see each other a lot, but once freshman year started somehow we were busy every weekend till November, when I saw him at the Gators/Seminoles game. By then it was too late.

Three months after that, Grandpa Dave died and Grandma Sarah came down from New York to stay with Dad at his condo. During spring break, I took Grandma to the Broward Mall 4 to see *The Outsiders*.

Because Grandma had been taking care of Grandpa all those years he'd been sick, she hadn't been to a movie in years. So I guess it was sort of selfish to make Grandma see something I wanted to see, but she ended up liking *The Outsiders*.

Over cheesecake at Danny's afterwards, she asked me about the young actors in it and if I thought they were handsome.

In 1991, after business at the Broward Mall 4 had been bad for years, new owners came in and turned it into an art movie house. But nine months later, Hurricane Andrew struck and the storm damaged the building. The movie chain that leased the theater decided to close rather than make repairs.

The last film I saw here was *Mississippi Masala*.

A plan for the city of Plantation to buy this property for an art museum fell through, and today it's just another strip shopping center with a parking lot.

Art Towne Twin

This tiny theater, in the back of a little enclosed shopping center on Broward Boulevard at NW 65th Avenue, opened in 1984 and closed three years later. It showed foreign films and art films.

At home on vacations from UF and then that year I lived with Dad and basically did nothing, I went here by myself to see *Fred and Ginger*, *Sid and Nancy*, and *My Beautiful Laundrette* (twice).

The same kid who sold you tickets also took the tickets from you, and later he'd be running the little candy counter. I felt so bad for him that I bought their overpriced popcorn and Coke.

I saw *The Official Story* and *Tampopo* here with Edward, who was the youngest person in the audience—not that there ever were that many people.

I think watching so many foreign films is partly what made Edward decide to go to Israel when he got old enough. That and what happened to our family.

Rachel and her boyfriend took me to the Art Towne Twin on my birthday to see *The Dead*.

The little mall burned down in 1996. They said the owners didn't want to put in a sprinkler system because they thought it cost too much.

A giant Publix supermarket stands on this spot today.

Inverrary Five

It seemed as if every time I would go to this Lauderhill theater, I'd meet one of my great-aunts or great-uncles who had condos nearby. On Oakland Park Boulevard in a little strip shopping center, the Inverrary Five drew mostly senior citizens.

Sean and I saw the last movie we ever saw together here, at the end of a day that we'd spent mostly in bed. At *Poltergeist* he grabbed my hand only at the scary parts and he didn't hold on long. Mom's Aunt Rose and Uncle Manny were three rows in front of us.

When the Inverrary Five closed on Christmas Eve in 1993, Rachel said she was surprised it had ever made money because ninety per cent of the theatergoers received senior discounts.

By then all of Mom's aunts and uncles were gone. Grandma Sarah had died the month before in a nursing home.

Sometime in 1995, this theater reopened, and the new owners tried to make a go of it by programming black-oriented films such as *Ride* for the blue-collar African-Americans who lived south of the theater and films such as *Odd Couple II* for the surviving seniors who lived to the north.

You could see the staff worked hard, scrambling to clean the theaters as soon as the audience left. Ushers escorted people to their seats with flashlights, a good thing with such an elderly clientele. They charged only five dollars for full-price admission at night.

Rachel and her husband didn't live that far away, but they said they never would consider going to a movie here.

"It's a dinosaur," Rachel said a few weeks before it closed for the last time.

Pembroke Pines 8

I can't remember when this theater opened. It was on Pines Boulevard west of Flamingo Road, long before the Pembroke Lakes mega-mall and various power centers made this the worst intersection for traffic accidents in the state of Florida.

By 1987, I didn't go to many movies with Dad, but just before I moved out of his condo because his girlfriend got on my nerves too much, we went here—him, Mireya, and me—to see *Platoon*.

I was always told that Mom and Dad put me in a stroller when they went on antiwar marches during Vietnam. I think I remember this one rally when I was about eight years old. Edward was the kid in the stroller by then.

Outside the theater after the show, we noticed a group of Vietnam veterans, some of whom I recognized from the army/navy store where I worked. They were huddled together like members of a football team, crying and hugging each other. Dad said they probably all had their posttraumatic stress disorder triggered by the movie.

About five years later, Dale and I saw *Malcolm X* at this theater. I thought he would like it better than he did, but Dale said that growing up in St. Kitts, he paid more attention to music and cricket than to African American history.

Malcolm X was too long, Dale said, and anyway, he preferred comedies. To Dale, Spike Lee went downhill after *She's Gotta Have It*, which he found very funny.

The last movie I saw here was *Planes, Trains and Automobiles*. I was very surprised when they closed this theater in September 2000 because it had seemed so new.

Coral Springs Mall 4 and Coral Springs Triplex

When we first moved to Broward, the Coral Springs Mall was the place to go when we used to drive all the way north up University Drive. But by the mid-1980s, it was overshadowed by the larger regional mall at Coral Square.

On our second date, Dale and I saw *Peggy Sue Got Married* at the four-screen theater inside this mall. He told me afterwards he couldn't relate to straight white people's love stories. I told him I didn't think *Peggy Sue Got Married* was a love story, unless a person could be in love with the past.

Eventually moviegoers didn't want to walk past all those depressing empty stores. The Coral Springs Mall 4 seemed tacky and cheap and was always playing pictures like *Ernest Goes to Camp* and *Creepshow II.*

In the early 1990s, after her fiancé died, Mom ended up working at one of this mall's few surviving stores, Uptons.

One night when Mom's car had broken down again and I was teaching a night class at FAU, Dale came to pick Mom up when the store closed.

Somehow he and Mom got to talking with Hamid, the guy who owned the theater in the mall. Hamid told them how he fled Iran in 1979 with $700 in his pocket.

Mom told him that 1979 was the year our family came to Broward County, the same year the Coral Springs Mall was built.

The first theater Hamid bought was the triplex a few miles south on University Drive and Royal Park Boulevard. He thought it would be easy to make money, but four months later a national chain opened an eight-screen theater down the block. Hamid had to turn the triplex into a dollar theater.

Mom worked at Uptons only a year before deciding to move to Ocala. She could sell the town house for a lot of money and live in a place where the cost of living was lower.

The Coral Springs Mall closed. The city took over the land, and on the property now are a charter school and a regional Broward County library.

Today Hamid's company owns only megaplexes like the Egyptian-themed Paradise 24, at the corner of I-75 and Sheridan Drive in Davie. It averages 100,000 patrons per screen per month and on some weekends is one of the ten busiest cinemas in the country.

At the Paradise 24, Dale and I usually buy our tickets with a credit card from a machine and head for the cappuccino bar before the show starts. The theater has a Dolby surround sound system, oversize stadium seats that rock back and forth, curbside valet parking, and a façade and interior as imposing as the pyramids.

Even though Hamid is now a multimillionaire, Dale swore he saw him behind the counter frying popcorn shrimp when we took Rachel's twins to the Paradise 24 to see *Shrek*.

As for the Coral Springs Triplex, after it closed, nobody leased the space in the little shopping center on Royal Park Boulevard at University. If you look through the glass doors, you can see lots of dust and faded old movie posters.

Sometimes I go on this Web site called Lost Treasures, which celebrates fondly remembered theaters that are now gone. But they're all old city theaters like the Loew's Paradise of my childhood in the Bronx: a majestic 4,000-seat theater with an Italian Baroque–style facade, Corinthian columns, sweeping staircase, etched-glass lighting fixtures and gilded railings.

Multiscreen suburban shopping-center theaters built in the 1970s and 1980s are not considered Lost Treasures, and I can understand why. They weren't handsome or imposing or well-built or historically significant.

I'm none of those things, either—which is probably why I identify with them.

3

Viewfinder

THE ELIZABETH TAYLOR PUZZLE

Wayne Koestenbaum

Quoth Elizabeth Taylor, in and out of her roles:

> It's got to be told and you never let me tell it.
> I am pretty enough. I try not to look like a slob.
> I'm best from the back.
> I loved it. Every awful moment of it, I loved.

So I got into my costume, which seemed to weigh hundreds of pounds—a huge thing made of twenty-four-karat gold thread. The headdress itself weighed about fifteen pounds and was two and a half feet high. I got the whole drag on and climbed up on the Sphinx, feeling totally trembly.

1.

Once I had a jigsaw puzzle of Theda Bara in *Cleopatra*. Her makeup looked like soot, applied with blind, crazy fingers. It wasn't a maquillage that any realism required. I required it.

From the slumber of fragments I woke Theda Bara; I kissed her by assembling her. I loved patiently putting together a star from pieces that looked, individually, like branches, or estuaries, or shuddering birds.

The puzzle sat without an audience. I am the only one who saw it. If you don't exhibit a puzzle to a friend, who will solve it?

2.

Whenever I was sick, and only when I was sick, my mother permitted me to read movie magazines. Feverish, nauseated, convalescing, I read them in bed. I am talking about the 1960s.

In *Photoplay*, I discovered Elizabeth Taylor, whom I'd never seen in a film. Columnists clucked about Liz and Dick and an expensive disaster, *Cleopatra*, which I'd not see until I was grown; but I worshipped it, as an abstraction, because her salary had been $1 million, and because the film had nearly ruined Twentieth Century Fox. *Cleopatra* seemed a feat of weight and waste for which I was suited. Or so I fancied, in the silence of 1965.

I read John O'Hara's *BUtterfield 8* because Elizabeth Taylor had won her first Oscar playing its "slut" heroine, Gloria Wandrous. *BUtterfield 8*: I thought about butter and the number 8, which, placed on its side, was the sign of infinity, and a hieroglyphic representation of two breasts. I touched the words *wondrous* and *wandering* stored in the name *Wandrous*, and planned to pick up a prostitute at the pharmacy's paperback-novel rack.

During a garage sale, I confided to my mother's friend Rita, a block lady with black bouffant, tanned thighs, and raucous laugh, a lady who later left the block to run massage workshops in the mountains: "You look like Elizabeth Taylor." I knew it was a compliment but I pretended not to know. Rita had a resemblance; I had a longing. Rita laughed, and my mother, who overheard the confidence, laughed, too, and I asked, with feigned naïveté, "Is Elizabeth Taylor beautiful?"

On the school bus, on the way to Santa Cruz's dilapidated boardwalk for a field trip, I overheard a dirty-minded boy say, "Liz Taylor has big boobs." This comment was a clue. I memorized it. "Liz Taylor has big boobs" taught me what boys wanted, what girls gave. I hadn't known that Elizabeth Taylor and "boobs" were synonymous; I'd thought Elizabeth Taylor was an atmosphere, a stature. On the bus I had learned otherwise. I was learning about her body and my body. I was learning about size.

3.

After watching Elizabeth Taylor movies I feel eerily masculine. Her beauty shoves me out of maleness and compresses me back into it, as if I were an astronaut losing gravity and then regaining it, or a sea voyager suffering the bends. When she appears on screen, she alters scales of dimension: we're not wearing 3-D spectacles, but her femaleness leaps out at us, and her gorgeousness seems a suicide cult we are drugged into wanting to join. I have the temptation to wear her beauty like a campaign button ("I like Ike"); to adhere to her beauty as a philosophical program or a party platform. Elizabeth Taylor is beautiful by objective standards, so my fandom isn't madness. To espouse Elizabeth Taylor as gorgeous is to take credit for her beauty, to nominate oneself as its shadow and consequence, or even its cause.

Voting for Elizabeth Taylor in the adoration sweepstakes, I dream I'm getting credit for heterosexuality, fictionally fitting into it; if I adore Liz, aren't I 1/100th straight? Staring at her, I hallucinate that she is an extravagance I am presenting to the world; that she is my responsibility; that her breasts and her hairdo and her glamour in a Richard Avedon photograph (circa 1964) enthrall because Liz's dominatrix aspect upsets the photographic balance of power. I, her advocate, cheer her sadistic beauty: with my eyes, I say "Get 'em, Liz!" Gender, carried to extremes, is compellingly extraterrestrial.

You will say, "He has an Elizabeth Taylor fetish," and I will meekly smile, and you will either discountenance my love, or will admit that years ago you adored her, but outgrew the crush. Or did you sink deeper into it and never surface? Did you grow sluggish, watching *National Velvet* for the thirteenth time?

4.

Elizabeth Taylor and masturbation: recall the marvelous scene in *National Velvet* when she plays invisible horsie in bed, pretending to ride a horse, making it go faster and faster, panting as it accelerates and she guides it over hurdles, her screen sister Angela Lansbury in bed dreaming of boys but Elizabeth Taylor as Velvet hot for a horse named Pie, as in mincemeat pie.

References to eating, hunger, and gluttony mark most of Taylor's films. In *A Place in the Sun*, she enters the pool room where Montgomery Clift is playing, and she nibbles. In *BUtterfield 8*, she says, "Waitress, could you bring us some french fries?" In the first scene of *Who's Afraid of Virginia Woolf?* she eats cold meat straight out of the fridge. "Eat, Velvet," says her screen mother, austere Anne Revere, in *National Velvet*.

The elephantine giantism of such vehicles as *Giant* and *Elephant Walk* signify that she's a star, that the emotions she inspires are huge, and that her figure is large. (Is it really? The allegedly "large" Liz often seems tiny. Liz is a matter of perspective.) It has always been considered acceptable to comment on her size. Stanley Kauffmann in *The New Republic* described her Cleopatra as "a plump, young American matron in a number of Egyptian costumes and makeups." She was called plump long before she was actually plump. Fluids and solids that pass through Elizabeth Taylor's body, or that stay in her body, are part of the public record.

5.

In childhood, in *Velvet's* wake, to capitalize on her association with animals, Elizabeth Taylor wrote and published a book, called *Nibbles and Me*, about her pet chipmunk. The word *nibbles* turns easily to *nipples*, and the phrase *nibbles and me*, or *nipples and me*, seems an equation: Nibbles = Me, or Nipples = Me. The "me" emotion—narcissism, identity—comes to fruition in the young star's love of a pet whose name signifies a "cute" orality. It's charming to nibble. It's less charming to gorge. (Nipples: the public has been permitted to see most of Elizabeth Taylor's breasts, but never her nipples.) In 1946, at fourteen, in *Nibbles and Me*, before she developed the body whose bosom and salary and appetite became fable, Elizabeth Taylor sketched the matrix of eating and being eaten, of mouth and breast, of cannibalism and nourishment, that would define her body in the public imagination.

Voted "Mother of the Year" in 1953 by America's florists, she said, "To me the most beautiful smells in the world are babies and bacon." She tries to pass as a model mother, but she seems, instead, to take easy, profound, scandalous delight in the human body as meat. She sounds like a cannibal, her baby a rasher sizzling on the grill. ("I'm a wolf," she says in *A Little Night Music*.) What do babies smell like? Sometimes, shit and piss. Elizabeth Taylor at her most acceptable, the Mother of the Year, the Bride of the Year, Elizabeth Taylor before the Betty Ford Clinic, was she-who-nibbles, was the sign of *our* desire to nibble, was bacon inside a body so bounteous in its beauty and its significances that only an ungrateful public would ever consider a performance of hers to be poor, or a sum bestowed on her to be wasted.

6.

But *Cleopatra* outraged the scandal-hungry public because it wasted money, and because Elizabeth Taylor was blamed for the waste, and because her performance was considered lousy though she was paid a million for it, and because, having "stolen" Eddie Fisher from Debbie Reynolds, she dumped him for already-married Richard Burton, instigating "*Le Scandale*," causing the Vatican to publish a letter denouncing Elizabeth as a home wrecker and an erotic vagrant, and *Photoplay* to run a reader's poll to discover whether its audience "could ever forgive what Liz has done." And a U.S. congresswoman to suggest that Taylor be refused entrance into the United States "on the grounds of undesirability," and a minister to advocate that Liz be burned in effigy.

To understand "*Le Scandale*," we need to consider Elizabeth Taylor's tracheotomy.

In 1961, during the early months of *Cleopatra*, Elizabeth Taylor almost died. To save her life, doctors opened her throat at the windpipe. The tracheotomy scar shows up in most of her subsequent movies, including *Cleopatra*: "I make no attempt to conceal it," she says. (And yet she underwent plastic surgery to erase it.) We see the scarred throat in a famous photograph that originally appeared in Vogue (with an article heralding "The New Cleopatra Complex"). Elizabeth is in Cleopatra drag, a snake brooch hardly joining the two halves of her dress over her cleavage, and she stares wearily and confrontationally at the viewer. Is she bored? Is boredom a part of beauty?

Nearly thirty years later, the photo was included in an exhibition called "The Indomitable Spirit," compiled by "photographers and friends united against AIDS." The scar is a symbol of Elizabeth's "indomitable spirit": she survived MGM, the star system, multiple marriages, and near-fatal illnesses. The scar marks her throat: site of voice, self-articulation, autobiography. She is scarred when she is most beautiful (in 1962, during the production of *Cleopatra*), when she is considered worth $1 million (more than anyone had ever been paid for doing anything, according to *Time*). Look at the expense and expanse of Taylor's creamy skin: stare at the cleavage, the Cleopatra makeup, the strange quaint bangs, and see the scar.[1]

7.

Follow the metaphor trail of the scar:

Elizabeth on a stretcher, carried blue and breathless into an ambulance (*Newsweek* called her "Sleeping Beauty"); Elizabeth Taylor looking like *Goldfinger*, gold and dead at the end of *Cleopatra*—her body so expensive ($1 million) that her allure *is* bullion; Cleopatra laid out for the viewer and the camera, as our eye pans slowly up her body, the money shot, to prove that Elizabeth Taylor was worth what Fox paid; Elizabeth Taylor as a face-lift patient in *Ash Wednesday*, real surgery footage to show beauty's connection to mutilation, and then convalescing Taylor swathed in mummy bandages, her face—the little of it we can see between the bandages—made up to look black and blue and genderless; Elizabeth Taylor falling off Pie in *National Velvet*, convalescing in the hospital, flat on her back, trying to pass as a boy jockey; Elizabeth Taylor fund-raising as national chair of the American Foundation for AIDS Research.

Her Oscar for *BUtterfield 8* was supposedly a sympathy prize, awarded because she had almost died. The scar, like her Oscar, proves that she is a power, that she has passed through puberty and ritual scarification. Elizabeth Taylor debuted as a child, and made films during every stage of her physical development. Consequently, her films are a piecemeal commentary on the meanings of a body's maturation, and the mysteries of that abrupt descent or nosedive we call puberty, when, by acquiring the stigmata of secondary sexual characteristics, we're deep-frozen into gender.

8.

Elizabeth Taylor's voice doesn't match her body; critics pan her acting on the grounds of vocal incongruity. She has a vestigial British accent; her voice sometimes curdles, as when she screams at the end of *Suddenly, Last Summer*, and we hear a dip or hollow or indentation inside the scream, and her scarf, blowing in the screen wind, covers her throat.

Critic Brendan Gill wrote in *The New Yorker* that *Cleopatra* would have made a great silent film. Elizabeth Taylor is an "effective" Cleopatra (what is the effect?) until she speaks. Her voice kills her as icon, and brands her as "a ward heeler's wife screeching at a block party." Critic Judith Crist condemns Taylor's voice in *Cleopatra* for rising "to fishwife levels," and associates this shrillness with her physicality: "She is an entirely physical creature, no depth of emotion apparent in her kohl-laden eyes. . . ." *BUtterfield 8* opens with a long voiceless sequence; Taylor as Gloria wakes up beside a blue phone off the hook; and Taylor stays off the hook, too, silently smoking, brushing her teeth and rinsing her mouth with liquor, writing "No Sale" on the mirror, stealing a mink from the closet of her trick's wife. *Secret Ceremony* and *Ash Wednesday* have long sequences without dialogue.

The scar on Elizabeth Taylor's throat demonstrates her indomitability, her survival, but it also announces the limits of her voice, or the mutual exclusivity of these two experiences: seeing a star, and hearing a star.

9.

In *A Place in the Sun*, Elizabeth Taylor's face is a blotter for gay beauty. She doesn't shut her features against her gay costar; she listens to Montgomery Clift and admits affinity with that lovely, homoerotic, pining loner. (Clift's biographer, Patricia Bosworth, thinks that one source of their affinity was hirsuteness. Hollywood couldn't tolerate body hair, which took away cinematic skin's connection to the inanimate—to sculpture, canvas, screen.) Taylor reflects Clift's beauty back to him and makes it speak: difficult in 1951 for a male body or face to radiate loveliness, to solicit desire, and to remain motionless and acquiescent while we stare.

In 1956, after a dinner party at Elizabeth Taylor's house, Montgomery Clift drove down the hill, and his car crashed; she arrived at the scene and found him bloody and mutilated, his head swollen, his face turned to pulp, and she reached into his mouth to pull out a tooth that was hanging by a thread and cutting his tongue. Thought it happens outside cinema, that image of Liz's hand in Monty's mouth is the inheritance of anyone who looks to Elizabeth Taylor for a complex and not a schematic sense of gender and sexuality: admire her lack of shame (no rubber gloves), her willingness to reach into the maw of his suffering; admire Liz before her years of "gluttony" reaching into another's mouth; admire her understanding of the "scar" underpinning star status, Monty's car crash preceding and prefiguring her scar. She liked Clift's ruined face, thought it more "poignant."

His accident tore *Raintree County* in half. Some shots (mostly interiors) show him before the accident, but other shots show him afterward: face frozen, jaw wired, he has lost his looks and his kinesis. Clift's crash disrupts the film's narrative—the temporality we're supposed to trust, to make our own; for us, *Raintree County* is ripped into Before and After, a schism written on the gay star's face. We reedit the film in our heads, to construct an alternative, sensationalist chronology, to figure out when the scenes were shot, to place each scene against the real backdrop of the crash. (Similarly, we'll reshuffle the scenes of Liz's later films to arrange them on a thin/fat axis; she gains and loses weight during filming, destroying realism, or introducing the higher realism of the star's body.)

The schism in *Raintree County* between Clift's perfect face and his ruined face gives us a literal image for his closet, divided between onscreen heterosexuality and offscreen homosexuality. (Another closet, another crash: In *Giant*, the film she made right before *Raintree County*, she is cast opposite closeted Rock Hudson and bi James Dean, who dies in a car crash right after filming ends.)

In *Raintree County*, Elizabeth Taylor's character has problems of her own. She imagines that she is the daughter of an African American slave: In childhood, her parents died in a fire, from which she saved a doll with a half-melted face. The doll's divided countenance is symbol of the Liz character's fear that she is racially "mixed," and it is also an image of Clift's closet and of Clift's accident, which divided his face and made his screen demeanor effortful, as if every moment he were considering, before the camera, the problems and agonies of presenting a "pretty but ruined" gay face to the world.

In *Raintree County*, morose Montgomery Clift must lovingly extract Elizabeth Taylor's secret. He is her husband, but he behaves like her shrink: he tries to make her remember what happened long ago in the fire. But because Hollywood confines him in the closet, he depends on Elizabeth Taylor *not* remembering, *not* speaking.

10.

Elizabeth Taylor, in her first two Tennessee Williams movies, *Cat on a Hot Tin Roof* and *Suddenly, Last Summer*, is a nymphomaniac with a taste for gay men; her sexual hungers function as a tuning fork, setting the pitch of male bodily catastrophes. During the filming of *Cat*, an actual event underscored her link to male disaster: her husband Mike Todd died in a crash of his private plane, named *Lucky Liz*. In *Cat*, Maggie (Taylor) knows Brick's (Paul Newman's) gay secret, but the screenplay can't tell it, and this enforced silence drives Maggie nearly mad. She tries to open the closet: in one of her climactic "cure" scenes, in which she remembers the trauma that she has repressed or that her family has forbidden her to reveal, she says, "The laws of silence won't work about Skipper and us . . . I'm going to say this. . . . It's got to be told and you never let me tell it!"

Cat on a Hot Tin Roof makes homosexuality seem illogical or lunatic. Paul Newman won't touch Elizabeth Taylor. What a waste! Taylor embodies a sexuality all dressed up with no place to go: she is a melancholy figurehead for the lost energies of Tennessee Williams's gay generation. Elizabeth Taylor's voluptuousness hurts; to be sexually hungry, according to the Taylor mythology, is to be an animal (Nibbles the chipmunk, Pie the horse, Lassie the dog, and now Maggie the cat)—or a queer child who, living outside heterosexuality, images he or she lives outside alloeroticism, too, and is therefore "doomed" to autoeroticism. (Auto Eroticism: Elizabeth Taylor drives a beautiful blue car in *Cat on a Hot Tin Roof*, the same baby blue as the princess phone in the opening scene of *BUtterfield 8*; she drives an orange convertible in *BUtterfield 8*, and, at the film's climax, hits a highway roadblock and dies.)

In *Suddenly, Last Summer*, again Elizabeth Taylor maintains a gay man's secret—her cousin Sebastian's. (The actor who plays Sebastian is unbilled, and almost entirely invisible.) Katherine Hepburn (Sebastian's mother) wants surgeon Montgomery Clift (Dr. Cukrowicz) to lobotomize Liz, to slice out Liz's knowledge of Sebastian's homosexuality. Clift stands to gain by silencing the gay secret: if he operates, Hepburn will give him money for a new hospital. But he is a noble ear, a sacred listener, as in *I Confess*, another closet part; he wants to help Taylor remember Sebastian's death.

Sebastian, a gay man, was torn to pieces by a horde of native boys he was accustomed to paying for sexual favors. After Taylor saw the boys devour him, she hysterically imagined that the world was devouring *her*. Later, the media will imagine Elizabeth Taylor to be a devouring mouth: they will locate her outrageousness in her size and hunger. The boys point to their mouths, asking for bread. Deprived of bread, they will eat Sebastian instead. Because Sebastian, like his saintly namesake, may enjoy arrows and mutilation, his castration/death is a sexual high, like a boy who hangs himself while jerking off. "Eating" may be code for gay oral sex and, by extension, homosexuality itself, but "eating," in this plot, is gay bashing. Additionally, the mob of boys murdering Sebastian represents Elizabeth Taylor's fans. Liz's dilemma: Do I want to be looked at? Are my fans going to eat me alive? To stare at Elizabeth Taylor is to eat her: critic

Andrew Sarris compared watching close-ups of Monty and Liz in *A Place in the Sun*, to "gorging on chocolate sundaes." When I look longingly at a photograph of Clift and Taylor taking a break from filming *A Place in the Sun*, I am beyond sundaes: I am eating time itself.

In *Suddenly*, Elizabeth Taylor accidentally enters a rec room of madmen, who leer at her through coke-bottle glasses and reach up to the gangplank to maul her legs; she is vulnerable to voyeurism, just as Sebastian is vulnerable to cannibalism. In a scandalous scene, Sebastian makes Liz expose her body in a flimsy white bathing suit, to procure boys for him. But in the final sequence, she jettisons her body and becomes just a head, a talking cure. As Liz describes Sebastian's dismemberment, her face, without her body, is juxtaposed on the screen with footage of the crowd of boys pursuing Sebastian up a hill to devour him, while her problematic voice, the voice that belies her voluptuousness, narrates the story of Sebastian's gay immolation: "It looked as if they had devoured him, torn bits of him away and stuffed them in their gobbling mouths." If we urge Liz to lose weight, if we value Liz's slenderness and not her plumpness, we are siding with Hepburn, and wishing Liz to be lobotomized, to lose a "heaviness" (a secret) that weighs her down: the weight on her chest is a scene of fatal homoerotic devouring. She resists lobotomy by remembering the lost scene, by outing Sebastian, by screaming. But, at the end, the closet returns: when she walks offscreen with Clift, we understand that they are now a couple. Clift has been cured of his homosexuality by Taylor's memory aria; now, on-screen, he wants Liz, though in life they were "just friends."

After *Suddenly*, Liz plays Gloria Wandrous, almost dies, gets a tracheotomy, recovers, displays her scar, wins an Oscar, and moves on to *Cleopatra*, where the gay secret becomes so loathsomely heavy that the media turn on Liz and invest her body with the imagery of waste. It took a movie as huge and pointless as *Cleopatra* to display the engorged nature of the secret, which could only speak through cinematic circumlocution, through waste, and through the body of a queen, Elizabeth Taylor's body, that surpasses what we expect of visual pleasure.

11.

The world pretended to be outraged by Elizabeth Taylor's adulterous liaison with Richard Burton; to be outraged by Elizabeth Taylor stealing

Eddie Fisher from Debbie Reynolds (BLOODTHIRSTY WIDOW LIZ VAM-
PIRES EDDIE, read one headline); but the fiercer scandal is *Cleopatra* itself.
The film has no meaning more multiple than the pleasure of watching
Elizabeth Taylor in Egyptian drag. Don't sneer at that pleasure. There are
too few occasions for publicly indulging that taste—a taste for nothing
in the body of something. Judith Crist wrote in the *New York Herald Tri-
bune* wrote, "Certainly, if you want to devote the best part of four hours
to looking at Elizabeth Taylor in all her draped and undraped physical
splendor, surrounded by elaborate and exotic costumes and sets, all in the
loveliest of colors, this is your movie." This is my movie. I loved *Cleopatra* (even before I saw it) because here at last was a movie as large and
extravagant and wasteful as every love. Here was a movie in which Liz,
not subsumed, embodied the whole system; nor are we subsumed. The
movie crowns us little Cleopatras for loving Liz. I anticipated *Cleopatra*
as a chance to prove to the world (as if the world were listening) that Liz
was grand and that I was grand, that we, together, were huger than old
definitions of star and kid.

In particular I loved the picture of Liz signing her *Cleopatra* contract:
she is wearing black suede or silk gloves, a simple black dress, and pearls,
and her hair is jet; seated, she's flanked by studio executives, who humbly
stand; she is absolutely in power, though she also seems to be signing her
life away.

We pretend it is a joke that Liz is monumental; but I have news for
you. She really *is* monumental.

What Elizabeth Taylor couldn't remember, in her films from the late
1950s, was the gay secret surrounding her (Montgomery Clift's, James
Dean's, Rock Hudson's); but she was also offering *amnesia* as a substitute
for history, and for the responsibilities that come with memory. *What happened? I don't remember. I can't remember. Even if I remembered, and told you
what happened, you wouldn't believe me. So I will forget history, and give you
costumes instead—or give you my body.*

12.

Elizabeth Taylor's bottom lip droops, as if it were a rose petal burdened by
a raindrop. The lip's underside—I think it's called a "bleb"—is bulbous,
shining, hungry, full of gravity and lip gloss, sick of shadows. It wants to
fall down, to rest, to speak.

13.

In *Cleopatra*, Elizabeth Taylor knows male weakness. She spies on Rex Harrison as Caesar and watches him fall down in epileptic convulsions. She gives Caesar the severed head of his beloved Pompey. With the aid of her seeress, played by the demented-looking Pamela Brown, Elizabeth Taylor hallucinates the scene of Caesar's assassination. She watches Richard Burton fall for a double of Liz at the banquet on a barge; poor Dick kisses the Liz double—not a convincing stand-in, but he believes the ruse. Elizabeth Taylor is a spy in her own house, and we understand her spy nature because her eyes are so compelling and huge, and because *Cleopatra* is shot in Todd-AO, for which she held the patent; because of Todd-AO, and because of her astronomical salary, the film is literally shot through her pocketbook's eyes. She is the seeing center, the pipe in the plumbing where all the funds are routed, the golden one who winks, who knows why everything is going wrong.

Everything went wrong with *Cleopatra*. That is its charm. England's hairdressers struck, because Elizabeth Taylor insisted on importing Sydney Guilaroff to do her hair. The production company started to shoot *Cleopatra* before the film was cast, or the script was written, and had to scrap expensive footage. Elizabeth Taylor almost died, and the production shut down entirely, and started again, but in another country. Executives were fired. Twentieth Century Fox sued its stars. Elizabeth Taylor sued Fox. The film was the costliest, and the longest, ever made. Eventually, the director cut it down to two four-hour-long movies, but Fox insisted on pruning the unwholesome mass into a single truncated, hard-to-follow epic that, though bloated, remains a fragment—suggesting a chance to stare at Elizabeth Taylor *at greater length* (but we never get to stare enough, the moment of staring always stops). One reviewer suggested that the movie be called *The Amputee*.

Elizabeth Taylor's nearly fatal illness (the tracheotomy, the Sleeping Beauty moment) haunted *Cleopatra*'s production. The film project was a disease: in his diary, producer Walter Wanger called the film "a cancer that would destroy us all." Elizabeth Taylor described it in her autobiography as "an illness one had a very difficult time recuperating from." She writes, "The whole thing was sick: people spying, spying on each other, unseen factions." Taylor also connected the film to waste and vomit. "God, that was a filthy house," she wrote about Casa Taylor, the Roman villa she inhabited during the making of *Cleopatra* (a house so large she had a separate room for her wigs alone); "one day the sewer erupted and the whole kitchen was floating in sewage." During the making of the film, her stomach was pumped (she had overdosed on pills), and after she saw the film for the first time, she vomited: "When it was over, I raced back to the Dorchester Hotel and just made it into the downstairs lavatory before I vomited." To say "*Cleopatra* is a piece of shit" is to offer an aesthetic judgment, and to make a reasonable if bitter assessment of the fantasies that Elizabeth Taylor's body has provoked during her career.

Though an amputee, *Cleopatra* was a blimp. According to Taylor, "And what ballooned the unbelievably Wagnerian, insane quality of everything was the insanity going on at the *Cleopatra* set every day." But there was a meaning, a moral, to the ballooning. The film's immensity represented Liz's independence and power, and the irreal, engulfing, and nearly psychedelic dimension that overtakes the viewer of *Cleopatra* and that overwhelmed its makers: the outer space on the other side of gender, an empire of signs, like the kingdom of toy boats over which Queen Cleopatra reigns. (The men in the movie fight real battles, while Liz plays with tokens.) An ambulance was kept on standby when Taylor played her last scene, "lest Elizabeth collapse as the shock of postproduction reality set in." Was *Cleopatra* the sickness, or was reality the sickness? And do we, watching *Cleopatra*, inhabit reality, or are we the sick spies, like Liz's maid in Casa Taylor, who buried a camera in her bouffant? Liz discovered the camera and fired the traitor.

In *Cleopatra*, Elizabeth Taylor wore sixty-five different costumes, each an event. The movement from outfit to outfit is a dramaturgy, though *Cleopatra* is to cathartic tragedy what an escalator is to a hike up a steep hill. We move and we do not move; the structure beneath us climbs, but our feet are motionless. In one remarkable scene, she changes costumes between quips: "Is it wise?" Dick asks Liz, who is wearing costume #43, and when she retorts, "Is it wise?" (reaction shot) lo and behold she has advanced to costume #44! History advances and does not advance.

Of the attention to Taylor's costumes in *Ash Wednesday*, critic Vincent Canby disapprovingly writes, "Mostly the film is interested in what Barbara [Liz] is going to wear next. This is not a male chauvinist's conception of a woman, but her hairdresser's, full of envy, awe, and superficial compassion." Canby condescends to the hairdresser's vision, but we should revere films like *Cleopatra* that speak to the hairdresser.

Liz won't admit us to her interior; Liz won't produce sensations of depth and authenticity. She conveys naturalness, but she is also distracted, glossy. Her stardom has become lumbersome. Elizabeth Taylor is the economic and aesthetic scapegoat for *Cleopatra's* apparent failure to be dramatically convincing; she is blamed for stopping drama dead in its tracks. She is the enemy of *Cleopatra's* ambition to revise history into a series of romantic personal encounters; but by flattening the film's historical ambitions, she tells a more real story. She shows us that *Cleopatra* is about women's bodies in 1961, 1962, and 1963, about gay men, about race, about power, and about waste.

Any glimpses of "truth" that we get in *Cleopatra*—the truth of queens, gowns, hats, corpses, scars, breasts, butts—we owe to Elizabeth Taylor's refusal to be "deep." For its lack of depth, I adore the scene where her maids give her a body rub while she lies on her stomach; we can see the side of her breast, but not the nipple, and her body seems so soft it is almost genderless, no sex in sight, just a blank surface, like the first scene in John Waters's *Multiple Maniacs*, when, seeing Divine from the back as an odalisque, we almost believe that Divine is a woman. In the early scenes of *Cleopatra*, the Todd-AO color process is so spanking and absolute that it audibly breathes, and Liz is supposed to be nineteen years old, not yet the weary diplomatic queen, not yet in love with Antony; when she stands next to her femmy brother Ptolemy and his loyal eunuch, her skin is so creamy I want to eat it—if I may confess my own unremarkable cannibalistic fantasy, my association of seeing and eating. To stare at Liz is to ask, like Oliver Twist, for more, and to receive it.

A reviewer wrote of *Cleopatra*, "At four hours it is the world's longest coming attraction for something that will never come." The film's edgy, bored foreplay teases us into wanting to come, but our desire suffers no release. Elizabeth Taylor is extravagant as a person (that is why she cost Fox so much money), and her body is literally an *extra vagance*: she has wandered beyond bounds, and we long to follow her into that far shoal of embodiment.

"Oooh, look, Liz has a gay son!" shouted a queen at a revival-house screening of *Cleopatra*, in response to the appearance of Liz and a little Italian extra on the Sphinx. In a later scene, Rex Harrison tries to teach the kid how to walk like a man, as if *Cleopatra* were a remake of *Tea and Sympathy*; Taylor watches the boy at Rex Harrison's School of Masculinity, and wonders why the boy is wasting his time. She is always, implicitly, winking; and she actually winks at the end of the procession into Rome, an expensive scene, when the crowd of extras expressed their love for Elizabeth Taylor, and their tolerance for her peccadillo, despite the Vatican's thundering protest, by shouting "Leeez! Leeez! *Baci! Baci!*" (Perversely, I imagine the extras are yelling "Lez!") Of the "Leeez" processional, *Newsweek* writes, "To top a ten-minute procession, costing hundreds of thousands, with a wink is fairly tricky business." Indeed, Liz is playing a trick. All the spectacle, as history, is garbage, and she knows it. When Rex Harrison as Caesar unrolls the carpet containing Cleopatra, and Elizabeth Taylor falls out of it, and arches her back like Maggie the cat, or as if it were the first scene of *BUtterfield 8* again and she were rising from a bad night's sleep, hungover, alone in her bedroom, no one watching, then the nonsense of narrative falls apart, and we are facing, without blinders, an extravagance.

In *Ash Wednesday*, someone asks Liz, "Was it fun?" and she replies, with a wistful morbidity that I admire, "No, not fun, but on the verge of fun."

I am not Liz, but I am on the verge of Liz. I can't arrive at Elizabeth Taylor. How would I recognize that arrival, except that I will have ceased to be? I may look forward to a life entirely founded on reveries that begin and end with Elizabeth Taylor, but I am also in the midst of that life, even as I call it a future life. I will never know a life innocent of her singular, specific beauty—a beauty of 1962 and 1952, a torpor I can locate and research and review, but never change. No one, least of all myself, can alter my relation to Elizabeth Taylor—utterly private, utterly historical.

With Liz's Cleopatra, I murmur, "You are not supposed to look at me. No one is supposed to see me."

14.

Elizabeth Taylor as Cleopatra has an Asian maid, but Hollywood couldn't cast an African-American actress as Cleopatra, even though Leontyne Price opened the new Metropolitan Opera House at Lincoln Center in 1966 with a world premiere of Samuel Barber's *Antony and Cleopatra*—itself, like the movie *Cleopatra*, an expensive flop.

In *Raintree County*, Liz thinks she has forgotten her race (she goes mad because she believes she is black); in *Suddenly, Last Summer* and *Cat on a Hot Tin Roof*, she has forgotten homosexuality, or is forbidden to speak it.

Cleopatra's whiteness is the film's silent scandal—never mentioned, though the media scrutinized every other detail of the film's production and of its stars' conduct.

15.

After *Cleopatra*, Liz had to turn into a flop, to prove that Fox's investment in Liz-as-potentate was a miscalculation. After *Cleopatra*, she was never believable as anything except a "shrew" or a woman whom America compelled to lose weight. I find disheartening the photograph of a reduced lovely Liz beaming beside brain-dead Reagan after a stage performance of *The Little Foxes*; Liz's shed pounds seem a "figure" (as in full-figured) for the violent cutbacks and budget trimmings of Reagan's administration—the rhetorical emphasis on "spending cuts" and on stopping "liberal waste."

16.

Elizabeth Taylor's cleavage is "natural" (her body is built that way), but it is also produced. The camera emphasizes it; costume reinforces it. Her cleavage—as image—is a fact of culture. It is a darkness dividing two white shapes; it is a displaced cinematic representation of the vagina that even a scandalous film like *Cleopatra* can't show but that it wants, everywhere, to suggest; it is the schism of the Clift face after his accident, or the doll with half-melted face that Taylor cossets in *Raintree County*; it is the ground of an income (and all grounds are divided); it is the place where the camera lingers in the later films, when she is no longer Elizabeth Taylor of the 1950s, and so the camera, still wanting to make a fortune off her, demands cleavage as signature, proof that she is still Liz. Her films make much of her breasts; but cinema is the art of cutting, and so wasteful films like *Cleopatra*, which required severe editing, care more about her cleavage, about the process of compressing breasts to describe a line, a space.

Cleavage is very 1960s: it shows off the new permissiveness. (Look! We can reveal most of Elizabeth Taylor's breasts!) Cleavage is not nudity. Cleavage is a promise: not sight, but on the verge of sight.

Staring at cleavage, I am not straight, but on the verge of straight.

I pour resources of time and attention into her cleavage. I am not specifically aroused by it, but I am involved with it. It calls forth in me an elemental, curious response: it evokes, from my depths, a *yes*, a giggle. Her relationship to her cleavage—wise, indifferent—makes me want to walk into bright sunlight with a more positive attitude, makes me sick of equivocation and mirthlessness. Her cleavage, beyond attainment, beyond prose, is not sublime, but is what we bring to it, and is on the verge of me. Not me, but on the verge of me. I am not the only one who has looked at Elizabeth Taylor, not the only man or woman who has turned to her for the first, rudimentary lesson in how to imagine elevation, and how to endure division.

NOTE

1. Postscript, 1998: Elizabeth Taylor had a brain tumor, which was removed. She agreed to be photographed after surgery, bald, sans wig, for *Life* magazine, an extraordinary act of star abjection, shamelessness, and solidarity with the world's other sufferers. Said Liz: "I won't dye my hair for a while. I'll let it grow out white. In the meantime, I don't mind being bald. For years the gossip sheets have been claiming I've had face-lifts. Now they'll have to eat their words. Look. *No scars!*

HYSTERESIS

Elizabeth Hatmaker

Sources:

Good Luck, Miss Wyckoff (1979 theatrical release) D: Marvin Chomski, Bel Air/Gradison Productions. MMPA:R Release via Hal Roach Classic Videos 1986 as *The Shaming*. Starring: Anne Heywood, Donald Pleasence, Robert Vaughn, Carolyn Jones, John Lafayette. Copyright uncertain.

Photograph. subject: Carolyn Bryant seated outside the law offices of Breland and Whitten. Copyright 1955. *Memphis Commercial Appeal*. Viewed w/o permissions.

1.

A film plot. An abusive sexual relationship b/t white spinster schoolteacher and a young black janitor, a student at the local junior college, in 1954 Kansas, near Wichita. Complicates her grips with sexuality, heterodyne, emotion. Coping with violence is a violent plot. First seen, edited for Midwest, on St. Louis KPLR channel 11 at 11ish and I am like 13 or so. I am myopic, archaic, I am insomniac. I watch at decibels below my parent's eyelid, I push ear to static light. I am in A/V Club at school. I am, TV says, to buy furniture, two brothers high atop the Gateway Arch wave, and then I hear KPLR movie intro music upper sax, Spyro Gyra's

"Morning Dance" the gateway to Midwestern late night easy lay liberalism like grainy local ideology, low pitch, anonymous; my parents sleep through as I murmur in response. Later, 1994 in Massachusetts, lonely and bespeckled, salvation is vodka and a Friday night deal at City Video in Porter Sq. Miz Wyckoff again, uncut, this time called *The Shaming*. First video in which I see a full-grown black man naked. I have insomnia like history stretched over my head. Scrambled sound, grainy video replay. I keep my TV on low sound. Plot: A teacher like me, like a shard of lyric line. The film is like a wandering signal. Mixed and hesitant review—IMDb database source. I hear it like history muffled on the magnetic strip.

February 07. LeFlore County, MS. Grand jury refuses to indict Carolyn Bryant for manslaughter. "Her composition had/ disintegrated. That, although the pattern prevailed,/ The breaks were everywhere." Her picture: a woman suffering from eye strain, dark circles, set mouth. I half hear an imagined cracked voice emerging to tell about white woman desire, about failed "heterosexual whiteness." I push ear to photo. I once saw a picture of a 3/12 Wurlitzer organ circa 1920, its keys like eyes, pedals like broken teeth, like such a cracked argument before sound on disk, post on sill, sound on film, before high head-to-tape speed. The sounds of the century lag behind the desires of this white woman's organs. I listen hard for her confession. I am 37 in '07, a teacher, a white man's white woman, 16 mm in every way. My archival skills suck but I can splice tape. A fan of the paracinema in the alterity of my basement. I spent $16.98 plus shipping from Amazon to own. I want to own my own audience, my own goon squad. My comma is my slit on the material.

In the film, I hear subcutaneous. Pedagogy fingers through organ key through [hesitate] moan of door, moan of bloody Kansas, of loneliness, whiteness, intertitle reads *doctor tells teacher her cunt is almost dried up.* A joke you've heard. How many virgins does it take to screw well you know? The laughter covers over the punch, mangled by uncertain desire. In my desire I hear drone of Bel Air Productions, flute oboe voice strung taut on the tape. Ernest Gold Music. Vibe memory buzz. Hum over wind on mono; a lost city for ages. Lex Salus Populi Supreme Est. Adult whisper over rusty Mozart as Wyckoff and I cry softly at our inability to understand men's intentions. Sub B hiss motif of bad video transfer is ecstasy of dissonant tears. Trumpet overdubs distraught syntagm as Wyckoff teaches

Latin to disinterested Midwestern students. This school is wired for sound. "Dramatic music for your dramas, comic music for your comedies!" says a commercial. The city of Pompeii is buried in y Fe2 O3, CnO2, Nickel Cobalt, Magnetite.

Wyckoff is lonely, virginal, ripe for technological perversion. She devises a wideband, low deviation, low carrier f.m. signal with frequency components within the pass-band of the tape system. She visits white man gynecologist. Appropriate gloves hat dress. Beyond my glasses I see watered organs and voices. Her vaginal wiring betrays. White man's head falls below the beat of the speculum and as he rises I see him, the actor who played Napoleon Solo: The Affair of an Older Adventure. He offers a prescription; his tuning fork hits white vibrato. *You Should Get Laid. See a Shrink.* Identify. Define. Divide. In the next scene, behind his back, blurry photos of his loving white women denounce the spinster, the virgin, the dry, the syntax of endless noun clusters. He himself is blind to her. Later scene: I see her Friday night = Chinese food with other virgins, slides from summer trip to Italy, movie starring Marlon Brando, white man so sexy and heavy-lipped he's got to be poor and different and not from around here laugh the other virgins. Men with names ending in o. Affairs of photographed women in other photographic settings. Exotica of appliqué flowers shatter and sing on her proper collar. The picture snaps momentarily and realigns on the head.

2.

She is a good analysand. I overhear a phone call from Wyckoff to a Wichita psychoanalyst. Hands to throat like a wounded harpsichord—analytic dissonance lends decay, a drink and a quick decision. I recall bad dates in MA—moldering tablecloth, a candle, a drink and a quick decision. Dates are ashen commas. On the screen a bus ride to Wichita, a clever Eisenhower interstate highway system spreads out, streets in Wichita on a fall night, cities full of men set in ash, establishing a promise to virgins of all spaces and situations:

vermouth sophistication integration an office made of wood far-off cities the idea of liberal Danish modernism at discount on TV, fucking men in color w/sound, and psychoanalysis on the jukebox to lay out my confession. Quarter and Selection: the music of second-rate Midwestern club circa 1955. Ike Quebec and Orchestra, lovely as a beautiful date I can't remember, as progressive as Brown v. in far back history, a nostalgia for long dead musical organs, for better vision, clear video transfer with a faded and fragile soundtrack, ownership of the mechanisms of history, pulse width control of the a.c. supply. Strains of green-eye, anonymous tremolo. Bryant is either guilty or innocent, but something, the endless splices of continuity, comma, guilt. But this is my desire.

As Wyckoff conveys her primal scene I spy the teacher's beloved father as a masochist or a rapist, her mother's desire unclear: "a date not ending in sexual satisfaction." Later, the memory of her masochist father will become the idea of her own flesh lynched and burned. I'll be with you in this scene! says Carolyn Bryant through another channel. My spy adventure. I wilt as I fall deeper in and out of sync.

3.

X-Cut. Being alone on a bus/possibility, a drum, harp, flute, a thoughtful fist in velvet,

confirmation of Bryant's white voice in the dark historic night, "yes, that's the one."

the possibility of musical signifier w/o value, the establishing sound so far beyond the sight line of horizon, loose wires in my abolition. Mono crackling mono. A finger pressing the signifier, tenderly if firmly.

4.

Wyckoff's voice sours over writhing = a conjugation of verbs, a movement of vowels. She is wounded by music and racism alike. Why would she? Why is short for Wyckoff. I suppose that's a joke. My insomnia damns the beat; decay is the attack of pure tone. No, that's wrong. Decay follows attack. AC/DC. A frequency with an AC bias. Inversion is mangling of the lyric sensibility, the "emotional backdrop." Track 5: Rape Theme. No, it's Mediterranean Sunset. It's a night without fear. No, it's not. "In melancholia it's the ego itself."

5.

The James "Buddy" Milton Highway welcomes you. Dead guardian of the city, memorialized for his trouble. Blood wires the state like a six-track TODD mixing board. For trouble. Kansas Interstate over fields, Dwight D. himself, the triggering towns, the minor tragedies along the way, the sound of deep trouble coming down the way from other cities, integration, miscegenation, yes I said it clear, Topeka, the cities of the East, Quebec and the jukebox, liberalism on top of LaFlore Co, MS. Wyckoff on a short bus ride to Wichita. An aerial shot shows preference for moving patterns live as levers on a mixing panel. Bass up 3 cm as treble is grazed 1.2 cm, only a mild deceleration of frequency.

How to open an over-determined scene? How many misogynists does it take to bury a woman alive? How taut the rope around a throat? When to scream and when to keep your mouth shut? The primal scene: our father's nose is bloody, our mother complicit. 1955 and no convictions and Bryant speaks in the nights of 2007. How to tell a joke? Advanced Electronics. The idea of young white girl looking through a partially open door. Ahhh a long time ago. Daddy naked w/bloody nose and green-eyed excitement. The idea of the white mother, the sound of her fist, the danger in her throat. Seeing him beaten after so long. Seeing students bored with history. Seeing threat and wanting to account for it as a white woman. The wires finally exposed, the tubing sheared clean. Progress is about tolerance and understanding. Buy my primal scene is mangled by pornography, just like everyone else, mangled on TV. Spyro Gyra wakes me tenderly to ache with apparatus.

The sound of psychoanalysis = the mechanized gurgling of confession. There is no sound to the consonants that break my round vowels. Slow, compressed, settling on the soundscape. The door never closes. The punch line is this: Far far off in the building desire traces, pipes to radiator, miles to rest, aural decay to broken flesh. You shouldn't fuck your students regardless of their race or affiliation. A limited and hesitant review. An audion tube. The shards of naked on lonely. Brown v. The song of pedagogy, a rhythm to reading out loud, test test, a signal path. I'd like to pretend it didn't matter.

Objects. Slides from Italy. Strained Eyeball. Women in other contexts, other pictures, para other picture like Paracinema. A spy drama. A joke about history itself. I splice in my white sleep. Ideology protects at waking suddenly if heads accurately positioned axially. R-2 return to bias.

6.

Wyckoff and the black man—the primal scene of the fifties and white girl late night confession. What white boys don't want to hear or know I saw. Miscegenation sounded like this: Scale up violin, parched scandal is an oboe bridging sadness on desks. A door closes behind a student, the black man, the film itself screams. The crackling of a radiator is an off-key bounty, a miracle of failed intertitle. Sweat the song out, those registers of metals of universal heating systems over lurching flesh. He'll brand her on that radiator later, the radiator looks like a Wurlitzer, like broken eyes and teeth on the lyric line. Strangely sweet, it is filmed. The scale matching is right. Lovers caught in auditory ash and I think he's beautiful. His skin is as shiny as Miss Wyckoff's satin blouse as shiny as splicing tape. The frequency decreases to low ground noise, race jumps servo head wheel. I am hearing a deviation frequency alone in 1986, 1994, 2007, 35, 16, 8, Super-8. Over and over. A reverberation. This is the fantasy.

No. I should say. It's all more conventional and white man–friendly. It's a slammed door, metal scraping metal, crackling ground noise, desks skidding, shattered flowerpot, he slaps her. *I think I'm bleeding.* I want to lose rape in this commutation, always, always, sharp intake, long decay. A slap. Certainly they would have lynched him for this. The melodrama points that way, *Birth of a Nation*, white fear fingering the highway system, X-cut. But she doesn't scream, point, demand justice because she's been good for the negro students, helped them get served in the cafeteria. She's not our mother. Maybe she knew they'd hate her all the same, rope or no. This is where the via leads. The signifier remains salient.

The primal scene again: a half open door, or a keyhole even, mother, a series of naked black men replace Father until suddenly I am Father and I am guilty. I see the rope transfer hands. Then mother in a photo array, a series of photos of Carolyn Bryant in which she appears to come to life, to slowly open her mouth and say. A blood root of the wires. Ernest Gold Music. A series of unmemorable dates with white men. An underpaid musician played for these moments, anonymous tremolo makes whiteness tolerable. Wires intertwine tubes in a crumbling Midwestern building. I know the fiction of wire sweat; we are all earnest in our desires.

The miscegenation scene again. I am dry. I choke on dried spit. I'm splicing this in rhythm I swear. Wyckoff wants to lose that rope or it is their nexus. Naked black man. And he's angry, also, in this film. No *yes ma'am*. Alternatively he is sweet. No reason. Bel Air Productions casts handsome black face, a strong body, hung like. Not right to objectify. A black student at the junior college with a scholarship. Equal opportunities they say. The Eisenhower Interstate System welcomes you. In my mind Miz Wyckoff becomes Buddy Milton at the door; I'm a white man gynecologist in my dreams, Carolyn Bryant tells a joke and I laugh. Two white brothers ride the Gateway. My need is for confession, for a spy drama, trouble, a musician in a jukebox, how many black men does it take to fill the signifier? Scenes with subtle paradigmatic and syntagmatic transformations. My voice is hoarse, broken attack and decay.

No, let's roll that fucker again again again. Being bored and white and soft-focus. Again. Is this paracinema enough? Trouble between feed and take-up spools; Carolyn Bryant is my viscous damping. I'm pressed up against rage in my parent's house, my apartment, my photo array.

7.

Curriculum explain Liberalism, The Lure of Miscegenation Is Evident in Pedagogy, The Superego Has Strong Links to the Rise of Stable Western Culture. Don't mix metaphors. No teaching with sex on the brain. Acting loco parentis, my life is a drink and a quick decision, an anonymous date, I need a vacuum guide, students all look alike, the decision to confess or to stay quiet and protected, a palm pressed into a scarred desk. The tape loops on. The pressure is on the lever, I murmur softly. Psychoanalysis can be practical advice too. *I take a drink once in a while, that doesn't mean I get caught with the bottle* replies Wyckoff's principal. The vacuum guide should have a fixed position. Playback. Record.

Getting caught. The door, the sharp intake, every primal scene is written as history on late-night TV, VHS, no DVD available at present time. (Amazon will contact via email if it becomes available.) I hear the breeze as Kansas decompresses. The sharp intake chalked and clear: *miz Wyckoff fucks niggers*. So what is the pitch of miscegenation in the dark? A rasping of wood or metal key or dull green eyes. The optic nerve under my closed eyelid. My ear to the machine, I hear a low B-flat wavering. A drone of stale prairie air pushed over my liberal sentiment. How to create is bound in local musicianship. Integration is a horizon, an audition tube of race, a wavering signal of past. Getting caught as an audience, the sync word indicates the direction of tape travel. "A failure to indict does not limit the future direction of justice."

THE VICTOR SALVA SCHOOL
OF FILM THEORY

Bard Cole

There are few things more intolerable than an intangible desire. It leaves only two choices: to substitute, through pretense, a tangible object; or to continue to pursue the intangible while pretending that your efforts serve another purpose altogether.

Neither choice helps a man attain that mysterious aim, but they make failure less humiliating.

They are also the basis for fiction—substitution and misdirection. And these two lines of fiction, crossed in a perpetual tension, form the x and y axis of hardcore porn—that is to say, all movies.

A tracking shot of the jockey shorts of a pubescent boy soft with baby fat and golden lighting as he strides down the upstairs hallway of an impossibly typical colonial-style suburban house. A second bedroom door swings open in the background so that another underwear-clad teenager can enter the shot—this one is taller, slightly older, slimmer; he fumbles for his nerdy wire-rimmed glasses. The camera pulls out. "Did it happen again?" he demands, not unkindly, hustling the younger kid into the shelter of his room. An older male, late teens early twenties, lurches into the frame. "What's going on?" "Quick," says the slim nerdy teen, and the chubby kid quickly strips off his jockey shorts and wads them up, hiding them. For a second or two, his bare buttocks are exposed.

Because they all tend to be blond and are walking around in their underwear in the upstairs of a well-appointed house, we deduce these are brothers. The narrative justification for this scene, the opening scene of the movie, is that it shows that the youngest brother has nightmares about clowns, prefiguring later developments in the film—after all, it is called *Clownhouse* (1989). While sleeping he has peed himself in terror, a fact that his gentle older brother wishes to protectively conceal from their oldest brother, who is a harsh stand-in for their absent parents.

But these are facts we assemble moments later, not during this unusual sequence which focuses so directly on the vulnerability of young bodies and the way clothing reveals as much as it obscures.

The oldest brother, around twenty, has the conventional good looks of a television lifeguard. The middle brother has some of the floppy-haired androgynous charm of the teenage River Phoenix. The actor looks to be somewhere between fifteen and eighteen.

The youngest brother, the one the most thoroughly ogled by the camera, is a pudgy adolescent with no visible hair on his legs. The actor is twelve. When the movie is not filming, he is performing sex acts with the director, who videotapes them.

When I was twelve, I came up with the idea of buttfucking. I can hypothesize now that this idea developed from overhearing an offhand joke about buttfucking but that is not what I actually recall. I remember coming up with the idea totally out of nowhere. I didn't know if it was really possible, if you would be able to kiss in that position, if a person's body would bend like that, but it seemed like a neat idea.

One of the earliest subjects to occur to the mind of a film director and to appeal to the tastes of the public, in the time when the length of movies was measured in seconds, was the kiss. It was likewise a popular subject among the college-age student filmmakers I knew as an undergraduate. Nothing could be more delightful than including a scene of two actors in intimacy in your student film, except for the moment of choosing the two actors from the realm of your social acquaintances.

What desire was being enacted when the student director chose the persons he would ask to kiss on his say-so for his camera? The person being kissed was perhaps someone the director would like to kiss; the person doing the kissing was a friend of the director, an equal—a proxy?

This seems too obvious when applied to my friend C., asking another male friend of ours, especially good-looking at that age, to kiss a girl we all liked, who was frequently comically flirty but ultimately non-committal. Despite awkward thoughts of boyfriends and girlfriends back home, we all knew they liked each other, but it gave C. an interesting experience of power to be the one who brought about their kissing.

But what was going on when he asked me to tie up a boy, J., in Christmas lights and French kiss him? My problem coming out in college was basically there weren't a lot of gay guys that were good enough for me. I guess it's the same thing, but what gave C. his motivation to force us to act out this scenario?

Nobody even had a TV in their room when I was in college. When we wanted to watch a movie, our own or one rented from the pharmacy in town, we'd reserve a viewing room at the library—seriously. Our parents back home had VCRs but we didn't think of getting our own, any more than we'd buy a cooking range or a lawnmower. We didn't feel the constant need for them. I had an electric typewriter with memory storage, and looked at pornography in magazine form. I did not watch an entire porn movie until I was at least twenty-two. This was, of course, a different age.

The essence of a hardcore porn movie is that people (actors, models, performers, prosubjects) engage in authentic sexual displays for a camera in order for that footage to be used in a movie that will be shown for the titillation of an audience.

As should be clear, this is a wide definition. Who are these people? What kind of displays can be judged as sexual? As authentic? What kind of reaction may be classified as titillation? What makes an audience?

With the slow, pause, and zoom features now available on DVD players, there are now a lot more porn movies out there. It is perfectly credible to me, for example, that the entire point of the movie *White Squall* (1996) was to frame a three-second-long shot of a distraught Ryan Phillippe on a bed on his hands and knees wearing soaking wet white jockey shorts with his ass angled toward the camera.

He is the youngest-looking of all the high-school-age "boys" on this character-building sailing jaunt, and from the beginning the attempt to portray his emotional vulnerability has been mingled with an interest in his vulnerable private parts. When he overcomes his fear of heights through impromptu scream therapy with Jeff Bridges and begins to climb the boat's rigging, the boy pisses his pants, dampening the front of his Kennedy-era khakis. All of the actors in the movie are too old by five years at least, and it is in part the attempt of physically and sexually mature young men to embody adolescent immaturity that gives the film its strange eroticism. In place of genuine teenage boys struggling toward physical and mental maturity, *White Squall* gives us a boatload of twink bottoms as if they are the same thing.

Take for comparison a shot in *Dodgeball* (2004) that showcases Justin Long down on his hands and knees in a tight bathing suit scrubbing a truck's tire for a bearish car wash customer openly ogling a young actor's boypussy. Despite providing a good outline of Long's gonads and perineum, the display does not read as erotic. It's a joke. There is no subterfuge to the display of his ass; that it is being ogled by its viewer is essential to the joke, and likely to arouse self-consciousness in any audience member temped to do the same—the ogler is particularly ugly and Long's character particularly obtuse. Nor does his red bathing suit encourage us to feel, as Phillippe's wet white shorts do, the warmth of the skin underneath. Additionally, the character's teenage vulnerability, such as it is, is treated comically and not sentimentally. He may be goofy, uncoordinated, and a touch naïve, but he is not weak, does not invite protection and love.

I have no doubt that everyone who worked on *White Squall*, from Ridley Scott on down, would deny that they were making a film about Ryan Phillipe's damp boypussy, but come on, lads—those underpants didn't pick out themselves. *White Squall* can only be as dirty-ass a jerkoff movie as it is because of its grasp of the idiom of the so-called "quality picture," in which innocence translates visually into the appearance of being sexually submissive, and in which familiar sentimental constructs substitute for complexity of character. It is a kind of emotional porn, in and of itself, that takes nice people and shows terrible things happening to them while pretending that there is some sort of deep and deliberate meaning that the story embodies. The quality picture, evoking literary models but without depth itself, is what we are left with since melodrama is split into TV movies and non-TV movies: in the old days, the whole shebang would have been called "weepers"—movies designed to evoke a particular physical response, the expulsion of a particular bodily fluid.

The transformation of desire that is personal and hidden to one that is manifest involves two critical fictions.

First, there is the fiction that the desire (for example) to kiss someone is a straightforward and self-sufficient desire, adequate in and of itself, not merely the outward sign of a complex of desires—for human
warmth; for love; for security; for an ego boost; for power; for status; to
name just a few probable constituent desires. This complexity is obscured
in the simple apparent clarity of the visible and performed kiss.

Second, there is the fiction that the opportunity for the kiss (to continue with the example) has come into being through an external process
of reasoning—that the kiss is necessary, proper, and at root impersonal.
While the director does have a reason for wanting two people to kiss, it
is a reason of economy; aesthetics; truth; symbolism; good storytelling;
proper imitation of an admired model; or popular expectations. That the
director himself, considered as an individual person with a history and
psychology, desires the kiss—this is the formulation that must be avoided
at all costs.

This was the real crime for which director Victor Salva was sen-
tenced to three years in prison: a crime against filmmaking.

Some people in the world would be happiest knowing they are in no
way different from everybody else in the world. Some people won't rest
until they've proven their uniqueness in the world. Some people go back
and forth. Most people try to reason their way out of that dilemma, pretending that they don't have any crazy longing for absolute belonging or
absolute solitude. They're liars, but who isn't?

There's two kinds of people, as Divine said in the 1972 movie *Pink
Flamingos*—filmed surprisingly near my childhood home—my kind of
people, and assholes.

When Jerry Falwell and the remnants of the Moral Majority called
attention to the fact that Disney had employed a convicted child molester
to direct a movie about an adolescent boy—this was in 1995—I only felt
my usual raw contempt for Jerry Falwell, who also worried about characters on children's television shows encouraging children to be gay and
would later assert that terrorists had struck the United States on Sept. 11,
2001, because the Lord had withdrawn his protection due to the tolerance of feminism, homosexuality, and reproductive rights.

It was years later, when a photographer friend of mine played his
VHS copy of *Clownhouse* and told me the story behind it, that I realized
that in this instance Falwell was completely justified; that giving that man

the opportunity to create a movie like *Powder* (1995), which takes the motif of the vulnerable, special boy to grotesque new heights, was an act of stunning, amoral indifference on the part of Disney—which was, at the time *Powder* was being made, helping to mold a young Britney Spears into a future celebrity train wreck.

Only some porn movies have plots and scripts, but the idea of porn movies having plots and scripts is central to the general perception of porn movies.

The pervasive idea is of porn movies being stereotyped facsimiles of mainstream films with sex scenes inserted higgledy-piggledy. The average person knows that porn movies are called things like *The Sperminator, Edward Penishands, Bareback Mountain,* or *Hairy Pussy and the Sorcerer's Bone,* even if he or she has never seen a porn movie in his or her life.

When the gay porn actor known as Joey Stefano died of a drug overdose in November of 1994, he became the savior of the gay porn industry.

It's very obvious that some young actors have been served up, with garnish, as teen sexpots, to be the objects of desire. Ryan Phillippe, whose first notable role was as a gay teenager on *One Life To Live,* is one such. More recently, Disney gave the world—as a gift or a sacrifice, who can say—Zac Efron, in his shiny superficial constructedness a cross between an eighties teen heartthrob like John Stamos or Rob Lowe and the Mattel doll Totally Hair Ken. There are plenty of teenage girls and gay men who would love to fuck these guys raw, for much the same reason that there are people who'd like to munch down a bag of Doritos. That's what they're marketed for.

My tastes tend to lean toward the Justin Longs of the cinema. Today best known for portraying a Macintosh computer, Justin is the hot nerd of his generation, and was first noted by pervs—that is to say, me and my photographer friend—as a sort-of-cute teenage computer nerd in *Galaxy Quest* (1999). Long was already in his early twenties when portraying a kid obsessed with the details of a cancelled science fiction series. It is not at all obvious that we were intended to want to fuck him but it is clear to me now that one cannot dismiss the strength of the audience who wants to fuck Justin Long.

Since I will never meet either of them, it seems ludicrous to think

I prefer Long to Phillippe because Phillippe is out of my league, looks-wise, but it may just be possible. Appreciation is always shaped by experience, and I certainly have more experience with marginally sexy nerdy guys than with perfectly sculpted Adonises. When I was twelve I used to beat off looking at pictures of Calvin Klein models but it's been years since I've found anything especially erotic about posed pictures of perfectly well-developed bodies.

In *Sex, Lies, and Videocassettes* (1989), Joey Stefano starred as an aspiring model who is pressured to perform on the casting couch by Hollywood sleazebags. His story is contrasted with that of another aspiring model who willingly and without fuss takes part in a straightforward porn movie and is rewarded by a mainstream acting career.

Stefano, who bore a passing resemblance in type to popular young actors like Tom Cruise or Matt Dillon, was celebrated for being the first bankable "bottom." Before Joey Stefano, it was believed that only a cocksman could be a star, the holes he fucked being incidental and interchangeable.

Gay men—so it was claimed—idolized the phallus, the symbol of masculine power, and their favorite porn stars were hypermasculine figures who fucked readily and refused to acknowledge any such thing as sexual identity. They could not, or would not, identify with someone who took a dick, demonstrating pleasure in it—a faggot, in other words. Stefano proved them all wrong.

The ideal porn movie is a pastiche, a formulaic genre parody that provides a framework for sex scenes. Disney's *High School Musical* could be typical of this ideal porn movie if instead of breaking into song at certain moments, Zac Efron and Vanessa Hudgens got naked and fucked instead.

However, the reason porn movies came to have plots, in the days of the sixties and seventies when the genre first flowered as a legitimate commercial enterprise, was fundamentally pragmatic. Having a script and having actors portraying "characters" gives the footage the status of a creative work, something that is arguably protected as free speech.

The purpose, then, of a porn movie having a script and requiring performers to act is to attest to its being a performance and prove that it is something other than the mere documentation of real sex acts. Given that purpose, it is more advantageous to have these things done poorly, so the artificiality will be clearly noted. A truly effective fiction introduces dangerous ambiguities about the nature of the film.

Consequently, there are no movies as laughable in their ineptitude as those that seek to evoke fantasies of rape, domination, and violence.

Stefano portrayed a working-class Italian kid named Vito in a movie called *More of a Man* (1991), which purported to show the transformation of a self-hating homophobic thug into a self-aware gay man. Statements put into characters' mouths insisted that love and self-acceptance are the vehicles for this transformation. The narrative thrust—which would suggest some meaningful difference between anonymous restroom sex with a man you assault afterwards and a mutual experience with someone who loves you and wants to show you a connection between avoiding disease and self-respect—is undermined by the repetitive sameness of the sex scenes. There is rarely any individualized character to porn sex.

Strangely, a narrative medium that has the freedom to depict sex explicitly shuns the opportunity to make sex function as part of a narrative.

After *Powder*, Victor Salva made *Jeepers Creepers* (2001), a movie with few artistic pretensions beyond displaying some degree of cinematographic competency. Justin Long plays a kid on his way home from college with his older sister. He throws a sack of dirty laundry in the car. Later, when their car breaks down in a desert town, we see the first good glimpse of the horrifying monster that will pursue him to his death. The monster, winged and leathery but disconcertingly human in appearance, is seen holding up a fistful of the boy's dirty laundry to his nose, inhaling deeply. I would swear there are boxer shorts in that handful. Throughout the movie, the audience wonders whether the boy or his sister will end up the monster's victim, but it's clear from the ending that the monster never had the slightest bit of interest in the girl.

In the sequel, released in 2003, the monster feasts on a whole busload of high school athletes in a movie that reads as if *Varsity Blues* (1999)—a football-themed "quality" teen flick with an exceptional heavy dose of male nudity—had inexplicably transformed into a splattery snuff film. Which is more or less what it is, in as real a form as snuff movies have ever taken.

Certainly the Creeper must qualify as one of the most interesting alter-egos a director has ever created.

Porn stars dying of AIDS was a problem for the porn industry. Being reminded that through sex, gay men were contracting a virus that destroyed their immune system and killed them did not put consumers in a good frame of mind to enjoy pornography, which is by its nature escapist and is at a loss to portray real-life consequences of real-life actions.

Joey Stefano was one of a group of young porn stars in the early nineties who had become, in some sense, public figures, making appearances at nightclubs and on gay pride floats. Seen in company with then-closeted entertainment mogul David Geffen, Stefano made the gossip columns. He appeared in photos in Madonna's book *Sex*, a symbol of fame and indifferent polymorphous sexuality.

Most of the gay porn stars dying of AIDS died private deaths that were only learned of months later. Joey Stefano died a star, his death as public and as sudden, at least to gay men who followed porn even slightly, as the deaths of John Belushi, Kurt Cobain, or River Phoenix.

Some people honestly do prefer porn with narrative, stories where porn actors pretend to be jealous rivals, or vampires and victims, or members of a professional football team, or explorers, or brothers. They like the bad scripts and the inferior acting, the shoddy sub-sitcom-level sets, the fanciful porn star names. A few are ironic in this liking but most are deadly earnest in their shoddy porn tastes.

I have great difficulty understanding such people. I do not trust them. They seem to me to be victims of some dowdy notion of propriety, unable to admit what really attracts them to watching porn. Nevertheless, they cling to their preferences and many movies are made to satisfy them. Some are porn movies with plots and some are Hollywood movies like *White Squall*. Or like *Apt Pupil*, in which a seminude teenage boy pouts his way through budding teenage Nazi fantasies with Ian McKellen and an occasional goose step—poor Brad Renfro, at the beginning of his downward spiral, when he was first pegged as a cinematic bottom, ages before Larry Clark got to him.

The silliest satisfaction of porn is the same as the silliest satisfaction of mainstream film—believing in stars. Great actors are performers whose talent brings roles alive. Stars are performers you can't not watch. Like a porn movie, a star must always stop short of being convincing, otherwise you'd forget you were watching a star.

I have a tattoo of River Phoenix on my left arm.

I know better than to commit such things to print, but there have been moments when I felt the face of a porn actor was a face I could fall in love with. You never want them to stay a porn actor though—you want to rescue them. That's almost the whole point. Porn movies are like *The Perils of Pauline* (1914): Who will save the beautiful young man?

A sixteen-year-old from the rural south came to New York City to attend a performing arts school; he had agreed to do some photographs in Central Park with my photographer friend, and I had agreed to carry my friend's equipment around. In pictures the boy was as beautiful as a pre-Raphaelite model, dark eyes and strong nose, with ruby lips and masses of reddish-brown hair falling to his shoulders. As he told us a story about his sister failing her driver's license exam, I truly found it difficult to keep in mind that he was male. Not that he was faggoty—he simply had the physical presence of a slightly built, flat-chested fourteen-year-old girl.

My friend was very nervous whenever he felt he needed to adjust the way the boy's clothes hung on him, how much of his pale, goose-bumped chest the opening of his shirt revealed. The boy wanted to know if we knew where The Duplex was, because he heard Joan Rivers hung out there. My friend posed him in the Rambles, under the arcade near Bethesda Fountain, on the Bow Bridge. When it was dark, we walked him to the subway station and sent him on his way home. I told my friend he was a perv, but I was kind of joking.

Later, the boy described his first professional modeling session. He was to be photographed shirtless and shoeless in a pair of jeans. When he came out of the dressing area and stood where the photographer directed him, the guy started yelling at him. "Did you leave your fucking underwear on? I can see your underwear bunching up under the pants. Take them off." And when the boy started back toward the dressing area, the photographer impatiently snapped, "We don't have time—change here, please."

That man believed what it seems most people in the entertainment industry believe—that human beings are products and that sex appeal is a salient characteristic of those products. He is therefore doing no more than his duty when he orders a shy teenage boy to strip naked in front of him or lose his chance at the career he moved across the country to pursue. Therefore there is no reason to consider anything as irrelevant as whether he himself enjoys forcing sexual humiliation onto underage boys.

Victor is a professional model who works out of London now.

Some people, like an old roommate of mine and his friends, enjoy the falsity of narrative porn because it provides a comfortable mediation between private desire and public spectacle. How else can one sit down and watch a porn movie with one's friends? There must be something besides the sex to watch and comment on.

One of the movies my roommate watched with his friends, supposedly all straight, was a porn movie about a circus. There was a dwarf in the movie, and a fat lady, and a lady who danced with a snake—they told me about this, laughing. Later, I watched the movie myself. The dwarf never so much as took his clothes off. The snake was safely put away before his owner got sexual. The fat lady's scene was brief. And there were two longish scenes of homosexual ass fucking, starring actors I recognized from porn movies.

My roommate and his friends had sat around on somebody's birthday watching gay porn while asserting, and I think believing, that they were watching a zany porn movie filled with all kinds of oddities.

It wasn't, though. It was a gay porn movie with window dressing.

At one time the death of a porn star was distasteful, tainting his or her movies and rendering them unwatchable to people with normal sensibilities. Unironic porn fans worried themselves over rumors of this or that actor having AIDS or being HIV-positive.

Stefano's death from a drug overdose—he was HIV-positive as well, and his drug abuse and depression certainly not unrelated to this—sanctified him, saved him from being an AIDS casualty, and put him at the center of a new narrative, one that rescued porn from the taint of death by packaging death as a kind of personal allure.

The porn stars who left Hollywood to die at home, with family, under their real names, were talked about in shameful half-whispers. Stefano, on the other hand, was the light that shone so brightly we knew he was bound to burn himself out.

Like Marilyn Monroe and James Dean, Stefano became the tragic movie star, endlessly watchable. The story of his life, and his death, and his movies, became hopelessly intertwined, as if there was no other possible resolution.

His biography, *Wonder Bread and Ecstasy* (1995), became a best seller. Its Amazon reader reviews tell his story even more admirably.

Stefano had become famous because of "that good boy/bad boy persona that was able to reach out beyond the screen."

Stefano's death was "a warning about not loving yourself enough to do the things that are right for you."

His tragic death also spoke of "how a beautiful, talented young individual can be bled dry by a community that took too much and gave nothing back."

When the viewer watched his movies, knowing that Stefano was dead, the viewer thought, "I wish I could just grab him out of the TV set and hold him safely."

After all, "the tragic story of this 26-year-old gayporn sex godlet is the stuff that movies are definitely made of nowadays."

The last time I watched porn with my photographer friend—Jean-Daniel Cadinot's *Les Minets Sauvage* (1984)—we discussed how various scenes were lit and why the director had made those choices. It's still a mystery. Cadinot is the only person who ever made gay porn movies that looked like real movies. They are poorly plotted and scripted, perhaps, but they are shot like any number of nicely made European art movies of thirty years ago. The protagonist of *Les Minets Sauvage* is a young street prostitute remanded to a boys' reformatory where he is sexually abused by the other inmates. In shocking disregard to American conventions, the actor playing the boy puts up a struggle against his initial rape that it short-lived but not self-evidently farcical, and afterwards, left alone in his bunk, he weeps. The movie is shot in and around a massive French country house apparently adapted to some kind of institutional use.

In the end they are not good movies, but scenes of them do look like fragments of an imaginary good movie. Do you suppose that a link can be made between the aesthetics of a movie and the ethics of its maker? For all I know, Cadinot killed and ate the young men he put in his movies. Still, his technique seems less degrading than what Hollywood porn directors do, capturing shaved assholes and greased-up parlor tans on garish video for eternity, or distribution as short Internet clips, whichever comes first.

The name Nick Iacona Jr. is not as famous as that of Norma Jeane Baker, but the mention of it serves the same purpose—to create the illusion of an intimacy between audience and dead star; to suggest that, however intertwined personal and professional disasters were for this human being, however much producers, directors, general exploiters, and the whole dirty business may have pushed this person closer to the edge, the audience's love was true and selfless and real, *as was Joey's/Nick's love for the audience.*

By pronouncing this name and believing that in it we recognize a real person, we convince ourselves of our own innocence.

MULTIPLE JOURNEYS INTO HELL

Stephen Beachy

I'm saying I'm an insect who dreamt he was a man and loved it. But now the dream is over and the insect is awake.

Jeff Goldblum in *The Fly*

PERFORMANCE

In the 1980s, what had once been an incredibly rare condition became frighteningly common. From 1985 to 1995 there were an estimated 40,000 cases of what was then called Multiple Personality Disorder; thousands of women, and a few men, were habitually splitting into tens of thousands of alter personalities. The alters were named Sharky or Rabbit or Reagan or Renee or Nobody or The Kids. There were nuns, prostitutes, good witches, bad witches, the bride of Satan, infants, rabbits, lobsters, wolf-dogs, fleshless demons, God itself. There were alters with their *own* sets of multiple personalities. Since 1973, when *Sybil* was published, the cause of this continual splitting was increasingly understood as childhood sexual abuse. By the end of the eighties, the reported abuses included more and more vivid and detailed accounts of cannibalism, human sacrifice, serial baby breeding, vast conspiracies of sexual torture, pedophilia, and Satan worship, involving the highest levels of government, the CIA and the media. The conspiracies involved not just the patients, but the doctors. One doctor, Judith Peterson, who ran a Dissociative Disorders unit in Texas, believed that organized crime operatives were wearing masks designed to look like her face in order to bewilder and further abuse her patients—just like in *Strait Jacket* (1964), in which Joan Crawford's homicidal daughter wears a Joan Crawford mask to confuse witnesses about the true murderer's identity.

It is mother who splits the daughter's personality in both *Sybil* and *Strait Jacket*. In their primal scenes, Sybil is tortured in the kitchen and the barn; Joan's screen daughter witnesses her mother murdering with an axe. In movies like *Mildred Pierce, Berserk!*, and *Fatal Confinement*, Joan would turn out to be more virtuous, and thus more complex, than she originally seemed, and her screen daughters more willful and disturbed. There was always a sweeter, more vulnerable and caring personality lurking underneath Joan's tough-as-nails persona. The way that role-playing informs, intersects, and alters personality is a major theme of the Multiple Personality epidemic; *Sybil* would radically alter the understanding of a condition that had entered American consciousness in the fifties by way of *The Three Faces of Eve*. It isn't mother's sexual torture in the barn that splits the daughter's personality in *Three Faces of Eve*, but kissing her dead grandmother's cold flesh at the funeral. Eve was played by Joanne Woodward, who also played Sybil's doctor, Cornelia Wilbur, in the 1977 movie starring Sally Field in the title role. Like Eve's, Sybil's personalities came in pairs, but Sybil kept bifurcating until she reached 16, providing Sally Field a much broader range to demonstrate how badly she wanted an Emmy.

One reader of *Sybil*, a typist who'd set the book in print, got so involved with the story that she dreamed that she was Sybil—to which the new Sybil said that *she too dreamed that she was Sybil*. But if some of us make our dreams into movies and TV shows, more of us splice movies and TV shows—and books—into the content of our dreams. In 1957 Sybil had gone to see *The Three Faces of Eve*. Nancy, the heroine of *Nightmare: Uncovering the Strange 56 Personalities of Nancy Lynn Gooch* (1987), recovered memories of being ritually abused after reading *The Shining*. Seeing abuse depicted in *Crooklyn* provoked memories for Lindsey. With its possessions, spinning heads and projectile vomiting, *The Exorcist* (1973) created a compelling library of images, and several multiples developed personalities with the same name as Regan, the devil-possessed child played by Linda Blair. Billy Milligan's Ragen was "the keeper of the hate" and Nancy Reagan also personified hate in its rawest form. Absolute evil merges, in the Dream, with the administration that presided over the epidemic in its peak; Jo had a personality named *Reagan*, one of two who existed solely to provide a storehouse of information. The sophisticated brainwashing techniques of multigenerational Satanic cults frequently reference *The Manchurian Candidate*, and Ruth was treated by Dr. Pickens, a psychoanalyst who'd been influenced by *The Snake Pit,* starring Olivia de Haviland. And everybody, both patients and doctors, watched or read *Sybil*.

Had the other book on multiple personality that was published in 1973 had the success of *Sybil* and been made into a movie, we might have lived through a very different kind of epidemic. In *Splitting: A Case of Female Masculinity*, Mrs. G has only two alters, and experiences herself as having an erect penis inside her body all the time. Her life story includes armed robbery, car thefts, drag races, bad checks, porn, and four marriages by the age of twenty-three. Her associates include motorcycle gangs, criminals, drug pushers, thieves, and "bad cops," one of whom she shoots in the ass. Like Sybil, Mrs. G describes a troubled relationship with her mother, a woman who is more disgusted by her daughter's lesbianism than by her attempted murders. Unlike Sybil, Mrs. G can remember her sexual experiences just fine. Although a grandfather, two uncles and several strangers have had intercourse with Mrs. G by the time she is eight, her original split comes as a result of her own actions; she hits a boy with a rock when she is four, and "Charlie" appears as a voice who takes responsibility. Mrs. G's sarcastic doctor, Dr. S, doesn't coddle Mrs. G, doesn't go on endless searches through her mind for more personalities to name, or for repressed memories. "How come you were such a cooperative little piece of ass?" Dr. S asks, when Mrs. G tells him about having sex with her uncle at thirteen.

A very different approach from either the real Dr. Wilbur or the version of her played by Woodward, a psychoanalyst who used hypnosis, among other tactics, to uncover repressed memories of abuse. In recent years, Wilbur's tactics and diagnoses have come under increasing attack; it is said that she encouraged, even insisted on role-playing on the part of Shirley Ann Mason, the real Sybil, and that the intense bond the two of them formed was a part of the illness itself. After the publication of *Sybil* in the seventies, Wilbur became a pioneer in the field and made an appearance as a consultant in most every multibiography published during the eighties. "I keep expecting her to look and act like Joanne Woodward," said Nancy Gooch, when she met with Dr. Wilbur at her institute in Kentucky. Dr. Eugene Bliss is typical of the small number of doctors who followed Wilbur's lead and who diagnosed a huge proportion of cases early in the epidemic. His first encounter came after urging a patient to look for someone inside herself. The "unexpected happened," and a "quiet matron" transformed into "a gum-chewing, brassy-voiced slattern." After that, as "his detection of these cases grew keener, he began to spot clandestine multiples hiding behind a battery of complaints and diagnoses," including Andrea, the heroine of *Prism: Andrea's World* (1985). He found the process exhilarating, "part archaeology, part magic. Never had he enjoyed such exciting 'live theater.'" One of Sybil's personalities was an actress, skilled at dramatizing and playing roles. Nancy was an actress too; she planned a show at her community college, where she played *all* the parts. Although many multiples were interested in drama, and certainly no more convincing than Field, their doctors would continue to distinguish between the sort of performances that happen in movies and those that happen in real life. Ralph Allison described his patient Janette. "It was like something out of a movie. It was Joanne Woodward changing from Eve White to Eve Black. . . . But this wasn't a movie. This wasn't an actress playing a role." In *Suffer the Child* (1989) when Jenny showed up for her appointment in a miniskirt and tight sweater, contrasting with her conservative appearance of the week before, cocky, but chewing nervously on bubble gum, her therapist noted the marked difference, "as if they were allowing themselves to be seen clearly." And yet, "the changes in voice tone, appearance, and ways of moving were more than role changes."

What exactly constitutes "more" than a role change? There was always different handwriting, there were often different prescriptions for glasses, even different eye colors, IQs, and brain waves. Evidence that the condition was "real" was especially an issue when the subjects were trying to use their diagnosis to avoid punishment for the crimes of their alters. Henry Hawksworth from *The Five of Me* (1977) was the first in a string of multiples who would try to use Multiple Personality as a defense against legal charges. In Henry's case, *dogs* knew the difference, and attacked Henry when he was Johnny. Henry left an impressive trail of corpses, car crashes, raped women, and jilted lovers behind him, all the time maintaining a personality called Peter Pan. It was *The Minds of Billy Milligan* (1981), however, by novelist Daniel Keyes that most successfully merged the multibiography with True Crime. Milligan, a studious reader of *Sybil*, used his diagnosis to win time in mental institutions, as opposed to the harsher regimens of prison. It wasn't Billy who had raped women, but his affection-starved lesbian personality, Adalana. In the Dream, causality can be so complex as to be indeterminable; we are both one thing and another, neither this nor that; everything is flux. Our institutions and our legal system require accountability, however; a name is attached to a body, and it is assumed that if the body commits a crime, the body should be punished—or cured. After the trial, in a mental institution, Billy's system mutated anew; the system became both more interesting and more practical, as his fusing allowed him to tell the whole story to Keyes.

Something is happening in these cases, and that something seems to be "more" than the role-playing we all do as we move through different social worlds. The question of whether Multiple Personality is, or has been, real or not is not exactly the issue, however, at least not my issue. Just because a great deal of splitting has been encouraged by a few pioneering therapists, like Wilbur, Bliss, and Allison, and their overzealous use of hypnosis, doesn't mean that the personalities that form in their patients' minds are any less compelling. Just because some recovered memories are demonstrably false doesn't mean that none of them are true. Just because the way Multiple Personality is experienced depends on the available models doesn't mean that it somehow doesn't exist. I'm less interested in the distinction between fantasy and memory than in the places the multiples go, as explorers of psychic space. If multiples were once just overly sensitive to the trauma of kissing a corpse—the sheer, physical fact of death—they have since undertaken vivid journeys into hell. Their guides on these journeys have been Sybil, Eve, and a cohort of enthusiastic therapists. The hell they visit is the hell of memory, the hell of childhood, the hell of abuse. By the time of *My Father's House* (1987), for example, the horror of kissing dead or aged flesh had shifted; kissing her grandmother horrified her as a child, Sylvia Fraser decided, because grandmother's caved-in cheek was the same texture as daddy's scrotum, a scrotum she'd come to know intimately. I'm interested in the evolution of these journeys through time, and I'm interested in the degree to which these psychic spaces are collective.

In *Splitting*, Mrs. G's Charlie tries to torment Mrs. G, to kill her, but sometimes, and more and more as time goes on, he tries to help her. Charlie evolves. Although he doesn't want her to have a conscience, another voice telling her what to do, he himself becomes interested in figuring out the difference between good and evil. "He's away from me now. He's up in his room reading his books on morals," Mrs. G says at one point. Good and evil and crime and responsibility are constant themes in the multibiographies. Before *Sybil* or *Splitting* there was *Minds in Many Pieces* (1972), a collection of case studies by Ralph Allison. Allison's patients were sometimes possessed by entities other than mere personalities—dead junkies or the spirits of their dead babies or evil spirits who entered when they experimented with black magic as teens. Their actual alters were rooted in imaginary playmates, the birth of baby brothers, childhood beatings, or the sight of their mothers beheaded. Male alters commonly formed in girls whose fathers wanted sons. For Carrie, it was having her beautiful red hair shaved off by her mother when she was nineteen months old. In this way, Wanda developed, "born into violence, filled with hatred, and capable of acting out all the anger Carrie was unable to express." Allison's patients always had good personalities and evil personalities; rather than integrating them, like Wilbur, Allison cast out the negative alters and encouraged a spiritual fusion with the personality he called the Inner Self Helper. If the reverse happened, and the good personalities were cast out, the entity left behind would be a monster and capable of any crime. The ISH couldn't hate; it could only love and express awareness of and belief in God, and could often predict the future. According to Allison, the ISH had no gender or emotion, no date of origin, and wasn't born from trauma like other alters. It was basically the conscience, and *everyone* had one from birth. It was like a computer, pure intellect, a conduit for God's healing power and love, and it usually believed in reincarnation. Sometimes there were several, ranked in a hierarchy—the highest would speak of being next to God.

Allison would be enormously influential; Henry Hawksworth was one of his patients, and typifies his use of a metaphysical vocabulary. "Am I an evil person who should be cut off from mankind and destroyed in the Hell-Fire of Biblical description?" his personality Dana asked in *The Five of Me.* "Yet how can I be all evil and still love the sweetness of Spring, the colors of the petals of a pansy, the giant redwood trees?" How indeed? His personality Johnny wrote, "Reality is hate!" Henry's internal battle was framed as a war between Dana and Johnny, the empath vs. the sociopath, in a battle to the death; the hospital ward was a way station for lost souls, where worms became butterflies. After an epileptic seizure, Jerry wrote, "Dana has been to Hell. Johnny and the evil entity he represented have been consumed and damned. Dana has emerged clean and ready to bring Henry forth." For Allison, the id was just a mental sewer, and Hell wasn't a realm to be incorporated into the personality, a source of necessary energy or an engine of evolution, but a place to be annihilated in a personal apocalypse. For Wilbur, a whole person owned all of the anger and hatred and desire, all of the abuse and all of the transcendence. Does evil ultimately belong to a separate realm from God—something to be cleansed from the divinity, and from those humans who want to partake in the divine? Or is it an integral part of the fabric of the divine, ultimately useful or ultimately to be redeemed? Separation or integration, the wheat and the chaff or embracing the shadow, apocalypse or an endless journey toward the light—the question of whether evolution happens gradually and all the time or suddenly, in brief transformative cataclysms, is a central motif of the dream of multiplicity, as are those two figures who haunt the dream of future human evolution, the empath and the sociopath. But with or without the evil personalities, integration is only one aspect of the traditional happy ending to the stories of multiple personalities, stories whose heroes undertake shamanic journeys into the underworld where they are ripped into fragments and emerge to tell the tale.

HELL

The Kingdom of Darkness was never just patriarchal; in the early to mid eighties, unloving mothers caused more splitting than even raping fathers, and initiation into satanic cults involved Mom without fail. *Michelle Remembers* (1982) has been described as the *Sybil* of satanic abuse. Although Michelle didn't develop multiple personalities, she would have a profound effect on the experiences and stories of multiples for years to come. Michelle simply undertook a journey down memory lane, regurgitating for several years her explicit memories of abuse by a satanic cult in the fifties, to her trusting therapist, Lawrence Pazder. Michelle's memories didn't involve any identifiable human beings except for her mother, who'd been dead for many years and so could neither confirm or deny these stories of her child defecating on crosses, having dead babies cut open over her, and being buried alive with dead kittens. After months of hearing the bizarre details of these rituals, it finally occurred to Dr. Pazder that it might be a group with a long history. "The only group I know about that fits your description," he says, "is the Church of Satan." "My God," Michelle says. "You mean, like Satanists?"

Soon, a snake woman showed up in her memories whose eyes went back in her head; she had a long lizardy tongue, and her head spun around; then she was pretty again. She was possessed, it turned out, and at one point she stuck her snaky tongue in Michelle's mouth and it became a real snake. Michelle had visions of the Virgin Mary and of Christ himself. "He looked like all the things in the world that you ever love. He looked strong, but like a rabbit too, you know . . ." Michelle began channeling the voice of Satan himself, just as he spoke during a seemingly endless festival in the fifties, the Feast of the Beast. He spoke in rhymes, a detail which a church father confirmed as his standard operating mode. "In Church history, we learn that it is usual for Satan to speak in rhymes. I have read his rhymes in French, in German, in Spanish, in English. I have read rhymes from the Middle Ages."

Both Rhonda, from *We the Divided Self* (1982), and Lia, from *The Healing of Lia* (1982), presented models of Multiple Personality seemingly uninfluenced by *Sybil*—Manichean visions, of good, meek personalities juxtaposed to destructive ones in battles to the death. *We the Divided Self* included recorded conversations of Rhonda talking to her Evil Twin, Mary—more evidence of what is real. Mary said, "Rhonda, I've got to hurt you. That's the way I live. That's the only thing that keeps me living is to hurt you." "There is, within me, another woman, whom I fight to keep deeply hidden, but who is stronger than I," said Lia. "Black, evil. Like a malignancy, one who lives only to destroy. And it is I she is bent on destroying." Hatred and abuse formed a kind of fuel, a rich energy source. Along with the other concepts that intersected Multiple Personality, their hell-worlds fell well within the mainstream of American spiritual belief systems—discarnate entities, demonic possession, and vast invisible dimensions of spiritual warfare. The parameters of hell were being mapped. How much further could we descend? On and on and on . . .

Multiples put razors into their own vaginas, cut themselves in the lower abdomen, downed pills in the school restroom, and burned their arms with cigarettes. They were hung on meathooks in the barn, beaten and raped by their fathers, raped by their fathers with ice picks, raped by their stepfathers, and raped by strangers too. They remembered religious rituals with their babysitters in the bathtub, at the age of two, in which the babysitter put brushes full of Lysol inside them until they bled. Dad might fuck a milk cow and have the cow perform cunnilingus on the child. Mom might lock the child in boxes, electrocute her vagina, pimp her out, give her ice water enemas, and neglect her for her boyfriends; abuse was understood as a generational chain—maybe Mom was also raped by several men in her family, and abused in several barns. If a girl, Mom might put the child in the oven, bury her alive, and lock her in the closet, where her bad personality would smear shit on the walls. If a boy, Dad might rape and beat him or Mom might repeatedly have sex with him and involve him in the crucifixion, burning and drowning of babies. She might sell him for sex and involve him in satanic cult rituals during which his uncles would have sex with a horse, and eventually so would he—although what that entails exactly won't be explained. Grandma might molest him too, or he'll be anally raped by "the man with the hairy hands."

After decades of these stories, the introduction of *Multiple Journeys to One: Spiritual Stories of Integrating from Dissociative Identity Disorder* (1999) assured us that if we were looking for lurid tales of abuse, this wasn't the book for us; these eight stories focused on the process of integration. If an occasional detail of abuse cropped up, it was because it couldn't be avoided; the abuse was centrally tied to the integration. An occasional detail *did* crop up: Carol, for example, remembered that her step-grandfather tied her in the barn, peed in her mouth, threatened her with a pitchfork, and raped her. Margaret was sold by her dad to friends for a bottle of whiskey, sodomized over the kitchen table, then forced to clean the shit off dad's dick with her mouth; he held a knife to her throat, and threatened to serve her to Mom for dinner as goat meat. At eight, she was left tied spread-eagled to the bed for hours, penetrated with popsicles and cucumbers, and left sticky during the day so that the ants and flies could come to get her. And on and on.

The abuse was almost cosmically tied to the integration; an empathetic therapist was another requirement. Multiples and other victims of Satanic Ritual Abuse are notorious for the amount of empathy they provoke in their therapists, the amount of energy and bonding they require. If their bad mothers tortured them, they needed good mothers to love them unconditionally. Therapeutic empathy had become the *opposite* of evil, the balm the victimized soul required. Sybil and Dr. Wilbur lived together for a time, along with Flora Rheta Schreiber, the journalist who wrote the book. At one point Dr. Pazder started crying with Michelle, not because he felt sorry for her. "It was empathy. He had entered her pain and was there inside it with her." Pazder and Michelle would later divorce their spouses and marry. *The Flock*'s Jo underwent "a radical program of reparenting therapy" with her doctor. In *Voices*, Christopher's therapist

Trula wrote, "As I walked through the psychiatric unit the next day, I noticed that my perception of the other patients had changed. Their pathologies seemed mundane. They grouped around the television, played pool or Ping Pong, or hammered their initials into pieces of leather. None of them compared with Christopher. None could have caused me to disrupt a night's sleep with anticipation of what I might encounter the next day." It was really only the four-year-old Timmy and the core Christopher that Trula was fond of, however. James, who talked about "nasty things," was difficult for Trula to empathize with, she found it difficult to bond with the female personalities, and the snobbish Ernest bored her.

It doesn't surprise us anymore when we hear that the arsonist who set a forest fire was a firefighter who needed work or that most of the kiddie porn on the Internet is created by FBI agents trying to catch pedophiles or, as in Philip K. Dick's *A Scanner Darkly*, that it is the undercover agents selling most of the drugs. It shouldn't surprise us either that therapeutic empathy, a process in which an intimate bond is formed around the memory of abuse, came to resemble exactly what it was trying to heal. Critics have suggested that many of these vivid memories were products of therapy itself, created by unspoken agreements and suggestibility within that empathetic bond, and that the painful reliving of violent and pornographic scenarios itself constituted a form of abuse. *Magic Child*, for example, is a story primarily about Carole Smith's willingness to believe every tale of abuse her adoptive son Alex tells about his biological mother and every other caretaker he's ever had, even though he tells similar stories, at times, about her own husband, which she knows to be false. Carole's interpretations of Alex's drawings sometimes suggest her own troubled imagination more than Alex's. "Much later, I happened to learn how the combination of semen and other bodily fluids smells exactly like fish. It wasn't until then that I knew the meaning of the fourth drawing, the one that had been so puzzling. The fish with the human eyes." By book's end, Alex's biological mother, a woman who originally seemed like simply another dysfunctional, incompetent, narcissistic, and abusive woman, was revealed to be a cult leader, a kind of priestess of Death and a symbol of absolute horror—perhaps Carole's more than Alex's. Mother and son drowned babies together, and Mom taught Alex that that was what life was about. "This was the ultimate horror," Carole wrote. "Mother. Mother was the negation of being. Mother was the antithesis of existence. Mother was death." In *Strait Jacket*, Joan

Crawford plays a mother who isn't really a psychotic killer. She's just a woman, like any other woman, who'd made a murderous mistake in her youth, transformed by her daughter's imagination into Death itself. It is the daughter who finds her own psychotic power in the act of donning a Joan Crawford mask and inhabiting Death. It is sometimes only in the imaginative lives of children that parents blur into angels and demons, and in the imaginative lives of adults who inhabit childlike realms of belief. Carole and Alex are not unsympathetic; their suffering is all over the page. While the afterword to *The Magic Castle*, written by Alex's therapist, suggests other possible readings than actual Satanic Ritual Abuse, it never questions the idea that it is therapeutic to let a child believe that he has murdered babies, raped children, and had sex with every member of his family—and their horses too.

THE DEVIL IS A WOMAN (1935)

Robert Glück

There is no real story and the beautiful and the arbitrary reign together in the form of Concha Perez.

From the Internet:

"Adapted from the same Pierre Louÿs novel that spawned Luis Buñuel's *That Obscure Object of Desire, The Devil Is a Woman* is set in an intricately conceived studio version of Spain and situates Marlene Dietrich in the middle of a love triangle with an older military man and a young revolutionary, both of whom suffer the exquisite agony of being snubbed by her. Dietrich, a cigarette factory worker, tells one of her admirers, 'If you really loved me, you would have killed yourself.' *Devil* is a fascinating juxtaposition of decadent romanticism . . . of 30's left-wing activism . . . and of Von Sternberg's own preoccupation with authoritarianism and freedom."

Director Josef von Sternberg and his greatest discovery, Marlene Dietrich, worked together for the last time on this notorious and controversial box-office flop. Antonio Galvan (Cesar Romero), a young military officer, meets mysterious and alluring Concha Perez and soon falls under her spell. Antonio confesses his love for Concha to his friend Don Pasqual (Lionel Atwill), an older and higher-ranking officer. Pasqual is horrified when he learns of Antonio's infatuation; years ago, he met Concha and started a long and disastrous relationship in which the cold-hearted woman would repeatedly lure him into her romantic web and drain him of his wealth. The film was thought to be lost for some time until Dietrich provided a print from her personal collection for a Sternberg retrospective in 1959; the movie has since been released on home video. John Dos Passos coauthored the screenplay.

CONCHA

Arturo, a cup of coffee.

PASQUAL

My emotions seem to make little impression on you. Aren't you afraid of anything, Concha? Have you no fear of death?

CONCHA

No, not today. Why do you ask? Are you going to kill me?

PASQUAL

You play with me as if I were a fool. What I gave gladly, you took like a thief.

CONCHA

I thought you would be glad to see me. I'm sorry I sat down.

The Devil Is a Woman was the single most controversial movie of the 1930s. The Spanish government demanded that Paramount pull the motion picture out of circulation and destroy all the film. Paramount only withdrew the movie when the U.S. State Department asked them to do so. The movie lost heavily at the box office and the careers of star Marlene Dietrich and the other cast members, as well as many of the production crew, were irrevocably damaged.

During the years 1930–1935, the single most successful tandem in Hollywood was that of Director Josef von Sternberg and star actress Marlene Dietrich. Between the two of them, they made one big box office success after another. *The Blue Angel* (1930), *Morocco* (1930), *Dishonored* (1931), *Shanghai Express* (1932), *Blonde Venus* (1932), *The Scarlet Empress* (1934) were all big money makers. Added to this mix was a short documentary titled *The Fashion Side of Hollywood* (1935).

However, all was not well between director von Sternberg and his star actress, Dietrich. Director von Sternberg was in love with Dietrich, yet her reaction to him drove him up a wall. He became completely frustrated in his relationship with her. He decided that there would be one last movie that would reflect his opinion of her. He also decided that this last movie with Marlene Dietrich would be his masterpiece.

In *The Devil Is a Woman*, Marlene Dietrich plays a charming female who is completely devoid of character. With all her scenes fully lighted, and clad in the most flamboyant clothing imaginable, she is impossibly beautiful. Von Sternberg did the photography himself, and Dietrich comes across like an evil goddess, her beauty on the edge of absurdity. Dietrich considered this film her all-time favorite.

The interesting thing about *The Devil Is a Woman* is that its themes and ideas do not come from what you hear, but what you see.

> CONCHA
> What did you do?

> ANTONIO
> Politics. A little bit revolutionary.

> CONCHA
> Is that all? I thought it was something important.

I have no trouble crying, but I need this story because of its glycerin tears. I cry very easily, all I have to do is begin making the motions and in a minute I am crying deeply. Possibly I am depressed—but more often I have the pre-tears feeling that comes after reading a long Russian novel. How impossible to contain, as one must, all the time that has passed, generations, and the characters, their childhoods, adulthoods, and deaths. The great events of history and the arbitrary ways history impinges on individual life. That is why I associate these tears, which seem to contain so much distance, with the experience of aging. It is the expression of intolerable distance, distance impossible to contain, so while the feelings may be congested and suffering and the body clenched and even wracked, there is also a delicate filigree, a pattern mostly empty, which I enjoy with a kind of recognition, the spatial equivalent of a death's head, but lovely, or rather, harder to endure. It is often said that people who age best live in the moment, or even that one lives in the moment as one ages, whether intending to or not, so maybe as I grow older any awareness of larger amounts of time equals mourning.

PASQUAL

I love you, Concha. Life without you means nothing.

CONCHA

One moment and I'll give you a kiss.

In particular I cry after movies, not so much in the theater, but at home at my dining room table, even over dessert. Any movie really. I associate this with my aging because movies compress so much time, and I wonder if I am more "in touch" with my feelings, as we used to say. We used to say, "we've got to get ourselves together," and nothing seems more improbable, since we never got ourselves together and we are less likely to do so now. "I've got to get myself together"—nothing is less likely. How will Ed, who is no longer alive, get himself together? In that era, the early seventies, we went to movies that supported an overall sexuality and esthetic position that repressed the difference between figure and ground. I am thinking of the duel scene in *The Devil Is a Woman*. It was part of a Sternberg retrospective in 1973 at a theater on 18th Street in the Castro in San Francisco that has long since disappeared.

Pasqual has never been able to cure himself of his addiction to Concha, and when he encounters Concha with Antonio at a street festival, Pasqual is overcome with jealousy and challenges Antonio to a duel. The duel takes place in a forest at dawn. Dietrich wears black lace as though already mourning the death that is bound to occur, that she has instigated. She raises a black lace parasol. This is what Ed and I took from the film: In order to make the screen dazzle, Sternberg slid beads of glycerin down hundreds or thousands of invisible strings, slow rain, each drop catching its portion of the light and carrying it downward.

The languid drops and the roar of rain are out of proportion to the slow movement of light, just as the roar of sex is out of proportion to Dietrich's indifference, or to the act of penetration, an imbalance that gave her a fairy-tale passivity.

It is hard to write about that image without reverting to somber camp—to wear myrtle in my butthole. It was camp ten minutes after it hit the screen in 1935. What did it mean to fabricate such an elaborate spectacle for the act of penetration? To support it with so much beauty. To subvert it with so much melodrama. To support it with so much artifice.

To elaborate the pure and impure, saint and whore, love of flesh and horror of flesh, the perpetual dualism of hips pumping.

> CONCHA
>
> Ha! This is superb. He threatens me. What right have you to tell
> me what to do? Are you my father? No! Are you my husband?
> No! Are you my lover? Well I must say you're content with very
> little.

Languid descent, the slow beauty that Ed and I imported into our
slow hippie lives, slow and anxious, as though Sternberg were directing
Ed and me. That is, slow from arousal, slow from fear, arousal never completely expelled, fear never meeting its source in consummation.

I don't think we understood the deep mourning of this image, we
could not add that to our mix of decadent romanticism and counter-
culture politics. Romantic obsession was always my subject. What for?—
to distract myself from the knowledge of death.

The acting in the film is on par with a PTA skit. Dietrich is supposed to be seductive, but she has only one note: swagger rather than allure. She's almost macho, as though she were besting the men in a contest.
But it is her sheer indifference that sets her apart in the film, as though she
were indifferent to the costume drama on every level. Her indifference is
the story Sternberg tells: Dietrich's indifference to him, her indifference
to the other actors, to the script, to her immediate fate, but not to the
lighting man or to the light.

Not sex, but light—which Ed painted his way towards: the naked
men floating towards the edge of the canvas and then away—leaving
clouds, sky and light, experiments in empty space and arousal. That is
what the glistening drops meant to us. They were light and they were
tears. Not tears for the death in the film, those cardboard cut-outs were
never alive, but tears shed by the oracle as she blathers nonsense that
must be interpreted: Something bad is going to happen. Something bad
is coming our way.

Yes, it is an oracle of some kind. Align yourself with light and the
knowledge of death, thank the cameraman, the lighting man, make sure
they are on your side.

What was our confusion?—her makeup was grotesque, the white

skull dome, the pencil eyebrows in perpetual surprise, the jaw hollow at the corners. Like a Mario Bava witch, an Argento witch. Whatever protected the inside of her body against itself has vanished, the tendons snap over bone, the pain flares from her wrists and knuckles.

A few nights ago I had this dream: Hitler appears and I say to my friends, Hey, there's Hitler, let's kill him. They say, Oh yeah, Hitler, he's looking good. Hey guys, I say, it's Hitler, c'mon, we've got to kill him. They say, He's in good shape these days—yah, he looks OK. I was Bob and what does Bob know about killing someone? Hey guys, let's kill Hitler. Besides the worst already happened so what was the point? That was Dietrich's stance too, that was the Weimar expression: the worst already happened. I picked up a rock and threw it at Hitler, but it landed a few feet away from me. He wasn't even upset. That's what the skull face of Dietrich was saying, that the worst already happened—that's why we could not understand or interpret her at the time—the early 70's—the worst had not happened. That's what her passivity was based on, her indifference, bringing that news of mourning into the realm of the sexual, which, it seemed to us, was founded on hope and possibility. Obsession, which is the fear of death, obsessive love, erotic mourning. The skull was already laughing through the pinched starving face, the enlarged eyes.

CONCHA

Good morning. Good morning! Good morning! Good morning! I came to see if you were dead. If you had loved me enough you would have killed yourself last night. Bad. Not made properly. I can make much better chocolate.

Instead of commanding you to live, your lover commands you to die. She takes a lively interest in your death, since she is dead. You are left with nothing to grasp, nothing to believe, nothing to understand. Oh Ed, can I find my way to you through this fucked-up image, the lacy black parasol, the glycerin tears sliding down a thousand strings? (I break a promise—I promised myself that I would not speak to Ed in the second person, as though language could float me "over" to where he is. I am talking to his photo or his image in my mind. Not the Ed I saw last, but younger. Am I mourning my lack of access to his beauty—the glory of my own youth, arousal and glycerin tears—or his death which took place twenty-five years later? My feelings are hemmed in by the reversibility of childhood and set free by the irreversibility of death. Is that true? Sometimes I say Oh Ed. That sigh contains the whole story. If I could "unpack" that sigh it would cover this book and a lot more. Maybe there's a way of talking to Ed that I am not prepared to do in public. I'll make myself naked when company comes, but I am reluctant to talk to the dead in your presence.

FROM *UNEXPLAINED PRESENCE*

Tisa Bryant

Undercover of Darkness

Older Sister and Younger Sister climb the stairs of their childhood home. Younger sister flicks the hallway light. They drag their feet down the worn wood floor, and force their bodies into the too-small room they once shared as girls. The room smells of their mother's perfume. Younger Sister sighs, flops onto the twin bed, her head propped on pillows on the footboard, facing the old television. Older Sister turns on the VCR, pushes François Ozon's *8 Femmes* into the machine, staring as the black case of the tape is sucked down into the chamber. The house creaks, pine trees scrape their branches against worn shingles, still riled by the dregs of an April storm. The closets hold decades of their mother's clothing. She takes her space at the edge of the bed, her back poker-straight against the headboard. She will not sleep tonight. The night is already gone. The tape whirs and wheezes.

The film begins. Its opening credits are reminiscent of George Cukor's *The Women*. Instead of a parade of farmland creatures, the sisters are led on a twirl through the garden. Danielle Darrieux is a violet. Catherine Deneuve is a yellow orchid. Isabelle Huppert is a tight red celosia argentea, also known as cockscomb. Emmanuelle Béart, the white orchid. Fanny Ardant, the red rose. Virginie Ledoyen, a pink rose. Anthropometaphorphism. Ludivine Sagnier, a young, lithe daisy fluttering in the breeze. Then the strings tremble deep, drop low, strike a chord of suspense, as if Joan Crawford's jungle red claws were about to slash through the screen, but that's not it. The vibrato of terror announces bright yellow petals surrounding an unfathomably brown center. The deepest notes produce Firmine Richard's name, quavering cursive white over the dark face of the sunflower, before it fades away.

Firmine Richard is Madame Chanel, the housekeeper. 'Madames' were once cinema's stereotype for dominant lesbian femmes. In the space of her name, cathouse meets design house. Together they dress Firmine's body in old stories of race and sex and servitude, all with high style, under a mansard roof filled with hothouse flowers. Her dress is slate gray, domestic *haute couteur*. Firmine is the shield that protects. The sisters watch the flowers sing and dance their numbers to each other as they applaud, react, respond.

"I hate that the housekeeper is black," Younger Sister says, glaring at Older Sister. "She has to take care of them. They don't listen. That's fucked up."

Older Sister makes an "mmmm" noise, not for delicious, but to signal a very old yes. Their mother is very recently dead. Hours. She loved murder mysteries. And sunflowers. The sisters stay awake and the subtitles roll. Their grandmother cleaned rich people's houses in Jamestown during the week. Stayed away for days, while her children ... While her children ... sang?

Firmine strides from the kitchen, smoothing her white apron over her slate gray dress, cooing and cajoling for the girls of the house she keeps. "Her" girls, the Pink Rose and the Daisy. They are not dark and comely, but pink and white, forever presumed innocent. Their aunt is all irony, the sexually frustrated Cockscomb, their mother, the glib Yellow Orchid. Firmine the Sunflower stands tall and smiles, giving self-assured womanhood where there is only shrewishness, maternal warmth where there is only icy materialism. She stands firm, baking her girls brioche. The coals in the iron stove quietly heat and glow. Orange is a healing color. None of these flowers Firmine tends have it.

But they sing about love and money and dance for the man whose eye they imagine to be constantly upon them. Just where is the source of all this passion, anyway? These women cannot be self-generating. As in Cukor's film, the Big Daddy of Ozon's *8 Femmes* is never seen. He is a sleeve in a smoking jacket, a leg jutting from his study's polished armchair, a hand writing a check at his desk. He is nearly invisible, but evinced in each woman's actions. Except Firmine's.

Younger Sister eyes the Daisy bobbing on the screen with derision. She looks over her shoulder at Older Sister. "Are you freakin' kiddin me here, or what? What *is* this?" Older Sister shrugs, shaking her head, the thin rasp of air escaping her lips passing for a laugh. They look at each other gently. Older Sister's eyes drift slowly around the room. Younger Sister remembers something; her lips tremble, and she turns back towards the TV screen, resting her head on the pillow of her folded hands.

The scene is the morning after a night of many acts. Someone has killed the Big Daddy of the house. He's found in bed with a knife in his back. Whodunit? All the flowers gather round a glossy hardwood table, questioning, deducing, exchanging sideways glances, nursing suspicions, pointing the finger. At the mention of Big Daddy's sister, the Red Rose, sexy maid White Orchid and Firmine exchange glances.

Firmine lives behind the big house, in the hunter's cottage, where at night she entertains the Red Rose, a "fallen" woman who plies her wares on the wrong side of the tracks. In her hunter's cottage, Firmine is madame, silky, sprawled across her duvet in a black negligee, a cigarillo between her lips, mooning at her love. Red Rose sits perched on the edge of the bed, laughing from deep in her throat. They play cards; one trumps the other. Firmine's eyelids grow heavy with waiting for the moment when this innocent game will end and another, more satisfying one will begin.

Beneath the sisters' bedroom is the basement, the laundry room, the coal stove, now cold, and the fourth television set, where Younger Sister once sat thumb-sucking and mesmerized in front of the screen, deaf to the bellowing of her own name. Where Older Sister was tricked by their mother to come down and watch *A Movie for a Sunday Afternoon* with her . . . and iron with her . . . and fold clothes, film after film, Sunday after Sunday. And here she is, home again and awake in the dead of night, hoping that this summons might turn out to be a ruse, that their mother might reappear, laughing as she steps out of hiding.

Estranged from her brother, and accused of being a money-grubber, Red Rose is a suspect in his murder. In the interest of justice, the sexy maid White Orchid outs madame housekeeper Firmine as a lesbian and Red Rose's lover. The girls instantly shun Firmine, stepping away from her in disgust. She looks to Red Rose for support, but the Red Rose averts her gaze.

"She is . . . a sapphist!" Grand-mère Flower hisses at Firmine.

And only her. Somehow Red Rose is not a sapphist. Older Sister smirks. She too is a sapphist. She remembers the Southie Irish girl from high school who sat on top of the dryer in the basement, asking, *daring* Older Sister to give her pleasure. She hesitated then, immediately feeling that once the inevitable happened (word got out), and the finger pointed (sapphist!) she would never be seen in the pink-white light of innocence, of youth, as one of two equally culpable participants. Older Sister knew, as she bit her lip and made a move, that she would be seen as inexplicably dark and singularly corrupting.

Younger Sister dozes, wet lashes crusted with new salt.

Older Sister's gaze wanders away from the screen. She had recently spoken about this film to Anne, critical how Firmine gets the short end of the stick throughout the film.

"What did he mean by all that?" she asked Jeanne, speaking of the director, François Ozon.

Anne waved her hand dismissively. "Pfft."

"Come on. He's deliberately using these stereotypes, the repressed lesbian housekeeper, the criminal lesbian madame, the loyal-yet-suspect black domestic, all rolled into one. All punished. He *must* be saying *something*."

"*Non, non, non,*" Anne insisted.

Older Sister bristled, but let it drop. This was to be cocktail small talk between strangers with a friend in common. Then Anne's hands waved more animatedly, as if orchestrating the *8 Femmes* soundtrack. Anne loved the all-star celebration of her country's actresses.

"And the trio of Deneuve, Emmanuelle Béart, and the picture of Romy Schneider, ah!"

No picture of France's equivalent to actress Madame Sul-te-wan falls out of Firmine's pocket in the midst of her playing the role of housekeeper, Older Sister thought. And *who* might that *be*, anyway? No portrait of Caty Rosier hangs over the fireplace in Firmine's hunter's cottage.

"I thought the film was just *lovely,*" Anne had said. "And the bits with Danielle Darrieux were *hilarious*. It was special, rare, to see all of those women acting together."

Older Sister nodded, poured herself another glass of *veltliner* and smiled, chewing a strawberry and imagining other possibilities for Firmine, ensconced as she was, as they *both* were, in the realm of other people's nostalgia.

I know this is not my future, Firmine thinks, but that somewhere else, at the edges of swamps and the mysteries of dead men, women grow true to their own desires. They know their worth. *Traversée de la mangrove*. There is another side, and a love that mirrors my skin, a child loyal to my blood, a sensuality that does not mock or damn, a vision that does not require my flesh as scrim. I cross back, to that other side, and stars are returned to my pockets to light my hips' curves with memory, with Time's continuous sway.

Younger Sister turns in her sleep, pulling the entire bedspread around her curled body, her hand close to her mouth. They have been returned to this position, fetal, blind, grasping, still dependent, suddenly alone, in a room too small to contain them. Older Sister watches the Pink Rose and the Daisy sit on the Daisy 's bed, talking about sex, after they try to force Firmine to tell them all her secrets, she, the only one among them, it seems, who has ever known love.

Older Sister's eyes turn about the room still alive with her mother's scent. She cups her palm to her own forehead with force, as if to keep her thoughts from running amok, as if to keep her brain from bursting from her skull and splattering all over the walls. Love has two faces, she muses, one white, the other dark, each with an alibi. The mask of Art hides the devouring gaze, the vacant stare, the rapid blink in the face of History. The heavy cloak of Desire drapes over impassioned bodies as they crawl, panting with slick teeth, toward the border of Custom and Taboo. Dark shawls, pots of greasepaint and discarded wigs litter this repressed landscape of sexual identity and moral culpability. Who is protected, in narratives in which certain desire is deemed perverse? Who shields, when taboo is tinged with the threat of social or physical Death? "Have I ever let you down?" Firmine implores. "Without me," Firmine says to the Yellow Orchid, "your girls wouldn't have had much."

Yellow Orchid makes to slap her.

Firmine flinches from the blow, and turns to Red Rose, in a gesture of love, even begging forgiveness, though she's done nothing wrong. Red Rose rebuffs her in a bewildering act of violence. Older Sister leans forward. Rewind. Play. Rewind. Play. Red Rose grabs Firmine's hand, then Firmine is suddenly flung bodily to the floor, crying, disgraced not by loving another woman, but by having that woman violently deny her. She scrambles to her feet, her heel catches and tears the hem of her dress. Pink Rose suppresses a giggle. Firmine runs sobbing into the kitchen.

Older Sister holds her nose, punches her pillows, then leans back against headboard, eyes on the screen, intent on smelling nothing. In denying Firmine, she realizes, Red Rose, the "dark" lady from the wrong side of the tracks, uses Firmine's body as a shield. Firmine absorbs all the disdain and punishment for her love of Red Rose. Under cover of darkness, Red Rose runs away from any admission of sex with a black woman, but runs toward a very public display of sexuality, and taboo, with her dead brother's wife. Firmine, exiled and singing alone in the kitchen, tears streaking her face, maintains her balance throughout the farcical, musical murder mystery, though she's hurtling, *being hurtled* in each scene, from social to certain death.

"You need treatment," Grand-mère Yellow Orchid says to Firmine.

"It's the domestic's revenge!" Grand-mère Flower huffs.

Older Sister's eyes burn. Younger Sister stirs, returns to sleep.

Firmine sings "so as not to be alone." She sings her song to no audience but the falling snow outside the latticed kitchen window.

Pour ne pas vivre seul
On s'fait du cinéma
On aime un souvenir
Une ombre, n'importe quoi

Pfft, said Anne. Ozon meant nothing by the flow of Firmine's story. Yet Firmine sings that she's made herself into a cinema, a movie house, a place for other people's projections. That, so as not to be alone, one loves a souvenir, a shadow, anything.

None of the other flowers look on with compassion as she sings of desire in spring and death and spring again.

Firmine's crucifix glistens. She is the diviner of truth, for it is she who discovers whodunit. And yet she's still there, staring into Red Rose's flashing eyes, her treacherous, dimpled cheeks bridged by lips painted thick, hoping that there might still be a trace, a chance. . . . *I wait, I love you, so as not to be alone.* But instead Red Rose pushes up on Yellow Orchid, her own brother's wife, claiming, now, avowing, her same-sex desire, rolling on the floor with Yellow Orchid, kissing her, their breasts pressed together, for the eyes they imagine watching them, despite the eyes of the other flowers actually upon them. There is no disgrace, but a kind of mild wonder that passes through the room like hypocrisy, like the sun through the clouds.

Firmine bursts from the kitchen excitedly, the key to her redemption from social death on the tip of her tongue. "I know who did it!"

Blam!

Younger Sister jerks awake. "What the fuck?"

She stares at Older Sister, as if in sleep she might have changed the world. But the gray night is still the night; no one has returned. Not childhood, nor their mother's hands. Reality hasn't at last ceded control and left the world to the healing power of their dreams. Younger Sister's glassy eyes follow Older Sister's to the screen, to where Firmine grimaces in disgusted shock.

"Oh, so she's shot now, too?"

"Mmmm."

There is no wound; Firmine has been hit, but no blood seeps between the fingers she clutches to her breast. Her eyes close slowly, in the fluttering throes of cinematic death. Then they flash open again, eerily undead, staring blankly out, as if transfixed by something, a vision, magic, a secret in the Continuum being kept from us.

FOOD OF THE GODS

David Trinidad

From *Phoebe 2002: An Essay in Verse*, a collaboration with Jeffery Conway and Lynn Crosbie. *Phoebe 2002* is a mock-epic based on the 1950 movie *All About Eve*, starring Bette Davis as Broadway star Margo Channing. This excerpt is from Book 7, "Pistol Packin' Margo," in which Davis confronts several other characters onstage after an audition. She lights a cigarette and smokes furiously in this scene.

There's no way Davis could have known—raving on the stage of the Curran Theatre in April 1950—that a quarter of a century later she'd be back in San Francisco filming her eighty-fifth motion picture, *Burnt Offerings* ("a trite, murkily-plotted and talky supernatural epic"[1]), and that she'd be sitting in her hotel room spewing "unprintable sizzlers"[2] into the tape recorder of "saucy, snoopy, bitchy"[3] journalist Rex Reed. Reed's profile is, in a sense, all about Davis as smoking gun: Her "[n]ostrils flare, eyes dilate like targets on a rifle range, and each word and gesture is emphasized by a blast of cigarette smoke that makes her look like she's walking in a cumulus cloud."[4] He compares her to "a locomotive, puffing and smoldering through the room." And she, naturally, breathes nothing but smoke: "[I]f I played bitches, or certain types of women who were nervous or angry or full of energy, I worked with cigarettes as props. If you're a woman who smokes, you can't just smoke one in the first scene and never be seen smoking again in the whole movie! You've gotta *stream* it out of your mouth and blow it all over the *screen!*" In the pantheon of Hollywood deities, Rex Reed maintained—from the mid-1960s through the late 1970s—the status of Ganymede, the only mortal who had complete access to the gods. Zeus fell in love with the beautiful Trojan shepherd (cf. Liz Smith's description of Reed as "sleepy-eyed, slickly tailored, blue-black hair sometimes falling in a forelock over a boyish face"[5]) and sent his eagle to abduct and carry the adolescent up to Olympus. There Ganymede replaced Hebe (the Goddess of Youth) as cupbearer. But the nectar Rex poured into the golden goblets of the gods and goddesses was far from sweet. Known for his wickedly hilarious humor and his rapier-sharp sarcasm, Reed "singlehandedly turned the [celebrity] interview into a deadly weapon,"[6] stripping the stars of their pretensions and leaving them clothed only in the naked truth. "@*%!&*!#@?&¢%!!"[7] was all Ava Gardner could utter when she read what Reed had written about her. Even his friend Jacqueline Susann once commented: "If I had an affair with Jack the Ripper, the offspring would be Rex Reed." Still, all the superstars in Tinseltown allowed him to catch them with their psyches down: Barbra Streisand, Warren Beatty, Lucille Ball, Marlene Dietrich, Ingrid Bergman, Paul Newman, Burt Lancaster, Elizabeth Taylor, Sophia Loren, Audrey Hepburn, Robert Redford, Natalie Wood. And Bette Davis—twice— though Ganymede clearly loved Artemis (smoking gun Goddess of the Hunt, Lady of Wild Things): "They come and go in their sarongs and skates and sapphire sunglasses, but there is only one queen of the silver screen. She always was, still is, and always will be."[8] In the end, Zeus granted Ganymede a somewhat dubious immortality. Rex appeared with Mae West and Raquel Welch in the ill-fated adaptation of Gore Vidal's *Myra Breckinridge*, "an outrageous story about a man-hating transsexual."[9] After a sex-change operation in Copenhagen, New York film critic Myron Breckinridge (R.R.) becomes Myra Breckinridge (Welch) and moves to Hollywood so she can immerse herself in the movie industry, con her randy Uncle Buck Loner (played by the venerable John Huston) out of half a million dollars, and symbolically destroy the American male. Myra checks into the Chateau Marmont, then calls on Uncle Buck, a former B-film cowboy star, and tells him that she is the widow of his late nephew Myron. She's there, she says, to collect on Myron's share of the property on which Buck's acting academy is built (which has passed on to Myron on his mother's death). Buck is appropriately suspicious ("I never knew that Myron had an eye for feminine pulchritude") and

says he'll have his lawyers look into it. To occupy Myra until things
are resolved, he offers her a job teaching posture and empathy, which
she gladly accepts. Myra identifies the dim-witted Rusty Godowsky
(Roger Herren), a strapping young ex–football player in her posture
class, as her sacrificial bull. Rusty is an easy target, for he has a posture
problem worthy of Myra's "special attention." In addition to picking on
him during virtually every class, she makes substantial progress during
a private session in her office. Then she goes in for the kill ("A sudden
blow: the great wings beating still"[10]) with the climactic after-hours dildo
rape in the school's infirmary. "Yes, it's lonely down here in the Hell of
Fame," said Vidal in 1995, "but there are compensations, the odd perk."[11]
Unfortunately, *Myra Breckinridge* is derided as one of the worst movies
ever made. When it was released in late June of 1970, the critics had a
feeding frenzy. *Time*: "About as funny as a child molester." *Newsweek*: "A
horrifying movie." *Look*: "A new low in amateur squalor." *Variety*: "The
bad taste is beyond belief." The film was littered with old movie clips,
many of which were juxtaposed with unorthodox scenes like the *Rape
of the Jock*. When Loretta Young heard that a clip of her was used in the
context of the posterior assault, she filed a suit in Cleveland and won.
It took Michael Sarne twenty years to get another directing job. The
only other known follow-up work by the very attractive Roger Herren,
apparently irreparably stigmatized by his role in *Myra Breckinridge*, was
as "Cowboy" in the West Coast stage production of *The Boys in the
Band*.[12] Rex, too, suffered a fall. Long after he'd lost his standing as "the
Now Kid, the jet set's latest instant celebrity,"[13] he was arrested for
shoplifting (shades of Hedy Lamarr[14]): "A Tower Records security guard
apprehended the 61-year-old critic as he allegedly removed three CDs
[Mel Torme, Carmen McRae, and Peggy Lee], police said."[15]

NOTES

1. *Variety*, 1976.
2. Rex Reed, "Bette Davis" in *Conversations in the Raw: Dialogues, Monologues, and Selected Short Subjects* (New York: World Publishing Company, 1969), p. 16.
3. *The New York Times Book Review*, 1969: "Rex Reed is a saucy, snoopy, bitchy man
who sees with sharp eyes and writes with a mean pen and succeeds in making voyeurs
of us all."
4. Rex Reed, "Bette Davis" in *Valentines & Vitriol* (New York: Delacorte Press, 1977),
p. 127.

5. Ibid., p. xi.

6. Jacket copy on paperback edition of Reed's *Conversations in the Raw* (New York: Signet, 1970).

7. Promotional quote for Reed's *Do You Sleep in the Nude?* (New York: Signet, 1969), p. i. In his piece on Ava Gardner, Reed quotes her saying such things as "I lost my goddamn mantilla in the limousine"; "Don't tell *me* about *God!* I know all about that bugger!"; and "Drink time, baby!"

8. Reed, "Bette Davis" in *Valentines & Vitriol*, p. 127.

9. Quotes and information about *Myra Breckinridge* taken from two Web sites: "Myra Breckinridge: The Web Site," http://members.tripod.com/~myrasite and www.geocities.com/myrabreckinridge [cited June 2000].

10. William Butler Yeats, "Leda and the Swan," line 1.

11. Gore Vidal quoted in Christopher Hitchens's "La Dolce Vidal," *Vanity Fair* (November 1995), p. 68.

12. *The Boys in the Band*: Mart Crowley's groundbreaking play about a homosexual birthday party, which opened at Theatre Four in New York on April 14, 1968, and was produced as a motion picture in 1970.

13. *Time* magazine, 1968.

14. Exotic movie star Hedy Lamarr was arrested for shoplifting in 1965, long after her screen career had become nonexistent.

15. From *Daily News*, February 12, 2000: "new yor k—Movie critic Rex Reed was arrested on Saturday after he was caught by store security allegedly removing three compact discs from a midtown Manhattan record store, police said. The 61-year-old critic, who was charged with criminal possession of stolen property, was spotted by store detectives at 4:45 p.m. at Tower Records on Broadway allegedly taking the three CDs, police said. Authorities said they found him carrying CDs of Mel Torme, Peggy Lee and Carmen McRae. Reed was expected to appear in court in March, police said."

And from the *Associated Press*, April 21, 2000: "NEW YORK—If Rex Reed can stay out of trouble for the next six months he's off the hook. That ruling came from a Manhattan judge on Tuesday. The 61-year-old film critic was arrested in February after he allegedly tried to steal three compact discs from a record store. Reed, a columnist for the *New York Observer*, denied the allegations but said he'd abide by the ruling from Judge Suzanne Mondo, who agreed to dismiss the charges and seal the record if Reed is not arrested again within the next six months. During a preliminary investigation of the acclaimed critic, it was brought to light that he was once detained for questioning in connection with an attempted house break-in at the estate of television legend Shirley Hemphill. Miss Hemphill was staying at her summer estate on Fire Island during the height of 'What's Happening!!' when her co-star Fred Berry noticed a man lurking outside the front gates wearing what appeared to be a Geisha outfit. Later that evening after running a red light in his Mercedes Reed was pulled over and not only was a Geisha outfit discovered in the back seat of his car but a harem costume. Said Reed at the time, 'So I dress up a bit, is that a crime?' Charges were never filed in connection with the incident. Hemphill years later confessed on *The Tonight Show* that she 'felt his shame.'"

4

Between Pictures

BEHIND-THE-SCENES (1982)

Masha Tupitsyn

For one to whom the real world becomes real images,
mere images are transformed into real beings.
The Society of the Spectacle

I don't dream about anyone, except myself.
The Smiths

I spent the summer afternoons of 1982 pretending to be Olivia Newton John singing "Physical" up in a barn loft in Maine because I liked how bossy Olivia sounded. In the music video, she threatens to fuck not just those fat losers in the gym, but if I wasn't careful, me too. Olivia's blonde-ness makes men put up with her aerobicized commands as she tries to act heartless. I'd only ever seen Olivia in *Grease,* so it was hard to reconcile the tough-love gym instructor of "Physical" with the cheerleading high school pushover. The only way to understand Olivia's behavior in "Physi-cal" is to view it as an extension of her transformation from goody-goody "Sandy 1" to spandex-clad "Sandy 2" at the end of *Grease.* "Physical" picks up where "Sandy 2" left off. Exhausted on the treadmill, men run to and from Olivia. Stranded in the song's call for a female sexual initiative, the true lyric of "Physical" reflects the loss of a strong male alliance—a fear that plagued the eighties. The body was shoved into fitness centers around the country and dealt with accordingly.

In the video, Olivia stands in front of a room full of frazzled men and harasses them into shape like circus animals with her voice and body, with her act; her image reflected six different times in the gym mirror. Her pseudo-aggression is reinforced through multiplicity and repetition. Six Olivias are better, hotter, sexier, and stronger than one. Like a magazine, each man gets a copy. Each one has something to look at.

In the afternoons, in between the beach and the girls at the cottage, I'd wear my mother's clothes and gold headband and hop around the hayloft to get in the mood. Like any decade, the eighties had a tone of voice. A color and an emphasis. Whenever I think about my mother's clothes, I remember the stars I pretended to be when I was inside them. Anything gold or metallic—fairy-dusted and shimmering—allowed me to morph into women like Olivia and Jamie Lee Curtis. Women arranged like chess pieces in a maze of locker rooms, dance clubs, and L.A. dramas. I imagined accepting the Oscar dressed in something from my mother's closet because at six it never occurred to me that I'd have my own money, my own clothes, and that time would make my mother's enviable wardrobe less desirable to me. By proxy, I'd also long for John Travolta, who was dark like me, and whose name is mixed into Olivia's (Olivia Newton *John*) like a final ingredient. John had cut songs on 1983's *Two of a Kind* with Olivia after they'd made *Grease* together. Neither of them believed they could pull the album off on their own, so they combined, using the recipe of two to get down to the power of one. Inside the album's fold-out cover, which I'd peeled open and tacked to my wall, their heads are twinned, fused together, like flowers knotted on a single vine, making them Siamese twins; one blonde, one dark.

Olivia and John had starred in things together, had shared screen-time, sang duets, vouched for one another; fucked, or acted like they did; fucked or acted like they did on-screen; fucked or acted like they did off-screen, because that's what everything is anyway, an act. Unlike in *Grease*, on *Two of a Kind*, Olivia and John are modern adults. They are present-tense (eighties), instead of vintage (fifties), so things aren't just suggested, they are stated and contrived. The entire album is a clue. Only I wasn't interested in the pair's singing, or the songs themselves, which they sang but didn't write, but in what the songs revealed about their relationship and its market-mythology. What were Olivia and John doing in the recording studio that I couldn't see? And what could I see by listening to them sing? Instead of watching desire play on screen, I went backstage, behind the curtain, to listen for signs. Seeing things offscreen allowed me to assemble an on-screen story for what was happening. The body is a melody that often makes a lyric irrelevant.

In *Blow Out*, John, as Jack Terry, takes the denotation of sound and turns it into a forensic science as a sound man who discovers a crime by listening to it. Out catching noise for a film one night, he accidentally records, and therefore witnesses, a murder. In the movie, John spends most of his time alone in his car, aurally stalking his surroundings on his headphones, while a microphone is planted somewhere like a trap. Trees and birds swish and brush against John's atomic tape, a sponge that sucks up both the tiniest and biggest of historical forces and happenstance: Kennedy at Chappaquiddick, Watergate, the JFK assassination. In Jack Terry's bag of sound effects, harvested for horror movies, car crashes fall like trees in a forest that no one hears and testimonial sound becomes a stand-in for vigilante justice. Unlike the male vigilante films of the 1970s, the 1980s hard-body films, explains the film scholar Susan Jeffords, suggest a different social order. Heroes, like Jack Terry, don't defy society, they inadvertently defy governments and institutional beauracracies "who are standing in the way of social improvement." The vigilante hero is thrown like a football past the threshold of society and is alone, a primary theme of Reaganism.

Blow Out is a remake of Michelangelo Antonioni's 1966 film *Blow-Up*, a title that refers to the photographic process of enlargement. In the Antonioni version, a series of prints are repeatedly reproduced, blown up, viewed and re-viewed, in order to increase perception. *Blow Out* refers to the reverse, a surfeit of sound that requires distillation in order to pick out the almost inaudible tone of certainty. Both films are preoccupied with return and repetition as the mechanism for recouping social relevance, and new technologies allow for unexpected encounters with history and historical trauma. In her book *Death 24x a Second: Stillness and the Moving Image,* Laura Mulvey points out that "a return to the cinema's past constitutes a gesture towards a truncated history . . . Such a return to the past through cinema is paradoxically facilitated by the kind of spectatorship that has developed with the use of new technologies, with the possibility of returning to and repeating a specific film fragment." In both films, narratives move around the stasis of death in order to unearth a previously unnoticed detail. And the delay in time—between the sequence of events, the murders in question, and their register (sound and photographic still) through mechanical witness—reveals some element that has lain dormant.

The title *Blow Out* refers to breakdown, while *Blow-Up* connotes climax and embellishment—the irresolvable problem of constructing history and framing the past. Recording a more recent historical trauma (Watergate), *Blow Out* is anchored in real government corruption and conjures power outages, blown fuses, blackouts, power failures; breakdowns in communication, narrative—history. Thus, in light of the Watergate scandal, sound acts as the more substantiative and historically relevant evidence, forcing both Thomas and Jack to cobble their narratives (verisimilitude) out of darkness and in darkness. When John was signed for the role, studio executives at MGM wanted to cast Olivia for the part of Sally to cash in on an on-screen rapport jump-started by *Grease*. But Brian De Palma vetoed the request and instead cast his real-life wife Nancy Allen in the role, with whom John had also shared a cinematic assignation (albeit a more sexually explicit one).

★

After singing "Physical," I'd pretend John had stayed after class to talk to me. He wasn't like the other students. He is a male anomaly, though signs of difference are never coherent. The movie says I want him. I was dressed in the clothes Olivia wears on the album cover: red-hot tank-top peeled back over her shoulders, white headband sliding her moist hair from her face. Her California visage—a mini sunset—in profile and tilted back, mouth unfastened like a seatbelt. She is blissfully fatigued after a workout, sex, or sex with herself. You can't see the rest of picture. What's there, what's not.

Upstairs in the barn, I'd sit on a block of hay in the dark and let John feel me as Olivia which I did by feeling myself, or imagining a movie scene I could crack open like an egg and scramble; walk into at some precise moment by splicing myself in. I longed for John because Olivia did. I wanted what she wanted. Or I wanted what she acted like she wanted, because it's often easier to act on an established desire. Easier to borrow and reuse than to build and test from scratch. I could work off an already existing script, material, group of people, set of circumstances, and then I could recycle and edit. I could alter. I could switch.

I assigned roles and personalities to parts of my body so that they could act the parts or the body of some other body. Mine played multiple roles. My eyes would end up being my mouth because they were what I was actually using to kiss with. I was looking at myself kiss and seeing the whole thing play on the screen in my head, or at least I'd see what I could remember seeing. I'd drag in a scene I wanted to work off of like some animal dragging another, smaller, dead animal into its cave in order to devour it in peace. I'd walk into a pivotal scene, into the point I wanted to start from, and hijack it. I'd sneak in through the back without paying. I'd climb in through the window and try to seduce the boy who slept in the bed below it. I'd mull over a part in a movie that I liked, stalked, wanted to grasp, or be in; that I'd circled and returned to for some unknown reason, a magnetic field pulling me, and then I'd draw that part back like a curtain—fast and swift—exposing a small, raw light of my own onto the poorly lit setting—dark because I wasn't in it.

★

Sometimes while I was up there I thought about the way film boys kissed film girls and wondered if film girls and film boys did things differently—kissed differently—offscreen? Does one act a kiss the way one acts everything else in a movie? How much of a person is in an actor and how much of a person isn't? The body is a disadvantage because it can never remove traces of itself. It changes by being bigger or smaller, shrinking or enlarging, like *Alice in Wonderland*, but otherwise the body is locked into place. You can change the person you want to play, but you cannot trade the body for another body. In her novel *Indivisible*, Fanny Howe writes, "a form cannot be recognized unless its image already exists in the body that discovers it." In *The Karate Kid*, a movie I saw in Provincetown in 1984, the year Ronald Reagan was reelected and George Orwell declared the world irrevocably doomed, Ralph Macchio's real walk—all in the toes, pulling off from the Achilles tendon, so that the heel is always suspended—is never Daniel, it's always Ralph. And Ralph's kisses—make-outs, big mouth open wide, sloppy and chasmal, full-body embrace, Italian and working-class—might just be Ralph's offscreen desire for the WASPY Elizabeth Shue, who put Harvard on hold to make the movie.

But whose kiss is it? Who does it belong to? The character or the actor? Is it Daniel's or Ralph's? Does the kiss belong to the film or what's off it? Is desire diegetic or non-diegetic? In movies, kisses are rarely forged, and neither are birthdays and height, which are almost always non-diegetic because they're outside the given story. The body isn't required to act; it's along for the ride—the ultimate prop. It's merely a vessel, a form of transport, chauffeuring the person around from place to place, scene to scene, feeling to feeling, part to part, movie to movie. Maybe that's the only kind of life an actor ever really has.

In DVD commentaries, actors turn into viewers and become their own identificatory site (image). Actors often say they hate watching themselves. Is this because watching something they did while being inside from the outside snaps open the lock of dualism? On-screen and offscreen? Front and back? Here and there? Is it like being in two places at once? Many actors claim that watching their own performances makes them feel self-conscious—fatal for an actor, like looking into the eyes of a camera, which are really our eyes. Actors have to stay *in* the picture—a gated community—until they're out of it. Or is it because as viewers—more specifically, viewers of *themselves*—actors would be forced into our real shoes instead of fictitious ones? Is it too much to juggle the inside *and* the outside, the on-screen and the offscreen, when pretending? In commentaries, offscreen eyes inform and review the on-screen body disrupting the flow of contrivance, so that the offscreen exposes, or reveals, what's happening on-screen, and the inside comes from the outside. Actors take shape through representation; by physically materializing, so the absence of face and body requires a reimagining of the viewership role.

Fanny Howe writes, "the body is everything and everything is a body." On the 2005 DVD *Karate Kid* commentary track, John G. Avildsen, the same guy who made *Rocky*, mocks Ralph's noticeable gait, his perfect 50/50 boy/girl face, so that while loving him, I was simultaneously loving myself, and Ralph says, "Yeah, I always walk from my Achilles' heel. My Achilles' heel has always been a problem." This private admission—revealed not through promotional text, on-screen body, or image, but through a supplemental (non-diegetic) voiceover that wasn't there initially, but affixed later on—reinforces Daniel's cinematic struggle with physical vulnerability, linking on-screen and offscreen via a shared weak spot in the body. In the commentary, I can hear Ralph's discomfort the way I can see Daniel's shame acting out.

In *The Karate Kid* the individual male (ethnic and working-class) body itself is the Achilles' heel of the larger national body, and in order to understand it, Daniel's is deconstructed and slowly reassembled like an old car. His is a body that garners strength through a piecemealing of the deliberate, menial, and symbolic: sanding floors, waxing cars, painting houses and fences. It learns, trains, and becomes (emotionally, not necessarily technically) "skilled" via general tasks—labor—whose spiritual significance is slowly revealed. This, the movie points out, is the one thing the rich blond villains have never had to do. For them, the body is a playground, a prized possession, an inherited right; a joyride, like every other machine they cruise around in. Through labor, Daniel discovers the "divine" (karate), and it is intention, which leads to the rescue, rather than the triumph, of the body. As in *Rocky*, the "fight" is won via (immigrant) manual labor, thereby situating the body within a caste system. Bodies at the top and bodies at the bottom. "The more you watch him move, at night, working out, pushing the body against darkness and winter cold," writes Lidia Yuknavitch in her film-based collection *Real to Reel*, "the more it is true, it is the film of a man and not the man, or it is the man caught on film repeating himself . . . We do not want the movie of a man who is losing heart."

Daniel, the name of a real-life boy I loved, and whom I met in the same town I saw *The Karate Kid* in two summers later, has what Dorothy has, has what every hero/heroine in popular American cinema has, an inner compass that cannot be shoved or knocked out the same way that teeth can. In the Hollywood movie, what is beaten, tested, and deplored is the very thing that cannot be terminally destroyed; the thing we know will heal by the end of a film. Cuts and bruises are merely illustration in the Hollywood film; post-it notes that allow the viewer to track the fiction and determine how much further the hero/heroine has left to go in it. The worst injuries come at the end, and the face, a sacred movie paragon that never (except in the horror genre) risks defilement or obscurity, is routinely spared visible massacre. In Hollywood, pain is something a viewer has to imagine or take with a grain of salt, thereby, in some sense, avoiding it altogether. "Because the characters often live against all odds," writes the poet Claudia Rankine, "it is the actors whose mortality concerns me."

The shiner that Daniel Larusso hides behind his sunglasses the morning after his first beating marks him as the film's "body-with-a-heart." "In Sufism," writes Howe, "'the pupil of the eye' is the owner of each member of the body, even the heart, and each part becomes a tool under its lens. It is in and through and with the pupil of the eye that the catch locks between just-being and always-being. . . . You are progressing at one level and becoming more lost at another." This is how Daniel is trained to face not the adversity of his body, but the adversity of eye/I. "The less focused the gesture, the more true to the eye of the heart it is." Meanwhile, the militia of boys fights like soldiers at the SoCal Dojo and their Cold-War gestures collapse into the centrality of power.

The offscreen Daniel came into my life after the on-screen one did, and when he appeared, I felt I was finally being given the chance to fully enter, or exit, the cinematic frame. Rather than fight for a body's survival, like Daniel, a boy, I wrestled for the chance for my desire to see the light of day. My thoughts leaving the confines of a dark ship. If I could accomplish this, my body would catch up and be fine. In *The Karate Kid*, Ralph walks, from scene to scene—a nomad made up of borrowed moves—in Daniel's shoes. When I came out of the movie theater, after years inside, my eyes ached from the patina of the real world.

In 1982 Jamie Lee Curtis made *Perfect*. In it, she plays an aerobics instructor whose body is the point. It's the point of her character's life in the movie, of the movie's plot, and of Jamie's on-screen and offscreen livelihood. In *The Karate Kid*, the body is also required to win, but unlike Daniel, who has to reestablish his prowess with each new *Karate Kid* sequel like a bad dream, re-entering the costume of the body in order to activate its pendulous strengths, Jamie achieved her victory a decade beforehand, earning her right to flaunt and shed her accumulative armor in future roles. By the 1980s, it was maintenance Jamie was after, not a brand-new car. Although the body is a character in *Perfect*, or the role belongs to the body, the body, unlike the role, belongs to Jamie, not Jessie, who wears it like a costume for the part. Two equally similar androgynous monikers (Jamie/Jessie) allude to the diegetic aspect of the body, which struggles to be in two different places at once, as do the names themselves. (Jamie's name and body have both been famously mythologized for their ambiguity offscreen, which led to an opportunistic utilization that crossed over into film.) While actors are routinely asked what it's like to play a certain character or part, they are rarely asked what it's like to play another body. Unless that body has been theatrically reconfigured through special effect, costume, or makeup. Unless the *point* is to change the body, making the body subject rather than object.

Perfect came out after Jamie spent an entire decade in horror, which due to her mother's own horrific past—death in a shower—she became heir to. Their abject mother-daughter paths crossed in 1980 when they starred in John Carpenter's *The Fog* together. Equally, Jamie often referred to her famous absentee father, Tony Curtis, as "a ghost." By taking a name from both her mother and her father, Jamie makes use of her real and imagined ties with the spectral.

While a lack of explicit, or unspoken body (the body being a kind of elephant in the room in the horror genre) in *Halloween* saves Jamie from being murdered by her incensed, one-track-minded, sociopathic brother, Michael, it is her explicitly articulated body, disrobed in *Trading Places* and *Perfect,* that gave Jamie's acting career a second (after) life. Having managed to save her horror-bound existence on a diet of sexual modesty and repression that immunizes the female in horror and allows her to become eternal and indeterminate like the Monster, Jamie got to celebrate her endurance in the seventies in the 1980s. For years, Jamie was called "The Body." The body that survived? That wasn't destroyed? All throughout the eighties and nineties Jamie was asked about her body and told the press, "While they're up and firm [her breasts], why not shoot them once or twice." *Perfect* provides the diegetic link between the female body and horror.

★

Some time in the early eighties, John Travolta claimed Olivia broke his heart in real life, the way he broke hers in *Grease*. Given his trauma—diegetic pain overlapping into non-diegetic pain—and the baggage he was hauling around because of it, I tried to be extra compassionate, to put aside my jealousy and suspicion, to make it up to him. I interjected myself as a way to meet John and to get him to make it up to me by making my way inside at a pivotal moment in the movie. The moment it all goes wrong. It was similar to slipping into a disguise—drag—(the drag of acting) in order to assume someone else's identity in a Shakespearean play; tricking them into reciting their lines to you instead of the person assigned to play the part. Sometimes, as the movie *Shakespeare in Love* demonstrates, you have to enter the body of the beloved to become the beloved.

I was John and I was me. I was John and I was Sandy up to a point. In the dark, I asked John all the questions Olivia didn't, that she should have, that I wanted her to; that should have been in the script, or that I screamed at the TV set whenever John was acting like an asshole and a group song just wouldn't cut it. Questions that had Olivia asked would have made the film cease to exist. Things have to go wrong in order for there to be a story.

In *Grease*, John never listens to Sandy. He's too busy pretending he doesn't know her or asking her to change so that he won't have to let his guard down in front of all his friends. I imagined John looking at me. Hard, then soft. It was the hardness that made it feel good. It was the hardness that finally made it go soft. Underneath a sky of stars, I finally had one for myself. We'd switched places and John switched without objection, sliding right off the screen and into my seat. "I can't keep my eyes off you," he said. Then I closed mine and mouthed the words to myself until I could *feel* them, like any good actor trying to get their lines right. I lit up. From the outside of that dark room in the barn, up on the second floor, lost in a maze of hay, I must have glowed and flickered like a little screen.

I wanted to respond to John's touch, to climb right into it as though it were a car and drive off with it. To fly as though John's touch was the caged love-birds that Tippi Hedren drives to Bodega Bay in *The Birds*. But those "lovebirds" are more than just birds. They're part of a continuum between the kinds of brightly-colored acting birds that live in cages, and the liminal black birds that fly off the screen and wildly peck at all of our fantasies. I wanted a person somewhere between character and actor, between story and life. But I didn't kiss John or succumb to the new script because this is where people always get lazy in a movie. Instead of pushing through into some kind of understanding, they look for a quick exit and slip into a predictable comfort zone—kissing, silence, omission, happy ending, *The End*.

I felt like Whoopi Goldberg in *Ghost*. The part where Patrick Swayze has to temporarily break into her body (makin' whoopee) at the end of the movie in an effort to have one final talk/fuck with Demi, who in the film's possessory dénouement is actually having a lesbian, interracial erotic experience with psychic Whoopi, who ends up not being psychic at all, just symbolically permeable. She is the restorative conduit for Patrick and Demi's prematurely ended white romance. Like John, Patrick can't talk either, could not say what he wanted to say while he was still alive, just *ditto, ditto, ditto*. Swayze is the return of the repressed who comes back, via Whoopi, to say all the *right* things. As corporeal prime real estate, Whoopi is overflowing with language and her otherness is invaded as a neutral territory in which to resolve Patrick and Demi's pre-death marital problems. What they do requires a third person. A third person is often in the picture.

★

I remembered the first time I saw John. He was on TV helping Nancy Allen—who gives him blow jobs in the movie—dump a bucket of pig's blood all over Carrie who'd never sucked John's—or anyone else's—dick. I bet she could have torn it off and flung it across a room just by looking at it. I bet that was the problem. The power to freely do things with your thoughts that you cannot do with your body. In online chat rooms, the body is lost to language. You think your way through the body. You write the body down. You order the body around. You treat it like a script. In the 1980 movie *Scanners*, thoughts also kill, though in this case, the impulse to kill is entirely masochistic, and scanning involves a psychic identification and empathy that leads in pain—nosebleeds, nausea, stomachaches, earaches. Being "plugged in" (Carrie gets assaulted with a similar phrase while showering in a locker room and getting her first period in the opening scene of the movie. A gang of sadistic high school girls throw tampons at her, while chanting, "plug it up!") leads to intense psychic pain but is also an antidote to narcissism. ("With all those voices in your head, how can you hear your own voice?") Non-scanners force scanners to identify with them until their heads break off their bodies, which sounds a lot like love. Telepathy is heterogeneous, a kind of pluralism, because it allows you to hear and feel more than one thing, for more than one person, more than yourself. At the prom, coated in blood like a bird pinned down by an oil spill, Carrie hears everyone's voices and covers her ears.

Maybe the rehearsal for the blow job scene consisted of John getting his actual dick sucked by Nancy's actual mouth. Isn't he method? Aren't men usually method? John could come in Nancy's mouth, but not in real life, because from 1979 to 1983, she was both filmically and sexually contracted to Brian De Palma, who, as a director, watched his wife fake things. It was Nancy who was originally supposed to play the Carrie role, while Sissy Spacek read for the part of Chris Hargensen, the movie's incorrigible female "monster." But De Palma made them swap sides. A few years later, Debra Winger was recast as the female lead in *Urban Cowboy* because according to Winger, Sissy Spacek and John Travolta had a falling-out.

The night I saw *Carrie,* I was in some old man's (an art collector) TV den in Yonkers, N.Y., where Nancy was born, while my parents ate dinner with him and his guests. After I was done eating I asked my mom if I could watch TV. I walked into the room and sat down next to the screen, kneeling in front of it like the little girl in *Poltergeist,* who dies in real life but not in the movie, and, like her, used my body to imbibe the horror the way a thick curtain sucks up too much sun. Nearly the end, and I still had no idea what Carrie had been through before detonating in the gym. Under her spell, I was afraid to get up as she made the cars flip over and crash. Maybe if I moved, I'd flip and break too. She was already outside in the parking lot after having escaped the fire she started. She walked through it unscathed like a magician, arms out like a zombie, in this sexy white slip that wasn't sexy at all; that should have gone underneath something, but that she wore like a heart on a sleeve, immune to the flames and to the heat, which was finally inside her, rising out. No more guilt.

After *Grease,* it was reported that John liked Olivia, or loved her, or wanted to fuck her, or did, or talked about how he never got to. In real life, Paul, an older gay friend from Provincetown, told me that he used to hang out with John at the Paradise Garage in New York in the seventies, and that they got "physical" too. Or John did. Paul said John was "a regular" in a sea where only men were regulars.

"Put two and two together," he said and rolled his eyes.

He said, "You do the math," like we were solving a crime and he needed my help.

So much of knowing has to do with wanting and not wanting to know. Paul waited on tables. I followed behind him with a pitcher of water, refilling everything. He smiled at the customers, acting through his long shifts, while I didn't have to. He was in front of the curtain and I was behind it. He was the actor and I was the editor who came in afterwards to clean everything up. It's why I took the job.

I poured the water and replenished people's bread baskets and garlic butter, while Paul took their orders and asked me to get things. I carried tubs of dirty dishes back and forth, building the muscles in my forearms.

During my shifts, I'd fold my long hair up in a bun and throw on my re-quired *Bubulas* T-shirt, and after my shifts, I'd let my hair unfurl again like a roll of film. The day went back and forth, rotating, echoing the panora-ma of waves that surrounded us. Our skin was always covered in salt and the thought of water. I'd put on new clothes, a dress, and the cooks would ask me out, acting on the worn-out cliché of women who switch from cinematic outcasts to sexpots simply by letting their hair down or taking their glasses off. "*The looks on their faces when she goes from being the frump to the fox,*" Jean Rhys wrote. From blurry to in-focus, cinematic makeovers concern an erotics of seeing or *re*-seeing. Like a mirage in the desert of desire, what the male lead imagines, desires, and wants to see, magically appears before him. The change is supposed to signify a heightening of consciousness on his part, but in actuality is aided by the female lead morphing into the very thing he wants to see. By submitting to a cultural standard, it makes it easy for a man to finally love her. *How* he sees does not change; rather she changes into the thing he wants to look at. Sandy does the same thing in *Grease* and John gets all the credit. He loves her, but why does he love her?

When it was quiet at the restaurant, Paul would give me cigarettes to smoke and serve up more Hollywood dish. Before the Internet, he'd spent years reading tell-alls, authorized and unauthorized. He had dirt on people we only ever saw in an indirect way; people we saw, but never talked to. We'd sit on upside-down buckets of mayonnaise in the parking lot and look at the bay. Our thoughts would swim around the same sub-ject in different ways and then come up for air.

Paul said, "I never saw Olivia at Paradise;" she was in Australia with her family most of the time promoting her albums. In 1982, John and Olivia declined to star in *Grease 2* because what more was there to say and do? They'd graduated from the ultimate caste system and floated up into the clouds to die—or were already dead—so intense was the euphoria of everybody getting what they wanted. For no apparent reason, the high school gang had somehow died and gone to heaven in a flying car. All this made it easier to go their separate ways and for us to do the same. The end of a Hollywood movie is often equivalent to Nirvana. "It is when a movie is full-square on the wall," writes Fanny Howe, "that there is nothing more in life to chase after. There is no future. You have reached bliss."

Before putting his cigarette out, Paul told me that John used to hang out in the back of Paradise by the pay phones and red bathrooms. He said it reminded him of De Palma's menstrual interiors—all that red—the pig's blood in *Carrie*. John stood talking, not signing autographs.

"An autograph would have somehow been proof, evidence," said Paul.

I pictured his mouth all over John's five-o'clock shadow. During the *Blow Out* shoot, John suffered from insomnia. Paul would leave Paradise at six a.m.

"A lack of sleep helped him create a moody performance and it's why his character seems so downtrodden in the movie. I find his exhaustion very sexy. It's like he's sleepwalking, at the end of his wick. Melting like a candle. And the mystery is solved just before the candle blows out. The point is, what's on the other side of that sound? Just like in *Blow-Up*, what's *not* in the image? The image doesn't actually tell us anything, only arrangement does that. Do you know why?"

"No, why?"

"Because John is so weary that he's able to hear things. He's open. Towards the end, he doesn't even need a sound 'detector' because he's a dog, he can hear things without it. His body doesn't fight back anymore and he's no longer naïve about America."

"But he's not an insomniac in the movie."

"No, but offscreen he is, and offscreen tells a story that ends up on film. It's like an X-ray. It changes how he acts. What he can play. It changes the image that develops on film. That's why *Blow Out* is an elaboration on *Blow-Up*."

Then Paul changed the subject and said, "John tried to fuck me in the bathroom once."

"Did you let him?" I asked, excited.

"What do you think?"

In the end, I don't know what John really wanted, had, or got. Some wants and needs sound better out loud than others. But for years, he kept going backwards and forwards like he was dancing.

"He's such a liar," said Paul.

"Who?"

"John."

★

"Have you ever noticed how everyone one gets well by the end of a movie?" John asked me while reaching for places I shouldn't have let him go. Not off the bat like that. Not with our age difference and not with all the bullshit I put up with all year at school after traveling thousands of miles, hours on a plane, to find him again without knowing I'd find him. Not after one vague, half-assed apology in the dark, where no one could see us, where it didn't really count, where there was no camera.

While unzipping his black jeans. While slipping my headband off, my sweaty red T-shirt, turning me around. I liked it better when I couldn't see him, when I could only hear him whispering into the dark like a movie. TV with the volume turned low. It was the way I watched it sometimes, in bed, rolled onto my side, my back to the screen. Trying to fall asleep without shutting it off: afraid of the room without it, afraid of myself without it, afraid of the gap in between. I'd lie there hoping to not plummet down the black rabbit hole wedged between my life and the movie. I'd lie there with just the voice of the movie next to me, like a nightlight left on for children who need a compass for dark. A lighthouse waving circular beams across the water, the images appearing like security guards checking the halls of a prison ward before sleep. Only the TV light was on. From my bed, I watched it on the wall in the shape of a dust cloud, flitting; a black ball moving over everything, darkening the theater. A shadow over the forced-entry light. I wanted to stay in character. I could project anything onto that screen. I could play whatever I wanted. There was nothing else to do.

ECHO

Peter Dubé

The mirror is where it all begins.

It hung on a green wall for months—old, and tall, and narrow—before I noticed anything.

It was implacable in its finish. The glass was so smooth: a rectangular pool of uncertain depth. The slick, reflective surface like a body of water unstirred by submarine motion: no great predatory fish, no snakes or grinning crocodiles, just the relentless silvery images tossed back at us with a certain insolence. The carved wooden frame glowed gilded and knotted: vines and, at each corner, a horned, grinning face, lolling tongue out as if to drink from the shimmering surface with an ornamental nonchalance. But things were disturbed, finally.

The peculiarities began with a small, framed photograph on a console table behind the couch, an image of a friend—Adrian—and me sharing a weekend in New York. It's a silly photo of the two of us leaving one of the last porn theaters in the city, barely a year before they all closed, before they vanished, ghostly and forever. That was a few months before Adrian too disappeared to parts unknown.

We are dizzy, holding an open book before us, pointing at something in it. An acquaintance that'd traveled with us—and whose name I've since forgotten—took the shot. We are captured a little after Adrian snuck up on me in the men's room. I remember his face heaving into the glass in which I was running my fingers through my messy hair. It all—after all—begins with a mirror.

Adrian and I are laughing in the picture. We had spent the whole afternoon in the darkened hall, watching pink flesh flicker across the screen . . . and flash among the shadowed rows of seats, the aisles and the stairwells, each step sticky, crowded with gloom. We were quiet during our tenure in the movie hall, but we are laughing, afterwards.

Today, staring again, I come to my senses for a second and look behind me at the actual photograph whose mere reflection I encounter in the glass. It is the same holiday snapshot on the table, but we are laughing at a closed book. The silver world of the mirror is different, as it must be, however partially.

The difference stirs memory. I recall Adrian hissing at me in the darkness, whispering about his headache. He wanted to go home, and didn't. He complained, I commiserated. We stifled a laugh then, because neither of us would make the slightest move to leave the cinema, a throbbing in the head or no. We spent the whole afternoon in there. I want to say together, but most of the time we vanished, happy, from each other's sight in quest of handsome strangers. He caught me in the men's room though. I remember that, his face hovering over my shoulder as I pushed my fingers through my—suddenly—messy hair. And a few short months later, he vanished from my life.

I remember the film playing on the screen as I sat in the dark. An impossibly handsome man cruising a bright street, T-shirt peeled off, hung over one shoulder. He, why not call him Angel, struts across a pavement scintillating with heat, the sweat lending him light too.

Angel stops on a corner, lifts his hand to his forehead, scans the passing traffic, and leans against a tree. A tall palm takes all his light and drapes him in feathering shadow. It highlights his body. Great plastrons of pectoral muscle are etched with lines of black. A long, white car slows before him and he gets in. The driver and he make a pair. The pair makes idle talk; their hands wander; beneath the pale, worn denim of his jeans his cock hardens visibly, strains at the seam.

In a strange cut away, the dashboard clock flips digital minutes over. Twelve. Thirteen. The soundtrack mangles melody and a clearer, fleshly sound joins it.

A tanned hand slides up and down Angel's erection. Root to glistening glans.

Then his face fills the screen, eyes shut, mouth slightly open, lips bright with saliva. The camera shows us the rearview mirror. It's always about the mirror. Again and again and—in the other glass before me—a shift in my posture unleashes light, obliterating half the image. My eyes shudder, shift, scramble, trying to track the remnants of vision. Why do I stare into it at so much length? One of the horned heads in the corners seems to mock me now, tongue out.

His cock curves in the hollow of a hand as the car plunges into violent daylight and expansive blacktop.

The pair arrives at his apartment. The man who drove is darker, slightly taller. One hand cups the denim crotch again, and the other slides up the naked torso to grab at Angel's stubbled chin. They kiss, wetly. A long time. The dark man pushes Angel to his knees. His dress slacks are tenting a few inches below the belt.

In the mirror, in the darkened theater, on the screen, in the room where I believe I am standing. Music plays at a low level. Grows.

Angel sucks at the man. The man beside me in the dark grins and I respond. Strong digits rise to the back of my own neck—burning—in the hall of moving images, pull me down. The Angel vanishes. It is dark again; my face buried in shadows, my mouth suddenly full and only taste and smell signifying and this man's hardness. Until I rise, sight means nothing. A memory.

When I do rise, the dark man is done with the Angel; he exits a shower. He towels off, puts some product in his hair. He leaves the bathroom nude, the tube of hair gel still in his hand, a curious detail. He puts the tube down on a low table covered with postcards. Jumbled among the mix of iconic or lesser-known landmarks and self-conscious camp is one image the camera lingers on a beat too long. A carnival winds its way through a narrow street. Half-naked men wear huge planets on their heads that crack open to release—doves, balloons, exploding clouds of glittering paper. There are horses fronting the crowd, caparisoned with tinted sprays on brows. Everyone's mouth is frozen; open in an endless shared laughter, like Adrian's and mine, their bodies jumping to an absent music, their clothing shining in a light that is different from the buildings outside. But not more beautiful. The tops of the buildings are as red as alchemist's gold. I hold my breath, and let it out again.

The man beside me, nameless, with strong digits, whispers a "thank you," smiles, teeth bright in the dark. Unexpectedly, leans forward to kiss me on the cheek before leaving. The small courtesies of the court of shadows unfolding in the glass. Relentless, I hear the word make its way to me.

The apartment on the screen reminds me of something—a circus tent or a cell in a well-lit monastery—something that we want to find a miracle in. Just past all the expected furniture—the ample sofa, the coffee table and the books—in a corner, is a colony of plants, their baroque greenery and tiny purple flowers spilling out of the place assigned to them and threatening to seize a little too much space.

I lean back in dark and notice a door across the mediated room. A tall narrow mirror, framed with golden foliage and fauns, like mine, waits in the projected color and shade. Reflected in the center of it, at about eye level, is an illustration under glass. It depicts a strange, spiraling shape in blue and green and purple. From the edges grow other, smaller, spirals in similar colors that spawn again and turn until they meet the limits of the frame to disappear, gone somewhere else. They flutter, these shapes, their hues mottled and opaque. They breed new images. They escape. Briefly, a memory of a black bird that circled in the sky as I was sprawled across a lawn comes back. This weird image reflecting in that mirror, hanging on some unseen wall, reminds me of others I have seen, that gorgeous pull and ebb. Seen in books about fractal geometry. They all start with a mirror too.

Strange attractors, I remember only the phrase—the last of the light long gone now. Strange attractors broken down in an otherwise civil phase space pulling flows around with them. Water—asteroids—attention. The single new element in a closed system that ends its regularity.

A lit cigarette unleashes chaos in the cinema, in the room where I stand gazing into a mirror, at a reflected picture of that cinema, where I saw a mirror, where I gave a stranger head and Adrian whispered to me in the dark about the curious book he bought. Adrian whispering in the obscurity, about his headache and his desire to leave.

And he did leave, months later, vanishing utterly. Nobody knew where he went, though for the longest time occasional emails would arrive describing adventures in pursuit of the monstrous that seemed to cavalcade across Eastern Europe. Werewolves and vampires and ghouls, oh my.

Adrian whispering from obscurity again.

Strange attractors, I remember only the phrase—the single new element in a closed system that ends its regularity. And at that very thought, the lights flash for a second, in the room with the mirror, in the cinema, in the framed photo in the mirror on the screen, in the memory, in the whole gorgeous, tenuous, breathless, creaking, gilded, dizzy, massive imperfection of the ever-spreading continuum of all possible worlds, they flash, brilliant, fiery, obliterating sight—all of it this time—nothing but expansive blanching, then go out for a second, only to come back on. A sudden burst of illumination with a life span briefer than a mayfly's. Small irony. Slight violence and then nothing.

Then the cinema, its blackness, the murmuring and slippery sound of flesh felt odd to me, disconcerting. I felt myself sharing Adrian's headache, his nervousness, and his eagerness for light though none was present to beckon any longer. Angel walks off the screen, the lover he was with begins to stroke his cock. A white car drives backwards and a man kisses me on the cheeks, says "thank you," sits down beside me, Adrian vanishes, pulls out a book, points to a story about travel, about mirrors and disappearances. I take a seat and stare into a mirror, seeing the image of my empty room, its spartan furniture, the heap of unwashed shirts that clutters up a corner.

And as I sit there a murmuring begins. It seems to come from everywhere at once, but I can't be sure. A soft, vast susurration that pours from the shelves . . . like all the voices on the screen and in the darkened room began speaking at once, whispering things. I could make out certain words; "satiety," "absence," "pinnacle." As the moments tick by I hear whole sentences—discourses even, which I am not ready to repeat. Then a fiercer noise. A great, heavy knocking from the screen before me, or the space between the screen and me, that throws me off completely. A booming, hollow sound, almost frightening, that makes me want to turn and run through the slim rectangle of light at the end of the darkened hall, signifying "door."

In the men's room I stare into the mirror. I feel like Edward Kelley looking for the spirits. And I feel like I will feel like that for days to come, as I gaze and see nothing but the room, the chair, now vacant, the piles of clothes, the bookcases, the door to the outside world. I am gone, vanished from that hoary space, absent save in the photographic trace from one lost weekend.

I turn from the display. Behind me, there on the console table—once more—are Adrian and I, smiles overbroad and an unconscious pleasure apparent in us—everywhere. The plate glass of the movie house's entrance is still behind us, but the book whose open rows of type stirred us to laughter is closed now, shut against the frozen light, only its jacket displayed to the world. On the cover, I see the same curious pattern, the spiraling shape in blue and green and purple. From its edges grow other, smaller, spirals in similar shades that spawn and turn until they meet the jacket's limits and disappear, gone somewhere else.

I feel my damp eyes widen. I spin around in my seat to look behind me. The room reflected, every bit of furniture in place, an empty chair. I peer through the mirror's gilded frame whose mocking faces I cannot see from my position here, inside. Just the lolling tongues, lapping at me. I am gone from the chair. And the volatile photograph shows an open book. Inside. Outside. The click of the lock turning over. The creak of hinges and across the living room, past the alcove, I see the shape of Adrian shutting the door behind him, his long black trench coat dirty at the hem. He walks past the glass and into the kitchen like he has never been away. Like he lived in this apartment. More spacious than where I am now. Where I'm feeling very cold. It all begins with the mirror. And it all ends there, with Adrian passing by, eyes turned. Eyes turned.

AFTER WATCHING KLIMOV'S *AGONIYA*

Fanny Howe

The peasant crosses from the farm to a train
And enters a tunnel to the palace.
The future watches him coming
Like a child whose doll falls from her hands when the living approach.
Ultimately he will be autopsied by nihilists
Who act like God and photograph his corpse.
The state goes on with its grim task of arresting its critics.
"Find me a person, any person, and I will find a way to discredit him."
What was alcohol for a peasant was heroin for Stalin.

The photographs of Rasputin's face make me wish I could meet him
    and vomit.
They are like unwrapped gauzes imprinted with mummies.
His voracious gaze, his wild hair.
They poisoned his cake and wine and shot him and shot him twice.
But he wouldn't die so they tossed him
Through a hole in the frozen river.
When the police found him, his arms were raised to lift the ice.
People dropped buckets in that superhuman water and drank.
Without an element of atheism, no religion can be credible.

A black frost dapples his face and torso.

They pickled his lingam; it was so long, they wanted to watch it.
He started life as a poor agrarian boy who got in trouble with the
   authorities.
Then he had a vision and walked from Siberia to Mount Athos.
Now he represents a question. What makes one person
Unable to inhabit his own skin? Once there was metaphysical socialism.
Call it Christianity. Or Gnosticism? Images of munitions
And wolves were sewn into his vestments. Because he was uncultivated,
He was dangerous. A serf, a monk and a drunk haunting the royal family.

We have to face reality.
We are glad we were born in the west. There. We said it.
Shame of *embourgeoisement* covers us.
Shame on behalf of the women and children who defended their city
Digging trenches in snow, Tarkovsky's Ivan,
Who lived in rooms smelling of wood and urine. Garlic, salt and black
   bread for supper.
The fountains play at the western palace from eight to five p.m.
The spouts work on a system of gravity that God or someone invented.
This discovering will become important to missile development.

What went wrong when we were young?
We had friends who became enemies of the state with us.
Students who turned into deserters, then returned to capitalism.
All was forgiven. So what did we fail to do then?
Carry through! Reconstruction was the next ideology.
Proud-bellied white men from the west got the last laugh.
Since the invention of the laptop, disconnected figures flow
From discarded works, phrases are resurrected.
Isn't this blasphemy like showing a saint in ballet tights?

When these four words—*You look well fed*—are said
You are doomed by your revolutionary companions.
You have no right to complain, having chosen to seek
A piece of the pleasure.
Some moments in history last too long.
They could have been whims but they became plans.

Beauty is a despised agent for religion under these conditions.
I open my eyes and can't hear a word from the days of rebellion
But when I close them, I hear "continuing revolution."

The spoils of a lost war (all wars dry up into scabs)
Have turned libraries upside down and texts are turned into clips.
Every old misery holds interest.
Father got worried when I went to the far left
And called me self-indulgent. Mother laughed
When I became a Catholic. She didn't believe it. I left the blackened
     house
And walked in the dark, throwing ballast overboard
For the sake of a future of solitariness.
To the seeker all objects are lonely and dangerous.

Great films begin in chaos.
They are made in order to show the abyss emerging into laws.
Like Pope John Paul, certain directors only want the splendor of truth.
Turgenev wonders if it is possible that all the tears and prayers of people
Can be fruitless? No, he protests. The indifference of nature
Is a foretaste of eternity and its mercy.
On the steps of the Czech embassy in London there is a splash of bird shit.
I sit beside it reassembling the bits of sound for this poem.
Words know everything. That's why my fingers shake.

Nietzsche was a saint but he made a mistake. He believed in humanity.
Almost everything in that café is weaker than the air that surrounds it.
Glasses hang upside down drying, a mirror reflects the room like an artist
Who is blind to what she is making.
The operation of a Gnostic is pure sex
But love aches its way through the interstices.
Sticks there like a dent in an inchworm's back.
You can't take it out because it is the thing itself.
Love is the green in green. Does this explain its pain?

Since love came over and knocked me down,
Then kicked me in the side and fled,
I have suffered from a prolonged perplexity.

God is the object of my wonder and the closest to me.
Especially near sleep. My sheets are like the wings of a guardian angel.
There is no other fabric so close to my feelings.
I haunt a dark cathedral, its single light coming from the gift shop
And follow the priest's movements, for here is the truth: both worldly
And eternal, a heart of gold in the roaring vault.

Here a weeping Madonna is kissed all day while an old woman wipes
    away the stain
With a grey cloth. The mass is focused on the resurrection
Not the passion. In this place a grandmother is called white if she has
    healing powers.
Rasputin had the power in his hands.
Yet Akhmatova shared a train compartment with him and felt faint
Looking at his pale eyes. Each iris, in either eye, saw around the pupil.
I feel sick looking at the photos of his eyes, his penis, beard and blood.
Violent, skinhead, racist, nationalist, sexist illiterate men
Would appreciate him for the wrong reason.

Rasputin played dog and crawled into the royal dining room.
You smell like a mushroom, he barked and called on Jesus
To bless the soldiers who refused to kill the workers.
He was like dry rot in motion.
Women loved him and let him achieve ecstasy on top of them.
This was his Gnostic and Tantric obsession. He lived without hate.
He could stop a migraine with his hands and was seen
Praying in a forest for hours on end and by his bed alone.
If only he had never taken up wine.

Now the children climb over the rails around the station.
The siege of renovation raised them, blocks and forests razed
And built on. Cement units they can't afford to live in.
The kids have behaved like spawn born to be the end of the line,
Or not fully born. Porn-driven thugs, Mafiosi, right-wing Christians.
Only hope can save them, or an invasion by Muslims or oceans.
Who are dubbed the New Stupids? The workers!
The revolutionists were long ago strung up and the old did not survive
    the cold.

You could write music on the waterlines around their flooded
   tenements.

The peasant mocked institutions that Ratzinger would prize.
It was the student uprising of 68 that turned him against the Left.
Nowadays in every bureaucracy, including the Vatican, there are two of
   everyone.
Two of each who look exactly alike. It is the softness in the chin
That undefines them. Each one is the half brother of a twin.
Likewise Communism is secular Christianity.
Either you fear or thank someone and stay anonymous.
One poet re-created a new language out of his nanny's fireside stories.
This way his childhood survived, the way dinosaurs became birds.

While painting takes time and gives headaches,
A digital camera doesn't blink and this produces a lack of analogies.
It is not an open eye but an impure certainty.
Empty frames stand waiting under the stairs.
They wait for a thought that carried Dante with it, a long and difficult
   thought
Full of stains and imperfect figures, suffering and acid rain.
Don't plan any parties for Lent, a man called up in Italian.
And in the dream the shutter kept opening and closing
Like an anemone. Every hour was the same as the one before.

The roads we did not choose began in a town where we were born.
Here a gun might go off,
There perhaps a broom would brush away the sticks of spring.
It was not your fault where you were dropped
Or where you took your first steps.
The red church down the lane, the red sail on the bay—
These had nothing to do with you when you first arrived on earth.
A peasant might prefer smoking weed to whacking at wheat all day.
How else would a vision find and know him?

In a remote fishing village and on its wet stone steps
The clink of the ropes and rings on the boats was the only sound.

Then footsteps. The sun broke through onto buses and houses.
High up, a man and a woman, both old and on their own
Crossed paths without looking. Then she noticed him and he her.
A hurried exchange of recollections followed and half-promises to meet
    some day.
And then he continued to mount the side of the hill to his house
While she went down to the highway.
Absolutely nothing happened, except recognition.

The sorrowing face of the Theotokos blessed their simplicity.

ROMAN À CLEF

Brian Pera

A flash of light, and I was sitting in the kitchen of what appeared to be my apartment, hunched over. I seemed to have been dreaming, about some kind of ritual where a big hairy beast—was it a man?—labored over me. Was he fucking me? When I came to, I was staring fixedly into a tea kettle. In the dream I was looking out of my eyes so I couldn't see my face, only the man's. In the tea kettle, I was a blonde, slender, the picture of purity. Depending on how close I was to the stove, my eyes grew, or my nose did; parts of my face ballooned as if they might burst. A woman who claimed to be my sister arrived, calling me Carol. She and her boyfriend—a married man—were going on holiday, would be gone a fortnight, would send a postcard, they said, Ta. The thought of being alone with myself and my reflection and dreams terrified me. I pictured everything in the room falling around me, after the rush of activity caused by my sister's presence, as if she'd somehow animated the objects in the kitchen, and now, with her departure, it would all be perfectly still, limp and inscrutable. I begged her to stay. I appealed to her very much like a little girl, like the image of myself I'd seen in the den; in an old photograph, she and I are arranged around our seated parents. I stand apart, staring at the camera the way I had at the tea kettle, as if into a fun house mirror. Having no real, useful idea who I was, I had only the past, this picture, to consult, so in my appeals to my sister I stuck my lower lip out and cast my eyes down at the floor, and my sister behaved as any mother would, telling me to grow up.

Take a look at yourself, she clucked, rushing around with her suitcases. If you only knew what you looked like.

I'd been working at a beauty salon, and in my sister's absence I continued to show up for my shifts. In my sister's absence, I would make an effort to keep in touch with the outside world, I would endeavor to look at myself—and, if I was to see myself, I should surround myself with other people. But I felt very much alone at the salon. The girls I worked with had their heads full of boys. Their thoughts scampered around like birds on the pavement searching for food, too busy to be engaged. Their eyes covered in cucumber slices, their faces masked behind cold cream, the patrons were in another world entirely. Flat on their backs, even their hair concealed under towels, they checked out to such an extent that again I found myself drifting. I sat beside their beds, cutting their cuticles or painting their nails, massaging their hands. This might have gone on for several days. My sister had been gone—how long? My sister's name was what? She'd been living with me, but now she was gone. Would she be back? I was a blonde woman in my twenties, I told myself. I had a nice figure, probably, all things considered. Trying to remember what the woman who might have been my sister looked like, I suddenly saw something, some figure on the floor. Everything I saw hid another thing and aroused my curiosity. The black and white checkered squares of the linoleum collapsed, folding and reforming into something perversely, flickeringly hypnotic.

During such blackouts, I was other people. Someone who is unable to lead his life in the way he wants to starts to hide himself in different, imaginary persons and invent narratives that allow him to lead a parallel life or whatever, I suppose. How did I want to lead my life? Entering a door or a portal, I was never sure where I'd end up. At one point, I was a redhead whose name seemed to be Rosemary, a newlywed living at The Bramford, a stately old building verging on the gothic. The master bedroom of my apartment had the most unusual wallpaper, one of those sprawling flamboyant patterns committing every artistic sin. The color was repellant, almost revolting; a smoldering unclean yellow, strangely faded by the slow-turning sunlight. It was a dull yet lurid orange in some places, a sickly sulfur tint in others. I could hear street noise from the apartment. When I looked out the window, I saw that I was surrounded by other tall buildings with too many windows to count and a park, farther out, where tiny little dots which must have been other people made patterns. I was pregnant, and lonely. June 28th, I was due. New York City? This will sound silly, I know, but I believed my next-door neighbors, Roman and Minnie Castevet, were witches, although it took me a while to put that together. They were pretty adept at confusing me. I was seduced by their noisy confidence and trusted them implicitly, even as I laughed inside at their silly, colorful outfits, their busy, apparently mindless chatter, which made no distinctions between one thing and another, stirring fact and fiction into one big soup. They seemed like parrots, the Castevets, fluttering little comedies.

It took me a long time to recognize that their colorful inanity was in fact a refined camouflage designed to distract me, like the wallpaper. I remained at a distance from my own perceptions and thoughts, to the point of failing to recognize myself, my physical body, as belonging to myself. I'd been so sure who my baby was. I sang lullabies to soothe it, named it, named him or her, Andy or Jenny. Douglas. Melinda or Sarah. He or she would look like my husband, Guy, but also like me. All I had to do, I kept telling myself, was subtract what wasn't Guy. I was singing these lullabies, so that upon the baby's birth it would hear my voice and recognize me, and remind me of myself. Andy or Jenny or Douglas or Melinda. I bought a bassinet, a crib, had painters paint the nursery. I read books on pregnancy and childbirth. I saw myself in the wallpaper. I guess it was me, something taking shape, someone rooting around behind the patterns, which were like brambles or branches, a sort of camouflage. It took me a long time to realize that the lullabies were putting me to sleep as well.

A man started following me home from the salon. Tall and lanky, fairhaired, he hurried along like I'd left something behind and he was bringing it back to me. I couldn't understand what he wanted. If I couldn't name it, how could I give it? If I couldn't give it and he still wanted it, wouldn't he simply take it from me? I felt as though I were in a hall of mirrors, where every person was a reflection of another person, who was similar but not identical. I confused the guy with other men, for instance construction workers near the salon, leering, surly types who made lewd suggestions as I passed. It was clear I had what these men wanted, but I saw them behaving the same way toward other women, which left me feeling interchangeable and confused. If what they wanted was something we all had, what distinguished one of us from the others in their eyes? I watched other women on the street as if they might be me, reflections, trying to tell what I looked like judging by strangers. The man who kept following me seemed very sweet, but his insistence unnerved me. Ultimately, his compliments weren't much different from the catcalls I received from the men at the construction site. His insistence soon turned into relentlessness, and after a while I knew he'd be waiting for me, whenever I came out of the salon, he'd be planted right across the street at a pub, staring at me through the window. Finally, I agreed to a date, thinking at least this would make him disappear until an appointed time. Until that appointed time, I continued to work, though my trances persisted. I had episodes—more dreams, maybe—hallucinations, which I mistook for objective reality, in which I became other people. I had no idea, after a while, which person was me and which wasn't. I was highly suggestible, believing whatever I was told but deeply distrusting it too. It seemed like I'd had a sister at some point. I intended to keep my date with the man who was following me; though I'd merely made the date to avoid him, by the time it came around I knew only that I was to be at a certain place at an agreed-upon time. I was on my way to our meeting point when I noticed a splintering crack in the sidewalk and took a seat on a nearby bench to study it.

Minnie kept giving me drinks. She and Roman cut me off from the doctor my girlfriends had recommended, insisting I see Dr. Abraham Saperstein, a friend of theirs, a famous obstetrician I'd never heard of. Dr. Saperstein said pills weren't necessary— "an entirely natural expansion of the pelvis," he said when I complained of swelling and pain, as if I were simply mutating, rather than having a baby—the drinks Minnie made me provided all the nourishment and vitamins I could possibly need. The drinks were like milk shakes and contained Tannis Root, an herb (Minnie said) that was also contained in a curious locket the couple had given me. I'd seen the locket before. When Guy and I first moved to the Bramford, before I'd even met the Castevets, I'd been in the basement, doing our laundry. Another woman was there with me, also doing her laundry. Her name was Terry Gionoffrio. She was wearing the locket. I really related

to her and saw a lot of myself in her. She'd been living on the street before she ended up at The Bramford. She'd been taken in by Mr. and Mrs.
Castevet, starving and on dope and a lot of other things. The Castevets
were childless, she told me, and had become like parents to her. They were
the most wonderful people in the world, bar none. They'd picked her up
off the sidewalk—literally.

One night, as Guy and I strolled home, we saw a commotion up ahead. A
small, excited crowd had gathered outside The Bramford. Drawing closer,
we saw someone had fallen from one of the windows, splintering the
pavement. It was Terry, who lay there in a pool of her own blood. The
Castevets arrived, and Minnie identified the body. The police told her it
was a suicide. Terry left a note; Minnie verified the handwriting. Neither
of the Castevets was aware of any next of kin, but I remembered Terry
mentioning a brother in the navy, and said so. Minnie reached for her cat-
eye glasses, which were hanging from a cord, and squinted at me through
them. Several days later, she knocked on our door and properly intro-
duced herself. At night, Guy and I could hear her through our bedroom
wall, her brassy, garrulous voice, a voice that poisoned my dreams, passing
from person to person. She appeared in the patterns of the wallpaper, taking the guise of different people; the nun who taught and punished me in
grade school, authority figures. Maybe she was the figure I'd seen taking
shape. The Castevets were like parents to Terry, and her death was like the
loss of a daughter for them. Accepting the maternal attentions of Minnie,
I became a surrogate for Terry, whom I barely knew, and Minnie became
a reflection of my childish need.

The man who kept following me eventually found me sitting there on
the bench. I was late so he came looking for me. He was upset but sensed
something was wrong. Perhaps I was sick or wasn't feeling well. All this
time, I'd been staring at the crack in the sidewalk. It had a meandering,
insidious pattern, like the wallpaper in my bedroom at The Bramford.
I watched my life and Rosemary's like a movie there, waiting to see
what would happen next. Maybe I was in the movie, I wondered if the
man who'd been following me was my director, made the cars move
where they did and the pedestrians walk convincingly, disappearing into
the background. I felt safer, but at the same time insecure. He drove me
home, staring at me the entire time. He didn't have to look where he was

going. The view out the windows was like rear screen projection. Roads passed by, pedestrians, someone pushing a baby stroller. I turned to look, thinking the new mother might be Rosemary, hoping I might see myself—then I remembered that if this was a movie I was in it, not watching it. I tried to focus on my motivation. The man who'd been following me parked in front of my sister's apartment and kissed me, and I shrank away from his touch. It seemed like something someone like me would do in a situation like this. Someone like Carol. When he tried again, I dashed out of the car and straight into the apartment. I locked myself away, replaying the kiss over and over in my mind. I went to the bathroom and cleaned my face, trying to wash him off me. I locked myself away so I could keep everything else out. I was going to take a look at myself but I'd have to get out of the movie first, basically, was how I was thinking. But none of the walls or surfaces in the apartment seemed to cooperate and the movie kept seeping through. I barricaded the door with a wardrobe but men found their way in. At night, I was visited by the construction worker. I woke up or turned over and he was on top of me, inside me; I tried but I couldn't fight him off. The plaster splintered, as if unseen men were piling on the floor above, threatening to rain down on me. Maybe it was the Castevets. Perhaps they lived next door wherever I was. Hands—perhaps theirs—burst through the walls, groping me. I started scenes then forgot them. At one point, I drew a bath. Later, I discovered the floor had flooded. The man who'd been following me showed up again, knocking at the door. Had any time passed since I left him in the car? I peered through the peephole.

A woman and a young girl stood in the hallway, staring back at me. Confused, I opened the door. Our neighbors, this woman urgently explained, had initiated a smear campaign against her daughter, whose legs were in braces. I stared at the girl, wondering where I'd seen her before. Everything seemed vaguely familiar. Everything was such a cliché. The woman asked for my help, calling me Trelkovsky. I assured her I had done nothing to contribute to any such campaign and in fact knew not the first thing about it. I didn't involve myself in other people's drama, I lied. I knew not the first thing about anything. In the larger scheme of things, I said, I was just passing through. Faintly masculine, my voice surprised me. Shutting the door, I turned to face my sister's apartment, realizing it wasn't her apartment at all. It wasn't Rosemary's, either. I moved to the nearest mirror, where I saw a short, middle-aged man with a rather large nose and a visibly mousy demeanor, lending him the aspects of a rodent. Maybe it was me, I was the director, a man playing different women, only—now I was confused. I seemed to be obsessed with picturing women in meticulously specific ways: in peril, in their nightgowns, delirious and uncertain. I decided to keep as much to myself as possible. Surely, I would sooner or later end up back at the spa or The Bramford. In the meantime, over the next few days, I learned bits and pieces from the various tenants of the building. I learned that the woman who occupied my apartment before me had jumped from the window, an apparent attempt to kill herself. Her name was Simone Choule. Along with these reports, images rushed back to me, dreams I'd had or, perhaps, memories. I saw men repairing the glass roof below my window, which had been shattered by Simone's fall. One of the men I was sure I'd previously seen on the street, as Carol, on my way to the salon. When he looked up at me, I recognized him: it was the construction worker who'd broken in and raped me. I saw a bandaged figure on a hospital bed, several limbs in traction. Everything but the eyes and the mouth were obscured. This was Simone, I felt, possibly recuperating, though of course it could have been anyone. The neighbors told me Simone had died.

My neighbors were intrusive, pushy, invading my privacy. My apartment gradually appeared to shrink, closing in on me. What if it shrank so much that it squeezed me out entirely? Say I was this man, a director making a film, or in one, pretending to be other women; if I was squeezed out, what then? Would I go back to being Carol, or Rosemary, or would the movie end? The others didn't seem to know they were in a movie. I was asked by my neighbors to sign a petition against the woman and her disabled child, and I refused, setting the tenants against me. This made directing things very difficult, this mutinous attitude. I locked my door and stayed in my flat, seeing things. At night I stared across the courtyard to an adjacent wing of the building. I could hear someone practicing the piano. My window faced the communal bathroom, where I began to see figures, not just neighbors but others. I was certain I saw Carol, and Rosemary. I saw the men from the construction site in the shadows of the bathroom, and the man who followed Carol home. I saw Guy Woodhouse and the Castevets. They changed shape like the figure behind the brambles of the wallpaper. They seemed to be keeping tabs on me. At one point, I saw a mummy with a gaping hole where the mouth should be, which turned out to be Simone standing there. When I snuck out of the apartment and traveled the halls to the bathroom myself to see what things would look like from the other side, I saw hieroglyphs, secret messages scratched into the walls. What do I look like, staring out from my window, I wondered. I looked across the courtyard to my apartment and saw a woman inside, staring back at me. I saw yellow wallpaper where there hadn't been any. I rushed back, sure this woman was the key to all my disparate dreams and visions, someone who could tie them all together for me and make sense of the pieces, but when I entered the apartment she was gone.

I didn't have to go into trances anymore. I didn't have to fall asleep or be unconscious. Everything fused together. I am a director playing a man who thinks he's a woman, I reminded myself. I am a woman who is putting all this together. I am—Rosemary? Big as a house. Minnie and Roman isolated me from everyone, confining me to The Bramford. They wanted my baby. I tried to lock them out, to hold them back, but our apartments were connected by a shared closet at the end of the hall. The Castevets didn't use the closet but had access to it. I used it for my linens, learning to ignore the other door, behind the shelves, the way I ignored the sense I was being watched over and the faint sound of someone playing the piano somewhere in the building, which might have also merely been in my head, imagined lullabies, another blurred line between reality and fantasy. I imagined I was in a movie and the movie had an audience. I didn't want to be self-conscious. I wanted to inhabit my character. I learned not to look at myself, relying instead on Minnie to show me who I was and how I was doing. She fed me my lines, giving me reports on myself the way someone would bring you up to date on an out-of-state friend. She visited often, bringing me her shakes, my mail, news, and gossip from the outside world. She stood in the kitchen chattering away as I drank the shake, her eyes traveling me up and down. She probably knows I'm a man, I kept thinking. Maybe she's a man too. She waited there until I was done with my shakes, she said, to save her a trip—for the glass—though her trips were frequent anyway and she lived, after all, right next door. At some point it occurred to me that I could simply leave the glass on a shelf in the linen closet. That way, she could open the door on her side and retrieve it. I never mentioned this idea, however, as doing so would break what I felt was some sort of unspoken pact to avoid

discussion about the closet altogether. I could stand on my side of the
closet and chat with Minnie, I thought. We could stand with our doors
open and chat through the shelves, which would cut us up into pieces. I
could even hide in the closet, really, as due to our avoidance it didn't seem
to exist, and no one would find me. It hadn't existed for the previous
tenant, either. When Guy and I had first moved in, there was a wardrobe
pushed up against the door. The landlord told us the old lady before us
had put it there.

One night, I got very drunk. I think I was drunk. I put on a dark wig
I'd purchased down the street. The flat was still furnished with Simone's
things and in a wardrobe I found some of her old clothes. The wardrobe
had a mirror and I stared at myself from across the room. That's what
I look like, playing a woman in this movie, I told myself. I put lipstick
on, changing the shape of my face. I posed as Simone, imagining what
she looked like under her bandages. I directed myself. I didn't look a
thing like Carol, or Rosemary. Andy or Jenny or Douglas or Melinda.
Like faceless Simone and Terry Gionoffrio, I might run to the window
and fling myself toward the street, breaking the glass roof below my flat
all over again. Maybe Simone and Terry jumped because a window is a
frame, a screen, and by entering it you can cross over to the other side.
Maybe they had a man inside them and needed to get him out. Or they
were self-destructive, as women often are. Then it occurred to me that a
door is a frame too, and I became curious about the wardrobe. Maybe this
one was hiding secrets too. Maybe some old lady had pushed it there. I
moved it out of the way with the strength of a man, and found a hole in
the wall. Someone had shoved a tooth into it.

If I were a woman, I decided, I would be scared for my life. There would
be people hiding behind doors and windows and walls all the time, and
I would be helpless. In a sexy way I would be helpless, the way you can
be sexy when you're most vulnerable. When you're a woman. If I were
Guy and I had a wife like me, like Rosemary, and people were after her, I
would encourage her to need my protection, even if I were secretly after
her too. Women give way to fancy and as men we must caution them
against it, though it is horribly attractive to know they need our help.
It's good to feel needed. Without us, women wouldn't know themselves.
We show them who they are, what they look like, we're their mirrors,

their screens, their windows and doors. If I were a woman, I thought, I'd want to be distressed and helpless, with people after me, so that as a man I would be more likely to find myself attractive. Along with a woman's imaginative power and habit of story-making, her nervous weakness is sure to lead to all manner of excited fancies. A postcard came, for instance, from someone who claimed to be my sister. *Dear Carol*. It had a picture of a tower on it, and I thought how if I were a woman that might really offend me. Why were men always erecting monuments to their penises, I might think, seeing a penis where clearly there wasn't one. I would have to ask the construction worker about that, the next time he came through the wall. In the meantime, a woman kept calling. Tramp, she spat. Did I think I could just run off on holiday with her husband? She must have had me confused with the sister I sometimes imagined I had. The anger in her voice scared the hell out of me. What if she got so pissed off that she came through the wall too? I had no desire to be raped by a woman. What if she pushed me out the window, and I fell to the sidewalk, and the Castevets came along and identified me? Then I remembered I was a man. I felt relieved not to have to worry myself too much about it.

I woke from a heavy sleep, disoriented. Had I been dreaming again? What happens to the movie when you go to bed at night? Does it wait for you and pick up where it left off the next morning? My tooth was missing. I found it in my clenched fist. I heard knocking at the door and construction noises outside. Someone, one of the neighbors maybe, was playing piano. I found myself singing along. A ball was bouncing outside, keeping time with the music like a metronome. How boring women are, I thought. They wake and immediately they start worrying. Sexy, I told myself, as long as you don't have to listen to it. I decided not to trouble myself too much with whatever was bothering me. It was Minnie at the door, standing there with my shake. I welcomed her into the kitchen and drank from the glass, patting my belly as the liquid went down, plotting. I'm going to direct this movie so that in the end, the woman is doomed, I decided. What should happen is, Rosemary won't know whether anything she thinks is really happening or just something she's imagining. She'll be given a book on witchcraft and, using her Scrabble board, figure out that ROMAN CASTEVET is an anagram which stands for STEVEN MARCATO, the son of Adrian Marcato, the leader of a coven. She'll realize Guy is involved and pack her things into a suitcase, she'll put herself into a cab and drive over to another doctor for a second opinion and try to tell him very carefully everything she suspects, so he won't think she's crazy but rational, will believe her, will find her sexy and help her. Only he turns her over to the others, because he can understand how worried the men in her life must be, given how hysterical she is, and the thing about a second opinion is that even though men encourage it they find women pathetic and predictable for distrusting them. Roman and Guy will take Rosemary home and though she somehow locks them out of the apartment—"Open the door, my darling," Guy says very quietly—they of course don't need her permission and sneak in through the closet, which she forgot about, because it didn't exist. She gets herself so worked up that she induces labor, and they knock her out with a shot, and when she wakes, there is no baby, they tell her, the baby died during childbirth, even though she can hear the sound of it crying somewhere, slightly discordant like the lullabies she used to sing, which might have just been the neighbor's piano playing all along.

I decided to let the construction worker take me without putting up much of a fight, because the man in me believed that women secretly want it, and after all, if I didn't want it, why would I be wandering around in my nightgown, when people are coming through the walls? You know you want it, I reminded myself, so I put out. First I lay there, with my arms limp to my side, staring up at the cracked ceiling, but of course I quickly realized that women always mistake this sort of acquiescence for the participation men desire, so I tried to think what I would want out of somebody like me if I were someone like him. I wrapped my arms and legs around the construction worker as if my entire body were a vagina, a clenching, clinging, orifice, etc. And I let the walls grope me. I laughed to myself: What would these guys think if they knew I was a rat-faced little director in women's clothes? What would the Castevets think, the Marcatos, if they knew I was a sequence of letters that appeared to be one word but was actually another in disguise? Perhaps I'm simply the unborn baby boy and they already know this, it dawned on me. I considered all this in Simone's apartment, laughing so hard I fell to pieces. I stopped laughing when I realized I had no idea where I came from. Say I'm a man, I thought. Say I'm Trelkovsky. Where was I born? Where did I live before coming to Simone's building? From whose womb did I come? How do

I know it was Simone on the hospital bed, bandaged head to toe? How do I know I'm not Simone, when I don't know who I was before? How do I know I'm a man, not a woman? Which came first in this loop? "Will I still be me?" I whimpered pathetically when I considered what might become of me. I certainly sounded like a woman—or a baby. The neighbors seemed to know. Who I was, I mean. They seemed to know I was a woman. This woman named Simone, who looked like no one, really, but me, as I'd only ever seen her staring at myself in the mirror.

At one point, I was in the kitchen, ravenous. I was Rosemary at the time, if memory serves. I had the munchies, because I was carrying this rodent around in me, feeding for two, and I grabbed whatever I could get my hands on, and tore into it, and when I looked up, and saw myself in the toaster, I saw someone I didn't recognize. I saw, not a man, but a blonde woman staring into a tea kettle. *A loop*, she thought to herself. *So they think they know who I am.* This director, these tenants, think they can make me into something I'm not or don't want to be or whatever. Like I'm so malleable. It's unbearable, if you think about it, that you can't protect the women in your life from people who will hurt them, so they can continue to be sexy and everything and not too complicated but a little confused, which is fine, which is preferable, surely. You could be living on a hill in a house and be out of town, be a man away from home, and there your wife is on that hill, pregnant, perhaps, like Rosemary, with parties, bohemian vagrants wandering in and out because you want your women open, which is preferable, surely, but anyone could walk in. Just about anyone. A baby was crying. The door of the linen closet is a frame, thought Rosemary. She peeped through the keyhole into the adjoining apartment, where things were blurry, shifting objects like in the wallpaper. Minnie's voice and others, the sound of celebrating. A party. Rosemary has a knife in her hand and enters quietly, dressed in her nightgown. I am a blonde woman, slender, the picture of moral purity, she tells herself. I call into question the very nature of human integrity through splitting and doublings of a once unitary self. She approaches the bassinet in the middle of the Marcato's living room with the blade poised, eyes wild. If only she could see herself, how crazy she looks. With the top of the knife she parts the black sheers surrounding the bassinet and yes, it's a witch, Satan's son or whatever, but it's her little man, her spitting image, he's got his father's eyes.

WORKS CITED

Cronin, Paul. *Roman Polanski: Interviews*. Mississippi: University Press of Mississippi, 2005.

Feeney, F.X., and Paul Duncan. *Roman Polanski*. Köln: Taschen, 2006.

Gilman, Charlotte Perkins. *The Yellow Wallpaper and Other Stories*. New York: Dover, 1997.

Gorightly, Adam. *The Shadow Over Santa Susanna; Black Magic, Mind Control, and the "Manson Family" Mythos*. New York: Writers Club Press, 2001.

King, Greg. *Sharon Tate and the Manson Murders*. New York: Barricade Books Inc., 2000.

Leaming, Barbara. *Polanski: The Filmmaker as Voyeur*. New York: Simon and Shuster, 1981.

Levin, Ira. *Rosemary's Baby*. New York: Dell, 1967.

Mazierska, Ewa. *Roman Polanski: The Cinema of a Cultural Traveler*. London: I.B. Taurus & Co, Ltd., 2007.

Meikle, Denis. *Roman Polanski: Odd Man Out*. Surrey: Reynolds & Hearn Ltd., 2006.

Morrison, James. *Roman Polanski*.

Orr, John and Elzbieta Ostrowska. *The Cinema of Roman Polanski: Dark Spaces of the World*. London: Wallflower, 2006.

Polanski, Roman. *Roman by Polanski*. New York: Ballantine Books, 1985.

Sandford, Christopher. *Polanski*. New York: Palgrave, 2008.

Repulsion. Dir. Roman Polanski. Criterion Collection, 1965.

Rosemary's Baby. Dir. Roman Polanski. Paramount Pictures, 1968.

The Tenant. Dir. Roman Polanski. Parmount Pictures, 1976.

ABOUT THE CONTRIBUTORS

Stephen Beachy is the author of two novellas, *Some Phantom/No Time Flat* as well as the novels *The Whistling Song*, and *Distortion*. His short fiction and nonfiction have been published in the *Chicago Review*, *BOMB*, *Blithe House Quarterly*, *New York Magazine* and elsewhere. His Web site is www.livingjelly.com.

Dodie Bellamy has been celebrated among the literati since the publication of her epistolary masterpiece *The Letters of Mina Harker* in the 1990s. Unapologetic in her use of sexuality, politics, and narrative experimentation, Bellamy has written a number of innovative books, including *Pink Steam*, *Academonia*, the Goldie Award-winning *Cunt-Ups*, and, most recently, *Barf Manifesto*. Dodie Bellamy's essays and reviews have appeared in *The Village Voice*, *The San Francisco Chronicle*, *Bookforum*, *Out/Look*, and *The San Diego Reader*, as well as numerous literary journals and Web sites. She lives in San Francisco.

Rebecca Brown is the author of a dozen books of prose including *The Last Time I Saw You*, *The End Of Youth*, *The Dogs: A Modern Bestiary*, *The Terrible Girls* (all with City Lights), *Excerpts From a Family Medical Dictionary* (Univ. of Wisconsin and Granta), *The Gifts of the Body* (HarperCollins) and *Woman in Ill-Fitting Wig*, a collaboration with painter Nancy Kiefer (pistilbooks.net). Her work is translated into Japanese, German, Danish, Italian, and Norwegian and widely anthologized. Brown has also written a libretto for a dance opera, *The Onion Twins*, and a play, *The Toaster*, and *American Romances*, a book of essays. She lives in Seattle.

Tisa Bryant is the author of *Unexplained Presence* (Leon Works, 2007), a collection of original, hybrid fiction-essays that remix narratives from Eurocentric film, literature, and visual arts and zoom in on the black presences operating within them. An excerpt from her novella, *[the curator]*, a rumination on cinema and black female subjectivity, is third in Belladonna★ Books' Elders Series for 2009, published in a limited edition featuring the work of her "elder," writer, filmmaker, and *Semiotext(e)* publisher Chris Kraus. In collaboration with writer/journalist Ernest Hardy, Bryant co-edited *War Diaries*, the 2009 AIDS Project Los Angeles (APLA) anthology of writings on survival and HIV/AIDS in international African diasporic communities. Bryant is currently working on *Spectral*, a historical novel of image, archive, and memory, based on the real life of Old Doll, an enslaved, literate woman. The novel is set on the Newton Plantation, Barbados, 1796, and in our own twenty-first-century moment.

Bard Cole is the author of a collection of short stories, *Briefly Told Lives* (St. Martin's Press, 2000) and a novel, *This Is Where My Life Went Wrong* (BLATT, 2008). He is the former assistant editor of *Alabama Heritage* magazine, where he wrote the definitive article on a noteworthy rock.

Peter Dubé is a novelist, short story writer, essayist, and cultural critic. He is the author of the chapbook *Vortex Faction Manifesto* (Vortex Editions, 2001), the novel *Hovering World* (DC Books 2002) and *At the Bottom of the Sky*, a collection of linked short stories (DC Books, 2007). He edited the anthology *Madder Love: Queer Men and the Precincts of Surrealism* (Rebel Satori, 2008) where *Echo* first appeared. In addition to his fictional work, his essays and critical writings have been widely published in journals such as *CV Photo*, *ESSE*, *Hour and Ashé*, and in exhibition publications for various galleries, among them SKOL, Occurrence, Quartier Éphémère, and the Leonard and Bina Ellen Gallery at Concordia University.

Robert Glück is the author of nine books of poetry and fiction, including two novels, *Margery Kempe* and *Jack the Modernist*. His book of stories, *Denny Smith*, appeared in 2004. Glück was co-director of Small Press Traffic, director of The Poetry Center at San Francisco State, and Associate Editor at Lapis Press. Glück's poetry and fiction have been published in the *New Directions Anthology*, *City Lights Anthologies*, *Best New Gay Fiction 1988* and *1996*, *The Norton Anthology of World Literature*, *Best American Erotica 1996* and *2005*, and *The Faber Book of Gay Short Fiction*. His critical articles appeared in *Artforum International*, *Poetics Journal*, *The Review of Contemporary Fiction*, and *Nest: A Quarterly of Interiors*, and he prefaced *Between Life and Death*, a book of paintings by Frank Moore. This year he and Dean Smith completed the film *Aliengnosis*. He teaches at San Francisco State and he is an editor of *Narrativity*, a Web journal. Last year Coach House Press published *Biting the Error: Writers on Narrative*, an anthology edited by Glück, Camille Roy, Mary Berger, and Gail Scott.

Veronica Gonzalez's short fiction has been widely published in literary magazines and anthologies. She is co-editor of *Juncture: 25 Very Good Stories and 12 Excellent Drawings*, published by Soft Skull Press. In 2006 she founded Rockypoint Press, a series of artist/writer collaborative books produced in association with 1301PE Gallery. *Twin time: or how death befell me*, her first novel, was published by Semiotext(e) and was awarded the 2008 Aztlán Literary Prize.

Daphne Gottlieb stitches together the ivory tower and the gutter just using her tongue. She is the award-winning author of four books of poetry, most recently *Kissing Dead Girls*, and one graphic novel, *Jokes and the Unconscious*, and the editor of two anthologies.

Richard Grayson is the author of the short story collections *With Hitler in New York*, *Lincoln's Doctor's Dog*, *I Brake for Delmore Schwartz*, *I Survived Caracas Traffic*, *The Silicon Valley Diet*, *Highly Irregular Stories*, *And to Think That He Kissed Him on Lorimer Street*, and *Who Will Kiss the Pig?: Sex Stories for Teens*. He lives in Brooklyn and Phoenix.

Myriam Gurba is the author of *Dahlia Season*, which was selected by the New York Public Library as one of 2008's best books for LGBTQ teens, and shortlisted for both the Edmund White Award and a Lambda Literary Award. She lives in Long Beach, former home of the Spruce Goose and the Black Dahlia, and writes and teaches just a few blocks from the city's notorious shore.

Elizabeth Hatmaker teaches writing and cultural theory at Illinois State University. Her work has appeared in *Mandorla*, *Mipoesias*, *Bird Dog*, *Social Epistemology*, *ACM*, *Epoch*, *LLAD*, *L'Bourgeoizine*, *Mississippi Review*, and *Mirage*.

Fanny Howe's most recent book of poems is *The Lyrics* (Graywolf Press). Recent publications include *The Winter Sun* (essays) from Graywolf and *What Did I Do Wrong?* (fiction) from Flood Editions.

Kevin Killian, a San Francisco–based poet, novelist, critic, and playwright, has written a book of poetry, *Argento Series* (2001), two novels, *Shy* (1989) and *Arctic Summer* (1997), a book of memoirs, *Bedrooms Have*

Windows (1989), and a book of stories, *Little Men* (1996), that won the PEN Oakland award for fiction. A second collection, *I Cry Like a Baby*, was published by Painted Leaf Books in 2001. His latest book of poetry is all about Kylie Minogue: poets Michael Scharf and Joshua Clover published Killian's *Action Kylie* in 2008, and City Lights will issue a new book of stories, called *Impossible Princess* after Kylie's controversial, "experimental" 1998 LP.

Wayne Koestenbaum has published five books of poetry: *Best-Selling Jewish Porn Films, Model Homes, The Milk of Inquiry, Rhapsodies of a Repeat Offender*, and *Ode to Anna Moffo and Other Poems*. He has also published a novel, *Moira Orfei in Aigues-Mortes*, and five books of nonfiction: *Andy Warhol, Cleavage, Jackie Under My Skin, The Queen's Throat* (a National Book Critics Circle Award finalist), and *Double Talk*. His newest book, *Hotel Theory*, a hybrid of fiction and nonfiction, was published in 2007. He is a Distinguished Professor of English at the CUNY Graduate Center and currently also a visiting professor in the painting department of the Yale School of Art.

Donal Mosher is a writer, photographer, and filmmaker living in Portland, Oregon. His fiction and nonfiction writings have appeared in *Instant City, Satellite, Frozen Tears*, and *Still Blue* (an anthology of working-class writing.) He has a photo-book collaboration with Canadian writer Derek McCormack forthcoming through Artspace Books. A feature length documentary film, *October Country*, based on his photography, was completed in autumn 2008. He is also a principal subject of Robert Arnold's ITVS documentary film *Key of G*, which focuses on life and work with a severely disabled young man. Samples of his writing can be found at ghosttype. blogspot.com. Film trailers can be found at wishbonefilms.com.

Maggie Nelson is the author of two books of nonfiction, *Women, the New York School, and Other True Abstractions* (University of Iowa Press, 2007) and *The Red Parts: A Memoir* (Free Press/Simon & Schuster; a State of Michigan Notable Book of 2007). She is also the author of several collections of poetry, including *Something Bright, Then Holes* (Soft Skull Press, 2007) and *Jane: A Murder* (Soft Skull, 2005; finalist, the PEN/ Martha Albrand Award for the Art of the Memoir). A book about the color blue, *Bluets*, will be published by Wave Books in 2009. A recipient of a 2007 Arts Writers grant from the Creative Capital/Andy Warhol Foundation, Nelson has taught literature and writing at the Graduate Writing Program of the New School, Pratt Institute of Art, and Wesleyan University. Currently she teaches on the faculty of the School of Critical Studies at CalArts in Valencia, Calif., and lives in Los Angeles.

Brian Pera is the author of the novel *Troublemaker* (St. Martin's Press). *The Way I See Things*, his first film, premiered at the Los Angeles Outfest Film Festival in July of 2008 and has traveled to film festivals around the world. He's currently working on his next film and a novel. He lives in Memphis.

Claudia Rankine is the author of four collections of poetry, *Nothing in Nature Is Private*, *The End of the Alphabet*, *Plot*, and *Don't Let Me Be Lonely*. She teaches at the University of Georgia.

Abdellah Taïa is the first openly gay autobiographical writer published in Morocco. Though Moroccan, he has lived in Paris for the last eight years. His short stories and novels (*Mon Maroc*, 2000; *Le rouge du tarbouche*, 2005; and *Salvation Army*, which was published in French in 2006, and is due out with Semiotext(e) in 2009) have been translated into Dutch and Spanish. He also appeared in Rémi Lange's 2004 film *Tarik el Hob* (released in English as *The Road to Love*).

Lynne Tillman is a novelist, short story writer, and essayist/critic. Her books include *Haunted Houses*, *Absence Makes the Heart*, *No Lease on Life*, *The Broad Picture*, *This Is Not It*, and most recently, *American Genius, A Comedy*, published by Soft Skull Press.

David Trinidad's most recent book of poetry, *The Late Show*, was published in 2007 by Turtle Point Press. His anthology *Saints of Hysteria: A Half-Century of Collaborative American Poetry* (co-edited with Denise Duhamel and Maureen Seaton) was also published in 2007 by Soft Skull Press. His other books include *Plasticville* and *Phoebe 2002: An Essay in Verse*. Trinidad teaches poetry at Columbia College in Chicago, where he co-edits the journal *Court Green*.

Masha Tupitsyn is the author of *Beauty Talk & Monsters*, a collection of film-based stories (Semiotext(e), 2007). She received her MA in Literature and Cultural Theory from the University of Sussex in England. In 2004, she worked as the Assistant Literary Editor at *BOMB* Magazine. Her fiction and criticism has appeared or is forthcoming in *Animal Shelter*, the anthology *Wreckage of Reason: XXperimental Women Writers Writing in the 21st Century* (Spuyten Duyvil Books), *Make/Shift*, *Bookforum*, *Fence*, *Five Fingers Review*, *NYFA Current*, on San Francisco's KQED's *The Writer's Block*, and *Drunken Boat*. She is currently working on her new book about the actor John Cusack, *Star Notes*.

Heather Woodbury is an award-winning solo performer and published playwright known for her ground-breaking "performance novels"—epic, multicharacter works which combine the immediacy of performance art with a novel's length and scope. Her critically acclaimed 10-hour, 100-character solo performance, *What Ever: An American Odyssey in Eight Acts* (published by Faber/Farrar, Strauss & Giroux) toured the United States and Europe—from Steppenwolf Theatre in Chicago to London's Royal Festival Hall—and was subsequently adapted as a radio play hosted by Ira Glass. Woodbury has received multiple awards, grants, and fellowships for her subsequent works. The premiere production of her ensemble work *Tale of 2Cities: An American Joyride on Multiple Tracks* (published by Semiotexte/MIT Press) won a 2007 OBIE for ensemble performance. In 2006 she was awarded the Spalding Gray Award honoring writer/performers who are "fearless innovators." Her current solo work, *The Last Days of Desmond Nani Reese: A Stripper's History of the World*, was commissioned for development by the City of Los Angeles, which awarded her a C.O.L.A. 2007 Performing Artist's Fellowship.

Lidia Yuknavitch is the author of three collections of short fiction, *Real to Reel* (FC2, 2002), *Her Other Mouths* (House of Bones Press, 1997), and *Liberty's Excess* (FC2, 2000), and a book of criticism, *Allegories of Violence* (Routledge, 2000). Her writing has appeared in *Postmodern Culture*, *Fiction International*, *Another Chicago Magazine*, *Zyzzyva*, *Critical Matrix*, *Other Voices*, and elsewhere, and in the anthologies *Representing Bisexualities* (NYU Press) and *Third Wave Agenda* (University of Minnesota Press). She has been the co-editor of *Northwest Edge: Deviant Fictions* and the editor of *two girls review*. She teaches fiction writing and literature in Oregon.

ABOUT THE EDITORS

Brian Pera is the author of the novel *Troublemaker* (St. Martin's Press). *The Way I See Things*, his first film, premiered at the Los Angeles Outfest Film Festival in July of 2008 and has traveled to film festivals around the world. He's currently working on his next film and a novel. He lives in Memphis.

Masha Tupitsyn is the author of *Beauty Talk & Monsters*, a collection of film-based stories (Semiotext(e), 2007). She received her MA in Literature and Cultural Theory from the University of Sussex in England. In 2004, she worked as the Assistant Literary Editor at *BOMB* Magazine. Her fiction and criticism has appeared or is forthcoming in *Animal Shelter*, the anthology *Wreckage of Reason: XXperimental Women Writers Writing in the 21st Century* (Spuyten Duyvil Books), *Make/Shift*, *Bookforum*, *Fence*, *Five Fingers Review*, *NYFA Current*, on San Francisco's KQED's *The Writer's Block*, and *Drunken Boat*. She is currently working on her new book about the actor John Cusack, *Star Notes*.

PERMISSIONS